CW00523776

Madalene – The Dark Goddess

Helen Franklin

Prologue

Madalene irritably ran a hand over the shaft of her rifle. It was warm and strangely comforting. Looking up at the roof of the tunnel, she thought of those above ground. They'd be getting ready to celebrate the two day festival that had once been called Christmas, but was now known as Wintertide. Houses were being decorated with greenery and multi-coloured paper chains. Barrels of newly brewed beer were being opened, as were bottles of home-made wine and spirits. Feasts were being created from whatever food people had managed to get hold of and children were rushing around excitedly, willing the festival to start so they could open their presents.

Her own family would be the same, but they would be wondering where she was. Wondering if they should wait for her to get home. She hoped they wouldn't wait; this was going to take a long time. She'd told them she was doing some voluntary work with the elderly and it hadn't been a lie - the assumption that she would be taking soup and blankets to poor old folk was theirs. When Wintertide was over, people would look forward to celebrating the coming of 2060, a new year full of hope and prospect. How deluded they were. Personally, she couldn't see any cause for celebration.

Looking down the tunnel, she watched her group of elderly fugitives, twenty five in total, grumbling their way to safety. They were nearly all in their seventies, and though they were driving her mad, she had to admire their courage. In their youth they had believed the future held increasingly sophisticated technology and they were all going to live happily ever after as a result. Instead economies had crashed and progress had faltered. Their golden future had become their grandparents past and increasingly looked like it would bypass centuries and take them all back to medieval times...

"Is it much further, dear?" said, Ivy, turning around to glare at her. "Only I'm riddled with arthritis and I'm finding it hard to walk."

Swiftly, she moved to Ivy's side, relieved her of a heavy bag of belongings and took her arm. Ivy's glare instantly became a benevolent smile.

"You're such a good girl, but you've got to stop doing this. It's dangerous. Those men nearly killed you." Madalene smiled, those men hadn't stood a chance. "Look at us. We're old fools with not much longer to live. Why do you bother?"

How should she answer? She'd been doing this for more months than she cared to remember and for reasons that were too complex to be noble. She wasn't good, that was for sure. A good person could never do what she did...Ivy looked at her waiting.

"Everyone has the right to die when it's their time, not before. That's why I bother."

What a bloody stupid thing to say. It wasn't as if she thought that Sanctum Guards had a right to die in their own beds, or anyone connected with the Sanctum come to that...

A shout from the group drew her attention, "Mr Bligh's wet himself again."

Her hand touched the rifle again, but she removed it quickly. Mr Bligh had been a nuisance from the beginning, but shooting him wouldn't help. Fixing a false smile on her face, she let go of Ivy's arm and headed towards the undelectable Mr Bligh. With him around she'd be lucky if she made it home for Wintertide at all.

Chapter 1

A Meeting of Minds

Elgin entered the warehouse quietly, then stopped and looked around. It was a bitterly cold night, yet nearly a hundred people had ventured out to hear him speak. He was humbled by their presence. Wintertide festival, with its usual demands on time, was close. Also it was risky to get caught in a meeting like this. Yet not only had they come, he could see they'd also erected a stage for him to stand on.

"Elgin?" said his wife, Bertha, who stood by his side, along with her sister, Grace.

"So many," he said thoughtfully, moving forward, acknowledging the cheers and applause that greeted his arrival. Slowly he headed to the front of the room, stopping sporadically to speak to those around him, as did Bertha and Grace. At length, Elgin stepped onto the makeshift stage, ignoring the shaky feel and the movement of an odd board or two. Bertha and Grace moved to either side of him, staying clear of the stage, which Elgin thought was probably a good idea. He acknowledged his audience and waved a massive hand for silence.

" I want to thank you for coming here on such a bitterly cold night. I'm sure most of you would rather be sat at home with a warm drink, wrapping Wintertide presents for your loved ones." This was greeted with murmurs and nods. "However I'm glad you're here. I can't oppose the evil of Peter Shadow alone. Or should I give him his nickname – Shadowman. A better name I think for a dictator whose intent is to bring fear and darkness to this land. A dictator whose intent is exemplified by his idea of mass entertainment, the atrocity that is the Arena..."

The Arena was impressive, built at the beginning of the twenty-first century and at one time, the site of musical excellence and sporting triumph. Presently, it was a parody of what it had once been; execution was not a sport in Elgin's eyes. Tickets were cheap, five engles for the back rows, ten nearer the front. Elgin had no choice but to pay ten, the place was packed. The air of excitement and the chanting of the crowd were abhorrent, but he stayed put. As the show started, into the Arena came marching bands, followed by a variety of entertainers. Hawkers moved through the crowd, selling unidentifiable food and drink, for prices far greater than the cost of a seat. Elgin ignored all this; he was transfixed by the sight of ten wooden stakes set into the Arena's centre. The grass below them covered with blood...

"It was the first time I'd been there and it will be my last. The carnival atmosphere appalled me." He heard gasps of shock echo off the walls and ceiling. "How can I describe to you the horror of what I saw there...?" Elgin paused, taking a deep breath while he fought to control his emotions.

Silence descended as a group of eight men and two women, all of them showing signs of having been tortured, were led into the Arena and tied to the stakes at its centre. Strangely, they were silent; as if they had already embraced death. One of the men was a friend-Robin Jones...A large group of people, wearing masks to hide their faces and known widely as 'The Choir' began to chant the charges made against these people. Murder. Abduction. Child Abuse. Rare crimes become commonplace. Treason. Elgin's mind had begun to wander, but now he listened carefully. 'Members of the abhorrent Provoke group, sworn to bring down our beloved government and thereby our beloved country...'

"Two of the people were allegedly members of this group, though I didn't recognise them." Elgin stopped as some people headed for the door. A small part of him wanted to head for the door too...

"So Peter Shadow's decided it's time to eliminate us," said a pale-faced man near the stage. "Surely he doesn't fear our opposition."

"He doesn't fear us," said Bertha, "This is an act of spite."

"When I joined the group, I never thought I would face death. I have a young wife, who knows nothing... I have two small daughters..."

"We all have families," said Mary, a young girl next to Joel.

4

"You have no children," said Joel. "What if my wife and children starve because I've been sent to the Arena? Or worse, if they get sent to the Arena because of me? I can't take that chance."

"We knew opposing Shadowman was dangerous.

"Easy for you to say. You've a wealthy family. Someone would buy *you* out of the Arena. Who will buy me out?"

Elgin had heard enough, "Quiet all of you. Those who wish to leave, do so with my blessing. Each of you must do what is right for yourselves and for your family."

Men with guns in their hands walked over to the stakes and waited, while a long trembling note was played on a flute, a note to indicate to the public that retribution's moment had come. With the note's end came the shots. Not cleanly to the heads of the victims, imparting instant death, but fired into their stomachs, so that death would be long and painful. It seemed to Elgin that he sat for hours listening to unending howls of anguish. Tears rolled down his cheeks, but he made no move to wipe them away, it did not seem right. At least the baying mob around him had gone silent, disturbed whether they liked it or not.

What made it worse was knowing that in his friend's case the charges were false. His friend Robin, along with his wife Alice had been dining with him and Bertha at the time of his so-called 'crime'. But no verifiable alibi would have saved him. There was no longer trial by jury, only trial by the Sanctum's torturers...

"I believe the people I watched die in the Arena were innocent, murdered by the Sanctum for reasons only they know. Sanctum! It means a holy place, but there is nothing holy about our new government. Their atrocities grow, yet they remain unchallenged. It is *we* who must challenge them, regardless of the danger."

"And how are you going to do that, old man?" came a voice from the back. "Bore them to death with your speeches."

As Elgin searched the room, a woman in her late twenties stepped away from the door, so she could be more easily seen. A dark cloud of hair swirled round her face and swept down her spine. Icy blue eyes sparkled with contempt from the confines of a flawless face. Her only visible imperfection, a jagged red scar across her throat.

Elgin couldn't identify her, but there were many in the warehouse that did.

"Madalene!"

People moved as far away from her as possible and a cacophony of different conversations filled the air. He'd never seen anyone create this much uproar before. He tried to listen to what was being said, but could only catch the conversation taking place in front of him.

"What's *she* doing here? I thought she was still in prison."

"I heard she murdered her father…"

Elgin saw a sweet smile cross Madalene's face while the gossip around her continued. It was obvious that she didn't give a damn what they thought of her. As he watched, she came to the front of the room.

"She spat on her mother's coffin when they buried her last year. What kind of a woman does that?" The man who spoke these words looked up in horror to find her cold eyes staring at him.

"The woman of your nightmares," Elgin heard her answer, making the man shudder. "Enough! I have not come here to be talked about. I have come to listen to the words of Bertha, Grace and Elgin. I am interested to hear how exactly they intend to challenge Shadowman. Well?"

Elgin stared intently at her. What he had heard had been horrific, yet it didn't match the woman who now stood in front of him. He had never seen anyone like her. How could *this* woman be accused of such terrible deeds?

"Appearances can be deceptive, old man. Most of what they've said about me is true."

"Some said your husband works for the Sanctum. Are you a spy then, come to find out what we are doing?"

At this the woman they called Madalene laughed loudly and scornfully, "If I was, I could tell them nothing, since you do nothing."

"Then why have you come here, Madalene? It is Madalene isn't it?"

"To join your pathetic group, if I like what I hear," she said, nonchalantly.

"And what makes you think that our group, sorry our 'pathetic' group, needs you?" said Bertha, angrily.

"Don't ask stupid questions. Of course this group needs me if it intends to offer any worthwhile opposition to the Sanctum."

There was fire behind her words and as she slumped onto a nearby rickety chair, folded her arms and waited, Elgin saw how powerful and dangerous she was; beauty was a mere façade to cover it. Sighing, Elgin turned his attention back to the room.

Elgin watched Bertha and Grace give *their* speeches, and he was proud of the way both women inspired the audience. They received well-deserved rounds of applause from the enthusiastic crowd, who seemed to have decided to ignore Madalene's presence, yet kept glancing curiously at her. He noticed that she did not applaud or cheer, in fact she looked increasingly bored. As the crowd left the warehouse, she remained on her chair looking intently at the three of them.

"Why did you call your group Provoke? You should have called it Irritate, for that is all you will achieve."

"At least we're doing something," said Grace, "We write letters of protest, so our views get heard. And we risk putting up posters and handing out pamphlets, so the public knows someone fights for them. That's more than anyone else is doing."

"Meetings like this one are held regularly; despite the fact that such meetings are unlawful. Our membership is large, so we rarely congregate altogether, though we do have a place we can use if we wish to do so. Meetings take place across London most nights, and we have deputy leaders assigned to take these meetings. The Sanctum knows it's not unopposed," added Bertha

"Your letters and pamphlets will be ripped up and your petty acts of civil disobedience will lead to the Arena," said Madalene, frowning fiercely. "Your group is splintered into many separate groups, so you have no unity. How the hell do you know you're not all writing the same damn letter?"

"What would you have us do?" said Elgin, as Madalene stood and began pacing, seemingly undecided.

"I know Peter Shadow. Shadowman? Good name. Makes him sound like a comic book villain, which is all he really is. I'm also familiar with most members of the Inner Sanctum, especially Michael Vertex."

Elgin stared at Madalene in amazement, wanting to ask her many questions, but staying silent in case she stopped talking.

"At the moment the Sanctum courts a credulous public and quietly they execute those sections of the public they despise, such as the elderly and the mentally handicapped. The prisons are a different matter; many violent psychopaths have been enlisted into the Sanctum Guard, or trained in the delicate art of torture."

"How do you know so much that we don't?" said Elgin, finding it hard to believe her words.

"I was an intelligence officer in a special army unit. I didn't lose my skills in prison." He noticed the arrogance that accompanied these words.

"Why would you gather information on the Sanctum? What makes a person like *you* care what they do?" said Bertha. Elgin could tell she was thinking Madalene sounded perfect for the Sanctum Guard; another violent psychopath.

"A person like *me* has my own reasons for attacking the Sanctum, but I need help. I thought your Provoke group might provide that help, but I would have been better off going to a Woman's Institute meeting, at least I'd be going home with a pot of jam." Madalene gave a contemptuous laugh and sat down again. Bertha and Grace glared meaningfully at Elgin.

"Well I'm scared of you and it seems you're on our side, so Shadowman should be terrified," Elgin said lightly, meaning every word.

"You want us to become terrorists, use violence to achieve our aims, but we're a peaceful organisation. History shows peaceful protest can work," said Grace, in her usual firm, but gentle fashion.

"You're not the only person who's fought in the army; both Elgin and I were soldiers for many years. Our group has many members who could fight, brave people that risk getting caught at an illicit meeting because they care about what's happening. You don't seem to care about anything or anybody. All you want is an excuse for violence. We're not giving you that excuse," Bertha said, turning away from Madalene, dismissively.

To Elgin's horror, Madalene calmly rose from the chair, picked it up and smashed it hard against the stage. "I don't need an excuse for violence," she smiled. The smile chilled Elgin to the core. One of the broken legs flew at Bertha's back, hitting her with a resounding thud. Seeing Bertha turn and pick the piece up, intending to retaliate, Elgin stepped in.

"You have to understand, Madalene, that even though no democratic process was involved, most of the general public are ignorantly content with the Sanctum. If the horrors you speak of are happening, the public are not aware of them."

Madalene began to protest, but Elgin didn't give her a chance to speak. "The Provoke group oppose his media takeover and the barbarity of the Arena among other things. But the Arena has become a popular form of entertainment, and outwardly the media seems unchanged... We would find the majority of the public allied with the Sanctum and end up fighting people we seek to protect."

"Foolish old man," said Madalene, speculatively eyeing Bertha. So she's not given up the fight yet, thought Elgin, only to become bewildered when in a cheerful voice Madalene asked, "Well? Am I in the gang or not? I've decided you need me to liven things up."

Elgin took Bertha and Grace over to the other side of the room, to discuss Madalene's involvement with the group. Looking across, he

9

saw Madalene sit nonchalantly on the floor, as if she had no interest in what they said.

"No, Elgin. There's something not right about her; you saw what she just did. I don't want her to be part of this group," said Bertha, furiously. She was obviously still enraged at being struck with the chair leg.

"Bertha's right, Madalene's a madwoman. Look at how the group reacted to her. If she became a member, the others would leave, and there would be no more opposition to Shadowman," said Grace, glancing nervously over to where Madalene sat.

Their mouths were firm unmoveable lines and their eyes dared him to deny them. Elgin knew they were right. Carefully controlled, Madalene could be an asset to the group and he was reluctant to lose her, but who among them could keep such a woman controlled?

"We are decided then?" said Elgin, staring wistfully at Madalene.

"Agreed," said Grace and Bertha, with relief.

Madalene's eyes no longer held contempt. To Elgin's surprise, she was now looking at them with renewed respect; clearly she already knew their decision.

"It's your loss, not mine. I'll fight the Sanctum alone. Not much chance of succeeding, but I'll worry them more than you do. Goodnight, may your endless letters prove fruitful." Without looking back Madalene strode out of the door into a blizzard that had just started.

"She doesn't have a coat," said Grace.

"Why doesn't that surprise me?" chuckled Elgin.

Chapter Two

Unforeseen Chance

Madalene simmered with suppressed rage, as she retrieved her rifle from its hiding place. Bertha was a bitch, Grace, a nonentity and Elgin...Elgin she liked. The rifle was covered with snow; she brushed it off and slung it over her shoulder. What would their reaction have been, if she'd walked into the meeting carrying a rifle, her presence alone had been enough to upset them? To hell with the Provoke group, they could keep their little creative writing club; she wouldn't have gone to their meeting at all if it hadn't been for the death of her friend, Robin Jones in the Arena that afternoon.

It hadn't been easy to identify Robin; he'd been beaten so extensively he could barely stand and his hair had been shaved off. The damp urine patches that flooded the front of his trousers revealed his terror. For her it had been almost been a relief when they shot him. If she'd had her rifle, she'd have done it for them, and she would have given him a faster, cleaner death... Whatever they said, Robin's only crime had been to cross Peter Shadow a long time ago on her behalf...

Shouts echoed through the trees. Like a pack of wolves they howled instructions to each other, and the air was dense, filled with feral excitement. Despite the certainty of capture she kept running, hoping that a freak chance of evasion might occur. It wasn't to be. A wild figure appeared in front of her, bare-chested and covered in war-paint. Still she ran, Robin Jones was not going to stop her. But he did.

"I won't hurt you, but you've got to hide...quickly..."

She'd found Robin's wife sitting alone at the front of the main stand. Alice's face had been expressionless as Madalene approached, her eyes firmly fixed on Robin's body.

"Can I sit with you, Alice?" Madalene had said, sitting down anyway. There'd been no response. "He died bravely. Be proud of him."

"He died." Alice had said, tonelessly.

"You have to be the brave one now. It's going to be hard living on your own." Madalene had known she was spouting platitudes, but what else could she do?

"I don't have to be anything. The only difference between me and Robin is my heart's still beating." A single tear had run down Alice's face, quickly followed by another and then another. Madalene had held Alice tightly as she cried bitter tears and silently vowed that this would be avenged.

Robin had been a good friend over the years. He was her first and probably only love, and at one time she'd believe she'd marry him; a time before her world had gone insane. He'd ended up married to Alice.

Madalene had been in prison at the time and during a regular visit, Robin brought Alice along with him to introduce her. She had been incredible jealous and behaved badly as a consequence. Undeterred by her hostility, Alice continued to accompany Robin on his visits. Slowly Alice and Madalene had become friends, so when Robin made it clear that he intended to marry Alice, Madalene had genuinely been delighted. The wedding took place five days after her release and it was an eventful day in more ways than one. At the wedding she'd been introduced to Robin's friend, Bren. He was a boring accountant, who turned out to be good in bed; as she liked him, she decided to marry him; hoping that marriage would bring normality and peace into her life.

Any peace gained had been taken from her that afternoon and the innate violence that she tried so hard to bury had emerged. It needed release and hoping that the Provoke group could provide that release, she'd gone to their stupid meeting. Simply thinking of the 'fishwife' gossip she'd overheard made the violence threaten to spill over. However, one bit of gossip *had* interested her; it appeared that her long time unseen sister, Holan, was a prominent member of the Provoke group. Now there was a surprise. Hadn't her sister always been a good girl, clever, well behaved, liked by everyone...

Madalene began to run through the fierce blizzard, her thoughts racing. If Peter Shadow was prepared to torture and kill Robin, he could possibly do the same thing to Alice. Not only could Alice

12

prove Robin's innocence, she knew the real reason behind his death. Robin had told her he was an enemy of Peter Shadow, shortly after the tyrant's ascendancy to power. It would be embarrassing for Peter if Alice decided to present this information to the public. He could deny it and say that Alice was a madwoman, but there would always be people who believed her version of events, which made Alice dangerous. It was vital that she made plans to get Alice to safety, and those plans had to be made quickly.

Madalene knew that Elgin and Bertha had had dinner with Robin and Alice on the night Robin was, allegedly, kidnapping and abusing infants at such a rate, the most demented of paedophiles would find it hard to keep up with him. Elgin had seen Robin die in the Arena with the others and he wasn't stupid, he knew the people who had died were innocent, so why insist that a violent response wasn't necessary?

Violence was the only answer to Peter Shadow. It was the only thing Peter would understand, because *his* answer to problems was violence. The man was a sadistic thug and a bully. The letters the Provoke group were sending obviously irritated him; otherwise he wouldn't have decided that Provoke group members were suitable Arena fodder. And if the letters were irritating him, that was good. But only meeting like with like would lead to his overthrow. Violence was the only way to get rid of the man.

She stopped for a moment to catch her breath, it was getting harder to run; there was at least four inches of snow already underfoot. Hearing the crunch of footsteps, she looked up and saw two rough-looking men coming towards her; they were young men, possibly in their early twenties. She tensed believing them to be members of the Sanctum Guard, but as they got closer she recognised them; they'd both been at the meeting.

"Well look who it is! Bad time to be touting for business, Madalene. Still if you don't mind doing it in the snow, I'll give you twenty engles for five minutes," said the shorter of the two.

"Okay, it's a deal. Come closer and give me my twenty engles," purred Madalene.

He fumbled in his pockets for the coins, leered at his friend and walked forward; the next moment he was flat on the ground with a cocked rifle held at his chest.

"I-It was a joke. P-Please..."

"Leave him alone, you psychopath. I heard what they said about you tonight. Got quite a name for yourself, haven't you?" said, the friend.

"I've got quite a name for you too, but I don't think you'd like it. Are you both mad? Did you happen to miss the part about me murdering ten men? Now you and your little friend here had better start running because if you're in my sight after two minutes, I'm going to shoot the pair of you." Lowering her rifle, she helped the man on the ground up, and then kneed him fiercely in the groin.

"I'm worth a lot more than twenty engles, you idiot."

Turning away from them, she began to run again; if that was the calibre of Provoke's members, she was definitely better off without the group. It wasn't long before she had to slow down; her legs ached from running through deep snow and the force of the blizzard made her face feel like it had been stung by a hundred bees.

As she was passing the Astoria hotel, an exclusive Sanctum member's only establishment, a transporter drove up and stopped outside. Curious about its occupants, she hid behind a nearby tree, so she could watch, without being seen. It was difficult to see through the flying snow, but a man and a woman stepped out onto the pavement, closely followed by three bodyguards, and stood there for a moment chatting affectionately and laughing together. Madalene gasped as she recognised the man; the blizzard could get worse, yet still she would recognise this man, he was Edgar Heaton one of Peter Shadow's life-long friends and a member of the Inner Sanctum. He'd been with Peter on the night she'd been attacked.

"Well what have we got here?" He'd grabbed her by the hair, pulled her out of the hiding place, and then howled in triumph. "A rat in a hole... and a robin with her...Robin Jones. Not trying to protect the rat were you Robin?" He'd pulled her hair harder until she squealed and then he'd reached under her shirt and squeezed her breast...

"Leave her alone, Edgar."

"Or you'll do what? I'd run if I were you. Peter's not going to like this."

This was her chance to strike a blow against Peter Shadow and the Sanctum; there might never be another one. A life for a life; his life for Robins'. She couldn't stop, all the emotion of the day spilled over inside her; gently stroking her rifle, she removed the safety catch, took aim and fired one shot. It went straight through Edgar Heaton's head, dropping the man instantly. Bending down she picked up the casing and ran back the way she had come; elation soared through her and she began to laugh wildly. It had not been a coincidence that she should think about her past, and then bang into it. Maybe Robin's spirit had sent Edgar Heaton to her.

The route she took home was a long one and the blizzard still hampered her progress. Finally she reached the large detached house that was her home. Slipping in through the back gate she headed for the greenhouse, where she hid the rifle in its usual hiding place. Bren hated gardening so there was little chance of him finding it there, or of him finding the other stuff she kept hidden in the garden. Fortunately Bren never questioned her activities and therefore did not realise the danger she put him and their two children in. The man was passionately in love with her, had been so from their first meeting; Madalene could get away with anything and that included murder. From time to time, it had crossed her mind that Bren did have an idea of what she was up to, but ignored it while he had no proof.

"Hi Maddy, you look happy," he said, looking up from a sheaf of papers he'd been reading. She'd managed to dry herself before coming to find him, but the cold had penetrated every part of her body and she was unable to stop shivering. "You're freezing, darling, come over here by the fire."

"Where did you get the coal from? That stuff costs a fortune," she said, moving to sit down beside him.

"I have contacts. We should have enough to get us through winter, if we're careful with it. So how was Elaine?" Bren casually placed his arms around her and began to gently fondle her breasts. Already aroused by the killing of Edgar Heaton, Madalene responded eagerly; coal wasn't the only way to get warm.

"Elaine was fine, but let's not talk about her at the moment," she said, moaning at his touch. She needed to call Elaine urgently and ask for an alibi, but Bren was incredibly distracting and his hands had wandered down to her stomach. The trouble was that the Sanctum Guard would not wait until morning to begin their hunt for Edgar Heaton's killer. She had to ring Elaine now, no matter where Bren's hands decided to go next. All she had to do was to pretend to have spent the evening with a fictional lover. Elaine was a silly woman who loved romantic intrigue and would provide an alibi to Bren or anyone else who asked, without question. With difficulty she moved away from Bren. He sighed and indicated their bedroom using his head. She nodded in agreement.

"You go on up, Bren and I'll be with you in a few minutes," she said, seductively. "There's something I have to tell Elaine. I won't be long."

Chapter Three

Revelations

Elgin was despondent. Bertha had kept him awake most of the night ranting about Madalene. Having seen the bruising on her back, he could understand Bertha's animosity; however he found Madalene intriguing and couldn't help wondering if her way was right and Provoke's wrong.

In the current situation there wasn't much Provoke *could* do to oppose the Sanctum. Any form of public protest was dealt with severely. The Sanctum had emerged from its womb in a tide of blood, as students, activists and ordinary people gathered and marched - protesting the loss of democracy - only to be shot in their thousands. Elgin had been on some of these marches and each time he'd escaped with his life, but the holes in his chest, legs and arms were a testament to the ferocity of the new government.

The Provoke group had been an alternative to getting shot. He'd set the organisation up during one of his many recuperation periods, and banned its members from any public displays of disaffection. Instead they wrote endless protest letters to annoy the government, and put posters up wherever they could, ridiculing Shadowman, and his policies. If Madalene wasn't lying about the extermination of the elderly and mentally handicapped, then this wasn't enough, and deep down he knew she wasn't lying; he'd seen the truth in her eyes.

The communicator buzzed and absent-mindedly he picked it up.

"Elgin, it's Alan. Have you seen the Sanctum papers today or heard any of their broadcasts?"

Elgin smiled; Alan Moore was a good friend and one day would be Provoke's leader. Alan's friends, Christian Peek and Torrin Spice also had leadership potential, but they were too volatile for the position, in Elgin's opinion.

"Edgar Heaton, the finance minister was shot last night. Whoever did it shot his wife too. They're saying Provoke members are responsible, that it was retaliation for the deaths in the Arena yesterday," said Alan.

"What. They know we're a peaceful organisation and wouldn't do something like that." Elgin was shocked at this news. It seemed the campaign against the Provoke group had started in earnest.

"I've spoken to some of the people who attended your meeting last night and they think Madalene's responsible for the shootings, that she's the person who shot Edgar Heaton."

Elgin was shocked by this accusation. Without a doubt Madalene was capable of doing it, but she hadn't been carrying a weapon at the meeting...

"That's ridiculous," he said. "She didn't have a weapon."

"She had a rifle, Elgin, rumour says she never goes anywhere without it. I reckon she hid it outside the warehouse and picked it up as she left."

Elgin felt uneasy, but surely all of this was supposition and rumour. He'd left the warehouse with Bertha and Grace shortly after Madalene's departure. There'd been no sign of her; surely Madalene couldn't have found a hidden rifle that fast.

"How do you know she had a rifle? I know Madalene's got a bad reputation, but that isn't enough to accuse her of murder." He heard Alan hesitate, as if reluctant to continue the conversation. "You've got no proof that Madalene had a rifle with her last night, have you?"

"Actually I have, Elgin; it's a bit of an antique from what I've been told, but a good weapon nevertheless. Daniel and Dave came across her in Mill Street and you know what those two are like. Daniel tried to be clever with her, thought he'd treat her like a prostitute. She had him on the ground in seconds, with the rifle shoved into his chest. Dave says she threatened to shoot both of them, and from the expression on her face, she meant it."

Elgin thought quickly. How near was Mill Street to the murder scene?

"Where was Edgar Heaton shot?" he asked, dreading the answer.

"Outside the front doors of the Astoria hotel, moments away from Mill Street. It has to have been her," said Alan.

"Did Madalene harm Daniel or Dave? She didn't shoot them, did she?" said Elgin, wondering if Madalene had wounded them as a warning to others, and unwittingly acknowledging her guilt.

"Daniel says she helped him up, and kneed him in the groin for insulting her; then without looking back, she ran off in the direction of the Astoria hotel."

"Leave this with me, Alan. I need to investigate and think over what you've said, I'll call you back." Elgin no longer doubted that Madalene had killed the Heaton's, but he had no desire to discuss the matter further, not until he'd had time to consider the repercussions.

"She has to be dealt with, Elgin; hundreds of Provoke members could die because of her. If you won't do it, then we will. If we have to lynch her to prevent further harm, that's what we'll do." Alan's voice had taken on a nasty edge.

"So, it's acceptable for Provoke members to kill Madalene, but we won't use that same violence against people we oppose, people like Heaton for example - the woman's not even a damn member of our group. I said to leave it with me, I am still leader of the Provoke group, am I not," said Elgin angrily, curtailing the call.

While the headline was suitably damning and the text sensational, it was the accompanying photographs that caught Elgin's attention. Edgar Heaton and his wife Mary were shown lying dead on the pavement outside the entrance to the Astoria hotel, and their bodies were almost unidentifiable. Only the wound on Edgar's head looked like it had been made by a rifle bullet, the other wounds appeared to have been made by a HIE (high impact explosive) weapon, a firearm carried solely by members of the Sanctum Guard. It pumped miniature bombs into its target, reducing everything to pulp in seconds; its use had been banned since the twenties. The Heatons' bodyguards were, according to the paper, unharmed; how could a weapon like that have missed them? Unless they were the ones using the weapon...

Looking again at the text, Elgin saw that a dark-haired man had been seen running away from the scene of the crime in the direction of Mill Street, but the severity of the blizzard had made pursuit and identification of the man impossible. None of it made any sense; Sanctum Guards wouldn't have hesitated to pursue an assassin. All Elgin knew with any certainty, was that Madalene *had* shot Edgar Heaton with one bullet to his head and then made good her escape, aided by the severe weather conditions.

It was vital that he find Madalene, before the Sanctum Guards or angry Provoke group members got to her. She had said that she would fight the Sanctum alone and her campaign had clearly begun. However he had to prevent her from any further action of this sort, or the consequences for the Provoke group could be terrible. The only way he could think of stopping Madalene was to make her a group member, though he paled at the thought of putting that suggestion to Bertha.

Bertha believed it was dangerous to have Madalene in the group, but he believed it was dangerous to leave her out of it. At least if Madalene was a member, they could control her to some extent; he fervently hoped they'd be able to control her. How to prevent Alan and others from a lynching, before he managed to recruit her was another matter.

Elgin left the house before Bertha stirred. It was cowardice, but he was not prepared to listen to her views on the Edgar Heaton situation, or Alan Moore's proposals - after last night's ranting, he knew she would gladly volunteer to put a noose round Madalene's neck. And he was *definitely* not ready to discuss making Madalene a member of the Provoke group.

He walked as briskly as he could through the deep snow, trying to clear his head and steady his nerve. The unnatural silence, which always descended after a large snowfall, followed him as he walked. The assassination of Edgar Heaton was an immense blow against the Sanctum. Heaton was reputed to be a financial genius and responsible for the high standard of living that the public enjoyed, after years of hardship under democratically elected governments. But what if the current economic climate had been aided by the annihilation of the elderly, a huge percentage of the population? Pension requirements had crippled economies throughout the world for decades, yet Heaton hadn't regarded pensions as a problem.

Had Madalene given the dead a small measure of justice? The thought plagued him. Her strike was more effective than anything Provoke had done. The invincibility of those smug bastards in the Sanctum, who thought they could beguile the public and get away with it, would be shaken. Elgin wasn't afraid to use violence in a just cause; he'd just grown tired of watching his friends die, and finding that all he had left were acquaintances. The events at the Arena had changed the way he felt. Thoughts of the Arena made him think of

Robin, so he decided to visit Robin's wife, Alice and see if there was anything he could do for her.

When she answered the door, he barely recognised her; she was thin and grey, a shadowy ghost of the plump, lively woman she had been only days ago. She shed no tears, her eyes had the look of a corpse; her speech was quiet and mechanical, her responses programmed. Elgin greeted her with a gentle hug then went and sat in the kitchen while she busied herself making him a breakfast of cheese, bread and beer. Elgin had not asked for or even wanted food and drink, nevertheless he saw her need and stayed silent. The bread was stale and the beer flat, but Elgin ate and drank without comment, until Alice suddenly grabbed the plate and took the glass from his hand.

"What am I thinking of, Elgin? That bread's old and the beer's flat. I'll cook you some eggs. No I can't, I haven't got any... I haven't got anything ...I haven't got Robin ..." Her voice cracked and she fell to her knees sobbing, dropping the plate and spilling beer over her clothing, which Elgin now realised was her nightdress.

"I was there, Alice, I saw what happened," he said softly, kneeling down by her side, trying to clean her up with a napkin he'd found on the table. Carefully he raised her up and sat her down on a chair. "I won't say it's going to be alright because it won't be, but if I can do anything to ease your grief, you only have to ask."

"My poor Robin had wet his trousers...Oh the shame he must have felt. I would have disgraced him further, by screaming and crying. But I knew I had to be strong; it would be the last time he'd hear my voice... and it wouldn't do for him to hear me screaming. Madalene found me afterwards. She said that Robin had been brave and I should be proud of him. That must have been hard for Madalene, she loved Robin nearly as much as I did, but I'm glad she came. After comforting me for a while, she took my hand gently, helped me up, and took me home. Then she gave me something to help me sleep and said she had to be somewhere, but she'd come and see me today,"

"Madalene?" Elgin nearly choked. "Long, dark hair, scar across her throat?" She'd gone to the Provoke meeting straight from Alice's. And she'd known all along that he was Robin's friend. She probably thought she could trust him, but he'd let her down. It was a bitter thought.

21

"Do you know her? She's wonderful isn't she? Robin loved her dearly."

Elgin couldn't believe what he was hearing. If Robin loved Madalene then she was worth loving, but before he could say anything, Alice continued.

"Madalene's a brave woman, while others talk she acts. I bet you don't know that she's saved thousands of the elderly from death? The Sanctum believes they're a burden, but Madalene gets them over to Ireland, to end their days peacefully. She's also saved the lives of others, finding them places to live in secret tunnels underground. She does all of this without expecting any kind of reward and at great risk to her own life, yet people say dreadful things about her. It makes me angry to hear her described as some sort of...of demon."

Elgin was so shocked by Alice's words, he stood up and fetched himself some more flat beer. He'd had no idea when speaking to Madalene that she was *actively* working against the Sanctum. She had to have a network of people that worked for her, so why did she want or need to join the Provoke group? Vaguely he became aware that Alice was still talking.

"...of course a lot of the stories are true, but Robin and I knew the facts behind them. You'll have heard that she murdered her father, but not that he beat her every single day. Worse still, he never touched Holan, her older sister. *She* was his favourite. Did you know Holan's a member of Provoke, by the way?"

Elgin wasn't aware that Madalene had a sister, let alone a sister that was a member of his group. Surely Alice didn't mean his dear friend, Holan; she was Alan Moore's second!

"Well you know what Madalene's like. She constantly defied her father, and the more she defied him, the more he beat her, until the day came when she stopped him..."

Alice seemed less grey and less subdued now. It was as if talking about Madalene helped her forget what had happened to Robin for a while. Elgin was happy to let her talk about Madalene for as long as she wanted to, he found the subject fascinating.

"I feel a little sorry for Bren, her husband. No matter how hard she tries, Madalene will never be an ordinary woman. It isn't in her,

Elgin; she wasn't born to be ordinary. But I fear for her future, it's likely to be just as unhappy as her past."

Elgin's head was spinning when he left Alice's. Madalene had shot Edgar Heaton to avenge Robin Jones, his friend. She'd come across him accidentally and taken her chance, he was certain of it. The bodyguards had been given instructions to make the assassination look horrific, and had killed Mary Heaton with a HIE weapon to make the crime look worse in the public's eyes. Elgin would have applauded Madalene for the killing alone, he even wished he'd been the one holding the rifle; as for the rest of it...Provoke needed Madalene badly if it was to mean something. His communicator buzzed and he pulled it out of his pocket. This time it was a man he knew only as Jackson,

"Elgin? Don't go home. Sanctum Guards have raided your house. They've killed Grace and taken your wife prisoner."

Chapter Four

A Warm Welcome

Like any good housewife, she waved goodbye to her husband, and then bustled around getting Hayla and Jinn ready for school. Hayla, twelve years old, was Bren's daughter. Jinn, fifteen years old, was her unwanted son; brought up by her Mother and returned after that vile woman's death. After their departure, she cleared the breakfast things and tidied the house. Then, like any good housewife, she wandered into the garden and used a shovel to clear snow off the path; fetched detonators, explosives and tape, which she carefully placed into a patterned shopping bag, and finally picked up her rifle from its hiding place.

Climbing over the fence, she entered the property by its back door.

"Madalene?" said Alice, brushing her hand over fresh tears on her cheeks, but failing to hide them. "I wasn't sure if I'd see you again."

Reaching out, Madalene embraced her friend, and then held her at arms length.

"Tears won't bring Robin back and you need to be strong, Alice. Your possessions are already in your new home, it's a cottage in Ireland. My friends don't give me any location details, which means if I'm caught, there's nothing I can tell the Sanctum torturers. Don't worry though, you'll be met at the docks and taken there."

"Are you certain the Sanctum Guards will come for me? All my memories are here, I can't bear to leave so soon after losing Robin." Alice began sobbing again and slumped dejectedly onto a nearby chair.

"They're probably already on their way over here. I haven't any doubt they'll come and arrest you, Alice, and I'll not let what happened to Robin happen to you," Madalene released her pent up anger by smashing her left hand viciously against a wall. That was not clever, she thought, as pain soared from her fingertips, across her palm and up through her wrist, but from the expression on Alice's face, she *had* made her point.

"I only spoke to Mr Braile, the butcher, and very sympathetic he was too, as were the other customers who were in the shop at the same time," said Alice, worriedly.

"And the rest, Alice?" said Madalene, moving over to the sink, so she could run cold water over her aching hand.

"I might have mentioned Robin's innocence to a few close, personal friends. But I haven't been condemning the Sanctum from every street corner, why can't they leave me alone?" A flash of anger crossed Alice's face.

That's more like it, thought Madalene, removing her hand from the cold water. "I wonder what falsehood they intend to charge you with?" she said.

Alice laughed bitterly, "Chopping up newborn babies, while drowning disabled women in the bath? Something inventive along those lines."

"Is that all? I don't think they're coming to arrest you, I think they're coming to hire you." Madalene laughed, and then became serious. "I didn't see any watchers, but that doesn't mean they're not there. Walk down the road, slowly, making it seem like you're on your way to the shops. Turn into Wainscot Drive and look for a shabby, grey transporter, one of the early models. A driver will be sat in it, reading something like the 'Sanctum Sun'. Greet the driver as if he's an old friend, and get in." For the sake of Alice's confidence, Madalene smiled. In reality she was sad to lose Alice's friendship. "We'll see each other again, Alice, and when we do, we can reminisce about Robin and his eccentricities."

Usually her plans were well organised, but this one had been rushed. Madalene despised words like 'luck', you either made things happen or you didn't. However she hoped Alice was lucky today.

"We won't see each other again, Madalene," said Alice, sadly. "Robin said you'd die young and violently. I believe he was right. You risk too much, Madalene."

"He always did know what he was talking about," Madalene said, with a wry grin. "Come on Alice, it's time."

Bravely and with one final hug, Alice picked up her bags and walked out of the front door, slamming it behind her.

Madalene watched Alice from the front room window, until she disappeared from view, and was relieved to see that no-one followed her. Hurriedly she started to work, moving with care around the still-furnished house; there'd been no time to get the furniture out, all Alice had been allowed to send on ahead were small, personal possessions.

Finally, Madalene let herself out by the back door and re-climbed the fence. Casually she strolled to the house opposite and broke in using a key she'd had made for that purpose. Pulling her rifle out from under her coat, she checked the place for occupants. Debris in the kitchen revealed that the couple who lived there had left for work hurriedly that morning; the house was as empty as she'd thought it would be. They'd never know how deadly an unwanted cold that day might have been. Helping herself to a large glass of whiskey, she moved to the front window, trying hard to ignore the nasty, green, triangular pattern of the curtains; their taste in furniture was equally revolting. Slamming the whiskey down her throat, she settled in to wait. They would come. She knew they would come.

She didn't have to wait too long. Less than an hour after Alice's departure, four transporters came down the road and stopped directly outside Alice's front door. Twenty men emerged from the vehicles, all with readied weapons. Madalene had known that Peter Shadow would see Alice as a potential danger, but was he really so pathetic that he thought twenty men were needed to pick her up. Twenty men or not, Peter would not get to put so much as a fingerprint on Alice.

A grim smile crossed Madalene's lips as she watched the men break down Alice's front door and rush into the house. They could have tried knocking, she thought, as her hand reached into her pocket; after all it wasn't polite to barge into other people's homes. She'd only expected about four visitors to turn up at Alice's house, which made the other sixteen and the four drivers a bonus. Well, as Alice wasn't around anymore, it was up to her to give them all a warm welcome. Gently she pressed a button, and then reached for her rifle.

Two drivers were dead before the house exploded into pocket-sized pieces; she shot the other two as they frantically tried to move their transporters away from the scene. Shame they were so arrogant they didn't think to use bullet-proof glass in their transporters. It wasn't pretty, body parts were scattered everywhere. As a couple of survivors staggered out of the wreckage, she shot them to ease their pain, proving that she had a heart after all.

Madalene shook with excitement; this was a huge success, twenty- four Sanctum Guards killed by one woman. Twenty- four. A frenzy of bloodlust came over her; she wanted to kill more, and began to consider the shocked people who now crowded into the road. Fortunately for them, her professional pride took over and, taking a deep breath, she calmed down. The place would be swarming with Sanctum Guards, Fire crews and Medics in less than five minutes; she had to get out immediately.

Carefully, she removed all traces of her visit, then ran down the back garden, scowling at the pink and grey rock slabs that covered this area; if she'd had any explosive left, she would have blown them up on the spot- she'd have to come back.

After bathing and changing into an elegant, blue, woollen dress, Madalene headed for the kitchen; killing was hungry work. Having fixed a plate of fresh bread and cold chicken, she sank into a chair and switched on the radio. Ferociously she tore at the chicken; while she listened to an over-excitable broadcaster describe the scene.

"…believed to be the work of the terrorist organisation, Provoke…"

Ha! The Provoke group couldn't blow-up a fireworks factory if they walked in there with their coats on fire. She was mad to think she needed them. She could bring down Shadowman's regime, single-handedly. Tonight Peter Shadow would know what it felt like to be afraid, she only wished she could see that fear. The communicator buzzed,

"Hi Maddy, it's Bren. Listen there's chaos here and if you listen to the news, you'll hear why. I'm going to be late home, so don't bother cooking for me; I'll eat in the restaurant. Sorry darling. I love you."

27

Would he still love her if he discovered, she'd neglected her household chores in favour of a little massacre and mayhem?

Madalene baked a large chocolate cake, filling it with thick cream, but this wasn't enough to curb her restlessness. The only way to deal with the enormous amount of energy inside her was to go running. Most days she ran at speed for at least two hours; today she felt that two hours wouldn't be enough. But that was the only amount of time was available to her; she had to be innocently, at home, when Jinn and Hayla returned from school.

As she went to fetch her running clothes, she heard heavy knocking on the door. Hurriedly she went into her bedroom, doused herself liberally with a floral perfume, and then went to find out what the Sanctum Guards wanted.

"Come in, gentlemen, how can I help you?" She smiled sweetly at them, flicking her long, black hair over her shoulder, to draw attention to it. Giving them time to notice the tightness of her dress and the way it moulded itself to her body, like an extra layer of skin, she beckoned them in. As they entered, shutting the door carefully behind them, she covertly studied them. They were not the usual Sanctum thugs and she wondered if they were members of the Secret Force that she suspected existed, but had never found any evidence of. Both of them were virtually dribbling at the sight of her; it was pathetic, but satisfying.

"We're sorry to disturb you, Mrs Agare, but we need to ask you a few questions."

"Is it Bren?" she asked anxiously, "Has something happened to my husband?"

"No, calm yourself, your husband's fine. There's been a major incident in this area and we're questioning everyone locally, in the hope of quickly finding those responsible."

"My goodness! Am I in danger? Are my children in danger?"

"No-one's in any danger, Mrs Agare, I promise you. If we could just ask our questions, we'll be on our way as quickly as possible."

"Well that's a relief. Come into the kitchen and I'll make you both a drink. You're in luck, I made a cake this morning, would you like a slice?"

Their eyes took in everything and Madalene knew how normal it all looked. As she busied herself, they began their questions.

-Had she been out at all that day?

-Of course she had. She'd gone to fetch the cream, she needed for her cake.

-Had she seen anything or anyone suspicious, when she was out?

-Not at all, but then she wasn't very observant. They had to understand that women's minds tended to wander when they were shopping.

-Was she a good friend of Alice Jones?

-Yes she was and had been so for a long time. Why? Had something bad happened to Alice?

This was the most dangerous question they asked. If these men were who she thought they were, they already knew of her friendship and her visits, just like they knew who her husband was; any denial would raise suspicion.

-Did she know that Alice Jones was a violent psychopath?

-Ridiculous. Alice was a gentle soul who wouldn't hurt anyone.

-We believe otherwise.

-Well everyone was entitled to their beliefs, but she could assure them, Alice was harmless. Now would anyone like another slice of cake?

Finally they seemed satisfied, and it was clear that all they saw was a beautiful woman, who had misguidedly befriended the wrong person. As they made to leave, one of them said, "We won't trouble you again Mrs Agare. Your husband is a lucky man, I hope he appreciates you."

Madalene simpered charmingly, "You're welcome to visit anytime, gentlemen."

Next time I'll give you a taste of something else- my skills with a rifle perhaps.

She changed quickly and was just putting on her running shoes, when she heard another knock on the door. This is getting irritating, she thought, opening the door to a dark-haired woman, who was eighteen months and two days older than her.

Madalene glared at her visitor. "Last time I saw you, I was in jail."

"They should have kept you locked up," said her sister, contemptuously. "Listen, Jinn and Hayla are staying with friends after school, and I've spoken to your husband, told him I'm taking you out for dinner to discuss old times. You're coming with me Madalene. My transporter's waiting outside."

"So, where are we going, Holan? I can see by your face I'm not getting dinner."

"I've been sent to bring you to a Provoke meeting. They believe you're the person who shot Edgar Heaton; they also think you're responsible for this morning's carnage. These people are incredibly angry, Madalene; they're talking about lynching you..."

Madalene looked questioningly at her sister. "Lynching me? How? By sending their letters to me, instead of Shadowman."

"That isn't funny," Holan snapped. "Your actions have led to the arrest of several Provoke members. For all of them it means death. They're friends of the people attending this meeting. Some of them are my friends."

"I'm not a member of Provoke; they have no claim on me. What right do they have to accuse me of these crimes without proof, and to threaten me? Their hypocrisy stinks. Your friends will die by Sanctum hands, not mine. Will the Provoke group lynch a few Sanctum Guards in reprisal? No they won't, they wouldn't dare." She had the satisfaction of seeing Holan flinch at these words. How could Holan do this to her? However estranged, they were still sisters.

30

As if Holan had read her mind, she said pleadingly, "Please come with me, Madalene. I won't let them harm you, I promise."

For a moment Madalene thought of refusing Holan's request, but aggravating Provoke members would be such fun... "I wouldn't miss this for the world, Holan; believe me, this is going to get interesting. I'll just change into suitable clothes and fetch something from the garden."

Chapter Five

A Bunch of Letter-Writing Sissies

Darkness fell, and snow began to swirl fiercely around the transporter; Madalene smiled, as Holan started to drive like a geriatric.

"We will get there before this meeting of yours comes to an end, won't we? I'd hate to miss it." Turning briefly, Holan glared fiercely at her. Madalene's smile became a cheerful grin.

"Shut up, Madalene, this isn't a social outing," said Holan, determinedly looking back at the road, as if to say I will not allow you to rattle me.

"It isn't?" Madalene replied, pulling a packet of bread and cold chicken out of her bag and beginning to eat. "Want some?"

"No I don't. How can you do that?" Now Madalene was beginning to enjoy herself, she'd forgotten how much fun it was to wind up her sister.

"What? Sit here eating? I'm hungry; I've had a busy day, or so you tell me. Isn't that why we're on our way to some juvenile meeting, where they intend to knot their skipping ropes together and hang me. I've got cake if you'd prefer it." Reaching into the bag she carried, Madalene pulled out a squashed slice of the cake she'd made earlier. Laying it down besides the chicken and bread, she continued eating.

"Cake! Where did you get the sugar to make a cake?" Holan's tone of voice showed she was close to being apoplectic. Good, that was just what Madalene wanted.

"I have friends in the black market; they steal it for me from ships that come in. I can get hold of almost anything; of course it's all meant to go to the Sanctum shops, which makes stealing it such a joy. Would you like me to get you some oranges or maybe a bag of coffee?"

Holan almost choked, but then she said quietly, "Doesn't Bren ask questions about your criminal activities?"

"Why should he? He gave me a pass to get into the Sanctum shops; of course it's rare for those shops to get sugar, unless I allow some to go through, but if I tell Bren they've got sugar, he believes me. I always make sure the shop I'm talking about has the stuff in stock, so I'm not lying to him."

"You're using him, Madalene, that's worse than lying. When I spoke to him earlier, it was clear that he adores you. Don't you realise how much danger you're putting him in? And what happens to Jinn if you get caught, not to mention Bren's little girl, Hayla? You don't care do you? Your grasp on reality went a long time ago, along with any genuine emotions you ever had."

Her grasp on reality? Holan had no idea what reality was like for countless people in the country. And Peter Shadow had only just begun. Worse was to come, she knew it. Of course she cared for her family and if anything happened to them because of her, then she was damned for eternity. It might be arrogance, but she was involved in something greater than family, and had been involved for a long time. It was too late to stop now.

"Always ready to think the worst of me, Holan; even though you know what made me like this? I don't want to endanger my family, but it can't be helped. Anyway, the Provoke group's about to lynch me, so my family won't be in danger much longer? Now have some cake, it might sweeten that sour disposition of yours."

"I'm driving; I don't want your cake," said Holan, snappily.

"You could stop the transporter and have something. You might as well, it's virtually stopped already. Where's the meeting being held by the way?" Madalene said, deliberately keeping her voice cheery, and therefore annoying.

"You don't need to know that, but it's not much further. Just eat your food and be silent."

Madalene chuckled, it was so easy to goad Holan, always had been. Genuinely hungry, she began to eat with relish, noticing her sister scowling as she did so. Did Holan really think she was scared of the Provoke group? Before she'd finished eating, the transporter came to a halt; Madalene noted they were on the outskirts of London, probably Amersham, though she couldn't be sure. To one side of the vehicle was a derelict computer factory, a typical venue for this sort of meeting, as there were lots of them around. Holan looked pointedly at her, but ignoring the look, she picked up the slice of cake and slowly began to nibble on it.

"We're here, Madalene," said Holan, impatiently.

"I can see that for myself," she answered through a mouthful of cake. "I'll finish this, and then we'll go in."

"There's no time for that. Put the cake away."

"I'm not wasting good cake." She took another mouthful, and then stepped out of the transporter, cake in hand.

"You can't go into the meeting, eating cake," said Holan furiously.

"Is that so? Try to stop me."

For a moment it looked as if Holan was going to do just that, but instead she spun around and headed angrily towards the factory.

Madalene followed Holan down into a basement, where a crowd of people waited; nearly three times as many as had been at the Provoke meeting she'd previously attended. A roar of outrage greeted her arrival, but nonchalantly she continued eating cake as she pressed forward through the crowd. Again she heard her so-called life story discussed in detail; a few brave souls even spat in her direction, but she ignored them. Holan however, was greeted warmly by everyone; she was obviously someone with status in the group. Once they reached the front of the room, Holan affectionately greeted a fair-haired young man, of stocky build, who stood there with two other, younger men at his side. Madalene smiled as all four glared at her, then took her last mouthful of cake, and, while Holan held a hand up for silence, she casually wiped her hands on her trousers.

"As requested I've brought my sister Madalene here, to answer your questions on recent events. Remember, there is no proof of her involvement in these events, so give her a fair hearing."

Madalene stepped forward slightly, contempt etched deliberately on her face; she had not brought her rifle with her, but was nevertheless armed with knives and a small handgun. They should have searched her for weapons; in fact Holan should have checked her before they left the house.

"I'm fascinated to meet so many members of the notorious and much-feared Provoke group. Surely you should all be at home,

34

scaring Shadowman with your mighty pens." Another howl of hostility started, but she ignored it. "I'm on your side, truly I am, but unfortunately I couldn't write a protest letter if I tried." She laughed, openly inciting them. "Now, now. I would have become a member of this group, if Elgin hadn't been afraid I'd get my spelling and punctuation wrong."

"We do more than just write letters," said the fair-haired man, furiously, moving to stand next to Holan.

"Oh yes, I forgot sticking up posters…"

Without warning the fair-haired man attacked her, and several men in the front row rushed to help him, but her reflexes were quick and in minutes most of them were flat on their backs, clutching their stomachs, and trying to stem bleeding noses.

Now she was angry and she watched with satisfaction, as the force of her anger was felt around the room; the crowd cowered away from her.

"You're right to fear me," she shouted. "I *am* the person who shot Edgar Heaton, I'm not however responsible for the death of his wife. As for this morning, I set a trap for Sanctum Guards, who were on their way to arrest a friend of mine. I thought only three or four would turn up, but twenty-four came instead, so twenty-four died. All those body parts flying through the air? It was thrilling. Twenty-four men killed by *me*. I thought I needed this group to help me build a proper opposition to our government. Now I find I don't need you at all. I'm a one woman war machine."

She let out a wild yell, only to find herself grabbed from behind by the two men who stood next to her sister, and the fair-haired man who was still trying to stop his nose bleeding. She didn't bother to struggle as they bound her hands and pushed her to the floor; she would be able to free herself at any time.

Well, well, there was some spirit in this group after all. To provoke them further, she let out another wild yell, and the crowd that had erupted into chaos with her supposed capture became silent. She could see them visibly wondering why she wasn't afraid. One of her captors, a dark haired man with strangely hazy, blue eyes, stood in front of her. She found him disturbingly attractive; he had to be at least ten years younger than her. She could see this attraction was reciprocated from the expression on his face as he gazed at her;

35

he was struggling to deal with it. To make life harder for him, she gave him her most dazzling smile. To his credit, he maintained his fearless stance.

"My name is Christian Peek. The fair-haired man you assaulted is Alan Moore, leader of this branch…"

"I assaulted! He attacked me."

"Your sister, Holan, is his deputy and the other man standing with us, is my good friend Torin Spice," he said, ignoring her outburst. "You speak with pride of your achievements, but let me tell you what you've actually achieved. Many of our members were pulled in shortly after the explosion. They'll undergo torture and die in the Arena because of *you*. Can't you see why we're so angry? We're getting blamed for things we didn't do and have no control over. You have to be stopped before more of us die. Promise not to take any further action against the government and we'll let you leave here unharmed. If you don't…"

"If I don't, what? You'll put a rope around my neck? Go on then, fetch your rope and get on with it. Your threats bore me. At no time did I leave any indication that this was the work of Provoke, that assumption is the Sanctum's alone. Why would I want a bunch of letter- writing sissies getting credit for my magnificent deeds?"

She ardently hoped no Sanctum spies were in the audience, but if there were spies, surely most of these people would have already been picked up. Putting the thought out of her mind, she continued speaking.

"You've already seen Provoke members die in the Arena, through no fault of mine; did you really think that would stop if you just kept writing letters? Whether you use pens or bullets makes no difference to Shadowman, he will annihilate this group anyway. He's never been able to take the slightest bit of criticism. I know I frighten you, but he's the one you should be frightened of."

Murmured conversations began, and a few people began to regard her with reluctant respect. Christian and his friends were studying her warily, and Holan was trying to indicate that she should shut up. When she'd got all this attention? No way.

"Listen to me. You can't fight Shadowman and the Sanctum openly, I agree with you on this point. It would be suicidal to do so; but neither can you wait for them to pick you up, torture you, and send you to the Arena. You shake them up with actions like mine, and you keep shaking them until they fall."

"We're not fighters, Madalene. You've had army training; you're skilled with weapons, know how to safely handle stuff, like explosives. That's why you have to stop; the people getting hurt aren't like you. I'm a University student, skilled only with books. And I have a conscience, it would destroy me to harm another human being..." said Christian. This one was beginning to grow on her. He had pompous ideas, but presented them so charmingly.

"Hypocrite! You intend to kill me! How is murdering me, different from murdering your pen-pals?"

Christian struggled to give her an answer, so Alan stepped in to reply; blood still trickling from his nose.

"Holan has told us a lot about you. She says you're little more than a crazed animal, and seeing your reactions here today, I believe it. It would be a kindness to put you down; a kindness to you and to all Provoke group members."

Madalene glared at Holan, who had the grace to blush, and turn away.

"My sister knows me well, but you're not listening. My death won't save you from Shadowman, unless it makes you realise that you are capable of the same level of violence that I am, and that you can use that violence against him."

"We don't want to become like you, Madalene. Yes, Shadowman will still try to prevent our opposition, but you're accelerating his attacks, and because we don't know what you'll do next, we can't protect ourselves. If you won't agree to quietly disappear, you leave us with no choice. We *have* to kill you. It's dangerous to let you live."

Before she could reply, Alan yelled to Torin and Christian to fetch rope. Holan followed them and began to argue, but they shook their heads stubbornly at whatever it was, she was saying. As they returned carrying a thickly corded rope with a pre-formed noose knotted into it, the crowd went wild and began chanting her name, preceded by the phrase 'Kill the bitch...' which was not very reassuring. She was hoping, fervently, that the Provoke group didn't have a clue how to hang someone, or she could be in serious trouble. She'd seen a few botched hangings during her time in the army, and they were sickening to watch, but her only chance of escape lay in a botched job. Her thoughts were interrupted by an argument going on between Holan and Alan; it was even less reassuring.

"I'm not letting her bring more destruction down on us. Your sister's insane; she won't even feel this," said Alan, trying to push Holan away, so he and some of the men in the crowd could throw the rope over one of the ceiling beams.

"I said she was crazed, not insane; there's a difference, Alan. Let me take her somewhere quiet and shoot her for you. She's my sister; I don't want to watch her die violently."

"The group's fears will be assuaged by this. They need to see her die to feel safe. Because of her, they have family members or friends suffering in the Sanctum's torture chambers, and they realise it could be them next. It has to be done, Holan."

"It doesn't have to be done like this, Alan." Holan went to attack him, but was grabbed by Torin and Christian. Madalene was delighted to see Holan fighting them, even if she wasn't good at it. It was also good to hear Holan defending her, although the 'quiet shooting' bit, was none too sisterly.

As Alan and his friends threw the rope over the beam, she freed her wrists, but left the rope in place hoping no-one would spot how loose it was. A few of the men who had helped Alan set up his make-shift gallows now came over to pull her up. Holan was still fighting Torin and Christian, and now doing a much better job. Madalene gave her sister an encouraging cheer, but received only a scowl in reply. The crowd was in chaos; fights had broken out everywhere; some people wanting to see her hanged and others trying to prevent it happening; the noise in the room was staggering. She was escorted to Alan and his apprehension was evident; nevertheless, he resolutely threw the noose over her head, and suddenly the room went silent, as people stopped fighting, and looked on in horror.

"You do realise that without a drop to break my neck, this is going to be messy? I could struggle for over half an hour up there, maybe longer," she said, smiling sweetly at him.

"Don't smile at me like that. I don't want to do this, Madalene. I have to do it. Will you agree to stop attacking the Sanctum?"

"What? And miss out on something so enjoyable? Get on with it, Alan Moore; find out for yourself what it feels like to murder someone. I already know and I tell you this, you will never sleep, trouble-free, again."

Alan released a frustrated sigh, and then signalled for the men on the other end of the rope to begin hauling her up. Before her feet left the ground, she let out a final wild cry of defiance, and then the rope tightened around her throat and cut it off.

"Let her go, Alan. I will not let you harm her." Elgin stood at the back of the room, a gun in each hand, rifle over his shoulder, and knives in a belt around his waist. Madalene let the rope drop away from her wrists and seized one of her knives; quickly she reached up and cut the rope above her. Dropping heavily to the floor, she loosened the rope around her neck and lay still, coughing and retching. Getting up shakily, she felt blood trickling down her chin; she'd bitten her tongue as they'd pulled her up. The crowd gasped, as Elgin walked quickly to the front of the room, and threw his arms around her. She threw him a quizzical look, but he ignored it.

"Are you okay Madalene?" he whispered to her.

"I wasn't going to let them harm me, old man, but it's good of you to come to my rescue," she said, hoarsely, wiping her chin with a trembling hand.

Ignoring Elgin, Alan and some of the others rushed to recapture her. She danced away from them, pulling the small handgun out of her pocket, it shook in her hand, but no-one doubted that she could hit any target she aimed at. "You've never seen anyone hang before, have you, Alan? When I said messy, I meant messy; my bowels would have declared 'Open day', and my bladder would have followed, not the most enthralling of sights, and with all its blood vessels popping, my face would have turned a lovely shade of purple. Watching me struggle to breathe and stay alive would have given you nightmares for months. Touch me again and I'll kill you; I don't have nightmares."

"I'll kill you, if she doesn't. You might be my friend, Alan, but this is barbaric. You know I would never sanction anything like this," said Elgin, moving once again to Madalene's side.

"Why have you come here armed, Elgin? Have you gone as crazy as this madwoman?" said Alan, heatedly.

"You have no idea what this madwoman is capable of..."

"Yes I do, Elgin," said Alan. "That's why I want her dead. Perhaps a careful word in a Sanctum ear will do the job."

"Then you would condemn us all. Madalene is the only opposition this government has at the moment, and they would be grateful for your help in disposing of her. Don't you realise how ineffective we are? Thanks to Madalene, many people live who should have died. Who have we saved?"

"I'm no saint, old man, and despite being called a madwoman many times today, my senses are intact," she said, still finding it difficult to breathe, let alone talk.

"They have my Bertha, and Grace is dead," he said softly. "What a fight they made of it though; apparently Bertha killed four of them before they captured her, and Grace killed two. I would have helped them, maybe saved them, but I'd gone to visit Alice to escape Bertha's nagging; she kept going on about you..."

To her dismay, Elgin began to sob; as he did so, the news of his loss spread around the room. "You'll be top of their most-wanted list, Elgin; if you've spoken with Alice, you know what I can do; I'll get you out of the country as quickly as I can, provided these idiots leave me alone. I'll also try to free Bertha, but make no promises, because I can't think how the hell to do it at the moment." Elgin gave her a fierce hug, which made her grimace; didn't he understand that a hug was the last thing a person who'd just been hanged needed? Trouble was that Elgin was a demonstrative man, she'd liked him instantly; he was the father she should have had. There was no love lost between her and his wife Bertha, she'd hated that bitch on sight, but for Elgin's sake, she would attempt to free her.

"I will not run," he said. "I will fight your way now, and I will train those who want to be part of a new Provoke group, to fight also. I want you to take my place in this new group, you will be responsible for Provoke members everywhere; Bertha would hate me for it, but it is the only way forward. I forbid you to attempt the rescue of my wife, it is an impossible task and the new Provoke group needs you."

Madalene barely heard his words. As Bren's wife, she had access to the Sanctum, at least to its offices. How hard could it be to reach the cells from there?

"I will not stay with the Provoke group, if she's to be its leader," said Holan, accompanied by many other voices, including Alan's. His friends, Christian and Torin were also shouting their refusal to be part of any group led by Madalene.

"And I was going to make you my second in command," she said, sarcastically, turning to look at her sister. "Bye, Holan."

"Now my dear Holan…" said Elgin.

"No, Elgin. You said it yourself, my sister is mad, she will destroy us all. Alan will take over this group if you no longer wish to be its leader, and I will remain with him, along with Christian, Torin and any others who want to stay with us. We will take on a new name and dissociate ourselves from the Provoke group. As it obviously aggravates Shadowman, the letter-writing will continue." Glaring at Madalene, she added, "and the sticking-up of posters."

But Madalene was no longer listening; as the noise and hubbub rose around her, she considered an approach to getting Bertha out. Bren had told her that security at the Sanctum was at heightened levels, since the attack on Edgar Heaton. Her only chance was that no-one would anticipate an attempt to free a prisoner; if it could be done though, it would be another huge blow against them. Mentally, she considered the layout from maps she had studied. Any open approach would harm her family, she could not risk that. It could only be done if one of the old tunnels beneath London went directly under the Sanctum. She needed to do some map reading before she could decide anything; that meant getting out of this ridiculous meeting and home fast. Though it had already been an incredible day, if she was going to rescue Bertha, it had to be tonight. And if that was successful, she also needed to get Bertha straight out of the country. There was a shipment leaving Liverpool at three o clock, the following morning; Alice would be part of that shipment. It was crazy to even contemplate this rescue, and the odds of it happening at all were huge, added to which, she was exhausted and her throat and neck were painful. Nevertheless, she was determined to try; there were pills to ease pain and exhaustion, and hadn't she just been called a madwoman?

"Madalene, do you accept the leadership of this new Provoke group?" said a harassed Elgin. "There are a few here who will join us, others will follow."

Madalene began heading towards the exit, almost immediately Alan chased after her, closely followed by Christian and Torin. To make her life harder, the crowd moved in on her as well. There was no choice, she grabbed a young girl standing nearby and held the handgun to her head.

"If anyone touches me or prevents my departure, she dies instantly. I will return here in four days time, hoping your manners have improved. You will have my decision then, Elgin. Holan, get him to a place of safety and guard him well, he's in great danger." She dragged the helpless, young girl through a crowd that now let her pass.

"What's your name?" she asked, surprised at how unafraid her victim was.

"Ellyn, madam," she answered.

"Aren't you afraid of me, Ellyn?"

"I'm afraid of being shot, but I'm not afraid of you, not if Elgin likes you. I want to be part of your new group, even if all I can do is fetch and carry things for you."

Madalene stopped for a moment to look at the girl and was stunned to see hero-worship in her eyes, maybe Elgin's idea of a new Provoke group could work. "I won't shoot you, and if I form a new group, I'll be glad to make you part of it and not just for fetching and carrying, but could you do me a favour and act frightened or I'll never reach the doorway."

To her delight, Ellyn winked at her and immediately let out an impressive wail of fear. The crowd quickly moved back further and within moments they were at the doorway.

"Thanks Ellyn," she said releasing her and beginning to run. "I won't forget this." As she ran, she could hear the crowd emerging behind her, but to her surprise they suddenly stopped. Looking back, she saw Ellyn lying prone on the ground and was about to return to check that she was okay, when the girl gave her a second wink. Laughing quietly to herself, Madalene ran on, until she reached the open air and Holan's transporter.

Chapter Six

Superwoman

Xybille was an amphetamine-based drug, available only on the black market; it had dangerous side-effects and was highly addictive. For days after using this drug, Madalene suffered severe exhaustion; she also felt like bugs were crawling under her skin, and would bleed badly as she tried to get rid of them with her fingernails. On the positive side, Xybille produced endless energy and incredible mental alertness, which was what she needed if she was to go out and rescue Bertha, instead of collapsing on the bed and falling asleep.

She needed to do a "run", repeated intravenous injections of the drug; it was the only way to make sure that she didn't run out of energy when she needed it most. It was going to be tricky to hide her drug use from Bren, and she also had rope burns on her neck to explain. Perhaps there was an excuse that covered both. However, now wasn't the time to contemplate Bren's disapproval, or how to avoid it; she had to rescue Bertha from the Sanctum torture chambers and send her straight over to Ireland. Quickly, Madalene arranged an overnight stay for Jinn and Hayla; and then rang Bren to tell him where the children were, adding that she was spending the night with Holan. Finally she rolled up her sleeve and became Superwoman.

Restlessly, Madalene pored over the maps, but she couldn't find what she was looking for. With a desperate need to move, she prowled up and down the room, holding one of the maps in her hand. Without thought, she switched the radio on, only to hear a solemn broadcaster relate the tragedy of the bombing earlier that day. He then began to praise the virtues of the Sanctum, especially the courage they were showing during this difficult time. In disgust she switched the radio off. With any luck, they'd need more of that courage, when she'd finished. Renewing her efforts, she finally found what she'd been looking for. There was an old sewage drain that led straight into the lower floors of the Sanctum building, and that was where the torture chambers were situated. Trying hard to control her euphoria, she changed into dark clothes, fetched a gun with a silencer on it, her rifle and several knives; and then made a few calls to various homes in Liverpool.

Leaving the transporter parked in one of the streets, near the drain's opening, Madalene ran to an area of derelict housing, where she thought she would find the manhole cover to the drain. It wasn't easy to find the one she needed, as there were several manhole covers in the area. And, when she finally decided she'd found the right one; it took ages to clear away the debris on top of it, and ease it open. So much for speed; at this rate, it would take days to rescue Bertha, not hours. Climbing down a rusty ladder, she was horrified to discover, that this particular drain was small and narrow; she could barely stand upright in it. The smell was atrocious and she retched frequently as she made her way along it, which increased the pain in her throat and reminded her that she'd forgotten to take any painkillers. Time and time again she had to stop and clear obstructions, as the drain was crushed in several places, probably due to new building work above it.

An hour passed by and still she moved carefully through claustrophobic darkness. Something was wrong. On the map the drain had seemed nearer to the Sanctum and weren't sewers supposed to be bigger than this. She must have taken too much Xybille and chosen the wrong drain, which meant her plan wasn't going to work, or had she? She'd used Xybille before, especially when helping the elderly go underground, and she'd made no mistakes then. Well this drain had to go somewhere and she had far too much energy simmering inside her to stop; besides she was, what had she called herself at that meeting? Yes. She was a one woman war machine. First there was Catherine the Great and then there was Madalene the Great. No, Madalene the Greatest, and Provoke had had the nerve to try and hang her. Bertha the bitch would enjoy hearing that particular anecdote once she was rescued; they could laugh about it together.

Her persistence paid off, when an hour later, she finally reached another rusty ladder. At this point, the drain was badly cracked and broken, and as she reached for the first rung of the ladder, she cut her left hand on a jagged shard that had fallen directly behind it. Coming out into a dirty, disused room, which might once have been a toilet block; she tore off a section of her shirt and used it to bandage the cut; it bled through in moments, so she tore off more to pad it further. She was glad it wasn't her right hand that was cut; she could use a gun with either hand, but preferred to use the right one. The remains of a mirror stood on a wall and looking into it, she saw a demonic visage; dilated pupil's filled bloodshot eyes, and her face was as black as her hair. Her appearance alone was enough to terrify any guards; hell, she hadn't needed to bring weapons. So where was she exactly, it was time to find out?

Carefully and slowly, she moved through deserted rooms, trusting to the luck that had brought her twenty-four victims that morning. It didn't fail her. Rounding a corner, she heard hysterical screaming coming from a nearby room. It was a female's voice, but was it Bertha's? As she'd only met Bertha once, there was no way of knowing. There could be only one attempt at this, followed by nearly two desperate hours back in the drain, possibly pursued this time. She had to be decisive, if it was the wrong woman, she had no choice but to help that woman escape, and leave Bertha behind. It wouldn't be the blow she'd intended; nevertheless, it would be a blow, and it would shake the Sanctum's complacency. She heard moaning and screams coming from other rooms, was it worth checking them? Instinct told her that Bertha would be given worse treatment than an ordinary prisoner. It *had* to be Bertha in that room.

Now she moved in a fluid fashion that was uniquely hers. Noiselessly opening the door, she saw three men, brutal in every aspect, standing around a large wooden block, burning the woman chained there with small metal rods. No wonder the woman was screaming frantically. Madalene knew, in this woman's position, she would scream too; probably louder and more frantically. It was a terrifying sight, but remaining impassive, she took out her gun and with speed, coldly shot all three men. Hurrying over to the block, she found the woman, lying there naked and badly burned, was indeed Bertha. Silent now, Bertha studied her saviour, and then groaned.

"Not you. Anyone, but you."

"Pleased to see me again? I knew you would be," said Madalene, with a sardonic smile.

Needing keys for Bertha's chains, Madalene began to check the dead bodies; the men disgusted her and she would have liked to mutilate their corpses, but there was no time for anything like that.

The keys were in the pocket of the second brute, she searched. Quickly, she released Bertha, and then half carried and half dragged her out of the room.

It was difficult, Bertha was a big woman and her naked body was covered with blood from earlier assaults. With her left hand cut so badly, it was hard for Madalene to get a grip on Bertha's slippery body, but there was no time to find garments for her. Struggling, Madalene finally got Bertha to the drain, she helped her down the ladder, and then went back to clear their tracks. Once she was satisfied, she followed Bertha into the drain.

"Listen Bertha, you have to help me. I can't carry you along this drain; you'll have to get along it by yourself. You told me you were a trained soldier, now prove it. Either get moving, or go back to that room with the wooden block and wait for some more Sanctum brutes to come along. Your choice."

"I-I-I can't...I'm hurt," said Bertha, trying hard not to cry.

"I don't care? Move it soldier. Get your fat backside down this drain, now."

The military approach worked. Bertha moved slowly at first, but gradually increased her speed until she was moving surprisingly quickly. Madalene followed, after wrapping the rest of her shirt around her hand. She would not leave them a trail, even if it was obvious that the drain went in one direction only. There was no pursuit, however, and no distant sounds of alarm; evidently the escape had not yet been discovered. It was just gone ten-thirty when they emerged from the drain; it had taken only an hour and a quarter to get back down it, as Madalene had removed all the obstacles on the way in.

Bertha stood, shivering in the freezing night air, Madalene felt sorry for her, but had no intention of letting her rest yet. Timing had become very tight; if they didn't reach the transporter quickly, they wouldn't get to Liverpool, until after the boat sailed.

"I'm driving you up to Liverpool and putting you on a boat to Ireland, it leaves at three tomorrow morning, but if we don't hurry, you'll miss it. Here, take my hand. No not that hand, the other one," said Madalene, grabbing Bertha and dragging her along.

"You're a maniac. Why would I want to go to Ireland? I don't need a holiday. I need to find Elgin and make sure he's safe."

"Elgin's safe, but you're not. The Sanctum will launch a huge manhunt for you; if you're not out of this country fast, they'll have you back in their cells by tomorrow morning. I have no intention of rescuing you a second time. You *are* getting on that boat, so come on."

Though Bertha stumbled and fell a few times, Madalene was impressed with the guts she was showing. Her dislike of this woman was rapidly being replaced by respect. When they reached the transporter, Madalene saw that Bertha was finished; she shook with the effort of simply breathing now. Gently, Madalene got Bertha seated in the transporter, then joined her and started the engine. It ran on alcohol made from food waste, as did most transporters. She had filled the tank using a funnel, before she left home and put an emergency can of the stuff in the back; still, it was a long drive to Liverpool and a boat to Ireland; she only hoped they made it

"Did you tell them everything you know about the Provoke group, about Elgin and the others?" asked Madalene, trying to keep Bertha awake to avoid any delayed shock reaction.

"I'm not you, Superwoman, but I'm not pathetic either. I told them nothing. Why were they burning me with metal rods, if they already knew everything I had to tell them?" said Bertha, defiantly.

"Elgin's taken up arms and made me leader of the Provoke group. You didn't even want me as a member. What do you think of that?" To her surprise, Bertha gave a weak chuckle.

"I was wondering why you bothered to rescue me, after our last little encounter. You wouldn't have wanted me to miss out on the news that you're my new leader. Well, surprise, I think Elgin is an absolute genius. If anyone can terrify the Sanctum into submission, it's you."

"My luck won't hold, it never does. They'll catch me fairly soon and when they do, I'll be lying in a torture chamber, just like you were, and talking non-stop. I'll tell them everything, even my knicker size and not many people know that. You don't know me at all; I'm not Superwoman."

47

"I know I hate you. A woman, who looks like you, should be a simpering imbecile, not a bloody heroine. It's not fair. Elgin's obsessed with you, did you know that?"

"Jealousy? I like Elgin, but as a father figure only. Besides, you're quite a heroine yourself. I hear you killed four Sanctum Guards before they captured you. You and Elgin should be proud of yourselves and proud of Grace too. You were the only ones brave enough to oppose our dearly hated government. Yes, I mock your group and its methods, that's the way I am; your way isn't my way. But one day you'll be in the history books; I won't be. Bertha the Brave, it has such a nice ring to it, don't you think?"

Despite her pain, Bertha laughed. "Bertha the naked. Isn't there a blanket, or something I can use to cover myself up, in this transporter?"

"It's Holan's transporter and I stole it, but have a look in the back, there might be something there." Madalene listened as Bertha rummaged around on the back seat, then saw that she'd found herself a blue blanket.

"Typical Holan. Only she would carry a blanket in a transporter. I bet there's a shovel in the back as well. There might even be food if you look carefully, Holan would protect herself against all eventualities." Sure enough, Bertha found some apples and biscuits.

"My sister, Grace, was the same," said Bertha, miserably. "This might sound stupid to you, but she was cautious about the activities of the Provoke group. I don't think she wanted to be a member, let alone a leader. It just happened and she went along with it."

"Grace died bravely. Be proud of her," said Madalene, meaning it.

"You're the one who inspired us to fight, even though we had no intention of becoming like you. And though my sister's dead, I'm glad she died fighting. You say I don't know you. Well Elgin likes you, though I don't know why, so tell me about yourself. That's if you can talk *and* drive in these dreadful weather conditions."

"I'm an evil woman with a beautiful face and no heart, that's all you need to know about me."

"That's what I thought when I met you at that meeting, Madalene, but I was mistaken. Your heart matches your looks, which is why you saved me. Yes I know it's a great strike against the Sanctum and you wanted to please Elgin, but subconsciously you've been very gentle with me. I'm beginning to see why Elgin thinks so highly of you. We have a long journey ahead of us, tell me more."

And so, during their long, desperate drive through snow-filled roads, Madalene told Bertha her history. Glancing over as she drove, she saw tears in Bertha's eyes and knew that Bertha finally understood her. Wanting to know Bertha better, Madalene demanded to know how Bertha had met Elgin, why Grace had no partner and what Bertha's experiences in the army had been like. Soon they were laughing and joking, as if they had known each other all their lives. When they finally reached their destination, Madalene and Bertha were firm friends.

As Madalene came to a halt, a transporter rolled up alongside her and two men got out and walked over. They greeted her with soft Irish accents, and then beckoned for Bertha to transfer to their transporter. Bertha hugged Madalene tightly, obviously unable to indicate her gratitude in any other way.

"Go on Bertha. Get well and prosper. I'll send Elgin over to you as soon as I can."

"I'll return to fight alongside you, as my leader, as soon as I'm better."

The expression on Bertha's face was so earnest, that Madalene had to smile; the new Provoke group had another member, a powerful new member.

"I would be honoured to fight at *your* side, Bertha. Goodbye my friend." She saw Bertha nod her head, an acknowledgement of their friendship, and then she was gone.

Her Irish friends would get Bertha onto the boat, even though they had less than ten minutes before the boat sailed, and no doubt they would charge her a fortune for doing so. And yet another fortune for the fuel she needed to get home. Mercenary they might be, but a man who worked for a fee was often more trustworthy, than a man who worked for a cause.

Filled with energy, she decided to wait for the men to return and get them to take her to one of the illicit night-clubs in the dock area. She was Superwoman and now she'd finished with the rescuing and dispensing justice, she wanted to dance.

Chapter Seven

In the Shadows

The room was dark; thick, black curtains preventing daylight's intrusion. A few flickering candles threw their light onto the occupants of the room, who sat in uneasy silence around a large oak table. Peter Shadow, or Shadowman as he liked to be called, sat apart from the others, hidden in darkness and deep in thought. His rise to power had been swift, almost unopposed, but now things had changed. It wasn't the Provoke group that worried him, initially they had been an amusement, then merely an irritation; they had never been a real threat. The events of the last week were a different matter - they were signs of serious opposition. Whoever was responsible had to be caught and dealt with quickly. His eyes fell on Barton Lacey, a skinny man with greying hair, whose looks belied the fact that he was second-in-command and responsible for gaining information from prisoners, or inventing information against them.

"Enlighten me, Barton. How does a woman, who has undergone hours of torture, manage to shoot three 'technicians', as you like to call them, who were working on her, and then calmly escape into the night.? What were your men doing? Teasing her?" He kept his tone mild, but as a pale-faced Barton stood, peering to find him in the darkness, he let out a menacing chuckle, making it clear that the answers to his questions had better be good.

"S-Someone came in from the outside to rescue her, Shadowman. We believe this person used an old drainage pipe to get into and out of the Sanctum cells. The technicians down there were shot so quickly, they had no time to raise the alarm. A gun with a silencer was probably used; no-one down there heard the shots. How could we have known that someone would dare to enter the Sanctum...?"

"We had Edgar Heaton killed without warning outside the Astoria hotel, and we lost twenty-four of our Guards in an unexpected explosion on an ordinary suburban street. Someone dared that," Peter answered, angrily.

51

He saw the silent men sat around the table recoil; they knew, as well as he did, that when he got angry he could become dangerously irrational. Controlling himself with difficulty, he continued. "You do realise that the woman who escaped was no ordinary female prisoner? We had *Bertha Thomas* in our custody - a woman who managed to kill four of our Guards, before she was detained. Do you want to know how she killed that many Guards? She used a sharp vegetable knife, got in close to them and quickly slit their throats. That alone makes her an extremely dangerous woman, but she is also deputy-leader of the Provoke group and the wife of Elgin, its leader. Didn't it occur to any of you that a bit of extra security might have been a good idea?" He glared from one man to another, before realising they could not see him in the darkness.

"B-But we kept her in chains from the beginning and there were three men in there with her at all times. We didn't lock the chamber door, because we couldn't see any need to do so," said Barton, desperately trying to defend himself.

"Exactly my point. You were too stupid to see that there was a need to keep this prisoner secure. You didn't understand that, properly guarded and tortured, she would have told us everything we needed to know. That this was our chance to finally eliminate the irritating Provoke group. Now, because of your carelessness, the irritation continues."

"My men did their job properly. Even with help, Bertha can't have got far…"

"Is that so? Bertha had to know her rescuer - a stranger was hardly likely to set her free; this rescuer could be the man who shot Edgar Heaton, and the man who set explosives in Alice Jones's house and helped Alice escape. He is hardly likely to leave Bertha where we can find her." Once again Peter struggled to contain his temper. Why was Barton so dim-witted, he didn't seem to realise the importance of what they'd lost? None of his Inner Sanctum realised they were now facing a serious threat to their government.

"I think Elgin's grown tired of writing incessant complaint letters and has turned to terrorism. I believe he's the man we seek. Our terrorist. Being Alice and Bertha's knight in shining armour is the sort of stupid, heroic action that he would find irresistible." For a moment Peter paused, considering Elgin; there was nothing he did

52

not know about his opponent, except where to find him. The man moved constantly and it was unfortunate that he had not been home when his latest hideout had been raided.

"Why has no-one yet discovered Elgin's whereabouts?" he shouted. "I want that man in my cells by tomorrow morning and I want his wife in there with him."

A bulky, hairless man further down the table, heaved himself onto his feet; wiping drool off his thick lips, he began to speak fearlessly. "We are not as stupid as you think, Peter. We realise that Bertha Thomas is a great loss; but even you could not have predicted this would happen. At the moment the drainage pipe is being examined for evidence, after which it will be destroyed, as will any other underground drains which lead into or near the Sanctum. We are conducting a nationwide search to find Bertha and Elgin and have even deployed the secret services to look for them. However, I do not think Elgin is our terrorist, even though he has the right background and training. The information I have received suggests that Elgin was elsewhere when Edgar Heaton was shot, and nowhere near the scene of the explosion."

"Ah Vertex! From you I would expect nothing less. It makes me wonder why I made Barton my second-in-command and not you. Don't worry, Barton, I don't intend to demote you yet, not when I have work for you to do. If Vertex is correct, and an unknown terrorist is causing all this mayhem, then I want the man caught quickly and made an example of. It's also time we crushed the Provoke group. There's still a chance that it's one of them who has turned to terrorism and others may join him."

Smiling grimly, he stood and walked slowly to the table. He saw the apprehension on their faces as he approached and went to stand by Vertex, the only one unconcerned by his approach. Hurriedly, Barton began to speak. "I will see to it personally that the Arena is filled with Provoke group members, Shadowman. My people will devise new, more horrifying means of execution for them. When this terrorist is apprehended, I will arrange a spectacular new show especially for you, one which will prolong his death for hours and terrify any who wish to follow his example."

"Will it include dancing girls? I do like semi-clad dancing girls. And there must be musicians to play appropriate music for a man's death; music that we can all dance to."

Barton eagerly nodded his head in agreement, failing to see the joke; the man was an idiot, but a devoted one.

"Be ready for power, Vertex. If Barton fails me again, he will take the place of our terrorist in this spectacular show of his and you will take his place at my side. However, I know how eager you are for power and I will deny you its taste for as long as I can. You have always watched my back, but I watch it too, Fat boy."

Growling angrily, Vertex pushed carelessly past his colleagues and left the room, slamming the doors behind him. Peter Shadow began to laugh and his laughter filled the room. No-one dared laugh with him.

"Only Michael Vertex would defy me like that," he said, looking angrily at his remaining ministers, including the offended looking Barton. "None of the rest of you would walk away from me, no matter how badly I insulted you. Fat boy is not afraid of me, nor has he ever been. Nothing frightens him, which is why he is effective and you are not."

Martin Brown, Minister of Public Affairs, stood up and shakily began to speak.

"I have ordered the media to malign this terrorist and imbue the public with horror. Tomorrow's papers will carry the news that five small children playing in a nearby garden were blown apart in the explosion, and of course there will be accompanying photographs. Sooner or later someone will give us the information to find him. The campaign against the Provoke group and its members continues. I hope this pleases you."

The news pleased him, but not the man. Any man who used obtuse words like imbue was a poof. If Martin Brown *was* a poof, he might well find himself in the Arena-and not as a spectator.

"It pleases me greatly, Martin, but what makes you think our terrorist is a man?"

"Y-You just said...T-The descriptions we have received...Surely only a man could have pulled Bertha along that drain? She was a large woman and too badly hurt to move by herself."

For a long while, Peter stared at Martin in silence, forcing the man to sit back down in terror, but then he smiled cheerfully. "At the moment I agree with you, Martin, but I don't discount the possibility of a terrorist group, or even the possibility that our terrorist is a woman. Now there's a revolting idea, there could be nothing worse than a woman who's forgotten her place - which is to keep her mouth shut and her legs open." He began laughing and dutifully the others around the table joined in, at which point he fell silent.

"I don't understand women in this country. With the exception of a few jobs, I have removed them from the pressures of the workplace, so why aren't they busy making babies? Our population numbers are reaching critically low levels, and something has to be done before they get any lower, or there will be no future for any of us. All fertile women *must* be forced to have babies; non-fertile women and lesbians can go to the Arena."

The meeting continued for another hour and his ministers told him everything he wanted to hear. They irked him, but where could he find people to take their places? Of course, he had three hundred Outer Sanctum members to choose from, but their chief function was to agree with every decision he made, and to allay any public fears about the country being run by a dictator - which it wasn't, he always discussed his ideas with Vertex before putting them into action. These people, both Inner and Outer Sanctum members, were tedious, but they did perform the mundane tasks that led, not only to the country being run well, but being run as he wanted it to be. They had all flinched at his decision to rid the country of its overly large elderly population, but had quickly seen the benefits of it - not seeing the inside of the Arena was one of them.

Soon he would go further, but for now he had to be patient, it wouldn't do to alienate the public at this moment, or there would be rebellion group meetings held in every village hall across the land. Then again women were probably already resurrecting the Suffragette group. Well, any woman found chained to railings this time round would be shot.

Later he dined with Vertex and several beautiful women in the State Dining Room, in Buckingham Palace, one of his many palatial homes. He allowed Vertex to have several rooms there, as Vertex had been his closest friend since childhood. He also let his elderly parents have a suite there. The majority of the place had been transformed into an exclusive, fee-paying brothel and was exceedingly popular. Other rooms acted as guest rooms for the occasional foreign leaders that visited, though he discouraged this as much as possible; their efforts at interference unwisely tempted him to send them to the Arena. The squabble of the afternoon was forgotten and the two men chatted warmly.

"I need a wife Vertex, but who will I choose for such a prestigious role?" He saw Vertex sigh and knew his friend thought he was being capricious again. Well perhaps he was, but at the moment having a wife of his own, rather than raping someone else's, seemed a good idea. If Elgin had a wife, he wanted a wife.

"There are plenty of beautiful women here tonight, why don't you choose one of them? None of them would dare refuse you."

"But I also want a child, Vertex."

"A what?" spluttered Vertex, sending a fine spray of the red wine he was drinking, over the white dress of the woman sitting next to him. She grimaced, but said nothing.

"After your little tantrum, earlier, we discussed women and babies and it made me realise that it's time I had a son and heir, someone to take my place eventually."

"All of these women are fertile, they've been tested, but if none of them satisfy you, I can always fetch more. Sooner or later, one will please you."

"No! These women have many uses, but the mother of my son is *not* going to be a whore. I want my wife to be a strong woman, with lots of courage. She has to be beautiful, because I can't stand ugly women, but she must also be feisty, difficult and hard to handle. That way my son will have two strong sets of genes and he will be a powerful man when he takes over from me. You know you would also get pleasure from this sort of woman, so where do I find her?"

For a moment Vertex looked taken aback, obviously unsure whether his friend could handle a woman who talked back, but then jokily Vertex said, "You need nothing less than one of the legendary Amazon women; someone who would cut a breast off to make it easier to handle her bow. I really don't think you'd like a woman with only one breast though - you are very fond of breasts after all."

More wine was brought to them and for a while they fell into a companionable silence.

"You have an employee in your accounts department called Bren Agare, who I hear has a very beautiful wife. Her name is Madalene and according to the men who interviewed her yesterday about the explosion at Alice Jones's house, she's not only the most beautiful woman they've ever seen, she's also fearless and agreeable. Most people were afraid of these men when they called, but she welcomed them into her home, and even admitted to being Alice's friend, which you have to admit, is pretty fearless given the circumstances. She sounds perfect for you, but unless we kill your hard-working employee on some false excuse, she's very much taken," said Vertex, wine dribbling from his mouth down his many chins.

"It could be easily arranged, Vertex," Peter said sardonically. "Didn't we know a Madalene once? That name bothers me, though I can't think why."

"We've known lots of girls called Madalene. Come, Peter; forget wives, babies and women called Madalene. See how Zara makes eyes at you, surely you don't intend to leave such a lovely woman unsatisfied?

Looking over at a nearby chair, Peter saw a woman with long dark hair and brown eyes gazing expectantly at him. She reminded him of someone. She reminded him of Madalene...

Chapter Eight

Not Again

Every word she spoke singed the air. Her eyes, like Medusa's, glared at anyone who came close turning them into stone. She was the vilest creature in Hell and she showed no remorse as Bren, her husband, left for work with a black eye and a bruised cheek. The children fared little better, leaving the house quickly after being slapped for making too much noise. Alone now, she raged around the empty house, leaving a trail of destruction in her wake, until finally, overcome by exhaustion, she collapsed on the kitchen floor and fell into a deep sleep.

"Madalene! What's wrong with you? Wake up, you bitch."

She was aware that she was being shaken violently, but had no energy to prevent it.

"Look at the state you're in. Wake up, Madalene. You're disgusting; you can't lie there like that all day."

A torrent of ice–cold water hit her body, making her gasp and open her eyes. Facing her and holding an empty bucket was her sister Holan.

"At last the monster awakes," said Holan, contemptuously. "How appropriate to find you lying in pools of your own vomit and urine, but not very pleasant."

Madalene's head felt as if it was stuffed with cotton-wool, making it hard to understand what was happening; even so, she realized that Holan was not exactly being nice.

"Can I get you anything, Holan? Tea? Coffee? Arsenic?" She groaned heavily. Even talking was an effort. "Tell you what, call your pal Alan and tell him to come over here with his rope. We can play Hangman again; I need someone to put me out of my misery."

Holan responded furiously, "I can't call Alan, even though I'd love to take you up on your offer. He was picked up by Sanctum Guards this morning, along with Christian and about eighteen others, and it's all your fault. You've caused all this trouble. All you've ever done is cause trouble."

"Elgin...?" Surely they hadn't captured Elgin, not after all the trouble she'd gone to freeing his wife Bertha; a woman she not only admired, but now also a firm friend.

"Elgin's safe for the time being, we keep moving him, so they can't catch him. By the way, where the hell's my transporter? How dare you steal it?"

"There's no fuel left to run it, but it's round the corner from here. Bren's got a can or two of fuel in his garage if you want to fill up. Please take it and go away, Holan." Shutting her eyes again, she began to return to the bliss of sleep.

"Oh no you don't. You can't cause all this trouble, and then forget it." Again Holan shook her; a habit that was becoming irritating.

"Go away, Holan. Shoot me if you think it would help, I'd welcome death at this moment, I really would." She said this with so much feeling that Holan released her.

"You're taking drugs again, aren't you? What have you taken?"

"A 'run' of Xybille..." Again she drifted off.

"How many injections, Madalene? How many?"

She felt Holan roughly pulling at the sleeves of her top, and then examining both her arms. "Eight injections!" Holan shouted in alarm. "That amount could kill you. Did you do this because of what happened last night?"

"Sort of. But you'll be pleased to know that I've decided to take up Elgin's offer. I will become leader of the Provoke group," she said dreamily, hoping this statement would make her sister go away.

"You're not going near the Provoke group again. A psychotic junkie isn't what we need right now."

"It's exactly what you need."

"Power, that's what this is all about. You want power because as a child you were powerless." Yet again Holan began to shake her. If only she'd got her rifle handy; not that her aim would be any good, but she only needed to hit a bit of Holan to make her stop.

"You seriously believe that I want to take Shadowman's place..." The urge to sleep was almost overwhelming now; it was hard to hang onto a single thought.

"Yes I do. Come on, Madalene, sit up. I'm going to get you into the bathtub and clean you up. Then I'll clean up this mess, before Bren and the children get back. It stinks in here."

Somehow Holan got her standing, walking, stripped naked and into a tub of water cold enough to revive her a little. She didn't understand Holan's motives. Yesterday her sister had talked of 'quietly shooting' her and today she was bathing her. Who was the psychotic in the family?

Gently Holan washed all the vomit out of Madalene's hair, and then, equally gently, she began to soap down her sister's body. As Holan rubbed, she began to talk.

"You have such a beautiful, ethereal body, Maddy; even the scars on your back have become elegant silvery lines. It's a shame there's something dangerously wrong with your mind. Even as a child you were badly disturbed, no wonder our parents hated you. Come to think of it, everybody hated you."

"Why do you hate me, Holan? I've never harmed you. It wasn't like this when we were children."

"Why do I hate you? Well, killing the father I adored didn't help. Then there's the rest of it, like hurting our mother, neglecting your son and the way you kill or hurt anyone who gets in your way or offends you. It's all you know, Madalene. Your biggest talent is death and destruction. The disturbed little girl has become a disturbed adult. I have a gun which Father gave me and one day I will use it and put you down for everyone's safety..."

To Madalene's surprise Holan began to cry; well her sister had certainly made her feelings clear, but why the tears? Feeling

60

uncomfortable Madalene began talking, her voice soft and somnolent.

"I can't deny most of what you say is the truth, but let me tell you something about your beloved father. I remember a day in the summer. It was one of those very hot days and you were sat on a blanket in the shade of the willow tree, revising for an exam. I was washing dishes and watching you concentrate, a little bit envious that you had escaped the chores."

Holan was already indicating that she remembered the day that Madalene was talking about. She had stopped crying and the cloth she was using to wash Madalene's body, lay still on Madalene's skin.

"You might have been concentrating, but I wasn't. I broke a jug that had belonged to our great-grandmother. Mother came rushing in and when she saw what I had broken, she slapped me hard and began shouting loudly. I reacted by throwing every dish I had washed at her; it was satisfying to hear them smash on the floor after hitting her first." She broke off her tale to catch her thoughts, unsure whether to tell Holan the rest. Damn it, why should Holan go round thinking he was some kind of martyr.

"Father suddenly came in; he stunned me with a blow to the head, and then dragged me into the shed. You remember the shed, Holan?" she said, looking directly now at her sister.

"Don't, Madalene! I know what happened next and it was horrible. I heard it all and you were unconscious when he dragged you out of there and took you up to your room. Mother sent me over to a friend's house for the night in case he started on me." Tears were pouring down Holan's cheeks now, but, remaining impassive, Madalene continued.

"Why? You were his favourite, he never touched you, nor would he have. About six in the morning, I dragged myself downstairs to get a glass of water...I was so weak, I dropped the glass and there he was again, as if he'd been waiting for me. He didn't see me grab a knife when he hauled me towards the shed. As he picked up the stick to beat me again I turned and stuck the knife straight into his heart. Can't you see, Holan, he would have killed me if he'd beaten me again that day? I picked up his stick and hit him with it, again and again and again…" Madalene's right arm moved up and down, physically demonstrating her words. In the mist of remembrance, she was unable to stop its movement.

"No! You're a liar!" Sobbing uncontrollably, Holan began to slap Madalene with the wet cloth she held. "You have to be lying. He wouldn't have done that to you. He wouldn't have… You're the evil one, not him…"

"Again and again and again…" Madalene was a prisoner of her own memory and though she heard Holan's words, she was unable to react to them.

Dropping the cloth, Holan grabbed Madalene's right arm, trying to forcibly halt its movement. "Stop doing that! Your crazy act's not convincing. Do you really expect me to believe that Father was hoping you'd break something that night, so he could beat you again? I'm not stupid. Madalene. He loved us and he cared for us, but you never stopped provoking him. You deserved what he did to you. Your plate-throwing left Mother bleeding and in tears, not that you cared. You deserved it, I remember …"

Faltering, Holan let go of Madalene's arm and slumped down the side of the bath tub. Speaking in a low whisper, she said, "I remember…everything. No-one deserves what he did to you. I loved him so much; I made excuses for him, told myself it was your fault you were always in the shed. Other parents smacked their kids when they were naughty, why shouldn't you be smacked? You were worse than any naughty kid, I knew. Only it wasn't smacking, was it? He got some sort of kick out of beating you and couldn't stop"

"Again, again, again…" Still the memory held.

"Ssh, I haven't changed my mind, I still think you're dangerous, but I understand now why you killed Father. Come on, let's get you dry and dressed."

Slowly the mist in her head cleared and she fell silent as Holan dried and dressed her. It wasn't good to bring up the past, at least not in her present state when she couldn't handle it. Holan was gently brushing her hair and talking softly to her, when she suddenly heard what Holan was saying.

"...I'm going to try to rescue Alan and Christian. Will you help me Madalene?"

Madalene was taken aback, this wasn't the sort of request she wanted to hear, not when she was still recovering from Bertha's rescue.

"They're in the Sanctum cells, Holan. You can't rescue them from there. It's not possible to get through to them. Besides which, what makes you think I'm capable of helping you rescue Alan and Christian? The fact that I've now had a bath? I can't even stand up Holan, without your help."

"I know how bad you are, but I'm scared to make the attempt alone and there's no-one else I can ask. Surely you'll feel better tomorrow. I know it's going to be almost impossible to get them out, but I have to do something."

"There's something between you and Alan Moore isn't there? That's why your usual commonsense has deserted you. I sensed it the other day, but dismissed it because you always told me you were a lesbian."

Holan smiled shyly at her. "Perhaps I'm bisexual, but I love Alan and he loves me. I can't bear the thought of him being tortured and ending up in the Arena. Maybe I could shoot my way into the Sanctum cells."

"Then you will end up in the Arena yourself, Holan. I don't want to see that happen." The itchiness of her skin attracted her attention; the bugs were back. She began to scratch her arms fiercely.

"Stop that Madalene. You're making your arms bleed," said Holan, pulling her sister's hands away from her arms.

"I'm thinking and this helps. Why the hell should I help you rescue the men who tried to murder me yesterday and will no doubt try to do the same again if this rescue attempt is successful?"

"T-They wouldn't try again, Madalene. I wouldn't let them...I'm asking you to help me, but I understand why you won't." Holan looked so downcast that now Madalene wanted to shake her.

63

"You know, I don't see you for ages, and then suddenly I can't get rid of you. You were right about me being crazy. It just so happens that I have some interesting ideas on how to free them, so I will help you, not because I care what happens to them – I don't. I do however care what happens to you. But understand this, Holan, everything gets done my way. In other words we won't be writing letters asking the Sanctum to let them go, and you have to promise to do everything I tell you, without question, starting now. Fill the transporter, then go home and change into some nondescript clothing. Return here as soon as you're ready." Holan gave her a worried look.

"Will you be okay on your own?"

"I'll eat something, clean the kitchen up and think about the best way to do this. Bring the gun father gave you, you'll need it. You still remember how to shoot a gun, don't you?"

"After all those 'Gun-club' lessons, father took us to. Of course I can still fire a gun accurately. In fact I think I was a better shot than you at one time."

"Don't push it, Holan or I'll change my mind. Now get going and be as fast as you can. And Holan…"

"Yes…?"

"If we should get Alan Moore free, don't trust that man with rope."

Holan laughed hollowly, and then left.

Holan didn't know about Bertha's rescue, if she had she would never have asked Madalene to make the attempt again, but Madalene didn't intend to tell her. This was a fool's errand, but she couldn't let Holan undertake it on her own. The only way Madalene could return to the chambers and attempt another rescue, was to take another 'run' of Xybille. It would ease her current pain, but leave her in a terrible state when it wore off. Wiping blood from her arms, she fetched the box she needed and did what she had to do. She could barely stand as she put the needle into a vein. By the time she'd finished she was bouncing around the room and managed to clean the house up speedily. Then she sat down to think.

Holan knew what she had done the moment she returned.

"Oh Madalene. How could you?"

"Don't lecture me, Holan. There's no other way I can do this and if we're going to help Alan and the others, it has to be tonight, before they're tortured too badly to move. I can't tell you how loathe I am to help Alan Moore," she said, rolling her eyes. "Please let me shoot him when he's free, just in the leg or the arm, nowhere lethal."

She was surprised to see sympathy in Holan's eyes, as she answered, "No you can't shoot Alan. I'll ring Bren and tell him it's safe to come home. You're going to stay with me for a few days, and then I can help you come down from this 'run' and stop you taking any more. I'll get a few resilient Provoke members in to watch you until it's over."

"Well that will encourage them to choose me as their leader," said Madalene, mockingly, but secretly she was glad that Holan realised that this 'run' had been done in response to her request. She was also glad that Holan was being nice to her for once, though she doubted it would last long.

"Er, Madalene, should I…?"

"No, Holan, it won't be necessary, I promise you. You're not the one who's hung-over from last night, so you automatically start with enough energy."

The plan was doomed to failure. Madalene had no doubt that after Bertha's rescue; even the smallest pipe leading to the Sanctum would have been blown up. She was going to try out an obscure tunnel she had found, in the hope that it was still open. They would probably get halfway down and find it blocked, but despite its doomed nature, Madalene made calls to her contacts getting them to stand by to take the rescued to safe houses or underground tunnels. There would be no boats available to take them across the sea for months.

Chapter Nine

Recovery

Madalene drove the transporter speedily through the snow—covered streets of London. Like a child going on an exciting family outing, she chattered non stop and squealed with delight every time the transporter went into a skid. A small voice in her head warned of the danger of drawing attention to herself, but she closed her mind to it and deliberately chose to drive down streets that housed Sanctum members and their supporters; she even roared past the Sanctum Guard headquarters. She felt like she was invincible and dared the fates to prove her wrong. Finally with a flourish, she threw the transporter into a spin and skidded to a halt.

After studying the maps she'd decided to leave the transporter in Monck Street; once a street filled with office blocks and the numerous people who frequented them, now a dilapidated place that no one had any reason to visit. It was also close to the Sanctum and an ideal place for her men to bring in their transporters and pick up the escaped prisoners. The manhole cover she was hoping to find lay in Medway Street nearby. She knew that a few Sanctum shops were located there, but hoped, at this time of the day, they would be closed or closing.

"Well, here we are. Unless you've changed your mind let's get moving," said Madalene, watching in amusement as Holan stuck her head out of the transporter door and promptly threw up.

"Appropriate, but not very pleasant," she laughed, echoing Holan's earlier words.

Holan glared at her, daring her to say another word; in response Madalene took a piece of cloth out of her pocket, wiped Holan's mouth gently, and then helped her out of the transporter. These actions helped to settle Madalene down and, as her sanity returned, she said, "It's important that we move quietly and carefully. I don't know what the security arrangements are for this part of London, but we take no chances. If anyone approaches us, it doesn't matter if you shoot them or I do."

At these words Holan was sick again. Madalene began to doubt whether her sister was capable of going through with this rescue; perhaps it would be better to leave her sat in the transporter...As if she sensed this Holan began to move forwards only to be grabbed by Madalene and turned around.

"Wrong direction. We need to head for Medway Street. Follow me."

There were several people walking along Medway Street, so Madalene decided to join them, moving purposefully, but keeping her eyes fixed on the ground as she hunted for the manhole cover they needed. Holan stayed by her side, looking perilously close to collapse. What was Holan going to be like if they succeeded and made it as far as the torture chambers? The smells and noises down there were nauseating and terrifying. It was like suddenly discovering that Hell actually existed.

"Over there, Madalene, just behind that pile of rubble. It looks like some of the rubble's fallen onto it."

"Stop pointing," snapped Madalene, pulling her sister's finger down, roughly. A glance in the same direction showed her quickly that Holan was right, but she groaned inwardly at the thought of having to clear rubble and snow off a manhole cover that was this exposed. There was also the problem of getting the escaped prisoners safely out of it later. Her only hope was that this street would be empty by then.

"Let's go back to the transporter for now. We can't do anything until the street's clear," said Madalene, impatiently regretting that they could do nothing for the moment.

"Can't we go into one of the shops? You said you had a card to get into them and it'll be a lot warmer than sitting in the transporter."

"I might as well leave a calling card in the cells. Don't be stupid, Holan. I can't use that card here. If we succeed and help members of the Provoke group escape, the Sanctum will quickly realise how it was done. They'll be here tomorrow asking questions, trying to discover who's responsible. If they find out I've been in this area, they'll put two and two together and get the right answer." She wanted to add that in all likelihood, the drain was probably blocked and they might as well go home now, but there was no turning back, not until she encountered the blockage.

Two hours later, after what seemed like an endless wait, they stood together at the foot of the ladder leading down into the drain. Holan froze, staring at Madalene with eyes dark and afraid, her skin devoid of even the slightest coloration.

"Let's get going, Holan we haven't got long to do this, not after the delay above." Pushing carelessly past her sister, Madalene moved into the drain; it was an ancient Victorian one, nice and high, damp and copiously filled with the biggest rats in England. She began to run, then realised that there were no accompanying footsteps. Turning, she found Holan standing where she had left her. Holan looked stupefied. Madalene had expected this to happen, but it still angered her. "What are you doing, Holan? If you haven't got the guts for this, then go back to the transporter and wait for me. If I'm not back in an hour, go home. I'll meet you there later if all goes well. This drain's probably blocked, but I need to see that for myself." She didn't wait for a reply; she had no patience left for anything Holan might say.

Time passed and with each new bend the drain took, Madalene expected to see the blockage. It remained clear and her hopes soared. As far as she was concerned, Alan Moore, Christian Peek and the others could rot in Hell, but Peter Shadow would be devastated if he lost prisoners twice in two days and that thought pleased her greatly.

The Sanctum had not been expecting any attacks on their torture chambers and that had given her the advantage yesterday. As the drain remained unblocked it was clear they were not expecting any further attacks, at least not today and that gave her the advantage once again. She expected to find the cells locked and well guarded since they couldn't be that stupid, but even without Holan's help, she was going to get all the prisoners out she could. If they were able to walk, then they could easily make it along this drain and out to the transporters, which hopefully would be waiting in Monck Street after midnight. It was a messy plan and a lot could go wrong. She almost certainly could do with some help from Holan, but as best laid plans sometimes went wrong so messy plans could sometimes go right- her rescue of Bertha was proof of that.

In less than an hour she found another ladder which she quickly climbed and, pushing up the manhole cover, she found herself in some sort of storeroom. A sudden noise made her slip back down again, but she realised that the noise was coming from the drain itself. Probably the rats. Satisfied, she went back up and into the storeroom. A quick glance showed her that this was no ordinary storeroom; in fact it resembled a chamber of horror. There were shelves of mixed clothing, men's, women's and even children's; shelves that held lengths of human hair, some cut off at the scalp; shelves of footwear; shelves of teeth. Other shelves held drugs or inventive instruments of torture. There were shelves of knives - she helped herself to a few of these - shelves of whips and pokers, a veritable Aladdin's cave of unpleasantness. The whole place was a testament to the atrocity that was Peter Shadow and his Sanctum and was justification for every action she took against them, including this one. More determined than ever, she moved to the storeroom door and glanced out. There was a grimy stone corridor that went both ways and many doors and other corridors seemed to lead off it. The whole place smelled like a charnel-house and the sounds of torment crammed the air, making her badly want to block her hearing. Aware of footsteps, she pulled back into the room. Shortly after two men entered, laughing and joking with each other.

"...Did you see that erection? He won't 'ave to worry about pleasing his wife, not that he'll get time to, what with the Arena and all, still I reckon we could charge for this service. A few carefully placed electrodes would put life even into old Barton's cock which I've heard is thin and shrivelled, like an earthworm."

"I heard your Brimmy says the same about yours, isn't that why you got the nickname Slug? I'll set up a few electrodes for you if you like."

"Giant slugs would be what you're referring to and my Brimmy's got no complaints, thank you. Didn't I tell you, she's expecting twins? We got a letter from Shadowman himself thanking us for our public spirit. It's being sent out to everyone who's procreating at the moment, so you'd better use your electrodes on yourself and get your Haney pregnant."

Madalene had heard enough. She shot both men before either of them drew their next breath. Brimmy would have to go it alone now, but it served her right for marrying a stinking torturer.

There were more guards around than the previous night, but it was fairly easy to elude them and as she had anticipated, all doors were locked except for the room Slug and his friend had come out of. In this room, she found three Provoke members; they'd been beaten and given electric shock treatment - and she had to admit that the erection was indeed impressive. They were able to walk – Mr Erection with difficulty - and she quickly got them into the storeroom, where to her surprise she found her sister – so it hadn't been the rats she'd heard - gazing sorrowfully at the two dead bodies.

"So you decided to come along after all," she said coolly. "Quickly, take these three and get them out of here."

"I'm staying with you, Madalene. Richard, take Daniel and Tom into the drain over there, turn right and head straight down it until you come to the next ladder. Two of Madalene's men are waiting there to take you to safety. Tell them there are more of you coming, so they need to get back here as quickly as possible."

"They're here already? Good. Let's go, Holan. You'll be okay if you do everything I tell you. Shoot guards on sight, using the gun with a silencer on it and don't have any qualms about doing so. If you hesitate you'll lose your life."

"Why kill them? Isn't there another way, Madalene? I-I've never killed a man before."

"So, there's a first time for everything. Shoot open cell doors, we haven't time to pick locks or find keys. We go in and out in ten minutes and anyone we miss stays behind, including Alan and Christian. There are to be no heroics, Holan, and if you can't do this then go with these three, because you'll only get in my way."

Surprisingly, they worked well together - though Madalene did all the killing - and in five minutes they released another twelve people, all in varying states of health, but mostly able to walk; those who couldn't were carried by others. They located every cell and torture chamber they could find; the cells deliberately placed near the chambers so their inhabitants got a foretaste of their fate; not a pleasant experience if the horrific shrieks that filled the air were anything to go by. It appeared to be a system of blocks of cells and chambers and Madalene had just found a third block when five armed guards came around the corner. Holan was inside a nearby cell, trying to pull a badly injured colleague to his feet. The guards stopped in amazement when they saw Madalene, but quickly came to their senses.

"You there, stand still and put your arms above your head." They didn't realise that she wasn't a prisoner, which meant they didn't know she was armed...Madalene raised her arms as if to comply, then dropped to the ground, firing three shots instantly, each one hitting its mark. Suddenly two bullets whizzed over her head killing the surviving guards. Spinning around in amazement, she found Holan standing behind her, a big man in a semi-conscious state leaning against her shoulder and a gun held in a hand that was shaking so much, it looked like she had palsy.

"That's enough, Holan. Take him and get out of here. We just ran out of time." She began to move in the direction of the storeroom, but Holan's shaky voice stopped her.

"We haven't found the other four yet. Alan....I can't leave him."

"I'll find him, but you have to get out now. Don't you realise this many men will be missed fairly quickly? I'm going to put the bodies into that man's cell, but I haven't got time to clear all this blood away...Go, Holan, I said no heroics." Madalene was now in an impossible situation, all her senses were screaming at her to get out, she'd already done more than should have been possible, but Holan's expression said that it wasn't enough. A rare moment of indecision came over Madalene, she hated Alan Moore and Christian Peek and hadn't a clue who the other two were. Why shouldn't she follow her instincts? However, she hated Peter Shadow more and was not inclined to leave him Provoke leaders to torture and kill; besides which she couldn't bear the thought of Holan's disappointment. Hadn't the whole idea been to rescue the man her sister loved?

"No heroics you said, Madalene..." Holan was still standing there, struggling under the weight of the man she was holding; uncertainty showing on her face.

"I meant you not me! Now get this man to safety, Holan, he can't do it alone. I'll do my best to get Alan out for you, even though it devastates me to do so."

It was instinct and outrageous luck that led her back to the block of cells and chambers that had held Bertha the previous day. Madalene quickly found two Provoke members unharmed in a cell, near a chamber where torture was obviously taking place. She recognised the voices of the tortured; a pleasant sound in this case. As she was a long way from the storeroom, she gave these men instructions and quickly sent them on their way. They didn't hesitate. Not hesitating herself, in minutes she found herself standing in front of the chained bodies of Christian and Alan Moore, both men naked and bloodied. Casually, she found the keys for the chains, and then walked over to the blocks to study them.

"Madalene!" groaned Alan.

"Yes, didn't Holan tell you about my new job?" She smiled, studiously picking up a long length of rope nearby and caressing it. "Well boys, I think this is what they call role reversal, except I haven't come to take your lives, I've come to save them. I believe, Alan, that puts you in my debt. You too, Christian." Still smiling, she removed their chains and helped both men onto their feet. It was difficult to get them to the storeroom in their condition and she was relieved when Holan met up with her halfway back and took over the care of Alan. Not only was she relieved, she was stunned to count the bodies of four men she hadn't shot as they made their way back.

"They came looking for the others," said Holan, by way of explanation. Madalene simply raised her eyebrows. "We'll have to take Alan and Christian to safety in my transporter as all your men have gone now," continued Holan. "They can come back to my house for tonight, it should be safe enough."

"Oh fantastic! I not only get to rescue them, I get to spend time with them as well."

Holan ignored her sarcasm and suddenly became excited. "Look, we've made it, we're back at the storeroom and no alarm's been raised yet. We did it, Madalene, we actually did it. You did it. I'll never forget this, Madalene, never."

72

At her side, clinging on to her so tightly she could scarcely breathe, a traumatised Christian finally spoke; although his voice was so hoarse, it was hard to make out what he was saying. "I won't forget either...I'm your man now, Madalene...never need to be afraid of me again..."

She didn't have the heart to tell him that she had never been afraid of him. Alan Moore said nothing to her though he spoke in whispers to Holan and glared at her from time to time with dark, bleary eyes.

"Alan's grateful too," said Holan, hurriedly.

Like hell he is, thought Madalene happily. Like hell he is.

Chapter 10

Should Old Acquaintance Be Forgot

Could this woman be *her*? Vertex's voice reverberated in his head, "...she is not only the most beautiful woman they have ever seen; she is also quite fearless and agreeable." Vertex's notion that they knew lots of women called Madalene was wrong. They knew Madeline's or Madeleine's. There was only one Madalene, and she could not easily be fitted in with others of a similar name. The Madalene he was thinking of was undoubtedly beautiful; she was also unusually fearless, but no-one sane could ever have called her agreeable. Mentally he began to conjure up her image in his mind; long black hair, shiny like a raven's plumage; sparkly eyes of cerulean blue; a tiny, perfect nose; plump lips – shaped like an invitation to pleasure. He recoiled as the image revealed itself further, bringing into being a pain he had not felt for a long time.

She had appeared in school halfway through the spring term, and had been placed in Second Sector – Second Sector was for students aged twelve to fourteen. Rumours about her had begun immediately; it was said that she had been expelled from First Sector for attacking an Educator, and only a substantial donation to the school from her father had allowed her return to Second Sector. At the time he was in Fourth Sector – this was for students aged seventeen and over –and about to take his Leaver exams. He was also Head boy. Michael Vertex was his deputy and his large gang of friends were his prefects. Harold Winters, Chief–Educator, was afraid of them, which made it easier for him to run the school as he wished.

One of his early decisions had been to levy a ten engle a term tax on his fellow students, telling them, and Harold, that the money would be spent on social events such as school dances – though not one student had to search out their dancing shoes during all his time in office. Failure to pay this tax meant punishment, usually a prefect's lashing. As this involved a painful beating from prefect's belts, everyone paid.

When the rumours about the new girl came to his attention, he made it his business to introduce himself and find out more about her. He also wanted to warn her of the consequences of not behaving herself. She was nearly thirteen and so stunningly beautiful that the sight of her made him catch his breath. However, if he'd expected her to cower at his approach as others did, he was to be disappointed. She'd pushed past him telling him that she knew who he was, and he could get lost as she was late for an art class, adding that if he thought he was getting ten engles out of her, he was psychotic.

Taking a swig of wine, he sighed at the memory. She'd been a feisty opponent and had paid dearly for it, never knowing that the ultimate victory was hers. Too late he'd realised that he actually loved her, and knew - after all he'd done - that she would never love him…

"There's a problem, Peter. You've got to get over to the Sanctum quickly." Vertex seemed to have appeared from nowhere and now stood by his side.

"What is it, Fat Boy? What sort of problem could possibly need dealing with at two- thirty in the morning?"

"The torture chambers have been attacked again. We've lost our best torturers and many guards. They've all been shot. It's unbelievable, but it's happened; the twenty prisoners we captured yesterday have gone." Sweat poured down Vertex's face, running into his clear grey eyes. Oh he was a fine actor but this was not a good jest.

"Very funny, Fat boy. Now go to bed, I'm not in the mood for this kind of joke." Turning away, Peter poured himself more wine.

"I'm not joking, Peter. Most of the underground entrances to the cells were blown up yesterday, but there were many old tunnels and drains that needed finding before they could be destroyed. The people working on the project ran out of time and stopped before the job was complete. They didn't worry because it seemed unlikely that anyone would attack the chambers again, not so soon after Bertha's rescue. The job would have been completed this morning," said Vertex, looking like he was girding himself for the angry outburst, he knew would follow.

"Who's responsible for this?" Peter leapt to his feet, spilling the wine, he had just poured down his shirt. "I'll have their body skewered on a pike and displayed outside the Sanctum as a warning to others. I said *all* drains, *all* entrances to the Sanctum cells were to be blocked. Get every member of the Inner Sanctum out of bed and into the meeting chamber, I'll be there as soon as I've changed my shirt. I want to speak to these incompetents, before I send them to the chambers. Did you say there are no torturers left to handle them? How hard can it be to hurt people? I'll deal with the Inner Sanctum myself."

"I'll get them for you, Peter, but you have to understand that they'll be as angry as you are, they have also been let down. Finding new torturers or technicians as Barton likes to call them isn't a problem. I have a long waiting list for jobs in the chambers, undoubtedly due to the high salary the job attracts; all vacated posts will be refilled by midmorning." An expression of disgust and regret crossed Vertex's face. "As they were not on duty last night, Partlin and his cronies are unharmed. They will see that these new men are trained quickly." Partlin was Barton's man and Vertex hated both of them equally. Vertex thought that Partlin's methods of torture were barbaric and unproductive. He often argued against them.

"Partlin is such an asset. I'm glad he wasn't harmed." Peter said, smiling vindictively. "Well don't stand there, go and do as I asked, and don't try to excuse the pathetic worms that you go to pull out of their beds. It was their duty to see that the work was done." Resignedly Vertex turned to leave.

"Wait, Vertex. Do you remember Madalene?"

"I remembered her almost as soon as I left you. Madalene was that arrogant girl from our schooldays. Acted as if no one was good enough to even look at her. If I remember correctly, she wasn't so arrogant by the time we finished with her. I wonder what happened to her after we left school."

"The last I heard, was that she was sent to a psychiatric institution after killing her father. That happened during my second year at university." He had tried hard to forget her, but the story about her father's death had been in all the papers and was impossible to ignore.

"Well then it's possible Madalene no longer exists. We shut down institutions like psychiatric hospitals and disposed of their residents," said Vertex.

"It's possible that Madalene no longer exists; then again, it's also possible she's the woman you mentioned last night. Find out what happened to her, Vertex. If she's still alive, I want her found and brought to me unharmed. Now, go and assemble the Inner Sanctum."

As Vertex left the room, Peter slumped down in a chair, staring at the empty glass in his hand. It was madness that a brief moment of reminiscence could make him long, so desperately, to see her again. He'd managed to forget her over the years, as other passions occupied his time. Yet she remained the only thing in his life that he wanted and couldn't have. Again he conjured up her image, but unlike before, her eyes were not cerulean blue, they were black with pain and hatred. Her bruised and bloodied lips offered not pleasure, but a silent threat of vengeance. Like a forgotten obsession, she returned to plague him, fill his dreams with desire and take away his peace. He didn't believe she'd been destroyed. No. She was out there somewhere and it was time to make her love him as he had once loved her, whether she wanted it or not.

"How could this have happened again?" he screamed, "Every one of you will go to the Arena in their place. Do you hear me? I'll find new people, people capable of keeping the Sanctum buildings secure. No-one will come in and rescue you, gentlemen. No-one!" To his amazement the members of the Inner Sanctum sat there looking defiantly at him. Exhaustion seemed to have temporarily overcome their fear - at least he hoped it was temporary. Barton didn't even bother to stand as he began to speak,

"Doors were locked and extra guards were put on duty down there..."

"What about security cameras?" he said, furiously. "Why weren't they operating? Other guards could have been sent in instantly, if someone had seen what was happening."

"The cameras down there are ancient and only a few of them work. It's not possible to get replacements for them, as you already know. Besides, unlike shops and banks, it's not normally the case that people break into torture chambers, and we have few worries about the prisoners escaping. Shortly after their arrival they are usually incapable of doing so." Barton sounded dangerously tetchy.

"And my instructions on the tunnels and drains below this building. Were they incomprehensible? Too vague for you to understand?"

Barton flinched at this sarcasm and for a moment looked like he was going to lose his nerve. "A few ancient tunnels and drains were left because they were hard to locate; they would have been dealt with today. Nobody was negligent, but if you want to lose our experience and weaken this government, then go ahead, Shadowman. Rumour is that the Provoke group now have a new leader and have changed their tactics, I think you need us more than ever."

"You do, do you? Well I think a few nights in the cells would make you do your jobs properly." His gaze swept across them, making it clear that this was no idle threat. Dickon Jones, Education Minister, looking alarmed, started to speak.

"W-We were working hard on dealing with this catastrophe when you sent for us. Vertex can confirm that he did not find one of us in our beds. Work had already begun sealing all the entrances leading to the chambers, and elsewhere in the Sanctum. It will continue until it's completed. The men involved have been told that failure to complete this work properly will end in the Arena."

Martin Brown was evidently not feeling as brave as Barton or Dickon; he stood before adding his own comments. "Newspapers are preparing to write stories on the twenty dangerous men and women who are at large. The investigation into their escape has begun and we should have some idea of how it was done by mid-morning."

"And for this you expect to save your skins?" He glared at the silent, but still defiant, members of his Inner Sanctum and was about to shout again in a bid to quell this defiance when a messenger appeared asking to speak to Barton. After speaking quietly to the man, Barton sent him on his way, and then turned smugly to address the room.

"Two of our escapees were recaptured an hour ago. Even as we speak, my man, Partlin, has begun to torture one of them. Like everyone else who works down there, he's very angry. I almost feel sorry for the prisoner, because Partlin's a brute at the best of times. I certainly wouldn't want to face the man when he's angry. You will have the name of the new leader by this evening, Shadowman." The man's smugness was unbearable, but there was no denying that this was what he wanted to hear.

"Well this is indeed good news for all of you." Peter spoke calmly and deliberately, but the undertones in his voice were still unmistakably threatening. "If I have that name by tonight then you are all safe. If not..." He let his words hang in the air, and then dismissed all of them, pleased to see that fear had returned to their faces, the exceptions being Barton and Vertex.

In moments the room was cleared, only Vertex remained.

"What are you still doing here, Fat Boy? Did you think you were exempt from what I said? No. You were included. Though Partlin would find it difficult to flay the skin off your bones, there's so much of it."

Vertex gazed at him calmly before answering. "Doesn't this resistance give you a thrill? You know you were getting bored with unopposed power." Mercurial as ever Peter Shadow began to laugh.

"There are some reasons to like you after all. This is much more exciting. Will Partlin get the name of their new leader?"

"Pah! Partlin is a barbaric fool. He'll probably cut the prisoner's tongue out, and then expect the man to talk. I was trained in the art of torture by the great Tom Bartzog. That man could create pain without leaving a single mark to show how he'd done it. He always kept away from the head area, so his victims could see what was happening, hear what was happening and talk freely when they were ready. This was always quickly." Peter was troubled; he was exceedingly fond of Partlin's methods and often went to watch the man when he was working. If Vertex was right, it could mean the loss of vital information.

"I will not upset Partlin, especially as he's already started. There's another prisoner down there and I give him to you. It will be interesting to see if you can get more information out of a prisoner than Partlin can. We shall find out if your method's better, won't we?" As Vertex left, Peter chuckled; Fat Boy was right, life had been getting dull. He almost hoped that the new Provoke leader would not be captured too quickly.

It was nearly midnight when Vertex returned. He entered Peter's private quarters with a strange expression on his face.

"The other prisoner was a woman, not a man, and she was not one of the twenty that escaped yesterday. Nevertheless, I have spent the day with her and we have had an amiable and enlightening conversation. Unlike Partlin's prisoner, she remains alive to provide entertainment in the Arena."

"Well? Don't keep me waiting, Fat Boy; give me the name of the new leader." He beckoned Vertex to sit down in the chair by his side and poured him a large glass of wine. Though Vertex sat, he did not immediately touch the wine, he seemed thoughtful and distant. When he did speak his voice was quiet and strained.

"There is no new leader. Elgin remains leader of the Provoke group..."

"Is that all you've got to say? Well it took you long enough to obtain that tiny piece of information. Partlin brought me the same news, hours ago."

"I haven't finished," said Vertex, picking up his glass and emptying it all in one gulp. "The capture of his wife Bertha changed Elgin's outlook, and it would appear that he no longer favours peaceful protest. He has proposed that Provoke becomes a militant organisation, led not by him, but by a dark-haired woman, whose name my prisoner did not know. She swears she was stood at the back of the meeting and did not hear it. Most members of Provoke seem to hate the dark-haired woman. They believe she's the one who's brought all the recent trouble down on their heads. Some of them even tried to lynch her, in a futile bid to prevent our attacks on the group. They nearly succeeded; only the arrival of Elgin saved her life. It seems that at no time did she show any fear, quite the reverse. She openly goaded and laughed at the deputy leaders and the group..."

Unbidden, the image he had conjured up earlier returned, but this time there was more. A dark haired girl stood facing him, and the gang of boys that accompanied him. As she opened her mouth, he rushed forward to prevent her screams attracting attention, but she didn't scream; her eyes of cerulean blue sparkled viciously and she laughed at them.

Chapter Eleven

A Dark Goddess

The closer Holan got to the transporter, the more volatile Madalene became. It was terrifying; Holan still had a sense of impending danger, and her sister's relentless, exhilarated drivel wasn't helping to allay it. Exchanging glances with Alan and Christian, she saw they both felt the same way. Once again Madalene insisted on driving, and the erratic journey to Holan's home was more torturous, and fearful, than anything the Sanctum could have devised. Holan's house was situated on the outskirts of London, just beyond a newly built township called Croon. It was a dilapidated, late-nineteenth century mansion house, surrounded by high stone walls and purchased with some of the large inheritance left to her by her mother – Madalene had been left nothing.

To any passer-by, the place would appear to be an unoccupied relic of the past, making it as safe from the prying eyes of the Sanctum Guard as any place could be. Relieved and exhausted, Holan helped Alan and Christian into the house, trying hard to ignore Madalene's incessant chatter as she bounded in after them. The house was freezing, nevertheless it was a safe haven, a place where they could all rest peacefully and come to terms with what had happened. Or so Holan thought, as they wrapped themselves in blankets and swigged large glasses of dandelion brandy. This had been made in a still Holan kept in her back yard. Holan explained that she ran a small business selling various, flavoured brandies and other types of alcohol, including a very smooth nettle beer, to near-by inns and public houses. The business was profitable as landlords could no longer import stock, and were reliant on expensive government supplies to stay in business.

Any relief the brandy gave Holan was short-lived, as Madalene's behaviour became more and more deranged. The same appeared to be true for Alan and Christian. Without doubt, Holan was indebted to her sister for everything she'd done that evening, but rapidly overriding that debt was the discomfort Madalene's behaviour was causing.

Madalene refused to sleep, and despite Holan's pleas, refused to let anybody else sleep, insisting that it was time for celebration, not resting. Leaping around the room, Madalene began singing, loudly and tunelessly. Tired of singing, Madalene next insisted that she needed to go outside for a run to release her pent-up energy. When Holan refused to let her run outside, she ran around the house instead. Holan flinched as she heard Madalene crashing into various bits and pieces, but was unable to stop her. Returning to the living area, a livid bruise forming on her forehead, Madalene had a fresh idea; she was going to go back down the tunnel and rescue the prisoners she had overlooked. Patiently Holan told her that she had already rescued all the prisoners in the torture chambers. Any others must have been transferred to the cells under the Arena, ready for their appearance in the next show.

At the mention of the word 'show', Madalene fell to her knees and began to incoherently tell them about the death of Robin Jones. Getting back to her feet, Madalene fetched a bottle of Holan's home-made nettle wine to toast Robin's memory. She drank most of it, and then dramatically smashed the bottle against a door, cutting her hand. Suddenly she became belligerent, she wanted a fight, but when no-one would oblige, insanely decided to cook instead. Staggering into the kitchen – blood still streaming down her hand - Madalene managed to make mountains of pancakes, only to declare them inedible, because she'd only had flour and water to make them with. Even so, she wasn't happy until everyone had eaten at least one of her - blood flecked - pancakes. And so it continued, on and on, and all Holan could do was watch, try to stop her from hurting herself and wait for it to end.

"I might sound ungrateful, Holan," said Alan, grimly, pushing the remains of his pancake, further under his cushion. "Let me shoot her. Please give me your gun, so I can shoot her."

Holan sat with Alan, watching Madalene throw up into a bucket - by and large missing it entirely. She'd sent Christian upstairs to a guest bedroom a few hours earlier, when it became clear that he could take no more of Madalene's behaviour. It was obvious that he was in a lot of pain, but apart from saying that he'd been given a severe beating, he refused to discuss events in the chamber. Neither would Alan, who despite his condition, insisted on staying by Holan's side, in case Madalene became violent.

83

"She's an absolute mess, Holan. I don't understand why we're putting up with this madness. It would only take me a moment to put an end to it," he said forbiddingly, turning away from the sight of Madalene and the bucket.

"This isn't madness. This is Xybille and I knew she'd be like this. It's not really surprising; she's taken dangerously high doses two days running. We haven't got to the worst part yet, that comes later."

"If you knew what she'd be like taking Xybille, why didn't you stop her?" The look Alan gave her clearly showed that his patience had run out. Like Christian, he could not stay near Madalene much longer.

"No-one stops Madalene when she's decided to do something. She took the drug while I was out, but she took it for my sake, knowing what the consequences would be. If you'd seen the state she was in yesterday, you'd know why she needed it and if she hadn't taken the stuff, you and Christian would still be in the torture chamber where she found you. The rescue couldn't have happened without it." She would never forget the state she had unexpectedly found Madalene in, not when she believed her sister to be invincible.

"So what was her reason for taking the stuff the night before? Is she an addict?" said Alan, scowling, and obviously trying hard to ignore the background noises of retching and moaning.

"She's too intelligent to become an addict. She's used different drugs in the past, but I don't believe she ever got addicted to any of them. It's hard to imagine, but I think the events at the meeting upset her. You nearly killed her, Alan. She knows you'd have strung her up again, in spite of Elgin's wishes, if you'd been able to get hold of her. You wouldn't have failed the second time, would you?" It horrified Holan now, to think that the man she loved had nearly killed her sister. Huskily, she said, "If she had died where would you and the others be now?"

"She's dangerous, Holan. Her rescuing us doesn't change that. If it hadn't been for her, we wouldn't have been in the chambers in the first place. I know something's changed between you two, but if your sister was dead a lot of lives would be safer. If we went to bed, she'd choke on her own vomit. We wouldn't need to feel guilty about an accident like that, would we?"

His comments angered her. How could he sit there calmly suggesting that they leave Madalene to choke to death? The trouble with Alan was that he was a stubborn man, one who didn't relinquish his beliefs easily. Madalene had this intransigence; they were more alike than he knew. Controlling her anger Holan said firmly, "Listen, when she took the Xybille, I promised I'd be there for her, until she was back to normal. I'll keep that promise."

Kissing her lightly on the cheek, as if to appease her anger, Alan sighed, "What's normal for Madalene? Insanity back to insanity? I have a better idea. Let's give her another dose of Xybille and keep giving it to her until she turns into a helpless junkie. Surely she couldn't cause much harm in that state."

Holan was shocked. "Alan! That's disgusting. I know you hate Madalene, but surely you wouldn't wish addiction on anybody. I can't believe you just said that."

"I'm sorry, Holan. I know she's your sister and I'm trying to be grateful that she rescued me, but if she carries on doing what she's doing, she's never going to see old age anyway. I can't understand why Elgin wants her to become leader of Provoke. I think the loss of Bertha and Grace has damaged his reasoning."

"I think so too, but Madalene won't recover in time for the next meeting, and by then Elgin may have regained his senses." Suddenly Holan began to sob.

"What is it, Holan? I know this is hard, but Madalene has to go to sleep sooner or later, and then we can get some rest." Gently Alan pulled her towards him and held her close. Turning slightly, he looked over at Madalene. "Look, she's still over the bucket, but she's not being sick anymore. It must be nearly over. She looks like she can hardly stand."

"It's not Madalene. It's me. Tonight I became just like her. You want to see her dead? What about me? I killed lots of men tonight. Not once did I stop to think that they had family and friends; that they do their jobs to survive, just like the rest of us."

"That doesn't make you like her. You reacted to the situation you were in and your own need for survival. You'll never be like her." Alan almost spat the last phrase out.

85

"You don't understand, Alan. After I killed the first one, it became easier to kill again. I learned how she feels...the elation... I'm no different from Madalene. It's in our blood, passed down by a brutal father who taught his daughters to play with guns, not dolls." The way Alan spoke so casually about destroying Madalene, frightened her. What if he ended up hating her like that?

Alan let out a heavy sigh, then softly said, "You're not crazy, Holan, your sister is. Nevertheless I understand how you feel. When I knew I had to kill Madalene, that no other choice was available, I was terrified. But when the rope went round her neck, a thrill of anticipation ran through me. I was actually going to do it. I was going to be the saviour of Provoke; hero of the hour...I'd still like to kill her, you know I would. But how can I take her life now she's saved mine?" His eyes wandered over to Madalene and there was longing in them. He was a cat watching a mouse. Pulling him towards her, Holan kissed him to distract him from his prey. Only later would she tell him that he touched Madalene at his peril.

Looking up, she saw Madalene had come to stand in front of them, her hands pointing wildly at her neck.

"See this mark on my neck; it's where someone tried to cut my throat open. Now I've got a lovely rope burn as well, thanks to your boyfriend. I'll have to spend the rest of my life, hiding my neck..." One minute she was standing and the next she was on the floor.

"At last," said Holan, "Let's put her on a mattress in the cellar, she'll make too much of a mess upstairs. Then you'd better go and see if Christian will wake up and guard her, so we can get some sleep."

Christian willingly agreed to watch Madalene, when he learned that she was unconscious, but it upset him when Holan loosely tied her to the mattress, despite his presence. Holan ignored him, Christian was too tired to be on guard duty and she couldn't risk Madalene coming to harm, not after her promise. But for the desperation of her own exhaustion and Alan's insistence that he wouldn't rest until she did, she wouldn't have left Madalene at all. Satisfied at last, she led Alan to her bedroom.

. "What about her husband?" said Alan, removing his clothes to reveal cuts and heavy bruising. She noticed him wincing as he did

86

so. "Does Bren know where you live? He's a member of the Sanctum after all. We could be in danger if he decides to come and find her."

"You worry too much. I'm not that careless. For one, after her performance yesterday he's unlikely to miss her for a day or two. When I rang and said she was staying with me, he sounded positively relieved. Secondly, he's never asked where I live and I've never told him. We should be safe." She'd forgotten that Bren was a possible danger, especially if he found out that she was involved with Provoke. She knew from talking to him that he wasn't happy with everything Shadowman did, but like most of the population, he couldn't see a viable alternative to the man's government.

"What if Bren traces your calls and finds you that way?"

Slowly and gently Alan pulled her down onto the bed and began to remove her clothing. "I've never used a communicator here. Stop that...I'm really careful, Alan. I own this house, but it's not registered in my name. The owner is a Betty Pringle, aged forty-four...Alan!"

"I do like older women." Alan leered at her and rolled his eyes.

"W-We can't... Look at the state of you...You couldn't possibly..."

"Oh I think I could. All this danger gives a man an appetite and I don't mean for your sister's pancakes."

"You're as crazy as she is. This is going to hurt, you know."

"I'll be gentle with you," said Alan, reaching out to hold her, while laughing at her mock indignation.

Later they nestled together and contentedly fell into a deep sleep; as time passed though, Alan began to shake and call out in terror. Each time he did this, she would stir and stroke his forehead gently until he returned to sleep. On a few of these occasions, she guiltily thought that she ought to go and check on Madalene. However, she was so weary... Surely with Christian there, Madalene could come to no harm. She would check later, when she had slept a little longer.

As he sat on a hard chair watching Madalene sleeping, Christian relived the terror of his capture and the torture chamber. He'd been badly beaten during his capture, even though he'd not resisted arrest. Then he'd been beaten again, with a knotted rope, inside the torture chamber. What had followed was nothing more than petty humiliation, so why had he wept like a child, crying for mercy he knew would not be given? He'd never deceived himself that he was tough, which was why he hated the thought of the Provoke group becoming militant; but neither had he imagined himself being so pathetic under duress. If Madalene hadn't turned up, he doubted he could have endured harsher treatment; he would have revealed the entire Provoke set-up, names, addresses, even what they liked for breakfast.... Silently he sobbed, and was unable to stop this outpouring of his shame.

"What are you crying for?" said a strangely subdued sounding Madalene. Looking down he saw her staring at him, with what was almost compassion in her eyes. "You're safe, at least for a while. If I can get you out of this country, you'll be completely safe, and then you can go back to being a student. Don't deny it. I know you're a university student, university students have always been idealists."

He couldn't answer her. One of her usual quips would have made him feel better than this gentle approach. He deserved her contempt – if it had been her in the chamber, she wouldn't have cried like a baby. How did she know he was a student? Universities were Shadowman's pet project and despite his opposition to the man, he'd enjoyed his time there. He couldn't go back now; that much was clear, and neither could Alan. Whatever Madalene thought, they were not going to escape abroad and resume normal life. They were embroiled in something greater and beyond their control. Though what part a pathetic being like him could play was debatable.

"I've imagined myself walking proudly into the Arena many times, defying the crowd and defying Shadowman. Of course, I've been tortured, but they haven't broken me." She gave a throaty laugh. "I'm so brave and defiant, I amaze myself. It's a nice thought, but it's not reality. Did you seriously believe you would be able to stay brave and defiant, once they got you into those chambers?"

Sobbing more fiercely now, he tried to answer her, but words would still not come. How did she know exactly how he was feeling and why, when he had tried to kill her, was she being so gentle with him?

"There's no shame, Christian. I would have been as helpless as you were. You're young and though you've read about evil, you've never faced the reality of it. The unthinkable's never pleasant, but you'll be stronger for this experience. Perhaps strong enough to help me form a new Provoke group. You said you were mine, so stop thinking you're pathetic and go back to bed. I have no intention of choking or coming to harm, if only to spite your good friend Alan. Please undo this rope before you go, it's irritating me..."

Her eyes began to close, so quickly he wiped away his tears and rushed to untie the rope. However, he had no intention of leaving her, so he sat back down on the chair. Again, as if she could read his thoughts, she spoke. This time her voice was slurred and hard to hear.

"I'd leave if I was you, you really don't want to be near me tomorrow or today. I can't think which is which..."

Carefully he watched her. Morning became afternoon, and afternoon became night, but she did not stir again. Lying there, pale and peaceful, she resembled a goddess. Sure, there was vomit and flour mixed in equal proportions in her hair, the bruise on her forehead had swollen, and a line of drool ran fetchingly down her bottom lip, but her beauty, in sleep, surmounted all these distractions. She intrigued him. Why had she rescued so many of the Provoke group, after their attempt to kill her? It didn't make sense.

Earlier on, she'd driven him to distraction, but then in contrast, she'd spoken to him with such warmth and compassion; she'd managed to ease his distress over his weakness. On the surface, it appeared she took nothing seriously; nevertheless she killed men like a wild animal did, without thought or conscience. Looking closely again, he saw that she was indeed a goddess – a dark goddess.

Chapter Twelve

The Show–Stopper

"Are you deaf, Bren? Can't you hear the terrified screaming coming from the room next to us? Here let me help you," said Vertex.

Peter smiled maliciously as he watched Vertex waddle over to a nearby door and open it. The sounds from the other room had previously been muffled, but now they were loud, clear and unmistakeable.

Giving his victim a sadistic glance, Vertex continued, "All that pain. It's heartbreaking. Would you like me to shut the door? Then again, perhaps not, because you know who's in there, don't you, Bren? Shall I describe what's happening to her, or would you prefer me to show you?" Turning dramatically towards Peter, Vertex held out his arms in an expression of disbelief.

"I can't believe this man can listen to his daughter's suffering and do nothing to help her. Such a pretty little girl and all he has to do is answer a few simple questions. If she were my daughter, I'd have stopped this long ago. The man's a heartless bastard."

Bren began pulling hard at the chains that bound him, obviously maddened by the sound of his daughter's torment. "I can't stand this," he wailed. "Let her go, Shadowman. I've been trying to answer your questions, but none of my answers seem to satisfy you. I don't know what you want to hear... Hayla's only a child. When did the Sanctum start harming children? Don't hurt her anymore."

"From the sound of it, she's enjoying herself. Why should I spoil her fun?" Peter nodded to Vertex to continue his work, and then he returned to the black and white photographs he held in his hand. The woman pictured in the photographs was exquisite, no woman he'd ever seen could match her, and she was definitely Madalene – the scar he'd left on her neck was proof of that. Looking up, he studied Bren. The man had not been physically harmed. That was not Vertex's way. Vertex was convinced that the sound of Hayla being

90

violently assaulted would be enough to get Bren talking. All they wanted was proof that Madalene was the dark haired woman mentioned by their prisoner, and to discover if Bren, her husband, had been involved in her activities. Yet so far Bren had told them nothing of significance. Was the man a hard-hearted bastard, like Vertex said, or did he genuinely know nothing? From the torment on the man's face, he suspected the latter. Bren was a tall, thin man in his late forties, with silver hair and an incredibly angular face. He wasn't ugly, but it was hard to conceive what Madalene saw in him.

Suddenly he felt irrationally angry. How could she have married this pathetic, older man? She'd rejected him on first sight, yet he'd been powerful and extremely good looking – he still was. What had there been not to like? "Take him next door. Show him exactly what's happening to his daughter."

Vertex unlocked the chains and Bren bolted out of the chair and into the next room before he could be stopped. A scuffle broke out immediately.

"Daddy!"

"Hayla! What have they done to you?"

Bren's bellowing combined with his daughter's screams and the sound of him fighting to save her grew increasingly loud. Listening carefully, Peter heard furniture breaking and shrieks of pain coming from his men. It sounded like Bren was doing surprisingly well, but he'd expected nothing less from a desperate man. Quickly he beckoned a reluctant Vertex to join the fray.

"I'll kill all of you for this outrage. Don't be frightened, Hayla. I'm going to get you out of here. Don't cry...Please don't cry...You're safe, Hayla...I won't let them touch you again..."

The bedlam continued, so extra guards were sent for. Bren continued to fight fiercely, but now he had too many opponents, he would not last much longer. Peter smiled in satisfaction; it was exactly what he'd wanted to happen. His smile broadened as Vertex and two other men dragged a bloodied Bren back to the chair and chained him down again. One of Bren's arms was broken, a bone was protruding just under the skin, and his face was so swollen, it had lost its angularity. The men returned to Hayla. Her frenzied screaming began again and this time it was worse; the men were obviously angry at what had just happened. Peter's amusement increased when he saw how furious Vertex was. Without warning, Vertex began shouting questions at the battered Bren.

"We'll start again, shall we? Your wife Madalene is a murderer..."

"No! She couldn't possibly be..."

"She's the one who shot Edgar Heaton and his wife in cold blood..."

"She was at home with me, the night Edgar was killed..."

"You told us earlier she spent that night at a friend's house. Which is it to be? Or shall we go back into the other room, watch your daughter suffer some more and then decide?"

"She did spend the night with a friend, but she was back home with me before the Heaton's were killed. I swear it."

"Your murderous wife then set the bombs in Alice Jones' house that killed twenty of our Sanctum Guard..."

"That's not true. I have a receipt that proves she was buying cream, to put in a cake. A receipt from a Sanctum food store, a long way from that house..."

"We also believe your wife is responsible for the loss of prisoners from the Sanctum torture chambers. I'm surprised you've seen your wife at all lately, she's been quite a busy woman."

"Don't be ridiculous. Madalene couldn't have done any of this...My wife's a drug user; she wouldn't be capable of doing the stuff you accuse her of. She'd taken a massive dose of Xybille and was in a terrible state when I last saw her. We argued about it. It takes days to recover from the sort of dose she took, and that was the day you say she helped prisoners escape."

"She's a leading member of the Provoke group..."

"She despises that group. You've made a mistake. My wife's a lovely woman, kind and gentle. I bet a woman accused her of these crimes. Madalene's so beautiful; she inspires a lot of jealousy. Look at the photographs; does she look like a killer? If you met her, you'd know the truth..."

Peter listened with interest, never once taking his eyes off the photographs. He wanted to believe Madalene was innocent, even though his instincts told him that she was the one they'd been hunting. If she was guilty, then he would have to make decisions he did not want to make.

There was dissidence up and down the country, despite the fact that people had a better standard of living under his governance than they'd had in over three decades. Small acts of disobedience and defiance were practiced daily, by people who were too scared to join a group like Provoke, but nevertheless hoped that someone would rise up and present the current regime with a serious challenge. Someone like Madalene maybe. Those unknown people were like a smouldering fire, they only needed someone to blow on them. The Madalene he remembered could breathe hard. If Madalene was the dark haired woman they sought, then she needed to be caught quickly, before she set the whole country alight.

"Kind and gentle! We've met your wife, Bren. We know her from our schooldays. She's not kind or gentle, quite the reverse. I've had my people do some research on her. She *kindly* blew up a barracks full of men. She *gently* killed her father with a knife and a lump of wood. Your wife has a history of violence. Her army records indicate that she's an expert bomb maker; apparently she's equally good at defusing them. She's renowned for her skill with weapons, particularly the old fashioned rifle. Somewhere she has a mountain of medals acclaiming her skills. Don't try to tell me that you know none of this, you're married to her."

The shock on Bren's face was enough to convince Peter that the man honestly knew nothing of his wife's past, meaning he probably knew nothing about her current activities either. Madalene had to be the dark haired woman, and the thought that she had been using Bren, for her own ends, made him feel a little better. Bren was an insignificant man who had aimed for the sun and underestimated its danger. He had been overly-ambitious and was now being burned.

Defiantly, the shocked Bren said, "I-I... I marry the most beautiful woman who ever existed and I'm the envy of every man

93

around me. They have their showpiece wives, but I've got the show-stopper. Of course I don't ask too many questions, I'm scared of losing her. Not only that, but she's a good, loving wife, at least she is when she's not taking drugs, and she's spectacular in bed…"

"Stop," yelled Peter, "or I'll go next door and slit your daughter's throat, right now." He didn't want to hear any more. *'I've got the show-stopper'*– the phrase made him feel physically sick. Looking down at the photographs he saw a picture he had missed. Madalene standing close to Bren, gazing lovingly into his eyes. Unreasonably, he felt like a cuckold. Violently he tore this picture up and threw the pieces to the ground. "She used you. I don't believe she ever loved you. She just wanted access to the Sanctum's secrets and you gave her that access."

"What secrets do your accountants have access to? I deal with hospital accounts. How were they supposed to help her in this imaginary campaign against the Sanctum?

Occasionally, I had to ring and let her know that I was going to be late home and I sometimes gave her a reason for it… W-Why has it gone silent…?" Bren tried to stand, but it was not possible. With an imperceptible nod, Peter indicated that Vertex should go and find out what was happening.

Vertex was so furious when he returned; his bulbous eyes appeared to be popping out of his flabby face. Ignoring Bren's pleas for information, he walked straight over to Peter and whispered bitterly, "Partlin's cronies have excelled themselves, as usual. The girl's dead. They ruptured her internally and she haemorrhaged. Do we tell him?"

"No. Not yet. Say they've stopped for a while. If he tells us where Madalene is at the moment, then they won't resume."

"He's already told us many times that Madalene's with her sister Holan, but he has no idea where Holan lives. He won't change that story. We've checked our records and we can't find Holan's whereabouts. According to the records, she doesn't exist."

"Holan does exist; we know that from your prisoner. Accidentally, or more likely, on purpose, she's fallen out of our record system; paper filing leaves a lot to be desired. What I find hard to believe is that Madalene's residing with Holan. Holan's a deputy leader of Provoke and was an integral part of the plan to kill Madalene. She also declared that Madalene was crazy, dangerous, and she had no intention of being part of a group that had Madalene as its leader."

Vertex looked surprised. "So you accept the dark haired woman is Madalene?"

"I don't want to believe the woman they tried to hang was Madalene, but after all we've learned about her, it can't be anyone else. And if they tried to hang her to save the Provoke group, it means that they believed she was guilty of the murders and the bombings." He took a moment to contemplate the various possibilities. Bren was too stupid to lie to them, and a large quantity of drugs had been found in the house. They had been hidden among her clothes, inside her shoes and even in cosmetic containers. It seemed that Madalene was a heavy drug user, but that didn't make her an addict. Nor did it rule out the fact that she had the ability to make bombs and was an expert with guns. Also, the photographs in his hand showed a clear-eyed woman, not a raddled addict. What didn't make sense was the rescue of Bertha and the rescue of Alan Moore in particular. Alan had put a rope around Madalene's neck and hauled her up; if he'd done the job properly, he would have killed her, according to Vertex's prisoner. He didn't remember Madalene being the forgiving type; she was definitely 'an eye for an eye' person.

"A lot of this makes no sense, but there's no use in questioning Bren further, I can see for myself that he knows nothing. Madalene shot Edgar Heaton. The Sanctum Guard then, rightly, shot Mrs Heaton to make the crime look worse in the papers. Guessing correctly that we would send her friend Alice Jones to the Arena, Madalene helped Alice escape. She then set explosives in the house, and waited nearby with a rifle to shoot any survivors of the blasts. She didn't have anything to do with the escapes from the chambers; I think Elgin's our culprit for them. Madalene's currently staying with Holan while she recovers from her latest bout of drug abuse. She'll return home when she's able to. All we need do is keep watch on the house and with luck we'll get both of them."

Vertex nodded his head in agreement, and then frowned. "What about the boy. Madalene's son? He wasn't in the house when we called and Bren won't tell us where he is."

"The boy may have seen us and run, or he may come back. Either way he won't be hard to find. Our conversation with Bren is over." He looked at the man, and again hatred seized him. This insipid, pathetic man was married to *his* Madalene; Bren actually believed that he was good enough for her, but he should never have been allowed to touch her. A moment of rationality informed Peter that he himself hadn't thought of Madalene for years. What did that matter? He remembered her now. The girl who had rejected him, because she had never given herself a chance to get to know him properly...

Pushing Vertex aside, he grabbed a knife from a nearby table. Guessing Peter's intentions, Vertex released the frantic Bren from his chains.

"Why is she silent? What's happening? Let me see her..."

"Oh you're going to see her alright. In you go." Brandishing the knife, Peter indicated the door, but the threat wasn't needed. Bren almost ran into the other room.

Following closely, Peter watched impassively as Bren pulled his daughter away from the men in the room and, despite his broken arm, carried her to a corner. Lying her gently on the ground, he wept silently and stroked her hair

"You can wake now, Hayla. It's over. We're going home... Hayla?" Bren began to shake her gently and suddenly Peter couldn't bear to be near the man any longer. Casually he walked over, knelt down and shoved the knife into Bren's spine, paralysing him instantly.

"If my wife's who you say she is, then be careful, Shadowman. Madalene loves me and she adores Hayla... she will avenge this..." gasped Bren.

Ignoring these words, Peter walked out of the room, leaving Bren - still holding his dead daughter - to bleed to death. His mind was full of dilemmas; the dark-haired woman was definitely Madalene, whether he liked it or not. His instincts had not been wrong. She was a merciless killer and as such, she had to die publicly and horribly after long hours in the chambers. It was not what he wanted, but there was no alternative; she had to be made an example of, in order to quell all those dissenters out there.

Yet wasn't he the most powerful man in the country? Couldn't he choose the time of her death? Of course he could. He would make her love him before she died. Maybe she could even be forced, or duped, into giving him a son. The child of such a match would be an incredible human being. Most of all, he wanted to be the man with the show-stopper on his arm, if only for a very short while.

Chapter 13

A Heart of Stone

With a pounding heart, Holan ran along the corridors of the torture chambers. She had to get Madalene out of this place, but which cell was she in? Suddenly she heard the sound of breaking glass, followed by Madalene screaming wildly. What the hell were they doing to her sister? She began to run faster, but it made no difference, the faster she ran, the more rooted to the spot she became... Holan woke with a start, relieved to find that she'd been dreaming. But Madalene's screaming continued, and so did the sound of breaking glass. She looked at Alan to see if he could hear it too, but he was still sleeping, albeit restlessly.

Suddenly she heard Christian, shouting to her from the bottom of the stairs. "Holan." He sounded desperate. "Holan, get down here now. I need your help." She heard the sound of something being smashed into pieces, followed by Christian cursing wildly. "Madalene's gone completely crazy; she's breaking windows, and everything she can pick up without difficulty. I can't stop her. When I try she throws the stuff at me."

"I'll be down in a few minutes, Christian. Just stay out of her way for now." Holan grabbed her trousers and crumpled shirt from the floor; she dressed rapidly and hurried down the stairs dreading what she would find.

A bomb would have caused less devastation thought Holan, as she wandered around the ground floor of her home.

"You were watching her, Christian. She was tied up to prevent her wandering: how the hell did she get out of the cellar?" His repentant expression was her answer. "You untied her! Why? I thought it was your body they hurt in the chambers, not your mind." She hadn't meant to be so scathing, but she was angry and close to tears. In the euphoria following the rescue she had forgotten Madalene's destructive nature. "Where is she now? I have to get her back into the cellar and tie her up again, at least until she calms down. As you untied her, you're going to help me."

"She went upstairs while you were getting dressed; I think she's gone to look for her rifle," said Christian, sounding extremely subdued.

"What? Why didn't you stop her?" Holan tried not to shout, but it was difficult.

"You told me to stay out of her way and as she said she wanted to shoot everything in sight; I thought that seemed like a good idea." He looked like he wanted to say more, but just then Madalene entered the room.

"Where's my rifle? I need it. Do you hear me, Holan? I have to have my rifle."

She would grace any asylum thought Holan, noting her sister's bloodshot eyes, unkempt hair and soiled clothing. Knowing it was important not to rile a madwoman, she answered casually,

"It's down in the cellar where you spent the night. Come on, Christian and I will help you look for it." Holan glanced at Christian, warning him to be ready when he was needed.

By mid-afternoon the vile obscenities coming from the cellar had ceased.

"I think our resident madwoman has finally fallen asleep," said Holan.

Breathing a sigh of relief, she cuddled into Alan, who sat by her side talking about the forthcoming Provoke meeting.

"This meeting's risky considering all that's happened recently, but at least Madalene won't be there. Please tell me she won't be well enough to be there," he said hopefully.

Holan shook her head. "The meeting's tomorrow night. There's no way she can recover her strength in time. In the state she's in, she's probably forgotten about it anyway."

"If she remembers we can always tie her to the bed in the cellar again," said Alan with a wry smile. "I assume you intend to set her free and clean her up when she wakes, or haven't you forgiven her for wrecking your home yet?"

"She definitely needs a bath, she smells horrible at the moment. Christian and I were gagging as we tied her to the bed. And no, I haven't forgiven her for the damage she caused this morning, but I'm only restraining her until she calms down. We can't tie her up again just to stop her going to this meeting. It wouldn't be ethical." Reading Alan's mind, she gave him a look that clearly said this last statement was not negotiable.

"Surely Madalene wouldn't have the nerve to attend the meeting; she nearly lost her life last time. I don't want to see her get hurt, but there are lots of Provoke members who do. If you think there's a risk of Madalene being there, it might be safer to keep her in the cellar," said Christian taking a swig from a bottle of nettle beer Holan had given him earlier.

Holan stared at Christian, speculatively. She had a suspicion that his feelings for Madalene went beyond simple gratitude. "Madalene isn't scared of anything and she never has been. That isn't normal, and it's why I keep telling you she's dangerous." It was a subtle warning. "Even so," she continued. "I will not leave my sister trussed up in the cellar just in case she tries to attend the meeting." She gave Christian and Alan a look that declared the subject closed.

"Elgin will be at the meeting," said Alan. "What do we do if he persists in this idea of making the Provoke group into a militant organisation? He'll leave us with no choice but to form a splinter group."

"Elgin's grieving for Bertha and Grace. No wonder he wants militancy. Let's give him time to grieve. We won't argue with him, just ask him to postpone any further discussion until Madalene can be there," said Holan.

"You're joking I hope," said Alan.

"No. I'm serious. Madalene will know nothing about it. And if she's not around, Elgin will drop the idea of militancy, I'm sure of it…Is that someone banging on my door? Quickly. Upstairs both of you."

Holan trembled violently as she answered the door, fearing to see a squad of Sanctum Guards stood on her driveway. Instead a lone male stood there, but such was her terror that for an instant she couldn't identify him. "Torrin! What are you doing here? Come in quickly before you're seen."

"I had to come," said Torrin, wiping sweat from his brow, despite the extreme cold. "I've been asked by Elgin to find Madalene. He thinks you'll know where she is. I thought I'd better be careful, so I used a borrowed transporter to get close to Croon, and then ran the rest of the way."

"No wonder you're sweating," Holan said, leading him into the living area and beckoning him to sit down. "I have a surprise for you. Alan and Christian are here."

"I thought the Sanctum Guards had captured them." Torrin sat down on a chair, looking at her with astonishment.

"It's a long story. I'll fetch you a drink and then we can talk. I thought you were one of the Sanctum Guards, so I sent Alan and Christian upstairs to hide. Let me call them down again, they'll be delighted to see you."

Torrin frowned and said reluctantly, "There's no time for that, Holan, even though I'm happy to hear that they're safe. I have news for Madalene from Elgin. Do you have any idea where she is?"

"I have a very good idea where Madalene is. She's currently tied up in the cellar of my house and that's another story. What's this news?" Holan was wary. Torrin was renowned for his outrageous sense of humour. It was not like him to be this serious.

His grey eyes looked deeply into hers and he sighed. "I'd love to tell you, but I can't. Take me to her, Holan. This news has to be given to Madalene first."

"I haven't got time to explain the situation," said Holan. "I'll take you to her and leave you both alone, but whatever happens, don't untie her or let her out of the cellar. Not without speaking to me first." Torrin looked curious, but he didn't question her.

Alan and Christian had heard Torrin's voice and come downstairs. Holan could tell how pleased they were to see him, but she gestured at them to leave him alone. Ignoring the puzzlement on their faces, she led Torrin to the cellar.

Torrin pulled a chair close to the bed and then recoiled, wrinkling his nose. Madalene smelt so vile, he thought he was going to be sick. Swiftly he moved the chair back again, but the smell stuck in his nostrils and wouldn't go away. With great reluctance he reached out an arm to wake her up, carefully pulling a sleeve over his hand to prevent contamination. It wasn't necessary, her eyes opened before he had to touch her.

"Who are you?" said Madalene. Torrin watched her try to get up, but she was unable to move because of the ropes that bound her. "Wait. I know you. You're one of the bastards who tried to hang me. What are you doing here? Have you come to try again?"

"I'd love to try again," said Torrin, bluntly. "But that's not why I'm here. Elgin sent me to find you. The Sanctum Guards picked up your husband and your daughter last night. They didn't get your son. Elgin thinks he must have seen them and run…"

"Quickly. Get these ropes off me. I have to find Bren and Hayla." Madalene began to struggle against the ropes that held her and he could see blood appearing on her arms.

"Stop that. You'll hurt yourself. I can't set you free. Holan's forbidden me to. Besides I haven't finished yet." It wasn't only the smell that made him feel sick now. "News came in late this morning from one of our sympathizers who work in the Sanctum. Your husband and your daughter are dead."

Madalene shook her head violently; from the expression on her face he could see that she refused to believe his words were true. "They can't be dead. The Sanctum doesn't operate like that. First they send prisoners to the torture chambers. When they're satisfied the prisoners have nothing left to say, they send them to the Arena. It never changes."

"Your husband and daughter weren't taken to the torture chambers. They were taken to Shadowman's private rooms. It's the talk of the Sanctum, though everyone's trying not to be overheard for their own safety. That's how our sympathizer got to hear about it. Your husband and daughter were dead within four hours of their arrival." The words choked him, even though he hated Madalene. He stood up, uncertain whether to stay or go.

"Wait," she said, looking desperately into his eyes. "How did they die? Does anyone know how they died?" It hurt to hear her anguish.

"We've heard rumours, but not from anyone who was there. They might not be true. What's the point of hurting you with them?" Making a decision to leave, Torrin walked over to the cellar door.

"Don't go," said Madalene, in a commanding tone. He automatically stopped and turned to face her. "How do the rumours say they died?"

"The rumours say that your daughter was raped so violently, she haemorrhaged... They say Shadowman's the one who stabbed your husband. No-one understands why this became personal...I-I can't do this..." The smell, the horror and the look in Madalene's eyes were too much for Torrin. Turning quickly, he walked out of the room.

Madalene knew why the deaths had been personal, but she couldn't grasp the information. Her brain had rapidly begun to switch off everything not directly connected with the functioning of her body. Nothing seemed real. She wasn't tied to a soiled bed in a dimly lit cellar. Bren wasn't dead. Hayla wasn't dead. Jinn wasn't out there frightened and alone. That shocking news wasn't real. She found herself falling into a trance.

Maybe it was time she looked after her own family, instead of other people. If she made the arrangements quickly, she could move her family to County Kerry, before spring came. It was a beautiful part of Ireland. They would be safe there. Bren would protest, tell her his job was important, but in the end he would go along with her because he loved her. It was strange to be loved after a lifetime of being hated and feared by almost everyone, including her parents. It was even stranger to finally love in return. Why had it taken her so long to realise that she loved Bren?

"I'm sorry, Madalene. Torrin's just told me about Bren and Hayla. Here let me untie you. If there's anything I can do…" Looking up she saw Holan had entered the room. *No. No. No. Not dead. Not true.* Then why were tears running down Holan's face? Madalene wanted to scream at Holan to stop crying. *Bren and Hayla were not dead. There was nothing to cry about.*

There was someone else she loved; her stepdaughter, Hayla, a bright-eyed girl with long brown hair and a cute button nose. A little minx who smothered Madalene with kisses and cuddles every time she wanted something and subsequently always got it.

"I have to fetch a knife, Madalene. I can't get these knots undone," said Holan.

Hayla who was…*raped so violently, she haemorrhaged…raped so violently…* Bren…*stabbed him…Shadowman stabbed him.* Because of her. Because Peter Shadow had found out about her. Her brain reconnected and unreality fled. This was her fault. Believing herself invincible, she had recklessly endangered her family and now they were dead. Jinn might have run, but it wouldn't take long for the Sanctum to find him. They would kill her son too.

"It's going to be alright. Look I've got a knife. I'll cut you free," said Holan, still sobbing.

Fierce physical pain began to course through Madalene's body. It was the pain of grief, but worse than she had ever experienced it before, because this time it was accompanied by massive guilt. She gasped at its force.

"Did I catch you with the knife?" said Holan, looking concerned.

Madalene relished the pain, even though its potency left her shaking. She deserved to suffer. Understanding pain better than she understood love, she knew what she had to do. As Holan cut the last bond away, Madalene sat up quickly and grabbed the knife out of her hands.

"Get out of here, Holan. Leave me alone," Madalene said in a voice that was distinctly not her own.

"Give me the knife back and I'll leave you," said Holan, cautiously.

104

"No. Get out of here, Holan, before I use it on you." Madalene waved the knife about feebly, knowing it was stupid, but not caring.

"Go on then. Use it on me. I'm not leaving you alone with a knife after what you've just learned about Bren and Hayla."

"Then I'll damn well kill myself in front of you," said Madalene crazily. "Go and call your pal Alan in; he wouldn't want to miss this. It's what you all want. It's what I want...It's what I deserve. I loved Bren and I've only just realised it. As for Hayla...." Though she hadn't cried since childhood, Madalene felt tears rolling down her cheeks.

"I didn't think you'd be like this, Madalene. I thought you'd want to avenge their deaths." Holan had stopped crying. There was now a look of dread on her face.

"I am avenging their deaths. You were right. I endangered their lives with my actions. I killed them, not Shadowman, or the Sanctum. I did."

"Bren wouldn't want you to kill yourself. If you found Jinn before the Sanctum finds him, you could go and live peacefully together in Ireland. Grandma's cottage in Cork is empty, you could live there. Don't worry about Shadowman. The Provoke group's got him riled. We'll keep on attacking him until he's overthrown."

Madalene had already drawn blood from her left wrist, but Holan's words stopped her. Holan couldn't seriously believe that the Provoke group was capable of deposing Peter Shadow. It would only be possible if the group became a combative force. If Madalene accepted Elgin's offer, she could make it happen. The time for fighting alone and paying mercenaries was over. A proper campaign was needed. It could only involve hit and run tactics and regular harassment to begin with, because the Provoke membership was small. But maybe if they had some success others would join them, others like the silent members of the public who currently sat in their homes fuming at the injustice that raged through the land. People who would fume more if they knew the whole truth. And if she was lucky a time would come when she could get close to Peter Shadow. That time would not come if she killed herself now...And she wanted that meeting. Wanted it very badly.

Ignoring Holan, Madalene placed the knife back on her wrist.

"Madalene. Don't." Holan lunged forwards with a yell that brought Alan, Torrin and Christian running into the room.

Pushing Holan away, Madalene continued with what she was doing.

"Don't stand there you three. Stop her," said Holan, but no one moved, they seemed stunned by what they were seeing.

Carefully Madalene carved Bren and Hayla's names onto her wrists. They would act as a constant reminder of why she had to fight until Peter Shadow was dead. And they would be the names that Peter Shadow saw when her hands went round his throat. While she cut her flesh, she hardened her heart, turning it into stone. Emotion would not stand in the way of what she had to do.

Chapter Fourteen

Howling At The Moon

Stand up. Ignore the bleeding and the shaking. Good. Now start walking and try to look dignified. *No.* Don't fall over. Get back on your feet. Slowly. That's better. Put one foot forward. Follow it with the other one. Look at their faces. They think you've lost your mind. You haven't. Pass by Holan. Now go past the lynch mob. There's the door. Damn! There's the floor again. Might as well stay down. *No.* Get up, Madalene. You have to get out of here. Mustn't let them have an excuse to tie you up for a third time. There are things to do. Meetings to attend. Peter Shadow to kill - not an easy death, a prolonged, painful one. First you have to find Jinn. *No.* Don't think about Bren and Hayla. Remember. No emotion. You're back on your feet. Forget dignity, stagger out. Nearly at the door…Almost there…

Strong arms grabbed Madalene as she fell again. Looking up she saw the grim faces of Alan and the man they called Torrin. She tried to pull away from them, but they dragged her upright and held her firmly.

"Come with me, Madalene it's time you had a bath," said Holan, gently. "Alan and Torrin will help you get upstairs."

"Do you really think I'll find a bath comforting?" said Madalene hoarsely. "I don't need any comfort, Holan… I never have."

"It's not your comfort I was thinking of, Madalene," said Holan pointedly.

An hour later, Madalene found herself alone in a small locked bedroom. Her newly washed hair was tied back and her wrists had been bandaged. She was dressed in one of Holan's jumpers and baggy woollen trousers held on by a belt. Her own clothes had been taken to be burnt, which was an insult; the clothes had stunk, but Holan could have tried washing them – she almost certainly washed Alan and Christian's clothes for them. It meant that for the moment Madalene didn't have anything of her own to wear. Fortunately she had clothes at various hideouts, which she could fetch later; she also had clothes at home. Not that going home would do her much good. There were probably people inside and outside the house waiting for her to do just that.

On a low table nearby was a loaf of bread, a large chunk of cheese and a cup of wine – apparently she'd broken all the glasses. As she took a bite of the cheese, she could hear a lively conversation going on downstairs. She guessed they were talking about their meeting. A meeting she intended to be at, even though it was obvious her companions had no intention of taking her with them. How she would get there wasn't clear, but her immediate concern was to find her son. Where had Jinn run to? A friend's house? Jinn had a lot of friends. Dare she visit the area and try to contact them? She was a wanted woman and fragile at present. Of course she dared.

Carefully Madalene picked up her rifle. Holan had obviously left it in this room for safekeeping and overlooked it. Her fragility wouldn't matter if her shooting was accurate. Checking the rifle was loaded, Madalene aimed at a photograph of Holan on the other side of the room. Right between the eyes, she thought. Instead her hands shook so violently, she dropped the rifle, sending a single shot into the cup of wine. Damn. Minutes later she heard the key turn and Holan and Christian came running into the room.

"What's happening, Madalene? Oh… You've tried to…with the rifle," said Holan, looking shocked and fearful.

Christian obviously thought the same. Madalene watched him pick up the rifle and place it as far away from her as possible.

"Don't be stupid, Holan. I'm not still trying to kill myself. I would have done that downstairs if your words hadn't given me a reason not to."

Holan gasped. "What words? When I talked about Provoke? You are not getting involved with our group."

Madalene smiled sweetly. "I don't want to get involved with your group. I'll have my own group soon enough." Holan squealed as the impact of Madalene's words hit her. Before Holan could come up with a rejoinder, Madalene continued and now she was serious.

"You promised you'd help me after the rescue. So far you've kept that promise by tying me up in your cellar and burning my only clothes - even now you're keeping me locked up. It's not quite what I had in mind, Holan."

"What was I supposed to do? You were trashing my house, Madalene. You were wildly out of control ..." Holan turned away, trying to hide the tears in her eyes. Madalene saw Christian give Holan a sympathetic nod. Either one of them would do, thought Madalene, though Holan was the better choice.

"I think Jinn might be hiding at a friend's house. If I give you the names of his friends, can you contact them for me and see if you can find him?" A sudden thought occurred to her. "Does Jinn know where you live?"

"Of course he doesn't. I didn't want to risk Bren finding out where I lived while he worked for the Sanctum." Holan turned and gave her a sullen look. "Jinn used to visit me regularly when I had my apartment in Golders Green, before you took him away from Mother to spite her."

"She begged me to take him." Madalene was angry, but controlled it. She saw Holan begin to muster the past. "No, Holan. This isn't the time for recriminations. There's a chance he still thinks you live in that apartment. You're closer to him than I am; it's possible he may try to find you there." As Madalene said this, the look on Holan's face changed becoming optimistic. "Will you go and find my son for me?"

"She can't, Madalene," said Christian. "If they're looking for you, they might be looking for Holan too; Bren could have told the Sanctum you have a sister. I'll go. Just tell me what to do."

Madalene studied him carefully; she knew what this was about, but wasn't sure if she wanted to allow it. "Oh and you're not an escaped prisoner on the run from the Sanctum?"

"I'm a commonplace prisoner on the run; I'd have to be very unlucky to be noticed. Finding you will take precedence over finding people like me," said Christian bravely.

"No, Madalene," said Holan. "Christian may be right, but he's still injured. Besides, Bren never met me in person; he couldn't have given them my description. You've seen what I can do. I'll go."

"There are photographs of you in my house. They're old, but Bren would have been able to describe you from them. And you're forgetting Peter Shadow knows you. Christian's right, the Sanctum will be looking for you. He will go," said Madalene decisively.

"You're sending him straight back to the chambers," said Holan, striding out of the room and slamming the door behind her.

No I'm not. I'm sending him out to regain his courage, thought Madalene, beginning to describe what Jinn looked like to Christian.

It was an impatient time for Madalene, each minute seemed like an hour and each hour seemed like ten. She didn't like sending others to do tasks that she was more capable of. Only she wasn't capable was she? Several injections of Xybille had seen to that. The longing to take more was great, but she denied it was addiction. She couldn't start a war in such a weakened state and she was going to start a war. The desire for vengeance had grown, becoming a conflagration that threatened to consume her. It could only be extinguished by Peter Shadow's blood.

Darkness fell and there was still no sign of Christian. Downstairs the voices were muted and it was clear that no-one would sleep until they had news. Madalene paced up and down the small room, willing her body's strength to return. She couldn't go further because Holan had locked the door shortly after Christian's departure. It was a petty act of spite because Holan was annoyed; there was a lot of Mother in her. Not that Madalene cared; Holan had forgotten the rifle again, she could blast her way out anytime. Suddenly she heard the transporter returning. From downstairs came excited voices, but were they excited because Christian was back safely or because he had succeeded? Furiously she pulled at the door handle of her room and was about to fetch her rifle when the key turned.

A dishevelled Christian entered the room, smiling happily at her. Behind him came a tall thin boy. The boy's long black hair fell into hazel eyes - his father's eyes - but it didn't hide the hostility in them.

She had never quite got used to his sullenness or his dislike at being in her company

"He was easy to find, Madalene. You were right, he was trying to reach Holan's apartment when I found him. He tried to run away, thinking I was a Sanctum Guard, but he's in a worse state than I am. I caught him easily," said Christian. "I was lucky because I tried his friends first with no success. None of them wanted to talk to me."

"You did well, Christian, and I won't forget it. Now leave us. I need to talk to my son alone. And Christian, leave the door unlocked, I have no intention of rampaging again," said Madalene, matching his smile with one of her own, amused at the effect it had on him.

"B-But Holan said…"

"I'll deal with Holan. Don't worry, Christian; I intend to stay in this room, I have no great desire to spend time with your friends downstairs."

"Don't keep the boy long. Holan's running about downstairs, getting food ready for him and he needs it, he hasn't eaten for nearly two days." With that Christian left and she noticed how proud he looked. She needed men like Christian in her army. Whether he would join her was another matter. Only he could decide that.

Jinn looked at her tentatively, and then looked towards the door and Christian's retreating back. He seemed almost frightened at being left alone in her company.

"Don't worry, boy. I won't keep you long. I'm sure Holan and the others are dying to smother you. Has Christian told you about Bren and Hayla?" she asked, trying to sound like a mother and failing.

Jinn nodded his head, fighting to stop the tears spilling down his cheeks. His hazel eyes blazed with a mixture of unidentifiable emotions. Then without warning he attacked her, hitting her with his hands and kicking her with his feet. "It's your fault. You made this happen. They didn't want Bren or Hayla, they wanted you. I've seen the posters on the streets and read what they say. Grandma told me you were wicked and I didn't believe her. But grandma was right…"

Madalene comfortably took the blows. Jinn was too weak to hurt her properly and he obviously needed to release pent-up grief and anger. Suddenly he stopped, threw his arms around her and began to wail loudly. Holan appeared momentarily in the doorway, but vanished as soon as she saw what was happening. Not knowing how to handle this erratic change of emotion, Madalene put one arm around him awkwardly and gently stroked his head. Recklessly she told him what she'd been doing, omitting only the details that affected the safety of others. Jinn knowing didn't matter now; his life was in danger anyway.

"So there it is, Jinn. I've told you as much as I can and you have to promise not to repeat my words to anyone, not even Holan. Listen carefully; I don't want you to suffer Bren and Hayla's fate. For your own safety, I'm sending you to Ireland..." Jinn went rigid in her arms then pulled away from her.

"I won't go, *Mother*." The last word was said with such contempt, she was almost proud of him. "I'm sixteen years old, I can look after myself. I'd rather be dead than go to Ireland."

Ah, the dramatics of the young. "Oh, like that is it? Let me tell you something, if I say you're going to Ireland you will go to Ireland."

"I won't go, *Madalene*," said Jinn, with a determination that surprisingly matched her own.

"Mother! I'm your mother."

"*Madalene*. You've never been a mother to me. I wouldn't have cried one tear if you'd died." Looking closely, she could see that this was bravado. Jinn's only intention was to hurt her.

"Well I'm glad to hear it, because I wouldn't have shed any tears over you either. That doesn't change the fact that you are my son." She could do bravado too.

Madalene studied Jinn, noting the defiance and hatred in his eyes and now seeing the vulnerability behind them. Something about him stirred her, Jinn was more like her than he knew.

"Okay you can stay with me, but you know what I have to do. I can't look after you. I'll teach you to take care of yourself, I'll even teach you how to fight, but that's it." Holan would have to be kept in the dark about the fighting lessons. "You'll have to learn to obey me without question." Jinn actually looked triumphant, but he nodded his head in what he obviously hoped was an obedient fashion. "First you can do something for me. There's an important meeting taking place tomorrow, but I need help to get there. The others in this house don't want me to be there, so you mustn't tell them what we're doing."

She expected immediate rejection, Jinn would never take sides against Holan, but as she watched him staring at her, she saw that he was excited and hope flickered in his eyes. Jinn didn't hate her as much as he thought he did.

Curious eyes watched Elgin as he walked towards the stage. There was no hostility, but neither was there the usual warmth. He noted that numerous people were present. Strange, given the current danger. Whispered conversations reached his ears and to his horror, he realised why there were so many. They had come to see Madalene, hoping Alan had his rope handy. Ignorant fools! This wasn't a game or entertainment.

Alan came forward to greet him. "You can see how they feel, Elgin. I've forgiven your interference at the last meeting and so will they if you say the right thing this time. Your *protégée* Madalene's ill. So you don't have to worry about her."

Elgin looked into the eyes of the man he once would have chosen to replace him and controlled his anger.

"That would be the *protégée* who saved your life and nineteen others in the group? Don't worry. I intend to say the right thing, Alan."

It was easy for them to dismiss Madalene as crazy and dangerous; they didn't know the truth. He hadn't known the whole truth until yesterday when an Irishman had arrived carrying a letter from Bertha. He had invited the man in for lunch and over a frugal meal had learned the full extent of Madalene's activities.

Madalene's need for the Provoke group became obvious. She couldn't keep paying men to help her and she couldn't save everyone alone. As Provoke group members were prepared to

113

antagonise Shadowman, she had thought they might be prepared to go further, but she had been wrong. He was ashamed that members of the group he had set up had tried to kill her, but of course it was easier than attempting to kill the real enemy. To then learn from Holan, before the meeting started, that Madalene had rescued twenty Provoke members as well as Bertha…

"Madalene is unwell and cannot be here." Elgin dispensed with his usual lavish greeting. "Therefore the leadership issue will not be settled tonight. Some of you are hoping that, as she is not here, I will see sense and change my mind. I will not do that. I still intend to make Madalene leader of this group…"

As he expected, chaos broke out. Alan, Holan and Torrin came over to him and started protesting vociferously. Christian followed them, but said nothing.

"She's insane, Elgin. You can't do this," said Holan.

"Of course Madalene's insane. The woman hasn't one sane bone in her body, even her heart probably beats out of time. But it is a big heart and if you all calm down, I'll explain my decision."

Alan spoke furiously. "We'll hear your reasons, but nothing you say about that woman will change our minds. We've lived with her and seen the madness first hand. You haven't."

Slowly the room became silent and Elgin began to speak again. "I would not lightly foist an unwanted leader on you. Until recently I believed Madalene was too dangerous to be part of our group. So why have I chosen her to lead us?"

"Because when Bertha was captured and Grace died, you went a little crazy too. Nobody blames you for that," said Alan.

"That would be a good reason, but try this one instead. What if I tell you that while we wrote letters, Madalene saved countless lives?"

He spoke about the annihilation of certain sections of society, such as the elderly and the homeless. And then he spoke of how Madalene had secretly saved as many of these people as possible.

"You keep saying she's mad as if it was a bad thing. Only a madwoman could have done this! At the last meeting you tried to destroy her, thinking her death would protect you. She barely escaped. What do you think she did after that escape? Do you think she crawled back to the asylum she came from and spent the night howling at the moon? Isn't that what crazy people do?" He paused for effect studying the faces of the people in front of him; sadly they were unimpressed and doubtful. "Hours after that meeting she made her way into the torture chambers and rescued Bertha." Painstakingly he added the details. Holan gasped loudly.

"Yes, Holan. The very next night, Madalene went into those chambers again because you asked her to. She must have been exhausted and reluctant to re-enter that hellish place, nevertheless she freed twenty prisoners, all of them members of this group. She even rescued Alan Moore, the man who'd put a noose around her neck. A madwoman indeed." In carefully measured tones he used the sympathy angle, finishing by describing the deaths of Madalene's husband and step-daughter.

"This is why I want her to lead us and change what we do. We have become one of those sections of society that Shadowman wants to annihilate. Maybe Madalene will save us," said Elgin, wearily. He had done his best, now it was up to them. He certainly intended to fight alongside Madalene and, looking at Christian's face, he believed Christian would too...

"Well I'm not saving *you* old man. I'd have to listen to your endless speeches."

"Madalene?" Elgin began to smile as he searched for her.

"I liked the bit about the asylum and howling at the moon though. That sort of thing keeps people on their toes."

Moving quickly through the crowd, supported by a young man, who held a rifle in clear sight to prevent any trouble; Madalene stepped into view and howled triumphantly.

Chapter Fifteen

Threads

Peter Shadow glared at the whore writhing on top of him; her shrill squeals of faked delight were jangling his nerves. She was a gift from Vertex, who had hoped her passing resemblance to Madalene would be pleasing. The whore bent down and blew softly in his ear. He reacted by turning his head away in annoyance. Admittedly the woman had long, dark hair and blue eyes, but she was no more like Madalene than a cat was like a dog; they were different species. Madalene had an aura about her that was unmistakeable; an intermingled air of arrogance and danger. It had been there when she was a child and it was there in the photographs of her as a woman. Damn her. Since he'd learned of her existence and seen her in the photographs he'd done nothing but yearn for her. He'd even lost his desire for whores and the countless other women who vied for his attention.

The whore's squealing became louder, and she began to claw wildly at his chest. He roared ferociously, unable to stomach her attentions a moment longer. For a brief second he wanted to strangle her, silence her for good. Instead he roughly lifted the whore away from him and threw her off the bed.

"Leave them," he said viciously as she went to retrieve her clothes. Ignoring her pleading glance, he beckoned to the two bodyguards stood impassively near his bedroom door. "Get her out of here. Get her out. Get her out." As he said this he threw a small glass jug at her. Satisfyingly it smashed into her face causing blood to flow wildly down her chin and onto her throat. She began to scream, but before he could throw anything else, the guards grabbed her, threw her out of the door, and then looked at him questioningly.

"You don't need to ask. She's yours. But I want to be left alone for a while so one of you will have to stand guard outside the door. Take turns with her." With lascivious grins the guards thanked him and left the room. He smiled; his leftovers were a perk of the job for these bodyguards. In return he received absolute loyalty from them.

116

Shortly after this Peter heard screams coming from a nearby room; this time the whore wasn't faking it, her terror sounded real. Irritably, he went to speak to the guard on the door.

"If he's disturbing you, Sir, I'll go and get him to stop and take her elsewhere," said the guard, snapping briskly to attention.

"No. Leave him. He sounds like he's giving her the hard time she deserves. When it's your turn though, for pity's sake take her elsewhere."

"Will do, Sir, and don't worry, we call him 'Two-minute Jenkins' in the barracks. He won't be much longer."

Turning back into his room, Peter slipped on a white robe and poured himself a glass of rare French brandy. After a few sips he felt his tension ease. Noticing that the screaming had stopped, he picked up a photograph of Madalene from his bedside table.

"Where are you?" he said, softly. "And more importantly, where's your army?" It had been six months since he'd first learned of Madalene's takeover of the Provoke group. Apparently she'd managed to form an army out of them. With Madalene in control there wouldn't be any written threats, only carefully calculated actions. Urgently he'd issued instructions that this army was to be found. The search had covered the length and breadth of the country, but there'd been no sign of them. Only when he had surprisingly continued to get protest letters did he realise that Madalene's army held only part of the original group and must therefore be small in number. It meant they posed little threat to his regime; but having seen what Madalene was capable of he couldn't afford to become complacent.

"You're doing this to excite me, my love." He spoke to the photograph in his hand. "I know you're going to attack, I just don't know when. Make it soon, my love. Your pathetic army doesn't stand a chance against mine. I'm going to destroy everyone in it, but not you, my love. Not you"

Holding the photograph at arms length, he imagined it was a picture of Madalene with a large belly, a belly that held his child. A shiver of delight ran through him as he imagined stroking that belly and feeling the strong kick of his son beneath his fingers.

"I may not destroy you, but I am going to hurt you. I'm going to enjoy hurting you, Madalene. You've been a naughty girl and you already know what happens to naughty girls." Peter thought back to the day when he had shown her what happened to girls who didn't behave properly.

"It's why you fight me, isn't it? Not for any noble ideas. For vengeance and hatred. But not for much longer, Madalene. Soon you'll learn to love me...Who is it? I said that I wasn't to be disturbed."

'Two-minute Jenkins' poked his head around the door. "It's Mr Vertex, Sir. He insists on seeing you at once. Says it's important and you'll want to see what he's got."

Peter sighed; Fatboy was the last person he wanted to see after his experience with that dreadful whore.

"Tell him I'm furious with him. It would be risky for him to come into my presence right now...

"Then I'll take this letter from Madalene and discard it," said Vertex, loudly.

A letter from Madalene? How ironic that she would do such a thing.

"Come in, Vertex. I want to see you anyway. You can explain to me in what way you thought that whore resembled Madalene."

Vertex entered waving a piece of paper in his hands. "This was found not long ago mixed up with letters from members of the Provoke group. How it got there I don't know. My understanding is that there are no connections between the group and the army."

"Shut up, Vertex, and give me that letter. I presume you've already read it." He noticed Vertex eyeing the brandy. "That isn't for you. It's rare and far too precious to go down your throat. Get some of that nasty Dorset red out of the cupboard over there, the stuff I keep to give my whores, talking of which..."

"Read the letter, Peter," said Vertex abruptly. "It's more important than you not liking a whore I've sent you."

118

Putting aside the photograph of Madalene, Peter sat down, beckoning Vertex to do the same and began to read the letter aloud.

Hello Peter, I know how you like receiving letters so I thought I would send you one. I'm furious about what you did to my husband Bren and my stepdaughter Hayla. It was unnecessary and harsh. Happily you didn't get hold of my son...

"She appears quite calm about their deaths, considering she probably knows what was done to them. Doesn't she have any feelings at all?" said Vertex, taking a large swig of wine from his glass and to Peter's amusement wincing as he caught the taste of it.

"The girl had no feelings, why should the woman?" Peter said, before reading on.

...You should have come to me if you wanted information. I would have been quite happy to tell you what I'd been doing. Though it would have been difficult not to boast. I didn't take long to realise that you were massacring the weak and helpless members of our society. So I began to rescue as many as possible, trying to prevent you destroying all of them. I've lost count of the number of your victims I've saved...

'What victims,' thought Peter? Was she referring to his cull of the extremely large elderly population? Had she no understanding of that ancient yet still relevant phrase, 'Survival of the fittest.' He was proud that he'd been capable of taking such severe, but necessary, action. The country didn't have enough resources to cope with the needy and useless. He read on.

...Then there was the just execution of your friend Edgar Heaton. It was an easier death than he deserved. I'm only sorry that you decided to kill his wife, though on second thoughts as she'd married such an evil man, she deserved it....

"Why is she doing this?" said Vertex. "What has she got to gain by telling us this?"

"Because she knows I already have this information, she's suggesting that if she could do it once, she could do it again. It's intimidation."

...I couldn't let you have Alice Jones; she was a good friend of mine, as was her husband Robin. How could you send him to the Arena? You were his friend once. Watching your Sanctum Guards get blown apart was exhilarating; I even got to shoot a few my bombs missed. They're evil men; the regular army wouldn't look twice at scum like them. Removing twenty of those bastards from the Earth was quite an achievement...

"Interesting," said Peter. "I thought she might have had help with those bombings, but it appears she worked alone. What the hell does Madalene need an army for? I think I might have underestimated her."

"You haven't underestimated her. She's a violent psychopath. We ought to pin medals on the Provoke members who tried to lynch her, starting with Alan Moore." Vertex seemed thoughtful for a moment. "His hatred for Madalene is well known as is his friend's Torrin Spice. We could use this hatred to our advantage. Alan must hate Madalene even more now she's forced her sister, Holan, to become part of this so-called army; it's said that Alan's deeply in love with Holan. It wouldn't be too hard to persuade both these men to help us catch Madalene."

"I don't believe it," Peter said, his tone darkening. "It wasn't Elgin who rescued his wife, Bertha and the others. It was Madalene." He'd thought Vertex's idea was excellent, but before he could respond the next few lines of Madalene's letter had caught his eye.

...Then there were my visits to your torture chambers, where I rescued Elgin's wife Bertha one night and returned the following evening to rescue twenty more prisoners. Two visits to your precious Sanctum building in two days and you didn't even notice me; just think where I could turn up next...

"I thought Elgin was responsible..." Peter was almost speechless. "She dared to enter the chambers *twice*?" Without a word Peter walked over to the side-table and, slamming down his glass, he refilled it with more brandy, lots more brandy. As he sat back down he saw Vertex looking wistfully at the glass, but said nothing as he picked up the letter and continued to read.

...Now you see that all you had to do was ask me and I would have answered all your questions willingly. Instead you chose to murder a man of far greater worth than you, Peter. A man I loved passionately. But what would you know of these things? Your love for yourself is so great that you will never experience the love of another...

Shaking now with anger, Peter dropped the letter and retrieved Madalene's photograph. "You have no idea of my worth; your pathetic husband could never have matched me. I will soon experience the love of another, Madalene. Your love. You will adore me. You will weep when I leave a room. You will do anything to please me. You will..." Looking down at his hands he saw only pieces of Madalene. In his anger he had torn up her picture. Compelled to hear the rest of her words, he dropped the pieces and returned to the letter.

...As for the abominable murder of my step-daughter Hayla, a girl I treated like my own child, I have only these words to say to you. A time will come when you will be at my mercy. When that time comes I will remember this crime and you will pay in kind, only your death will not be so swift. There will be no further words between us. Now I will let my actions speak for me. I declare war on you and your pernicious government.

Until the day we inevitably meet, Madalene.

"She declares war. How optimistic she is," said Peter, standing up and moving over to the large windows of his room. "A time *will* come when we inevitably meet, but she will be at my mercy, not the other way around."

"Her threats are preposterous. How can one woman with an army of less than fifty people propose to make war on us? At best she could only ever be a damned nuisance and even that's not going to happen. There are rumours that she's in Ireland training this so-called army, which would explain why we couldn't find them. I've seen to it that the ports are watched. We will have her and her ridiculous army as soon as she attempts a return. " said Vertex, walking over to help himself to more wine.

"Then where has this letter come from and how did it reach me...?" A loud explosion was heard in the distance. With horrified fascination Peter watched threads of smoke began to appear over a group of buildings in the distance. Turning, he saw Vertex's equally horrified expression as he came to look out of the window.

"What's over there, Vertex?" said Peter anxiously, turning back to the window and seeing the threads go higher and higher, weaving a tapestry of their own design into the afternoon sky.

"There's nothing important in that direction…No wait, the printing-presses of the Sanctum Sun newspaper are located around there. The paper was the first to condemn the murderer of Edgar Heaton; I can remember telling them what to write. Hundreds of people work there…" Vertex looked shocked.

"So Madalene's war begins. What was that you said about her not being in the country?" Peter felt both shocked and elated at the same time. Madalene was in the country and the start of hostilities brought her one step closer to his side. "She's made her move and it's a good one, the Sanctum Sun is our most popular newspaper and Madalene has effectively shut it down. However, to counteract this I will insist that other state papers allow the Sanctum Sun to share their presses. They won't like it, but it means the newspaper will be operational again in less than a week and its first headline will be news of the newly imposed curfew." Peter smiled; Madalene had just made it easy for him to keep the lower classes locked away at night.

"A curfew!" said Vertex, looking surprised. "You can't impose a curfew now; it will send members of the public running into Madalene's arms."

"For a long time now I've been infuriated at the problems caused by drunken agitators every evening. Many of my Sanctum Guards have been assaulted by people who have drunk too much Terpz."

"What's Terpz?" said Vertex looking puzzled.

"Common bars serve Terpz. It's a rough beer made from anything that will ferment. Its strong stuff and actually not that unpleasant after the third glass."

"You mean you've tried it," said Vertex.

"Of course. Leaders must be familiar with the habits of their people. Places like 'The Slug and Cabbage' even have an illegal still

122

that makes something akin to transporter fuel. That stuff is not so nice. It's caused more deaths than I have, which is why so far I've left it alone. It's time to close these places down and Madalene is our excuse. Can't you see, Vertex, it's not because these people irritate us. This curfew is necessary for their own safety. Of course the curfew will not affect Sanctum members or our wealthy supporters. Nor will it affect anyone who can prove they work for us or on our behalf. There's another reason for a curfew: if Madalene and her army move around at night time, they'll be so much easier to see."

Refilling his glass with brandy, Peter returned to the window and looked up at the sky. The smoky threads had finished their weaving and were now threatened by bigger plumes of smoke coming from below them, but in the threads he saw something that chilled him. Had he drunk too much brandy or was it his imagination? The threads had woven a word and that word appeared to be 'Madalene'.

Chapter Sixteen

Responsibility

"Mad old eye," said Ellyn, looking up at the smoke letters in the sky, that Peter Shadow had seen so clearly, and laughing with delight. "Why did you make it say mad old eye? Is it some sort of secret code?"

Madalene looked at the young girl jumping up and down with delight by her side and tried to hide her own amusement. Ellyn was mischievous, but a constant source of joy. Her presence had helped a lot to ease the pain of losing Hayla.

"It says my name, Madalene, just as I intended. In its way it is a sort of code," said Madalene, hoping if Peter Shadow was watching this, he wasn't seeing the same words as Ellyn. "It tells Peter Shadow I'm back; it also tells him I'm the one who set the bombs."

Casually Madalene sat down on the grass, cautiously surveying the others in the park. Not unusually for a warm summer's day, the park was full of people walking, sleeping or picnicking, and undoubtedly secret police members mingled with them. What did she care? The safest place to be was right under your enemy's nose. Laying down and stretching out, she gazed at the sky, watching the smoke threads unfurl, rejoicing in her own ingenuity. Her companions joined her and began to pass around the food they had brought along; mainly bread and cheese, their staple diet. It was nice to picnic in the park and comforting to know that they didn't look out of place.

"That's a fancy touch, Madalene. Why did you put *your* name up there and not the Provoke army's? This is supposed to be about all of us, isn't it? Not just the *great* Madalene," said Holan, sounding peevish.

"Peter Shadow isn't afraid of the Provoke army."

"You mean he *is* afraid of you? So what? Everyone's afraid of you."

124

"Putting my name up there makes sure the public gets to know me. It might encourage some of them to join us." Madalene turned languidly and stared into Holan's eyes, deliberately goading her to say more.

"The public already know you. You're on all the wanted posters. I hadn't noticed *them* sending people rushing to join us. Maybe people aren't keen to associate with a notorious murderess." Holan took a bite out of the chunk of bread in her hand. Talking with her mouth full she added, "So tell me *Great One*, how were you able to make smoke do that?"

For a moment Madalene considered starting a full-blown row with her sister. Holan was asking for trouble after all. Feeling indolent she decided not to give Holan the satisfaction.

"Remember firework displays when we were young? They'd always end with the word 'Goodnight' written in the sky. Well I did the same thing with smoke bombs. My idea was that smoke from the smoke bombs would be less dense and rise faster than smoke from the main blast. All I had to do was channel the smoke and hope no wind blew to disturb it. Did you understand that, or shall I explain it again?" In truth, Madalene hadn't thought it would work at all, but she'd no intention of telling Holan that.

"Its saying 'Moody one' now," said Christian, making Ellyn giggle. "So it definitely worked."

Ellyn's giggles were infectious, giving Madalene no choice but to laugh and noticed even Holan smiled. With mock indignation, Madalene threw a chunk of cheese at Christian. He responded by throwing a lump of bread at her. For a while food went to and fro between them.

"Enough," said Madalene, pulling cheese and bread out of her hair and sitting up. Come on, I think its time we went back to the hide-out and told Elgin and Bertha about our success."

"I don't think we should be laughing and throwing food around like children," said Holan, suddenly. "Innocent people died in that blast. That makes us killers."

This was so like Holan, Madalene almost spat. The eternal party pooper. "Nobody died, Holan. I didn't set the bombs to kill or maim. Along with the letter that Reynard put into the Sanctum post, this was just a warning."

"What are you talking about?" said Holan, standing up and walking agitatedly up and down.

"Sit down, Holan," Madalene hissed. "You're drawing attention to yourself. Sit down and laugh and play like the rest of us."

In an exaggerated motion, Holan slumped back down on the grass, glaring at Madalene. "Hundreds of people work in that place. Don't tell me that no-one got hurt. Of course it doesn't matter to you, but some of us still have feelings. Alan was so right about you. I should never have left his side."

Madalene began to laugh. In temper, Holan threw a glass bottle at Madalene's head that missed her by inches. "Tell her, Christian, before she makes me do something that I have no intention of regretting."

Christian's alarm at the tension between her and Holan was evident. Nervously, he began to speak. "You weren't there, Holan. Madalene set the bombs and then she went to find the fire siren. Even though it was in full view of everyone she turned its handle and kept turning it until she was sure the whole area was clear. Madalene's right, no-one got hurt."

"Oh," said Holan, her mouth open in amazement. "Oh…"

"A simple sorry would do. After all the sisterly fun we had in Ireland, I really thought you'd think better of me now. Especially as those idiots Torrin and Alan aren't around to poison you against me."

"They're not idiots. They're good men and given time they may yet join us. You need people like them to moderate your ideas."

"Hell will crumble into ash before I let those two join my army." Madalene knew that she was the one doing the glaring now. She watched Holan get to her feet and walk away and was relieved to see her go.

Holan stopped, turning back to look at Madalene with a furious expression on her face. "You could have told me that you would get everyone out. That simple bit of information would have given me peace of mind. But with you it's all *me, me, me*. Why did you bother training us? We can now run, use guns and some of us can make simple bombs. We're all capable of unarmed combat, and we've found out Christian is good with knives, but rubbish at shooting. What was the point when you intend to do everything yourself? You organised this mission and you're the one who set the bombs. Were we brought along to be your sycophants? Then listen carefully. Well done, Madalene. Good job. Didn't you do well? Are you happy now or do you need more?"

Before Madalene could get to her feet, Holan set off at a run. Ellyn and Christian gathered the remaining food into a bag and then also stood up; their silence speaking volumes. So they all thought they were soldiers after only six months of training in Ireland. They knew nothing. She'd been in the army for years and her skills had been hard earned. Didn't they realise she was trying to protect them and teach them at the same time? Scowling, she began to run after Holan, hearing Christian and Ellyn running in silence by her side. For a brief second she stopped and looked up at the sky. Her name had disappeared, engulfed by billowing clouds of black smoke. She smiled, knowing intuitively that he had seen it. He would have the Sanctum Sun running again within a week, but the effect of her message would stay around for a lot longer.

"Come on, you two. I thought I'd taught you how to run," she said, laughing as they both overtook her.

The mood at the hide-out was celebratory. Beer had been fetched and people stood around in small groups laughing and joking. They were not long back from Ireland and already action had been taken against the Sanctum. Successful action. Holan had to admit that, despite her misgivings, Madalene's leadership was faultless, even if Madalene did have a tendency to do everything herself. The members of the army were so closely knit; they were like an enlarged family. The Provoke group had never known such intimacy.

Assisted by Elgin, Bertha and ex-army colleagues, Madalene had trained over half the group to physically oppose Shadowman's tyranny. She had not however forgotten or demeaned those who could not fight. Valuing them equally, she had turned them into cooks, builders, medics, cleaners, intelligence gatherers. A couple had been made into scribes and these were the people who had not only written to Shadowman on Madalene's behalf, they had also made sure the letter was delivered.

Madalene had organised hiding places, setting up food storage areas and armouries. There were also meeting places and makeshift hospitals. All the hide-outs had escape routes to use in an emergency and were equipped with as many home comforts as possible. It seemed there was nothing Madalene hadn't thought of. Holan had been impressed and knew that Alan would have been impressed as well.

Holan spent a great deal of time worrying about Alan and Torrin, even though she was fairly certain they were still using her home as a hide-out. Large numbers of Provoke members were still being sent to the Arena, whereas so far the army members and their families were safe. Holan longed for Alan's company, Torrin's too, and wondered why she had ever left them and gone with Madalene, but in her heart she knew the reason. It was hard to forget the exhilaration she had felt rescuing prisoners from the chambers. It was also hard to forget the way it had felt killing people who deserved to die.

In a corner of the room talking loudly and drinking far too much beer stood a group of young men. Madalene had considered them exceptional during training. Their names were Mark Reed, Luke Stance, Adrian Brown, Adam Longbetter and Malcolm Short. With them stood Christian, regaling them with details of the day's events. As he talked, the group became louder and more exuberant. Holan noticed Ellyn going over shyly to join them. She was glad that Christian had found such good friends to replace the loss of Alan and Torrin. For her it was not so easy. Even so, she also enjoyed the company of these young men and several drinking sessions with them in Ireland had helped to ease her pain over what she saw as her betrayal of Alan. All of these sessions had ended with attempts to get her into their beds. So feeble were these attempts that it had been impossible to take offence. Looking at Ellyn's red face it seemed they were doing the same to her. Holan wondered if she should rescue the girl, but decided not to when she saw Ellyn firmly shake her head and begin to giggle. Ellyn looked like she could take care of herself.

Not far away sat Jinn. As always he was on his own, but she noticed his eyes straying wistfully towards Ellyn. Holan felt for him. Ellyn was the only one close to his age, but she was a lively spirit and tended to seek out those who were the same. Jinn was the opposite, quiet, introverted; someone who preferred his own company, or when he could get it, his mother's. It wasn't diffidence. In training, Jinn had proved to be just as fearless as his mother. Holan knew the problem: Madalene's rejection of him had shaped Jinn's character; he didn't trust people because he thought they would reject him likewise. Holan resolved to have a quiet word with Ellyn; maybe that lively young girl could help bring him out of his shell.

Thinking of Ellyn brought Holan's attention back to the men in the corner. There was now a lot of mock tussling going on as they each tried to impress Ellyn. Holan smiled, these extremely hormonal young men were currently running a competition to be the first to bed Madalene. The prize was a pot of engles which they had all contributed to and the immense status that would accompany such a feat. They didn't stand a chance, though Holan didn't like to tell them that. Christian had put his money into the pot, but Christian's intentions were different from the others; he was in love with Madalene and could no longer hide it, at least not from Holan.

Looking across the room, she found Madalene sat at a table near the kitchen door talking in hushed serious tones to Elgin and Bertha. Holan knew it wouldn't be long before Madalene sent the two of them up north to start conflict there. What would Madalene be like when their calming influence had gone? With them around the madness that lurked in Madalene had been quenched. With them around Madalene laughed even though pain still lingered in her eyes.

"Elgin and Bertha are taking a transporter and going north tonight," said Madalene, interrupting Holan's thoughts. "They want to speak to you before they go. I'm going to sit with Jinn for a while, but first I'm going over to speak to Christian and his friends. Give them hope. Do you know how big the pot is yet?"

Holan laughed, forgetting to be angry with Madalene. "I heard there was a hundred and fifty engles in it at the last count, but the boys keep egging each other on so it could have gone higher."

"Is that all I'm worth?" said Madalene, smiling. "They'll have to wait a lot longer for me in that case."

"Be honest, Madalene. They'll wait forever."

"Not necessarily," said Madalene, walking over to the group and beginning to tease them.

Sighing, Holan went to talk to Elgin and Bertha.

"My dear Holan," said Elgin in his usual booming tones, "I hear you're not too pleased with Madalene. Aren't you happy that her plan worked and no-one got hurt?"

"She did extremely well today," said Bertha. "I saw her name in the sky and was astonished. How did she do that?"

"Madalene's clever, wonderful and can do anything," said Holan, feeling her annoyance rising again. "So why did she bother taking us along? Like props in a play we stood in the background while she did everything herself, just like she always does."

"Did she keep watch while she set those bombs?" said Bertha, shrewdly.

"Well no. Ellyn and I did that, but..."

"Was her back covered while she worked? Did she know she had nothing else to worry about but doing her job properly?" said Elgin.

"Yes of course it was. We all carried guns, even Ellyn, but..."

Elgin persisted, "Were you ready to go to her defence if she was attacked?"

"Yes," said Holan. "But you don't understand..."

"Then you weren't just props," said Bertha, gently patting Holan's hand. "You were the valuable support team who allowed her to do the job and get it right and you all did exceedingly well."

Defeated, Holan sank into a chair beside them.

"Did you ever consider how much your safety means to her?" said Elgin, patting her other hand. "She's not going to let you risk your own lives until she's certain the odds are in your favour."

"I suppose I don't ever think of Madalene as a normal human being, but then you have to remember that I grew up with her." Holan looked over at her sister, seeing Madalene in a slightly different way. The way the young men were flirting with her was outrageous, but she noticed that Madalene was being careful not to hurt their feelings. Everyone in this room cherished Madalene and most of them were ready to die for her. Why couldn't they see Madalene as she really was? Insane and dangerous.

As if Bertha had read her thoughts, she said to Holan, "You have to start seeing the good in her. She's a great leader just like Elgin predicted. Soon more people will join this army and it will be her that draws them in. The trouble is she relies heavily on Elgin and I for stability. Now you have to take our place. She loves you and listens to what you say more than you think she does. She also has great admiration for you."

"She does not!" said Holan.

"You're her older sister and she looks up to you. We've heard her talk about you remember," said Elgin, beginning to smile. "I've lost count of the number of times she's told us about your exploits in the chambers, the night you rescued Alan and the others. She was definitely impressed."

Holan was stunned into silence. She saw Madalene walk over to Jinn and noticed the boy's happiness at getting his mother's attention. Holan felt the same way as Jinn at that moment. A ripple of joy ran through her, growing until it became a torrent. Her sister loved her. Wasn't that something? Then a discordant clang sounded.

"She's changed lately, I know that, but I can still see the madness and the danger in her. It frightens me. She doesn't have the restrictions that keep sane people safe. She's a danger to herself and others," said Holan, with tears welling up in her eyes.

131

"Not if she's kept stable, Holan," said Elgin, now looking desperately into Holan's eyes. "It's an important job and only you can do it. She has to be kept stable and sane for all our sakes."

Again Holan looked over at Madalene. Jinn was laughing at something that had been said and Madalene was smiling in response. Sensing she was being watched Madalene turned and looked over at Holan questioningly. Holan merely smiled in return already accepting the enormous responsibility Elgin and Bertha had given her.

Chapter Seventeen

Breaking Curfew

"Funny that Sanctum members don't have to obey this curfew. Surely they risk getting shot..." Madalene glanced at Holan and grinned, knowing that her meaning couldn't be any clearer. While ordinary bars, clubs and restaurants had been forced to close down, Sanctum-owned establishments had remained open for business. As Sanctum members and their associates weren't bound by the recent curfew rules, they were able to use them. To Madalene's way of thinking that didn't seem fair.

"We'd better go and talk to the council about this," said Holan, acknowledging Madalene's intent with a wry smile.

Madalene grimaced. She had been made leader of the hastily formed Provoke army, but only after agreeing to be overseen by an elected council. At the time she'd been half out of her mind with the after effects of Xybille and facing overwhelming hostility. With Alan Moore walking out, taking most of the group with him, and others threatening to follow, there hadn't been a choice. The council had been given the power to block any of her actions they considered too dangerous, which, when she thought about it, was all of them.

With Elgin and Bertha as leaders of the council, things hadn't been too bad: they had readily agreed to the demolition of the Sanctum Sun's printing presses, provided the lives of the people working there were spared. But now that Bertha and Elgin had gone to fight in the north of the country, their positions had been taken by two people Madalene despised, Hannah Brown, a sour-faced crone, and a squinty-eyed man called Tom Bragg. They were apparently old friends of Alan Moore and it seemed odd that neither of them had chosen to stay with him. Madalene was convinced that they had only joined the army to thwart her. Hadn't she seen Alan talking passionately to them before he walked out with his followers in tow? While they were in charge, her army wouldn't be allowed to squash a fly.

Hannah and Tom had quickly declared that Madalene's regular running sessions should be banned in case people on the streets recognised her from her 'wanted' posters. On the same theme, they'd urged Madalene to cut off her hair and bleach it in an attempt to disguise herself. They'd even had the nerve to suggest that her rifle remain in the armoury until it was needed, which if they had their way would be never.

Madalene had gone running every day of her life and wasn't about to stop to please them. Running calmed her down and helped her think. The colour and cut of her hair was her own business. As for her rifle, it wasn't negotiable.

She had defied them, arguing that their only power lay with the actions of the army as a whole, not her as an individual. She wouldn't be kept prisoner in the hide-out and if she needed disguising she would do it when she saw fit. Sarcastically, she thanked them for their concern over her well-being, but they had to understand that the photograph on her wanted poster was old, and most times she went out, her hair was tucked securely under a cap.

Since that time, Madalene had presented the council with lots of ideas, all of which had been turned down. It was frustrating. Madalene's rifle twitched every time it came near Hannah or Tom. There was going to be some serious ousting from power before too long. Either that or she would just shoot the pair of them.

"Why do we need to talk to the council? This isn't a planned undertaking for the group. It's target practice. We'll get rusty if we don't practice."

"You agreed to run all your decisions past the council," said Holan, trying to placate her and failing.

"You were there that night," said Madalene, knowing she sounded childish. "You know I was forced into it. Things were okay when Elgin and Bertha were in charge, but with Hannah and Tom they're impossible. How did that pair of tyrants get voted into power?"

"They were extremely efficient when they worked for the Provoke group. Look, the point of setting up this army was so you didn't have to work alone anymore. I know Hannah and Tom can be frustrating, but they're only trying to keep us safe."

"Safe! I didn't set up this army to be safe, Holan. Why didn't Hannah and Tom go with Alan, he likes safety? He must have ordered them to stay and frustrate me at every opportunity." Holan's response to this outburst was just to laugh at her.

Madalene thought up several vile curses, but didn't utter them. Holan had been good company since Elgin and Bertha had left. Madalene was not prepared to lose that at present, though she did wonder what part Elgin and Bertha had played in Holan's recent character transformation.

"Don't take all the fun out of this," said Madalene, plaintively. "The group aren't ready for this kind of adventure. What's the point of taking it to the council?"

"Jinn's ready for action and so are Christian and his friends. Ellyn's getting better each day," said Holan, looking questioningly at Madalene.

Madalene ignored the look. "None of them are as good as you, Holan. I know you'll keep your nerve if there's trouble. Despite that unerring conscience of yours, you can kill if you want to. I've seen you do it. If you'd wanted to be safe you would have gone with Alan. Killing's in your genes, Holan, you can't fight it."

Holan looked disturbed by these words, but after a momentary pause she said firmly, "In the chambers I did what was necessary to survive. What you're suggesting is different. You're talking about killing innocent people."

"Weren't you listening to what I said earlier? Sanctum people aren't affected by this curfew. Everyone else is. There won't be any innocent people to kill." Madalene started to laugh.

"What's funny, Madalene?" said Holan, angrily.

"The curfew is what's funny. Peter Shadow's put his affiliates on the line for us like wooden ducks in a shooting gallery. He's made it easy for us to distinguish between his cronies and the public. It's shooting season. Come on, Holan."

135

"Then take someone like Luke along, he's an expert marksman, or Malcolm, I know he's good with a gun," said Holan.

"No. They've still got that Provoke group mentality. I don't trust them not to go weepy on me at the wrong moment. It has to be you, Holan." Madalene sighed and used a final argument. "I'm bored, Holan and I've been good for such a long time. Just you and me. We'll pick a few off, make a brief impact and then leave the scene. You've heard what Elgin and Bertha are up to in the north of England. Why are we getting left so far behind? Please, Holan."

For a short while Holan remained stubborn. Madalene watched her fight the idea of going out and shooting Sanctum members; she could almost hear Holan's thoughts. *I'm not like Madalene. I won't ever be like her. Not all the people working for the Sanctum are bad.* Then Madalene saw a hint of excitement appear in Holan's expression. There was a struggle as Holan tried to deny it, but it would not be denied. To her delight Holan nodded her agreement.

"Okay," said Holan, looking manic now she had made her decision. "Let's go and do our citizen's duty. There's a curfew in place. Anyone breaking curfew is asking to be shot. Peter Shadow said so. Didn't he?"

Madalene grabbed Holan and began to swing her round and round. "The council's going to be angry with us. Are you sure you can cope with being in disgrace? It's not something you're used to."

"If you can cope with the disgrace, I can," said Holan, dizzily pulling away from Madalene's embrace.

Madalene made sure they were both armed with powerful weapons and then led the way out of the hide-out as darkness fell. She knew they were seen leaving, but no-one tried to stop them.

"I have a feeling those two are taking some kind of action tonight. They're too heavily armed to be just going for a walk," said Luke Stance, turning round in his chair to watch them leave.

"Nothing's been said to the council. Surely they wouldn't embark on any kind of action without council permission?" said Adrian, who was lounging on the floor trying in vain to attract the attention of a young blonde girl nearby.

"Madalene would. She said she reserved the right to work alone when she needed to. The council denied her that right, but that would mean nothing to her." Christian swore softly under his breath. "This has something to do with the new curfew laws. Why didn't Madalene ask us to go along? We're ready for action."

Christian was irritated. He spent a great deal of time watching Madalene and had seen the familiar look of madness on her face as she had spoken to Holan. He knew then that she was up to something. Why hadn't she included him in her plans? He'd been terrified during the mission to blow up the Sanctum Sun's printing presses, but he'd stayed by Madalene's side and done everything she'd asked him to.

"She doesn't trust us," said Luke. "She thinks our idealism will get in her way. If she's going on a killing spree then she could be right."

"But it's Sanctum members she'll be killing. The ones who put us in the torture chambers." Christian had only recently found out that all his new friends had been in the chambers with him that night. It was their reason for joining Madalene's army. She'd saved their lives, but there was no sign that she realised it. In her fevered state she'd probably pulled bodies out of cells without even looking at their faces. In spite of the joking that went on between his new friends about how great sex with Madalene would be: in reality they were in awe of her.

"Do you think they might need back-up tonight?" said Adrian, meaningfully, turning away from the blonde, unaware that he'd just managed to attract her attention. Christian smiled at the longing looks the girl was now giving Adrian's back.

"They may need back-up if something goes wrong. We'd have to be careful not to be seen. Madalene would be furious if she spotted us," said Christian, trembling as adrenaline began to race through his body.

By the time they'd armed themselves, they were about fifteen minutes behind Madalene and Holan. However, Christian guessed, correctly, that Madalene would head for Sanctum-owned restaurants; as the clubs wouldn't open until later, and it didn't take him long to find her. He deliberately fell back to leave some distance between them.

"Your identity cards, gentlemen. Now." A guard stepped out of a side street in front of them, his weapon raised. Christian went rigid, unable to move, but Adrian stepped round him and rammed the butt of his rifle down on the man's head.

"Get him back where he came from," said Christian, shamed by his reaction, but thinking quickly to atone for it. "Use those manacles in his belt and chain him to something. Don't forget to gag him." Luke and Adrian gave him funny looks, but they did what he asked without question. Minutes later they returned.

"There was nothing to chain him to, but we manacled his hands behind his back and gagged him with a piece of ripped shirt. His shirt, not ours," said Luke, looking scared, but managing to grin at his own weak joke.

"It won't be a problem. I hit him again so he'll be out for a while," said Adrian. Christian was convinced that Adrian was speaking coldly to him because he had proved to be a coward. Nevertheless he moved forward quietly, with them following behind.

Stopping to look around a corner, Christian saw Holan and Madalene take up positions outside the Hedgewick restaurant, a well- known Sanctum haunt. Three men walked out laughing and joking with women at their sides. What happened next was so shocking that it took every ounce of courage Christian possessed not to turn and run away. The gasps of horror coming from either side of him showed that Luke and Adrian felt the same way. There was a series of deafening bangs. It seemed like the noise would never end. For a second there was silence. Then the screaming started, banshee-like, inhuman. Looking down on the ground Christian saw the mess of flesh that a moment before had been six human beings. People tried to rush to their aid not only from the restaurant but also from other establishments nearby. They too were simply blown apart, their flesh joining the slick mounds on the street. It was a massacre. In his younger days, Christian had had a taste for novels that extolled violence. The reality was that there was nothing glamorous or heroic about violence. Violence in reality was bits of brain flying through the air and blood gushing in red fountains. Violence was noise that made your skin go clammy and your reason stop functioning.

"I have to get out of here," said Luke, throwing up before he ran off into the night. Adrian stood at Christian's side looking like someone had frozen him in a moment of time.

"Go after him," said Christian, thumping Adrian on his right shoulder. "Get back to the hide-out and tell them what's happened." He also wanted to run, but he wouldn't be a coward twice in one day. "I'll stay here and help Madalene and Holan get out."

"There is a curfew on," shouted Madalene. "It applies to everyone. If ordinary people don't dine out, then neither do you. Tell your leader, *Shadowman*, that Madalene, the leader of the Provoke army has said so." In blood-frenzy Madalene sounded more crazed than Christian had ever heard her before. To his surprise Holan seemed equally as crazy. Laughing wildly both women ran in his direction. For a moment Christian had the urge to hide from them. He was as afraid of them as the people watching from the safety of the buildings. In the distance there were sirens and he knew the Sanctum Guards were on their way. Suddenly he saw two men exit the Hedgewick and pull out HIE weapons. Madalene and Holan hadn't expected anyone in the restaurant to be armed and in their elation and certainty neither of them were looking back. They hadn't got a chance.

Two shots rang out clearly. Christian closed his eyes in horror. Hearing two bodies crash to the ground, he flinched violently, and then forced himself to look. Both men lay on the ground, their bodies jerking, twitching, reaching for death. Madalene and Holan stopped running and swung around. They seemed stunned at how close they had been to death and raised their guns ready for further action. Christian could see them hunting for the person who had fired the shots and he looked too. Then he saw that he was holding his rifle up to his shoulder. It couldn't be. He had been a poor marksman during their time in training. The men had been hit precisely in the middle of their foreheads. It must have been someone else who shot them. Turning he looked for Luke. Luke was almost as good as Madalene herself. He must have overcome his fears and returned. There was no sign of anyone behind him and, as he turned to look back, he was grabbed by Holan and Madalene and pulled along with them.

"Go Christian. Run as fast as you can. If anyone appears in front of us- *Anyone*- shoot them," said Madalene.

Both women were manic and elated in the aftermath of their bloodlust. Their emotions had not been dampened by the close brush with death. Rather their emotions had been heightened. Madalene rounded a corner and then dived behind a nearby wall. Holan followed. Having no choice Christian did likewise and saw there was an open manhole there. Holan leapt into it and Madalene followed. Not knowing what the hell was happening, Christian jumped in after them.

"Pull the cover over, Christian," said both women in unison.

Without thinking he did what they asked and in darkness followed them down a ladder into a drain. Using a piece of flint Madalene lit two rag torches. As light flared, Christian saw a section of drain that was carpeted and filled with cushions and blankets. Near the cushions were several bottles of home-made spirits. Now he knew for certain that he had joined Madalene in the asylum. The whole set up was surreal. Madalene passed him a bottle of red spirit and urged him to take a deep swig. What had he got to lose? His world had gone mad. He drank the spirit in great gulps hoping the world would return to normal.

"When did you learn to shoot like that, Christian?" said Holan. "You were terrible with any kind of gun in Ireland. You'd have missed me even if I stood right in front of you."

Christian couldn't speak. The shock, mixed with the alcohol and the strangeness of being in a carpeted drain, completely overcame him.

"You did well, Christian," said Madalene, softly. "I don't know how you made those shots, but I'm glad you attempted them. You saved our lives. I know you're in shock. The first sight of death is always bad. Ask Holan... Understand this, next time it won't be so hard..."

"Luke and Adrian were with me. T-They ran..." Christian drained more alcohol, feeling its warmth, but knowing it wouldn't take the chill from his body. *The first sight of death is always bad...* He'd seen his parents die and *that* was bad, but nothing like this...*the word 'bad' didn't even begin to describe what he'd just seen.*

"None of you were ready. It's why I didn't take you along. Holan wasn't really ready. Later on when she's thought about it, she'll be regaling me with bitter recriminations. But understand this, both of you: this is what we have to do to oppose Peter Shadow and the Sanctum. They won't hesitate to kill us in the same fashion. At least our army doesn't use refinements like torture. We kill quickly and painlessly. I'll talk to Luke and Adrian about this as soon as I can. I only hope they're not too inconsolable tonight."

Holan came over and put her arm around Christian. "I know it hurts, but you'll get used to it. I'm not saying that's a good thing, it just happens. We've struck a serious blow against the Sanctum tonight and while I might weep tomorrow, I'm going to celebrate tonight. Come on, Christian. We have to stay hidden here for a while. Let's enjoy it."

Christian finished the bottle of spirits. He would never be immune to the sights he had seen tonight. Tomorrow he would make his way back to the Provoke group.

Chapter Eighteen

A Rewarding Conversation

The witch was in his bedroom. He recognised her by the cloud of black hair that swirled around her head like a tornado. Over her shoulder hung an ancient rifle. He wasn't afraid, just curious to find out what she wanted. At first she didn't seem to notice him. She wandered around his room, running her hands over his possessions. He stayed still, following her progress with his eyes. Stopping by a large free-standing mirror she examined her neck, running her fingers across the scars there. He wanted to speak to her, but captured by her beauty the words wouldn't come. Without warning her icy, blue eyes fixed on him. She turned, her mouth moving slowly as if she was casting a spell, and walked over to him. He smiled invitingly, certain now he knew her purpose. With fluidity her rifle left her shoulder and slid into her hands and he knew he had made an error. Fear came too late to save him as her bullet eased out of the barrel and headed towards his heart...

Peter sat up with a gasp, his hands clutching his chest, sweat running down his brow. Another nightmare about Madalene and always the same ending. There was a feeling of premonition about it and it made him uneasy. He told himself that he didn't fear Madalene. And then he told himself again. These nightmares wouldn't end until she was in his possession.

A timid knock came on his door and when called to come in, a female servant entered with his breakfast. She was a new girl, fair-haired and around sixteen years old. If she noticed his distress, she said nothing. Nervously she approached his bedside, laid the breakfast tray across his lap and began to pour his favourite camomile tea into a cup. Silently he watched her, noticing how she fumbled under his gaze. She was young, sweetly pretty, and he needed comforting.

"Put the tray over there." He indicated a side-table with his head. "Then come over here and lay beside me." He noticed her eyes grow large, as the realisation of what he wanted struck her.

Having satisfied his lust, Peter yelled at the girl to get him a fresh breakfast. Bowing her head to hide her tears, she rushed to obey him. Indifferently he watched her dress, pick up the unused breakfast tray, and stagger to the door. Why was she walking like that? Had he hurt her in some way?

"I might have need of you again; make sure you're washed and fragrant before your return." He smiled as the door closed behind her. The girl had been clumsy, but the pleasure of taking her virginity had certainly eased the misery of his nightmare.

Twenty minutes later the expected knock came and he smiled in anticipation. His smile fading as a flustered Vertex entered the room without invitation, leaving the door wide open.

"You're supposed to wait until I tell you you can come in," he said, coldly.

"This can't wait. It's news we should have received last night, somewhere along the lines of communication, someone cocked up." Vertex heaved his bulky body into a chair by the bedside.

"What the hell is so important that it can't wait until I'm fed and dressed?" he said, angrily.

The fair-haired girl appeared in the doorway with a fresh breakfast tray. Her eyes were red-rimmed and she was visibly trembling.

"Well don't just stand there, come in," he said, seeing her hesitation.

Limping over to his bedside, she again laid the tray over his lap, desperately trying not to look into his face. Shakily, she poured tea into a cup. Most of it ended in the saucer. He made no comment preferring to amuse himself by trying to catch her eye. She couldn't escape him. Like a petrified little rabbit, she looked into his eyes and almost dropped the teapot.

"Leave us," he said to her, and then sensing her relief, he added, "Collect this tray in an hour. I'll be waiting for you."

As she turned to go, he caught a whiff of cheap perfume and smiled. The girl was obviously more eager to please him than she was letting on, but then he'd always had a way with women.

"That's a sweet looking girl," said Vertex, looking at him pointedly.

"You didn't come here to discuss my love life," Peter said, looking regretfully at the closed door. "So what are you here for Fatboy?"

"There was a massacre last night outside the Hedgewick restaurant. Look at this."

Vertex gave him the early edition of the Sanctum Sun. Under its headline 'Bloody Nightmare' were graphic photos of the dead. So many bodies littered the street; he thought the paper had tampered with the photos to make the scene look worse. It *was* their job to do so after all. He looked questioningly at Vertex, but the man shook his head.

"They haven't been touched. They represent the actual scene."

"Madalene's work?" Vertex looked at him, warily and nodded.

The woman was becoming a damned nuisance. Every time he foiled her she came back with another attack. Well let her do her worst. It was entertaining watching her feeble attempts to bring down his government.

"I haven't got the details yet, but her sister, Holan, is believed to have also been involved.

How could women behave like that? Madalene and her sister needed to be taught how to be more ladylike. Perhaps Partlin could show them how? Well maybe just Holan, he had other plans for Madalene. The last time he'd met her, he hadn't treated her kindly, but she'd only had herself to blame. She'd insolently rejected his overtures of friendship, and had mocked him and his friends. Admittedly it had gone too far, but they'd been forced to teach her a lesson. His heart ached and his mind filled with self-pity – and if she rejected him again? Quickly he brought his emotions under control, leaving them to simmer in the background. He needed to think instead about this current situation.

"Why didn't anyone try to capture Madalene at the scene? There must have been members of the Sanctum Guard around. What were they doing?" he said, angrily.

"From what I heard, two Guards dining in the restaurant ran outside to prevent further death. They were killed by an unknown person as they got ready to shoot Madalene and Holan..." Vertex's face went white as he realised the implication of his words.

"They tried to kill Madalene? I want her alive. You *know* I want her alive. Why don't the Sanctum Guards know I want her captured alive? Do something about it, Fatboy." Those men were lucky, if they'd brought him the dead body of Madalene, their fate would have been a great deal worse than death, they would have taken from him the only thing he desired. It didn't bear thinking about.

Throwing the breakfast tray across the room, he leapt out of bed and began to put on the clothes that had been laid out for him. Normally he bathed first, but today was not a day for bathing. In moments he was out of the room and striding down the corridor. What did his people think they were doing? It was time to sort a few of them out. Make it clear what he wanted and what he didn't want. Behind him he heard Vertex puffing in an attempt to keep up.

"Who died in the shootings last night? Name them." His words snapped out.

"Miles Turton and his wife Victoria, the woman with the braying laugh. We were thinking of bringing Miles into the Inner Sanctum. He was a talented minister."

"Anyone else?"

"Robert Morton, Outer Sanctum member. I believe you had a liking for some of his ideas. The worse loss is Martin Brown, our minister for Public Affairs..."

Peter couldn't help laughing, none of these people were big losses, in fact he despised most of them. "Madalene's done me a favour. No more Turtons and no more Martin Brown. Shame about Morton though. Let Madalene think she's harmed me. She hasn't." Peter stopped now outside the office door of the Commander of the

Sanctum Guard, another old school friend, John Fletcher. Vertex reached his side, looking near to collapse.

"Peter, you have to understand. The common people hate the curfew. They will applaud Madalene for this attack and name her their saviour," Vertex gasped, obviously having difficulty talking.

In between sucking in gulps of air, Vertex repeated the words Madalene was supposed to have shouted at the scene, *'There is a curfew on. It applies to everyone. If ordinary people don't dine out, then neither do you'*. "The people will love her and the ranks of her army will swell. Others will make moves against us, believing that, like Madalene, they will come to no harm. Can't you see, she has harmed us?"

He didn't want the people to love Madalene or call her their saviour. Hadn't he been *their* saviour? Wasn't it him who had given them more prosperity than they had known in a long time? His name would be the one in the history books, not hers, unless it was down as his wife. This had to be dealt with urgently, but not yet. John Fletcher had to be made aware of the consequences of killing Madalene, accidentally or otherwise.

Ignoring Vertex for the time being, Peter strode into the office and watched John Fletcher's face blanch as he hastily stood up and tried to get his jacket on. Vertex, still panting, could be heard coming in behind him.

"Shadowman. What a pleasant surprise…"

"No it isn't, John. I heard two of your men attempted to shoot Madalene last night. What don't you understand about taking her alive?"

"You-You didn't say that she was to be taken alive. W-We didn't know. She…They were killing so many people; my men would have reacted instinctively. I-It won't happen again. I will make your wishes perfectly clear…"

"Too right you will, because if one of your men shoots Madalene, they will not be the only ones punished. I will have you placed on a bonfire in the centre of the Arena and watch your agony as you burn alive. If you weren't an old friend, the punishment would be worse.

Now dress yourself properly and get out of here. I need to talk to Fatboy alone."

He watched John's hurried departure, knowing that John would make certain Madalene was captured alive. There was a streak of cruelty in John that Peter had never understood, even the toughest guards feared the man. No more mistakes would be made. Feeling his anger over Madalene's near miss with death ease, he turned his attention to Vertex. There was no doubt Vertex's assumptions were correct. But how to deal with them? An unorthodox approach was called for. He needed to react in a way Madalene wouldn't expect.

"Sit down over there, Fatboy, before you collapse. You know exercise is bad for you. I've made a decision and you won't argue with it. From today the curfew is lifted. It is to be explained that a mistake was made by a junior minister, who was only trying to protect people from the sort of terrorism we saw last night. Madalene won't expect that. She wants glory and for us to be an unpopular government."

Despite his warning Vertex started to protest. "You can't do that. Madalene will think she's won..."

"I can do whatever I want to. I am this country's leader. Not you." he gazed fiercely at Vertex, waiting until the man flinched and looked away. "Let Madalene enjoy her victory while she can. Why should I care? I'm going to send out squads of men, in disguise, to bring a cascade of terror down on the public as they return to the streets. Hundreds will die. After what happened yesterday the people will think it's the work of Madalene and her army. Instead of being loved and admired, she will be the most hated woman in this country. See how she likes that! Don't question me again. Your position isn't that secure."

"Forgive me, Peter. I sometimes forget that you have the ability to see a larger picture than the rest of us. Shouldn't we also increase the price on Madalene's head? No doubt by the time your men have finished, people will be queuing up to give us information about her, but it wouldn't hurt to provide some extra encouragement."

"It wouldn't, would it? Let me see. There's a reward of one thousand engles for information leading to the arrest of Elgin and Bertha. That should be enough to tempt the northern yokels to turn

147

those two in, before they blow up any more of my town halls. I think there should be at least a thousand engles reward for any information leading to Holan's arrest. So what does that make Madalene worth?"

"Two thousand engles?" suggested Vertex, tentatively.

"No. That won't do at all. Once we have Madalene in our custody, all opposition will collapse. There's the annoying Provoke group to consider, but *they* are hardly opposition." Peter closed his fingers together over the end of his chin, looking speculatively at Vertex.

"Four thousand engles? Her army members will turn her in for that sum of money. It's the sort of figure I'd been thinking of," said Vertex, eagerly.

"I think twenty engles will be a more than adequate reward for Madalene," he said, watching Vertex absorbing this figure in shock. It was amusing to watch the man trying and failing to regain his composure.

"Twenty engles? For Madalene? Are you sure?" He knew Vertex had wanted to say mad, but didn't dare.

Carelessly he shrugged. "By the time I've finished with them, the people will pay to give me information about Madalene. Why should I let that arrogant bitch feel more important than she already does?"

There was a risk of this backfiring. If the public saw such a small reward, they might not blame Madalene for the events that were about to transpire. But he could always raise the reward to a massive five thousand engles if that happened. He wanted to strike an immediate blow at Madalene and this was the way to do it. The more he thought about it, the more he was sure that such a tiny reward would upset Madalene greatly. She was too much like him for it not to.

"In fact let's increase Holan's reward to two thousand engles. Let's also get our newspapers to give Holan the credit for last night. There can be a few lines mentioning Madalene's involvement, but nothing more and make sure every newspaper has a photograph of Holan on the cover.

"B-But..." Vertex still seemed lost for words. Peter was amused at the man's expression. There was more than one way to attack an enemy and he would love to see Madalene's reaction to this.

"Yes Vertex? Are you questioning me again? What reward shall I put on your head?"

"But that's a wonderful idea was all I was going to say," said Vertex, sulkily.

"Of course it is. And I have another wonderful idea. I want our Secret Force sent out with one assignment only. They are to find Alan Moore and Torrin Spice and bring them here to me. It's time to persuade those men that we're on the same side and want the same thing." He'd suddenly remembered Vertex's previous words. *"It wouldn't be too hard to persuade both these men to help us catch Madalene."*

"B-But..."

"You're doing it again, Vertex. I presume you were about to tell me that's another wonderful idea."

Chapter Nineteen

Lonely At the Top

"You didn't have council permission," said Hannah, wagging one of her bony fingers so violently, Madalene thought it might fall off. If it came any nearer her face, she would help it along.

"I didn't need it," Madalene said coolly, gazing at Hannah with contempt. "It wasn't important. I just wanted some shooting practice."

"Everything *you* do has to be considered by the council. You know that." Hannah glared fiercely at Madalene; a pathetic attempt at intimidation. Unmoved, Madalene decided to show her the proper way to intimidate someone.

"Everything?" said Madalene, in the same cool tone she had used previously. "Then call a council meeting. I need to urinate and defecate soon, so tell them not to take too long deciding if that's okay. And if I'm not doing a lot later, which is more than likely, I'll probably masturbate to stave off the boredom." Madalene edged closer to Hannah as she was speaking, never once taking her eyes off the woman's face. She could tell that Hannah was unnerved, and when Hannah stepped away, Madalene followed.

"There's no need for you to be so crude." Struggling to maintain any composure, Hannah walked over and sat down beside Tom, who though present, had not yet taken part in the discussion. Madalene could hardly wait for *him* to start.

"There's every need." Madalene started shouting, even though she was aware the entire group could already hear their conversation. The trouble with the hide-out was there was too little space, for too many people. "This is an army, Hannah, *not* a nursery school. If you don't take my plans seriously and allow me to take co-ordinated action against Peter Shadow's regime, then I resign." It was impossible to miss the gasps of shock this statement created. "I'll return to working alone, and believe me; I'll wreak havoc before they capture me."

150

"There's no need for that," said Tom, entering the conversation. Tom had never been able to fully hide his fear of her, so she scowled at him with great effect.

"Oh. You're going to have your say now are you? Great. Look, why don't you and Hannah just go and find Alan Moore? You can sit and talk about revolution for hours, and then you can all write some lovely letters to dear old Shadowman. In fact I'll even go along with you and help you find where he's hiding. Alan and I are old friends. I know he'd be *so* happy to see me again."

Pausing for breath, Madalene was surprised to see that Hannah and Tom were looking upset, but she was past the point of caring how they felt. Madalene was proud of the action she and Holan had taken outside the Hedgewick restaurant. Reverberations would be felt all around the Sanctum and the curfew would come under immediate scrutiny. Hannah and Tom should be standing on the tables shouting her praises, not treating her like a five-year-old who'd spilt her milk.

"The council may oversee my actions, but I'm still the leader of this army. Get out of here. Go away. Why the hell did you come with me in the first place?"

Madalene knew she was ranting. Holan was walking towards her with that 'Let's calm Madalene down' look on her face. She didn't want to calm down. Christian had walked out earlier and was unlikely to return. He hadn't given her a chance to dissuade him, he'd simply left. As predicted, her schizophrenic sister had spent the last few hours weeping for those she'd killed - with precision, without thought, without missing. Enough! The whole Provoke idea had backfired on her. She only had half the group anyway, though numbers were beginning to increase as word got round. The half she had were inadequately trained and not nearly as good as her mercenaries... In frustration, Madalene's rifle slid into her hands and she shot a large rat, a few feet away. An action she immediately regretted when she remembered Jinn had made one of the many rats in the place into a pet. Looking across the room, she saw Jinn's look of horror. Damn! She *had* shot his pet.

"Don't, Madalene," said Holan, reaching out and taking the rifle off her. "Hannah and Tom aren't trying to aggravate you."

"They aren't?" said Madalene, sarcastically.

"They've spent a long time planning concurrent attacks on various institutions. Their plans are good and involve all of us, not just you. They're angry, because our action last night means security will be increased everywhere. It makes their plans harder to carry out."

Madalene was stunned. Holan had been summoned before Hannah and Tom, not long after their return to the hide-out. She'd looked so much like a mortified schoolgirl when they'd finished with her, Madalene had asked, sardonically, what her punishment was. Ignoring her, Holan had headed straight to their shared bunk and spent the next few hours sobbing incessantly. When Madalene's turn came to speak to Hannah and Tom, she'd been ready for them, but she hadn't been ready for *this*.

"What plan? This is a joke. You can't plan actions without speaking to me first. You don't know how to set them up properly."

"Don't be so arrogant, Madalene," said Hannah, crossly. "You spend all your time avoiding us or defying us. When were we supposed to discuss anything with you?"

"In Ireland we were treated with respect," said Tom. "But since we replaced Elgin and Bertha, your attitude towards us has changed. Why, Madalene?"

"Why? Because you thwart me at every turn," said Madalene, shouting once again. "Why are you here with me? You're Alan Moore's friends. I *saw* Alan persuading the two of you to obstruct me. You can't deny that."

"You saw Alan pleading with us to go with him," said Hannah, abruptly.

"No-oo..." Madalene said, ferociously, grabbing her rifle off Holan and aiming it directly at Hannah and Tom. Voices rang out in consternation and several members of the group reached for their own weapons, aiming them at her.

"You're spies...You're..."

"Members of your Provoke army and proud to be so," said Tom, shakily.

"Put the rifle down and listen to him, Madalene," said Luke. His pistol was shaking in his hand, but Luke was a good marksman. Shaky or otherwise, Luke would not miss.

"You've turned them all against me," Madalene said, looking grimly around the room.

"They're not against you. They love you. But they want you to listen for once in your life," said Holan, putting her own weapon away, and sinking into a nearby armchair with a loud sigh.

As Madalene watched, Hannah and Tom indicated that everyone should put their weapons away, including her. A small movement near the door caught her eye and looking over she saw Christian sheepishly enter the room, only to stop in amazement. She stared at him questioningly for a few minutes, then hearing expectant coughs, she took a quick look around the room. Everyone had put their weapons away, except her. Casually she lowered her rifle and slung it back over her shoulder.

"I'm listening. Tell me more."

"You didn't hear what I said, Madalene," said Tom, actually managing to look her in the face for once. "I'm a member of your army and proud to be so. The rumours say you and Holan killed a member of the Inner Sanctum last night. Despite the security implications for our plans, I can't deny I'm impressed."

"It still should have been put before the council, Madalene. And I have to say I would have refused to allow such a reckless action. Nevertheless, with reluctance, I admit that I too am impressed," said Hannah, boldly. "You have misjudged us, Madalene. I'll say what I have to say, and then Tom and I will leave. If you want to be a dictator with no reference point, that's up to you."

Hannah's bravado faltered. Madalene watched Hannah struggle, but the tears came anyway and it was uncomfortable waiting for her to continue. "You want to know why I joined your army. Why I didn't go with my good friend, Alan Moore. I'll tell you why.

153

You're the person who saved my Mother's life. I realised it when Elgin began defending you..."

As Hannah stumbled, too choked with emotion to go on, Tom came to her rescue. "My reason is the same, except you rescued my mother and my father. I managed to meet up with them when we were in Ireland and they told me about you. Why do you hide your goodness and your compassion for others, Madalene?" Tom looked at her in silence, and then he added, "Our fellow council members have the plans we set up, I hope you at least have the courtesy to consider them."

"Tom and I will say our goodbyes to the members of this army and then we will leave. Maybe Elgin and Bertha will be glad of our presence," said Hannah, brushing the remains of her tears away, defiantly. Swinging one arm around to indicate the people nearby, she added, "These are good people, Madalene. Brave people. Don't destroy them with your reckless hatred of Shadowman."

Madalene was taken aback and unable to react immediately. What she had been told was like hearing that the sky was now the sea and vice versa. The room was silent and everyone in it, including Christian, was studying her intently. How she reacted was important. Yet she couldn't pretend she was going to get along with Hannah and Tom, in spite of their revelations. If the two of them stayed, they would continue to irritate her, and there would be many more arguments...

Smiling to herself, Madalene strolled past the quizzical faces and pulled a bottle of potato whiskey off a shelf. Opening it with deliberate flourish, she filled three clay mugs and took them over to Hannah and Tom.

Handing them each a mug, she shouted, "To our council leaders, Hannah and Tom, and to the success of their plans. Long may these people live to annoy me." Draining her mug quickly, she threw it to one side and, accompanied by loud cheering, hugged both of them. Then believing she'd done more than enough to restore harmony, she ignored them and walked over to hug Christian. Now it was his turn to look questioningly at her.

"Just glad you came back, Christian," was all she said, before moving on to talk to others.

"What's he playing at? It's me he wants," said Madalene, furiously. Barely an hour had passed and she was ranting and raving again. Adrian had come in and, strangely apprehensive, had given her the evening edition of the Sanctum Sun. An old photograph of Holan occupied most of its front page under the heading, 'Cold Blooded Murder', and a reward of two thousand engles was offered for information that led to her arrest. Madalene carefully read the lurid accounts of the incident, and studied the graphic photographs, but there was no mention of her involvement anywhere. It only took Holan seconds to spot a paragraph which offered a twenty engle reward for information about *her*.

"The reward's not important, Madalene," said Holan, looking shocked, but sounding rather smug in Madalene's opinion. "Look, he's lifted the curfew. We succeeded, made him change his mind."

"The reward *is* important, because this doesn't make sense. If Peter Shadow were to put a sizeable reward on my head, even my army members, including you, would be tempted to betray me. He would have me on show in his Arena in days and this would all be over. If someone betrays you, Holan, nothing changes."

"Thanks, Madalene," said Holan, angrily. "I'd hate to feel I mattered in any way. Perhaps I should claim that twenty engles before your inflated ego blows up."

"Don't be stupid, Holan. It's obvious Peter Shadow's playing a game. We need to figure out what he's trying to do. It might be important."

"Isn't it obvious, even to you, Dark Goddess, that his intent was to attack your inflated ego and upset you? And hasn't he succeeded? He knows you well." Once again Holan looked smug.

"What did you just call me?" said Madalene. "Dark what?"

"Dark Goddess. It's Christian's nickname for you and it's sort of caught on with the rest of the army. They all mutter it under their breath when you're being particularly obnoxious." Holan now looked so unbearably smug, Madalene walked away from her before she did something she'd regret.

155

So they called her the Dark Goddess, did they? Vengeful Goddess would have been a better title, for Bren and Hayla were not forgotten and justice had not been served on their account yet. Well she would show Peter Shadow, despite his pathetic mind games, what a vengeful Dark Goddess could do. If Hannah and Tom's plans were any good, she would initiate them immediately.

Bad events tend to happen in threes, as Madalene discovered when she found Hannah and Tom had left her out of their plans. Once again she erupted, to the concern of everyone near her. She should be leading at least one of the attacks. It didn't make sense for her not to. It took the council and most of the army members hours to convince her, that as their leader she would be needed to coordinate the attacks from a central position. Wasn't that what leaders did? Not what capable leaders did, in Madalene's opinion.

"We go out in our groups at the allotted times. You stay here to co-ordinate everything and deal with the groups as they return. There may well be losses and you're the best person to deal with them," said Tom, bravely.

"You're not ready," said Madalene, wanting to say, 'You're not good enough'. Now the time had come, Madalene was reluctant to use her army. None of them had been tested yet, with the exception of Christian, Luke and Adrian. Looking around she saw scared faces; faces she had grown to like.

"Why train us to fight if you don't trust us?" said Adrian, loudly. The young men with him nodded their heads in agreement.

Christian, Luke and Adrian had reacted badly to being in a violent situation. Okay, they had all recovered quickly, but the others would be no better. Jinn and Ellyn were too young…She was the only one who truly knew what she was doing and they were planning to leave *her* behind.

"It isn't that I don't trust you, but you've seen what I'm capable of… Wouldn't it be better if I came with you?" She was trying hard not to seem arrogant, but it was difficult. "Understand - I don't fear death. I don't seek it, but I don't fear it. Why should any of you die in my place?"

Madalene went quiet and walked slightly away from the meeting area. They were like children who needed to show her what they could do. Deep down she knew that she had no choice but to let them go, whatever the consequences. It was going to be physically impossible to be with every group anyway. Hannah walked over to speak to her, the group looking on with interest.

"Elgin and Bertha will be conducting a similar series of raids at the same time. There'll be attacks in Sheffield, Nottingham and Birmingham. We haven't got as many people, so our attack has to centre on London. All those who go out know they could lose their lives and yes, they are afraid. What they're not prepared to do is lose you. You're too important."

Madalene was trapped. She looked over to Holan for support.

"I'm going with Christian. Though if he makes any more comments about what he intends to do to me when we get back, I'll make sure he doesn't return," said Holan, to the accompaniment of whistles and catcalls from Christian's friends.

"You know I want you, Holan," Christian yelled across the room. "Give in once and I'll leave you alone." Cheers rang out and Christian's friends were patting him on the back.

"Get us through tomorrow safely and I might give in. I'll give you so much pleasure, you'll die pining for me," said Holan, coquettishly.

Christian's eyes lit up. "Really?"

"No!" laughed Holan, as Christian slumped, then began to laugh too.

Madalene smiled. This was army banter. Necessary bravado. And it lightened the mood.

"Finally given up on me, Christian?" she said, joining in.

"You're unattainable, Madalene," said Christian, cheekily. "And I have needs. Luckily Holan's easy." Loud laughter accompanied these words and as Holan rushed over to deal with Christian, Madalene laughed too.

All around her was an air of tension and excitement. It was hard not feeling part of it, but the insurgence wouldn't work if she had to be its heroine all the time. The others had to have their chance.

Madalene worked alone through the night, checking and re-checking plans that had been made without her. She altered small details here and there, but mostly left the plans intact. It was said to be lonely at the top, and Madalene was definitely feeling lonely. Looking at the clock, she saw that it was six in the morning. Had she really been going over the plans for so long? She decided to get some sleep, knowing the rest of the group would be moving in another couple of hours. Casually she popped an 'Ease' tablet into her mouth, to help her sleep through their moving around. Then, leaving the revised plans where the council could see them, she made her way to the bunk she shared with Holan. It would be a long night following her protégées around and she would need to be alert. If they thought they were going without her, they were very much mistaken.

Chapter Twenty

An Explosive Night

One by one the allotted groups left the hide-out. Some were silent, others excitable. All of them were terrified. Madalene spoke a few words of comfort and encouragement to each group as they left, warning them not to be reckless. Holan's amusement at this was evident, and the angry look Madalene gave her in response did little to quench it.

"Reckless?" said, Holan, laughing as she moved out. "Did anyone else hear, *Madalene*, telling *us* not to be reckless?"

Holan was part of the last group to leave. Shortly after their departure, Madalene grabbed her rifle, put a small handgun in her pocket, and left the hide-out herself. Briefly, she wondered if she should take more weapons. If there was a problem, a rifle and handgun might not be enough. But arming herself further would take time she didn't have. Not if she wanted to get to the site of the first attack before the group, assigned to it, arrived.

The first attack was taking place at a private club in Soho. Using her personal transporter, Madalene arrived before the group and did a quick survey of the area. It was currently a large construction site, but had been derelict for years, until a wealthy businessman and close friend of Peter Shadow had decided to restore it.

The recently completed club was rumoured to be highly decadent; a place where any fantasy could be acted out if you had enough engles in your pocket. This was Hannah's reason for wanting to see it destroyed. But what caught Madalene's attention was that Peter had attended the opening ceremony. Peter Shadow was not in the habit of attending public functions; which meant he had to be an investor in the club. And that was a better reason for overseeing its destruction.

Security was minimal; five or six heavy-set men, patrolling the front of the building. From her hiding place, Madalene watched Hannah arrive with Tom, Malcolm and the other members of their group. Working in perfect unison they overcame security and began to set the bombs. Then to Madalene's surprise, Hannah and Malcolm rushed into the building, firing their guns in the air, to get everyone out – an unexpected deviation, which was probably due to Hannah not wanting to harm anyone. Chaos ensued as people rushed out in panic, many of them naked.

The bombs had only a five minute time delay. Minutes passed, but there was no sign of Hannah or Malcolm. Though she was angry at Hannah's deviation, Madalene was about to go in and rescue them, when the first bombs blew. Suddenly, Hannah and Malcolm, accompanied by six children came hurtling out of the front doors. Seeing the children, Madalene's anger faded. Hannah and Malcolm had *not* been wrong to go in like that. Proud of their courage, she got back into the transporter and moved on.

Ten minutes later she watched several Sanctum stores go up in flames, but only after having been cleared of the goods they contained. The Provoke army would be eating well for months thanks to this particular action. Like a proud Mother, Madalene nodded her head in satisfaction and moved on.

Thirty minutes later, she was delighted to see the, almost deserted, Sanctum headquarters reduced to rubble by several powerful explosions. Personally, Madalene would have liked the place to be full, but unfortunately its occupants were out on the streets dealing with the problems her army were causing. Still, Adam Longbetter and Mark Reid, both reticent young men, had made and set the bombs beautifully. The explosions were so incredibly artistic; they should have been captured on canvas. Reserved they might be, but Adam and Mark were adept bomb makers and she resolved to praise them personally on their return, as this was the most dangerous action being carried out that night.

Ellyn and Jinn were part of the group she watched next. Their task was to chase Sanctum whores and their clients out of a well-known brothel, and then blow the place up. This was accomplished with ease, but as the group made to leave, shots were fired. Madalene couldn't see who was firing, but as she prepared to interfere, her rifle cocked and ready; Jinn coldly turned and killed whoever was attacking them. The firing stopped and Ellyn went over, threw her arms around Jinn and kissed him soundly. Madalene was proud of her son, there had been no hesitation. Hadn't she told,

Holan it was in their blood? When she was sure the group were safely away, Madalene moved to the site of the last action.

This was the easiest undertaking. The group involved were going to rob The London Bank. Madalene knew a large percentage of the people's tax money ended up in this Bank. Little did the people know, they were about to get large tax rebates! With the Sanctum Guards occupied on the other side of London, their only problem would be opening the safe, which was known to have been in existence since Victorian times.

Madalene had spent the afternoon preparing two devices for the purpose; using her favourite recipe for home-made explosives and attaching booster charges. The timers were wind-up clock mechanisms. Without being able to study the safe, it was all done by guesswork. She hoped that her devices would blow the safe open and not the bank apart; although as long as her army members were clear; either outcome was acceptable. The alarm systems and the bank's security guards were covered by the original plans. Even the guard dogs had been taken care of.

When Madalene reached the scene, the bank was still intact. Christian, Holan, Luke, Adrian and two excellent fighters, Mary and Annie, were standing in the street surrounded by a large force of Sanctum Guards and Bank security members. Their weapons and the explosive devices lay on the ground nearby.

A bulky man, sweating heavily in his slate-grey uniform, was shouting loudly for transporters to be fetched and communication to be made to the, recently bombed, Sanctum headquarters. Nearby, several spectators emerged from a brothel and stood around in various states of undress, watching the events impassively. To Madalene's surprise, she recognised two Outer Sanctum members...

Without a thought, Madalene shot them and then reloading her rifle with great speed, she shot two of the men guarding the group. The spectators dispersed instantly, screaming in panic. Raising their weapons, the nearby guards prepared to fire them. Madalene dived to dodge their bullets, but none came.

"Don't fire," said the bulky man, loudly, looking panic-stricken. "It's Madalene." Getting back up, Madalene looked first in his direction and then back at the guards. Now they too looked apprehensive. Lowering their weapons, they looked to the bulky man for guidance. Madalene was puzzled, but reacted quickly.

"All of you run," she screamed at the group. "Get out of here." With no time for thought or reloading, Madalene pulled the small handgun out of her pocket and shot the bulky man straight through the head. The questions his men were putting to him went unanswered as his body hit the ground with a tremendous thud. Holan and Christian reacted in an impressive manner, the others were temporarily stunned. Moving quickly, they grabbed what they could from the pile on the ground and then ran. The sight stirred the others from their stupor and they too ran.

It was bizarre, instead of giving pursuit; the guards remained where they were, looking speculatively at her. Most of them had now got their weapons raised again, but they seemed morbidly afraid to use them. She turned to run, but shots fired ahead of her forced her to stop. Sirens could be heard and she had the feeling that these men were holding her in place until help arrived. She was so near to them, why didn't they just shoot her?

Again, Madalene made to run off and again several shots flew around her, but not one of them came close to hitting her. Sanctum Guards were good marksmen... Abruptly she realised that their objective was to capture her alive and unharmed. This had something to do with Peter Shadow... They began to edge closer, obviously hoping to take her by physical force. Two shots went into her rifle and she fired back at them, killing two, and delaying the others for only seconds. It was enough time to make a run for it.

"See if you can miss me now," she shouted, as shots rang out around her. Dodging the bullets, she kept going, making it harder for them to miss her. She made it too hard. One massive thud hit her in the side, another followed. She stumbled. It was like being kicked twice by a lead boot, only worse. Heavily, she fell to the ground, where she waited for the inevitable. There was only silence, into which gasps of pure horror came from the Sanctum Guards. Madalene tried to get back on her feet and had almost succeeded, when a nearby explosion shook the ground. As debris rained over her, she fell, losing her precious hold on consciousness.

"We can't leave her," said Holan desperately, ushering the others around a corner just two blocks away.

"We have to," said Christian, with tears running down his face. "There's nothing we can do. We've lost her."

"No! Not Madalene. She's our leader. My sister... We have to do something." Holan was also in tears, but she'd seen Madalene survive impossible situations before. Surely there had to be hope. "They were scared of her Christian. None of them wanted to shoot her. I don't know why, but it gives us a chance. Listen to that. Those sirens mean they've got help coming. We've got to act now." Looking down at her hands, Holan saw what she'd picked up and smiled. Next to her guns were the devices for blowing up the safe.

"The bank, Christian. We've got to blow up the bank. Luke! Adrian! Take these guns and cover us. Christian and I are going back to the bank. Mary, Annie, run to the hide-out and get help." A half formed idea was beginning to take flight. Holan was as terrified as the others and had no real desire to put herself in danger again. Nevertheless, if Madalene was still in front of that bank and alive, she had to try something.

"How's blowing up the bank going to help, Madalene?" said Christian, in a panicky voice. "Holan, we can't just casually walk back to the bank and throw bombs at it. You know that."

"Blowing up the bank will distract them," said, Holan, already moving. She knew that Christian was scared, but she also knew his feelings for Madalene would overcome that fear. "And we're going back a different way. Down these streets and turn left. Quickly, Christian, those sirens are getting closer."

Terror made them run like cheetahs, and as they ran Holan set the devices. If these streets didn't lead to the bank, she'd have no choice but to throw them and blow something else up. She hoped the houses she was passing were empty.

"Two minutes, Christian. Run faster and take this." He looked like she had thrown a white hot coal at him, nevertheless he held onto it. "Throw it when I throw mine and then find Madalene."

The bank loomed before them. Shots rang out and two guards went down. Luke and Adrian had spotted the guards in time. Holan had been concentrating, so hard, on the devices, she'd had missed seeing them and so it appeared had Christian. Unless they reached the bank in time more guards would come, and then all this effort would be for nothing. A feeling of unreality descended on Holan. It had happened on the night of the shootings at the Hedgewick restaurant. She felt like she was watching herself behaving irrationally, unable to prevent her own actions even if she wanted to. Thirty seconds, twenty-nine, twenty eight...The countdown seemed desperately slow, but the bank was now in view...

"Five, four. Throw them, Christian. Those windows there will do. Three, two, one..." Detonation. Dazzling light. Unbearable heat and noise. Guards landing in puddles of their own blood. Debris flying everywhere. Money fluttering in the sky, aping birds. Burning pieces of paper falling like snow. Luke and Adrian killing any guards left standing and grabbing weapons from the bodies to kill more. There in front of them the sight they dreaded to see: Madalene sprawled under a pile of debris, her blood flowing incongruously into a broken piece of guttering. Dead? She couldn't be. There was a roaring in Holan's ears, the roaring of dread.

Between them they cleared the debris, Luke and Adrian throwing the stuff to one side like maniacs. Seeing his desperate need, Holan stood back, as did Luke and Adrian, and let Christian gently lift Madalene's lifeless body off the ground. She watched as he softly touched Madalene's neck with his fingers, and then shook his head.

"She's dead, Holan. There's no pulse..." Convulsive sobs came from him; nevertheless he held Madalene's body tightly to his chest.

Madalene dead? Inconceivable! Madalene was too arrogant to die. As Sanctum Guards began to appear on all sides, Holan realised that they were all going to die. Incapable of feeling terror and still watching herself, she didn't care. It had all been a waste of time...

Suddenly, Mary and Annie appeared and with them were Tom, Hannah, and other army members; the group who had attacked the club in Soho. They'd, apparently, been on their way back to the hide-out when Mary and Annie had stopped them.

"Holan! What's the matter with you?" said Hannah, shaking her. "Listen, Malcolm's over there with a transporter. Get Madalene's body into it and go. We'll hold these guards until you're safely away, and then we'll make a run for it."

Mindlessly, Holan followed, as Christian ran to the transporter with Madalene still in his arms. Desperately trying to prevent them from leaving, the Sanctum Guards sent all their firepower in their direction, but supported by the new arrivals, Luke and Adrian were able to provide cover. As soon as Holan had squeezed in at Christian's side, Malcolm drove off, veering from side to side as bullets began to plough into the transporter. Holan heard him ask about Madalene and noted how concerned he was, but in her present situation she was unable to answer his questions.

"I can't believe she's dead," said Christian, softly. "Goddesses are supposed to be immortal."

"She isn't dead," said Holan, bleakly, refusing to accept the possibility. Her refusal given credence by a low gasp coming from Madalene's lips as the transporter hit a bump in the road. Relieved at being proved right, Holan, the spectator, gave herself a silent round of applause.

Malcolm drove them to the nearest field hospital, and then helped Christian carry Madalene in; Holan followed. When the medics saw who their patient was, they were horrified, but as the shout went up, people came running from all directions. Within minutes they had taken Madalene into their makeshift surgery. All Holan could do now was wait. She occupied herself watching Christian and Malcolm pacing up and down.

An hour passed. People ran to and fro, but no-one spoke to them. Then Hannah and Tom arrived. Tom had a minor flesh wound and while it was being treated, Hannah told Holan and Christian how they had managed to get away just in time. Several transporters, each one filled with Sanctum Guards, had turned up at the bank, just as the last of them were leaving the scene. Luckily they had managed to elude the reinforcements. Holan would have been delighted with this news, if she hadn't felt so distant from everything, and been so worried about Madalene.

Another hour passed and more people turned up to find out how Madalene was, including Luke, Adrian and the rest of Christian's friends. By the time another hour had gone by, Jinn and Ellyn had arrived, with the rest of the army in tow. It was obvious the army members were getting on the medic's nerves, but no-one had the heart to send them away. Two more hours passed before Doctor

Grey, their only surgeon, came out and announced that Madalene would live. Two bullets had been removed from her side and she was now sleeping peacefully. Holan nearly collapsed with relief. Christian put an arm around her shoulder and steadied her. The relief all around was tangible, though no-one said a word.

A bottle of spirit had been found for them and Christian and Holan sat together drinking it at Madalene's bedside. Jinn had wanted to stay close to his mother, but seeing how tired and emotional he was, Holan had got Hannah and Tom to take him back to the hide-out, on the promise that she would fetch him as soon as his mother woke up.

"You did well today, Christian. Madalene will be proud of you," said Holan, feeling normal again and glad that 'Holan, the spectator' had gone.

"We messed up, Holan. All the other groups succeeded and we messed up. And that's the second time Madalene's had to save my life," said Christian, morosely.

"You saved hers, remember. You could have refused to run with me, but you didn't. I had no real plan and you knew it, but you still came with me. And we didn't mess up. Hannah underestimated the security and Madalene didn't spot it." Holan began to stroke his dark hair, so like Madalene's. Visibly he began to relax. She smiled. "Well, I've made promises I'd better keep. One night only mind."

Christian smiled back at her, "You say one night now, but by morning you'll be wanting more… You were amazing today, Holan. I'll never forget running at your side. When you threw me that bomb…! You're more approachable than Madalene, yet just as brave and strong."

"Keep talking my brave warrior, it's working," said Holan, running one hand lightly down his chest while the other continued to stroke his hair. Suddenly all stress left her and they began to kiss. Kissing a friend was a strange sensation, but the events of the day had left her with a strong desire for this sort of comfort. As his hands gently caressed her breasts under her shirt, she sighed at her overwhelming need to use his body. A sudden groan pulled them apart.

"Go use our shared bunk, Holan," said Madalene in a hoarse whisper. "I salute your courage, Christian. Holan's going to kill you." She paused and coughed, "You got me out... thank you..." Her eyes closed again.

Christian and Holan stood up and looked down on her. The joy on Christian's face was unmistakable, proving what Holan already knew - Christian might not admit it, but he was undeniably in love with Madalene. Well in love or not, what did it matter. She needed sexual release and so did Christian.

"Like a lamb to the slaughterhouse," said Madalene, muttering in her sleep.

Holan laughed loudly. "Too right, Madalene. Too right." Taking Christian by his hand, she led him out of the room. There was a way to go before they got back to the hide-out. Wasn't there a convenient park nearby?

Chapter 21

New Arrivals

"Last night was a huge success and I'm proud of all of you. The incident at the bank was unfortunate, as we nearly lost our leader. A leader, I might add, who seems incapable of doing what she's told."

Wasn't that the point of *being* a leader, thought Holan, as Hannah paused for a second?

"However, fast thinking on Holan's part prevented disaster. Madalene's had a comfortable night and I've been informed that she will make a rapid recovery," said, Hannah, looking around with an over-bright smile on her face.

Holan had a feeling that Hannah was slightly disappointed by this news, but as Madalene treated Hannah so badly, that wasn't surprising. Her thoughts were interrupted by loud laughter from Luke.

"From what I've heard, Holan also had a comfortable night."

Holan had been expecting this. There'd been nothing but jibes and alternative offers from Luke and company, since her return to the hide-out.

"A more comfortable night than I would have had with you, Luke. At least that's what your girlfriend, Annie, told me."

For a second, Luke looked crestfallen, but then he grinned and she had to smile. Luke's grin was irresistible. He could make women swoon with that grin. "With me, you would have experienced passion, not comfort. Christian's whiskers have barely grown. What would he know of love-making? I presume you had to show him what goes where."

Everybody laughed, except Christian, who bristled with anger at Holan's side. Lightly she touched his arm and said softly, "It's only playing, Christian and it's easier than standing here listening to Hannah dissect last night's events."

As Hannah continued, Holan felt herself drifting off. On leaving Madalene's side, she'd spent several passionate hours in the park with Christian, and despite Luke's mocking words; he'd *definitely* had experience. Upon her return she'd been desperate to sleep, but Jinn and Ellyn were sat up waiting for her. So with a groan, she'd kissed Christian goodbye and taken them to see Madalene. Lately, Jinn and Ellyn had become inseparable, where one went so did the other. They'd been overjoyed when Madalene had opened her eyes and told them how proud she was of them, adding that good soldiers needed their sleep, so why weren't the two of them in bed.

A few hours ago, she'd returned to check on Madalene. Madalene had been awake and full of enthusiasm for the way her army had performed. She'd wanted to return to the hide-out and praise everyone personally. It had taken considerable persuasion from Holan and the medics to prevent this.

"Look at this," came a shout from behind her. She turned to see Malcolm waving several newspapers in his hands. He looked upset. Running forward, Malcolm handed Hannah the papers. As Hannah scanned them quickly, Holan saw a sombre expression appear on her face. Something was wrong.

"We've got trouble," said Hannah, abruptly. "There's a brief mention of our activities last night, but it's superseded by a massacre that took place on the streets at the same time. Over two hundred people were killed and they're blaming us for it."

Shouts came from everywhere. A few people *had* been killed by Provoke Army members, but not two hundred. What was going on? Tom took a paper from Hannah's hand and began to read it aloud. "As ordinary men and women returned to the streets last night, joyfully celebrating the ending of the curfew, they were attacked by the terrorist group that calls itself 'The Provoke Army'. They spared no-one, not even the children…"

"Do we have a rival group?" said Holan, grabbing the paper out of Tom's hand and reading it rapidly. Holan saw that Elgin's raids in the north of the country had been scathingly covered in detail; there was no mention of any massacres. Only Londoners had suffered. It had to be a copycat group, there was no other explanation. All around the room, which was now silent, people stood in groups examining the papers. Holan was horrified when she came across photographs of mutilated children and their mothers. What were children doing on the streets so late? Was it just excitement at the curfew ending? Suddenly she noticed something else. Her home had been discovered and two terrorists had been taken away for questioning. Alan and Torrin? She was going to be sick. Quickly she ran to the washroom, handing Christian the paper as she did so. As she finished heaving, a towel was handed to her and looking up she saw Christian's concerned expression.

"They've got Alan and Torrin," he said. The words she'd acknowledged, but didn't want to hear. She replied by nodding her head. "I thought today would be a day of celebration..." he added.

"It was meant to be," said Holan, beginning to cry. "It was meant to be."

Returning to the main room, Holan saw instantly that Hannah and Tom were at a loss. They didn't know how to comfort the group or what to do next. As they conferred with their fellow council members, the rest of the army hovered around them in a state of confusion. They wanted to know who this rival group were and why they had attacked the public. Had it been a mistake? No. You didn't accidentally kill two hundred people. What if there were other resistance groups they didn't know of. Would the Provoke army get the blame for everything these groups did?

The atmosphere was horrible. Ellyn was in tears and Jinn was trying to comfort her. Adrian had begun to push Mark and Adam around. Luke was arguing with Malcolm and fights were breaking out in all parts of the room. Too late, Hannah made a bid to get attention, but in the chaos no-one noticed her. Emotions were running high after the previous night, thought Holan. This isn't going to stop and when weapons are pulled out there'll be real trouble. Madalene was the only person who could stop this, and she was in a makeshift hospital on the other side of London. Glancing at Christian, she saw his thoughts echo hers.

"I could go and fetch her. If I took Luke and a few others, we could carry her here gently and not hurt her. All we need her to do is to speak and quell this panic."

170

"No, Christian. It's less than twenty four hours since she was shot. However gentle you were, the journey in the transporter could kill her. Maybe they'd listen to me."

"What can you say? Damn, Madalene, for not doing what she was told last night. If she had done, then she'd be here to stop this."

Holan touched him, lightly. "If she'd done as she was told, we'd be in the torture chambers and none of this would matter."

A rifle shot went up at the back of the room. It's started, thought Holan, turning around wearily to see who had produced a weapon, and coming face to face with Madalene.

Madalene was devoid of colour, her eyes filled with pain, nevertheless, she was a commanding presence and silence ensued as everyone stopped what they were doing and looked in her direction. A concerned, young medic at her side, propped her up, looking with concern at the red smudges appearing on the bandages around her middle.

"I'm sorry," said the medic, earnestly. "I couldn't stop her. The minute she read the papers, she insisted I fetch a transporter and bring her here. She's Madalene, what could I do?"

"Enough," said Madalene. "I heard some of your talk as I came in. There's no rival group. The people on the streets are Peter Shadow's men. He's cleverer than I thought he was. Not only does he discredit our army, he retains his curfew."

As Holan looked on, she saw Madalene begin to fall. Casually, she walked over and put an arm around her sister to keep her upright. Madalene acknowledged this assistance with a brief nod. Christian beckoned to a nearby chair, but Holan ignored him. Madalene needed to stand until the army came to its senses. Madalene knew it too.

"We don't argue amongst ourselves. We fight back. You all go out again tonight and you stop this. Everyone you meet, you send home. They'll be afraid of you, so they'll do what you say. If you come across the men who committed this atrocity, you shoot them without hesitation and you shoot to kill." Madalene sighed and looked around. Holan saw she was taking in every face. "This isn't

171

like last night. It's an unplanned killing spree. If the council even attempt to stop this, you are to disobey them. Forehead and heart, these are your targets. When you hit them, don't see the people you kill, see the innocent people they murdered yesterday."

Looking down, Holan saw the red patch on Madalene's bandages was growing larger. Madalene had done enough, it was time for her to rest, but as she went to tell her this, Madalene began to speak again.

"You stay out all night and sleep in the day. And you keep going out, until this ends and people can safely walk the streets again. To cheer you, know this, I have heard from Elgin and Bertha. Despite the newspapers contempt for their actions, they were as successful as we were. The powers in the north of this country are trembling. As is Shadowman."

The weakness in Madalene's voice was now evident and Holan was not the only one looking at her in concern.

"That's enough, Madalene," said Holan. "We've got to get you into bed. It's too risky to send you back to the hospital, so we'll have to find you a bed here. Christian, go and find some more medics to help her."

"One more thing...then I'll...stop." Madalene slumped in Holan's arms, but Jinn appeared from nowhere and helped lift his mother up again. He was rewarded with a weak smile. "I...I doubted you, but last night...you proved me wrong. I...cannot follow you this time...I have no need to..."

Madalene lapsed into unconsciousness, but her work was done. As people rushed around to get Madalene safely into a bed, Holan breathed in the renewed vigour and determination of the group. Elgin had been right, Madalene was a great leader.

A week passed and then another. The army was exhausted and depleted. Every night they went out and cleared the streets of Sanctum Guards, but always more came. There was no light-heartedness, no banter, only an unending nightmare. The good news was that the public finally seemed to realise the Provoke army was on their side, and more people began to join the army. Many of them former members of the Provoke group, lost without Alan's leadership. Trouble was that without any training, it wasn't possible to send these new recruits onto the streets, so the original army members had no reprieve. Holan had killed so many people she was immune and no longer wept for her victims. She slept with Christian every night, but only for comfort; sex was not the prerogative of the weary.

Gradually Madalene recuperated and it became harder to stop her from joining the action. Holan felt it was probably time to unleash Madalene, despite the medics warning that she needed more rest. They all needed more rest.

"My army's going to party tonight," said Madalene, checking her rifle and the other weapons she intended to take with her. "Though I haven't told them yet. I'll send a few people to fetch more drink from the West London hide-out. We've run low and everyone here deserves the chance to get drunk. If you want to join them, then I'll patrol alone."

Holan smiled, watching Madalene now checking the weapons *she* would be taking out. The army desperately needed what Madalene was proposing and it felt good to have her back in charge again. Looking around, she saw Christian making his preparations alongside Luke and Adrian. As usual his gaze was fixed on Madalene. He was becoming obsessed, despite the fact that Madalene gave him no encouragement. Holan was worried this obsession might get out of hand and damage the army's unity.

"That's a good idea, Madalene," said Holan, turning back round. "But I wouldn't enjoy myself knowing you were out there alone. I've grown strangely fond of my little sister."

Madalene smiled, "Sentimentality? From you?"

"Why not, Madalene? I know deep down, you're fond of me too."

"I don't have any feelings. But if I did, I'd probably say that I care for you, *deep* down, really *deep* down."

Holan laughed. Hostility between the two of them had lasted so long; she never would have believed they could have a relationship again. Yet it had happened and Madalene appeared saner because of it.

The party began almost the instant, Madalene announced it. Only Christian, wanted to patrol with them, but Madalene insisted he rest. Holan was grateful. Christian had not become immune to what they did, unlike the others, and his terror had not lessened. He needed this respite more than anyone. His obsession with Madalene had to be contained as well. It was good to see everyone cheerful, even if it was only for a short while, and Christian's scowling vanished after a few mugs of beer.

Once Madalene was satisfied that everyone was happy and had checked that Jinn and Ellyn weren't drinking too much, she gave Holan the signal to go. Holan nodded, and then noticed it was silent. The whole group had turned towards Madalene as she prepared to leave and there was concern in their eyes. Though she hid it well, Holan could see that Madalene was touched.

"Get on with your drinking and carousing. I don't need any babysitters..." said Madalene, gruffly.

Suddenly there was a commotion at the entrance. Madalene's rifle was loaded and cocked before Holan could blink. The men on guard duty rushed forward and with them came two other men.

"Don't shoot, Madalene. It's Alan. Alan and Torrin." Holan rushed towards them, hardly believing what she was seeing. Both men had obviously undergone terrible torture and were hardly recognisable. With difficulty she looked into the mangled flesh that had been Alan's face and in a croaky voice, he responded to the sight of her.

"H-Holan. It is you, isn't it? N-Not another of their tricks."

"What have they done to you? Oh Alan...How did you find us? Only army members know the location of these hide-outs," said Holan, looking at them in amazement.

"My Provoke group members," said Alan, croakily. "Some of them joined your army recently..."

"But they're not allowed to reveal the whereabouts of the hide-outs to anybody. We have them vetted before we let them in." Holan turned to look at Madalene, but she had gone cold and there was a strange look in her eyes.

"No vetting's been done while we've been fighting Sanctum Guards," said Christian.

"There wasn't time," added Luke. "If they were Provoke group members, we thought it safe to let them in."

"But they still had to swear not to tell anyone about the hide-outs…" Still Madalene hadn't moved or spoken. It was Alan and Torrin. Holan knew Madalene hated them, but she'd expected the usual sarcastic comments, not this silence. Something was bothering Madalene, but what?

"Alan's the leader of the Provoke group," said Torrin, weakly. "Don't blame the people who spoke to us. They would have believed that it was okay to tell Alan. This group was united, until Madalene came along and split us up."

Holan heard the hatred in his voice and looked at Madalene, knowing she would have heard it too. Surely now, Madalene would say something sarcastic, something funny…

Every member of the army looked to Madalene, waiting for her instructions; ready to show immediate loyalty if Madalene insisted Alan and Torrin be ejected. Holan sighed, *her* loyalties were divided. She was overjoyed to see Alan and Torrin again and their plight was desperate with both of them near collapse, but if Madalene wanted them out, so be it. She had to remain loyal to her sister.

Madalene lowered her rifle, and then looked intently at Alan and Torrin. "No one can withstand torture. Don't be ashamed. I won't be able to withstand it either. Listen to me both of you. Once I've gone out there, tell my army what's happened so they can get to safety. They know what to do and they'll make sure you get the treatment you need. Whatever you were told was a lie…"

Madalene had hit the crazy trail again. What the hell was she talking about?

"You're not coming with me tonight, Holan. Stay here and look after these two. They've suffered badly."

"There are plenty of people to look after them." Holan began to issue orders. "Christian, fetch a transporter, Mary, go with him. Take Alan and Torrin over to the field hospital. Doctor Grey will take care of them." Holan walked over to Alan with a smile on her face and carefully wrapped him in her arms. To her surprise he flinched away from her. He was more badly hurt than he looked. "We've a lot of catching up to do Alan, but it can wait until you're better. I'll come and see you when Madalene and I have finished clearing Sanctum scum off the streets." Moving away she kissed Torrin lightly on the cheek. He flinched also. Neither of them looked her in the eye. Puzzled and upset, she moved back to Madalene's side.

"No." Madalene's voice was actually sorrowful, but it was filled with authority. Holan had never seen Madalene look so powerful, yet seem so vulnerable. "I go alone, Holan. You're my sister and I love you. That doesn't mean I want you hanging around all the time. You need to rest. Besides, haven't you got a bit of a dilemma on your hands now?" Madalene looked pointedly at Christian and then at Alan. Softly, she added, "Deal with this tonight, for the sake of your own sanity."

Holan was aghast. Madalene knew there was nothing between her and Christian. They provided comfort for each other, nothing more. But at the moment Madalene wasn't saying anything that made sense. "You can't go out there without back-up. Luke or Adrian could go with you if you don't want me around."

Both young men stepped forward, ready and eager, but Madalene shook her head. Turning to them, she said, "You need to relax with Annie tonight, Luke. You've both fought too hard, for too long. And, Adrian, look at Lilia." Holan looked at Lilia too, she was the beautiful, blonde girl; Adrian seemed to have spent a lifetime trying to attract and she looked decidedly tipsy. "A few more beers and I think she'll be yours. She's been trying to get her hands on you for ages. You two have played cat and mouse for far too long and it's irritating me now."

Holan noticed how crestfallen they looked. Once again she was struck by how much the army loved Madalene. How they would do anything to please her, hear her praise or get one smile from her. Realisation hit her; she felt exactly the same as them. She still believed Madalene was dangerous, but weren't they all now?

"Let me go with you, Mother," said Jinn, longingly.

Madalene looked tenderly at her son. "Stay with Ellyn. You're my youngest and bravest soldiers and you need more rest than the others. Don't drink too much though; you haven't yet learned the price you pay for that pleasure." For a second, Madalene paused and Holan heard the catch in her voice. "Bren loved you like his own son. You already know how much Hayla loved you. Don't forget them, Jinn. Not ever. There's still a price to be paid for their deaths."

Now Holan was really puzzled, Madalene sounded like she was giving a goodbye speech. She wasn't her usual self either. Where was the sarcasm, the arrogance, the snappy comments?

"I'm going," said Madalene, moving out. She looked like someone who had accepted their fate and was now content... "Don't drink all the blue spirit," she shouted. "I've become partial to it. There'd better be some waiting for me when I come back in. And I'm not dealing with any drunks. You stay where you fall." This statement induced laughter and the party started up again. Holan saw Madalene turn in Alan and Torrin's direction and smile knowingly.

"No," shouted Alan. "You can't go out there, Madalene."

"It's a damn sight safer than staying here with you, Alan Moore. If you looked hard enough, you'd find our rope store sooner or later."

Alan tried to grab her and Torrin had run forward too, but Madalene was fast, despite her recent injury. Once again the party came to a halt. Holan saw Alan and Torrin were filled with shame and despair, and Madalene had gone. She didn't understand any of this. What the hell was going on?

"Why isn't it safe for Madalene to go out there, Alan?" He wouldn't speak. "Torrin?"

Torrin looked at her and shrugged his shoulders. "We had to do it," he whispered. "Madalene's a crazy woman. They were right... They promised they won't harm the rest of the army. They'll let you go. They only want her..."

"Had to do what?" screamed, Holan.

"They hurt us badly…You'd have done the same." Torrin began to weep pitifully. She turned again to Alan, but still he said nothing.

Consternation hung in the air like a lethal vapour. No-one said a word, but with the exception of Holan herself, comprehension suddenly swept the room and it began to clear. Jinn picked up his weapons and raced past her, the others followed. Christian walked over to Holan and grabbed her hand.

"They've betrayed her," he said, glaring at Alan and Torrin, before following the others out of the entrance.

The reason she hadn't understood what was happening, was that she hadn't wanted to understand. Alan was the man she loved and Torrin, her friend for many years. Madalene had known instantly, but had said nothing - why? Looking at Alan, she saw that he was crying.

"You can't have done that. Tell me you didn't do it."

"I didn't have any choice, Holan, and they promised that they would leave the Provoke army and the group alone, once they had Madalene. No repercussions for any of us."

"You Fool!" Blinded now by tears that she didn't even know were falling, Holan raised her gun and, without thought, fired it. Alan's death was instantaneous. Looking at his body she felt nothing. Turning to Torrin in disgust, she shouted, "Get out of here, Torrin. If I see you again, I'll kill you. Madalene's my sister."

Holan thought she was running to the entrance, hoping to catch up with the others, but she wasn't. She was on her knees at Alan's side staring blankly at his body. It was hard to comprehend why her body wasn't obeying her brain. She had tried to overlook Alan's hatred for Madalene. Easy when she had hated Madalene too, but not easy now…Hours passed by, or was it only seconds? Finally a loud wailing came from behind her. Without any real interest, she turned and came face to face with her nephew, Jinn. He stood in front of her shaking violently, and though he tried many times, he was unable to speak. As if a switch had been turned on again, Holan stood up and threw her arms tightly around the distressed boy. Over his shoulder, she saw that Ellyn had come to find him. The girl was covered in blood and equally distressed.

"They've got her, Holan. They've got Madalene."

Chapter 22

Let's Go To Heaven

So finally she'd been betrayed, and by Alan Moore of all people. An idiot who knew of her, but had never known her. The man who'd tried to lynch her, claiming it was the only way to keep the group he loved safe; but now most of that group would die: because in betraying her, Alan had betrayed his friends as well. The man who she had saved from the chambers, when she should have let him rot. A final thought occurred to her. He was the man who had been tortured beyond imagining…Remembering his face as he begged her not to leave the hide-out, she realised he had not betrayed her lightly. Torrin was a different matter…

Reaching the entrance, she acknowledged the men guarding it, and paused for a few seconds. Sanctum Guards would be out there in great numbers. Any moment they could attack the hide-out. Alan and Torrin would have been told the army would be left alone once they had her, but that was a lie. The only chance her army had, was for *her* to distract the enemy outside long enough to allow their escape. She only hoped Alan would warn them in time, even if he gave no reasons. It might have been better to warn them herself, and she still had time to do it. But their reaction would be, either not to let her go out there, or to insist on accompanying her. Both would have disastrous results. That she would be taken was almost certain. All she had to do was make that 'certainty' take as long as humanly possible.

Surfacing, she spotted the enemy instantly. There were hundreds of them and most of them made little pretence of hiding. A quick glance showed her an escape route. It did not appear to be guarded, and at the end of that particular route, she knew she would find a transporter - the one used mostly by Malcolm. Even if it was a trap, it was the only way to go, if she wanted to delay an attack on the hide-out.

Feigning nonchalance, she walked out of the hide-out, already sensing movement all around her. If she was correct, the Sanctum

Guards would still be afraid to kill her, they would fire their weapons only to contain her. This time they meant to capture her by outnumbering her and it was unlikely they would touch the hide-out until that had been accomplished. At least she hoped it was unlikely.

Coolly, she stopped walking, took a swig from a small bottle of spirit, she kept in her pocket and looked around. They began to show themselves. Spinning quickly, she shot three men coming at her from behind and ran towards the unguarded street, she had spotted earlier. Only at the last moment did she realise her error. They had not left any openings, it was a trap.

Men appeared in front of her, emerging from the buildings they'd been hiding in. They'd planned for her to go that way. Swerving quickly, she ran into a nearby house, raced through it and into the garden at the back. Climbing the fence, she found herself in another garden. Now she jumped fences, one garden to another, and the guards chasing her kept up; only one fence between her and them. She heard them yelling to each other, heard whistles blowing and sirens wailing. There was also a sound of guns being fired nearby. Had they gone into the hide-out? The leading guard reached her side; kicking him in the face, she dived into another house, ignoring the horrified looks on the faces of its residents. Glancing out the window, she saw the street was clear, so she ran back into the street. Peter Shadow's minions appeared in seconds. Again she ran through a house to reach its garden. Shots were fired at her as she tried to climb the fence, so she retraced her steps. Shooting the guards coming towards her, she raced past the rest of her assailants into the next street and through yet another house. Not once did she lose her bearings. She was close to a drain that had been set up as an emergency bolthole. All she had to do was get herself onto the street adjoining this one. But how?

They were keeping up with her, which was why she using the houses and gardens. It was limiting the numbers of those who could chase her at any one time. From the shouting that went on between them, she gathered that it was more than their lives were worth for them to lose her. This time she dared a fence despite the bullets that were fired at her. The problem was that she was getting tired, her injury too recent for all this climbing and running. The adjoining street and a few moments alone were all she needed. One street!

181

Carefully she climbed the nearest fence and peered over the top. The way was clear. One street. Lowering herself over, she ran, reached another fence and cleared it. The sound of weapons being fired and counter fired reached her ears. A battle was taking place. Her army were on the march. She knew it. They were fighting to save her. Silently she cheered them on. Part of her wanted to find a way back and help them, but the majority of the guards and police were still chasing *her*, she was certain of it. If she led them back to the hide-out, her army would be severely outnumbered. One street. She was close. All she had to do now was reach that drain. No more fences, only a clear run.

She finally reached the street she wanted, only to come face to face with a multitude of Sanctum Guards. Turning around, she came face to face with others who had crept up behind her. There was nothing left to do but smile, and she was happy to see her smile disturbed them. On another day, she might have made it. Not today however. Not today. Well she might as well shoot a few of them, while she still had the opportunity. Still smiling, she raised her rifle…It was knocked out of her hands. Falling to the ground, she rolled to get clear of the men trying to grab her. Rolled into the arms of others.

There was no way she was going to let herself be taken easily, so she began to fight them, in spite of their numbers and her own exhaustion. A net appeared over head and she tried to evade it, but she was surrounded by so many men, it was impossible. As the net descended over her head, her wrists were grabbed and placed into heavy shackles. No longer able to fight back, she snarled, and then laughed at the fear on the faces of the men surrounding her. It was over. She knew it was over; her only hope was that it wasn't over for her army. The men continued to punish her and their blows were harder now they were no longer opposed. The last thing she was aware of was a transporter arriving by her side, as she lay trapped in the net.

"Good morning, Madalene," said a voice she recognised. "Remember me? It's been a long time, hasn't it?"

"Some faces you never forget," she said with a defiant smile.

As she attempted to move, she realised she was chained to a slab, or was it a table, it was hard to tell. Her eyes were sore, her mouth

182

swollen and her head doing a tailspin. Wryly she studied his face, not even trying to hide her loathing. Those grey eyes had once been the stuff of nightmares, but no longer held any fear for her.

"I'd like to say it was nice to see you again, Peter, but it's not. It really isn't."

"You say that only because at the moment you are hurt and frightened. You'll feel differently in a few days time, Madalene," he said smoothly, bending down to look more closely at her.

"Frightened! Of you? You rate yourself highly. I'm the one lying here in chains because you're too afraid to talk to me otherwise." She laughed in his face and watched him withdraw. "I won't ever feel differently about you. So what's next? Torture followed by the Arena, or just torture and death. That's what you did to my husband Bren and my stepdaughter Hayla, wasn't it? Knowing what a sadistic boy you were, I guessed you'd turn out to be a monstrous man. I just didn't realise how monstrous. Do what you want. I don't care. My army have shown they can function without me. You'll remain opposed."

She watched him beckon one of the dozens of men stood nearby.

"Sir. Yes Sir," said the unknown man, standing to attention.

Madalene laughed out loud. "Not only do you need chains, you need several armed guards as well. Tell me again how unafraid of me you are."

He didn't respond to her taunting. "Take those chains off her and help her into the chair over there. Then leave. All of you."

"But Sir..." One look from Peter was all it took to dowse the man's question. In moments the shackles were removed and she was roughly hauled up and placed in a nearby chair. The men then left the room as ordered. Nevertheless, Peter looked unnerved at being alone with her.

"I'll deal with your army shortly. Now you're safely out of the way I don't fear them at all." He sat down opposite her, staring at her with an expression, she could not interpret.

"So you do fear me after all. I can't tell you how happy I am that my actions bothered you." Again she smiled at him and this time it needled him. She saw it in his face.

"You were an irritation, nothing more. What grandiose ideas you have, Madalene. Do you really think the things you did were important? You overrate your efforts."

"If my actions had no effect and were merely irritating, why send so many men to capture me? Why force Alan Moore and Torrin Spice to betray me?"

"They betrayed you willingly," he said, snappily. For someone who had succeeded in capturing a much wanted enemy, he seemed unhappy. She had no intention of cheering him up by weeping and wailing, begging him for mercy; the sort of thing he was obviously used to. "Your insanity frightened them and they believed you capable of doing great harm. They were tortured because they were leaders of the irritating Provoke group. You did me a favour forming your army. My mail bag lessened considerably after you took them to Ireland for what you call training purposes."

"Enough talk, Peter." Deliberately, she spoke in a commanding tone, watching his alarmed reaction. No-one ever spoke to him like this, she was certain of it. He did not know how to deal with someone more commanding than himself. "Not that I'm not enjoying our little reunion. I'm simply impatient to get to the torture bit. I want to test myself, see how much I can endure. I've been tortured a few times before, in my army days and I did quite well. Somehow they never quite managed to break me. I'm sure you'll manage though, so get on with it. We'll speak again when I'm a gibbering wreck."

Now it was his turn to smile. "Why would I want to torture you, my beautiful, Madalene? I have a much better use for you. I thought you were a beautiful child. As a woman, you are unsurpassed. Anything you want I will give you. All you *ever* had to do was ask." Once again that strange expression appeared on his face and Madalene felt uneasy. Her death wasn't going to be as straight forward as she had thought it would be.

"My freedom. Give me my freedom."

"Almost anything," he said, regretfully. "As wife of this country's leader, you risk attack from various terrorist factions. With that in mind, I have assigned five bodyguards to protect you at all times."

"Wife! I'd never agree to marry you. Send me to the Arena. Today if possible. I'd rather that, than be your wife." Madalene was horrified. Peter was a devious opponent and the game he was playing with her was not what she had expected. There were horrors greater than death and torture and she had the feeling she was about to find out what those horrors were. Peter Shadow moved closer to her, his eyes never leaving her face. In his hand was a glass of wine; she had seen him drink from it several times. Carefully he held out the glass and offered it to her, almost daring her to drink it.

Casually she accepted and drained the glass. "Oops," she said. "Looks like you'll have to pour some more."

"If you would like some more, you shall have it." His voice sounded menacing now, almost distant. Madalene was no fool.

"You drugged it, didn't you?"

"Did you expect anything less, Madalene? I know of your addictions. Numerous drugs were found in your home when it was raided."

Madalene was shocked. This was unexpected. She had imagined the vilest torture followed by a horrible death. Not this. Not this.

"What have you given me?" she asked, keeping her voice steady.

His own voice was equally neutral, but she sensed his delight. "Naztrolone."

Naztrolone! It was illegal and had been for many years. Users apparently went to Heaven and experienced wonders untold. They returned to Earth with a thunderous crash, unable to exist on the planet any longer. To re-enter Heaven they would do anything, absolutely anything – even marry the man they hated. Game, Set and Match. Already her aches and pains had left her and the world looked a prettier place. Peter Shadow looked positively handsome, almost genial. Had she maligned him just because of a petty schoolground incident?

Slowly she climbed up to Heaven, unable to resist its allure. A voice in her head told her to turn around, go back to Earth before it was too late. Uselessly she fought it; the urge to go on was too great. Looking back, she saw that Peter had laid her down on a bed covered with cushions. She laughed with delight, where had the bed come from? He didn't touch her; he just stood still looking down on her. He was an angel, taking her away to... He was an angel...No! He was a demon. Wasn't he?

Now he touched her and she welcomed it. She felt her shirt being undone and the chill of cold air on her nipples, or was it the coolness of his fingertips? Heaven came closer. Still there was awareness of earthly matters, even though she no longer cared for them. Her trousers had gone, her legs were pushed apart. Heaven appeared before her. As she stood in Heaven's green forests, a pulsating sensation came from inside her and she saw that seeds had been released into her body. Beautiful seeds. Feeling safe, she watched the seeds begin to race to her egg; eggs, there were two of them. Two seeds were the fastest and penetrated the eggs before the others arrived. Clever seeds. She applauded them, even as she began to pick the pale blue flowers that lay everywhere on Heavens paths. Now the seeds became cells and the cells divided. For two beings it was the onset of life, and already she knew these cells would be her sons. Like a spectator in a theatrical production, she threw her flowers down to earth to show her appreciation for this spectacular production.

Peter Shadow turned to accept her acclaim, his mouth sneering with triumph; in his eyes, a look of malicious satisfaction. The flowers and the trees turned black and she felt herself falling.

"No-ooo..." she screamed. "No-ooo..."

Chapter 23

Acceptance

Satisfied the battle outside the hide-out was over, Holan raced in the direction of the sirens. Creeping noiselessly, around large numbers of congregating men, her heart beating wildly, she finally found Madalene: trapped in a net and getting a terrible beating. Men were pushing and shoving each other, to get *their* chance to land a blow. It looked like she would be beaten to death, until concerned looking commanders stepped in and restored order. The men stood back, jeering and yelling, even after Madalene had been thrown into a transporter, like a piece of baggage, and taken away.

Holan longed to be heroic; to rescue Madalene from their midst: commit the sort of outrageous act, Madalene would have attempted, but she didn't have the nerve. Besides, it was suicidal to attempt anything with so many men near. Instead, she slunk away quickly, after hearing talk of 'Getting the rest of the bastards'. Approaching safety, she relaxed her guard, only to come across a bulky man, in the uniform of a Sanctum Guard, peeing against a wall. Before he could call to others, she fled and kept running, even through the pain of his bullet scraping her head. Fortunately, Madalene had practised emergency evacuations so many times; Holan knew where to go.

From the collective sigh of relief that greeted her arrival, she realised that her friends in the army had thought she'd been captured. It was comforting that they cared. Carefully, she examined the wound on her head. The bullet had scraped away skin and hair in a path, roughly four inches from the back of her head to the front; it would have been fatal if it had flown any lower. She'd been lucky. Using the back of her hand, she now wiped blood out of her eyes and looked around. Army members were slumped all over the place; weapons still clasped in their hands as if they were afraid to let go of them. Their eyes were bleak from sorrow and weariness, and no-one spoke. The only sound came from a corner where Hannah lay sobbing. Her tears had to be for Tom; he had foolishly turned his back on a man he thought dead. Maybe Hannah also cried for Madalene's loss, but somehow, Holan doubted it.

Many others had lost their lives, however the overall loss wasn't as great as it might have been. They had Madalene to thank for that; she'd led the majority of the Sanctum Guards away from them.

The new place was as comfortable as the old one, but at the moment it stunk. A lot of the silent people, slumped down on the ground, had vomited at least once, if not several times, and the smell indicated that many of them had also lost control of their bowels and bladders. Stale sweat, vomit and shit were the smells of life; the life they *still* had. Ignoring the eerie silence, Holan headed to the kitchen and grabbed the first bottle of spirit she could find, sending up thanks to Madalene for providing the basics. Pulling the cork out with her teeth, and wincing as she felt one loosen, she swigged the stuff back and then slumped down in a corner with the bottle. It was so rough, she thought it might, in reality, be transporter fuel, but as her senses reeled she forgot to care. She threw more of it down her throat.

Bleary-eyed and semi-blinded by an alcoholic haze, she looked over at Christian, who was gazing at her with alarm, and saw Torrin sat by his side. Why was Christian associating with that traitor? With difficulty, she reached for her gun. Hadn't she promised to kill Torrin if she saw him again? She had. But for the moment she couldn't be bothered; no emotion could cross the empty space in her head, and if you killed a man without emotion, that made you a murderer. Had she felt anything when she had killed, Alan?

Torrin had been fighting by Christian's side during the battle, and he had fought well, considering he was a man who had undergone torture and was untrained. Did it make any difference that Torrin had fought for the army, after all he had still betrayed, Madalene. Would Alan have done the same? Yes, was the word that came into her mind. Quickly, she took enough swigs of spirit to change that 'Yes' into 'No'; the vision of Madalene struggling in that net was still fresh in her mind.

"Ha," she said in a loud voice, which startled just about everyone. Swigging more spirit, she felt the floor beneath her stir. Earthquake? Strange thing to happen in London. "Ha. She didn't think we were good enough. Thought we had no hope of surviving without her. Well we're all here. Where's she?" Without volition, Holan dared the unsteady ground and got to her feet. "Where is she? Where is she?"

188

Christian looked at her mouthing the words, 'No Holan. Not now'. Pulling himself to his feet, he walked over and grabbed hold of her. Fiercely, she hit him, again and again and again.

"Where is she Christian? Traitor! Why are you associating with Torrin? I thought you loved Madalene."

Christian grabbed hold of her hands and Luke and Adrian came over to help him. Mark, Adam and Malcolm were on their way.

"Don't touch me," she said, breaking free; hitting out at Luke and Adrian, as they tried to get hold of her.

"We only want to help you, Holan," said Luke, anxiously.

Tears joined fresh blood streaming down her face. She could barely see. Before the other three men could reach her, she broke away with a wail. The pity on their faces was too much to take. Suddenly she fell, landing on a startled Mary, who squealed and moved away. Mary had also been drinking. Holan grabbed what was left of Mary's bottle and downed it.

"There's no point in crying," she said, wiping her tears away. "I saw her...They had Madalene on the ground, trapped in a net like an animal...an animal. They kept hitting her and hitting...an animal..."

Now she wasn't the only one with tears in her eyes. "It's over," she said in quiet, slurred tones. "We have to find a way to get normality back into our lives. Perhaps we should rejoin what's left of the original Provoke group..."

She crawled to a bottle of spirit she could see nearby, took it back to Mary's spot, and again swigged its contents. A soft hand touched her arm.

"Don't Aunty Holan...We need you...I need you..." Jinn knelt down beside her, his face damp with tears.

"Oh it's Aunty Holan, now your rotten mother's gone is it? No time for me when she was around, but now you need me?" She was lashing out, she knew it, but somehow she couldn't stop. Jinn said nothing, but he stayed by her side. Hannah walked over to join him, tears gently rolling down her cheeks.

"Jinn's right," said, Hannah. "We need you."

Slowly, Holan tried to look at everyone in the room, but there were too many of them and her sight was too blurred. Collectively they were holding their breath; they didn't want it to be over. Holan realised, with bewilderment, they wanted *her* to take Madalene's place.

"I'm Madalene's sister, not Madalene," she said, hoarsely. "Get Elgin to come down here and take over. He's the only one who can replace her. Or Bertha…"

"You've become more like Madalene than you realise," said, Hannah. "It doesn't have to be over…"

Madalene had more power and authority than Hannah realised. It couldn't be done without her…

"Go away," said Holan, angrily. "And get *that* traitor out of my sight." She pointed at Torrin. "See, even now he can't look at me."

Holan scrabbled for the weapons; Mary had left behind when fallen on. But she couldn't get hold of them properly; her hands weren't working. Torrin walked over and knelt down by her side. He selected a pistol and forced it into her hand.

"You have a gun now, Holan. Shoot me," he said, raising her face so she had to look at him properly.

Again it seemed like everyone was holding their breath. Blearily, Holan raised the pistol and fired it. The bullet flew past Torrin's ear and lodged in a wall behind him.

"You missed," said Torrin, heatedly. "Try again."

"Stop it," said Jinn, trying to get hold of Torrin and pull him away. Holan saw Torrin shrug him off.

"Try again, Holan. You were quick enough to shoot, Alan."

Gasps of horror indicated that many in this room hadn't heard that tasty bit of information yet.

"Try again, Holan." Torrin was shouting now, and in frustration, he raised her shaky hand and put the pistol to his chest. When she did not react, he pulled off his shirt, so the pistol made direct contact with his skin. "Do I have to do this myself? Pull the damn trigger, Holan. You can't miss."

Holan stared in horror at Torrin's torso. It was bruised and burned, not a patch of his skin had escaped maltreatment.

"Not a pretty sight eh? Don't let that stop you."

He moved the pistol to a blackened area. Glancing around the room, she saw the others were mesmerized by what was going on. No-one was going to intervene unless Torrin turned the gun on her.

"Shoot me, Holan. It won't hurt...Please do it...Please..." His anger and desperation had gone. Now all Holan saw was pain...Her hand shook violently and she dropped the pistol.

"What have I done, Torrin? What have I done...?" Christian and Luke came over, raised up Torrin, who was now sobbing uncontrollably and led him away. Jinn who was still by her side, grabbed hold of the pistol and threw it away. Then quietly he put his arms around her and hugged her tightly. Adrian and Mark, followed closely by Adam and Malcolm came over too.

"Come on, Holan," said Adrian. "Time for you to sleep this off. Help me get her up, Jinn." Holan found herself being lifted by many hands. Adrian turned from her for a second. "Do we still have a transporter, Malcolm? If we do, take Adam with you and get Torrin to the field hospital, he needs help. It's risky, but you should be okay."

Slowly, like a chick breaking free of its egg, the thin shell that had protected her sanity cracked and widened. As they carried her to a bed, Holan began to wail with grief and once she'd started, she couldn't stop. Gently, they placed her on an empty bunk and Mark leaned over and popped something into her mouth.

"What are you doing?" said Adrian, sharply.

For the first time, Holan heard Mark speak. "I-It's an 'Ease' tablet. I thought it might help her sleep..." The last thing, Holan heard was Adrian laughing.

"With all the alcohol she's chucked down her throat, *you* thought she'd need something to help her sleep?"

It was dark when Holan woke. She thought she'd been asleep for a few hours, but was quickly informed it was in fact the following evening. The bustle and chatter around her was evidence of some return to normality. So normal, she almost expected Madalene to burst in any minute with a sarcastic comment dripping from her lips. Like a stone thrown at her chest, it hit her that she would never see Madalene again. Another stone struck, neither would she see Alan, and she alone was the reason *he* was dead. Desperately, she wanted to turn the clock back, give Alan his life again. She'd loved him so much, it had felt like he had betrayed her, not Madalene...How could she carry on living...How?

Her head pounded violently as she walked through the communal area and her eyes would barely open; nevertheless she was conscious of being stared at and disliked the attention. Was this what it felt like to be Madalene? Heading directly to the wash room, she was sick, and kept on vomiting until her stomach had inverted. Looking into a mirror, she saw a hideous spectacle, but at least someone had washed her face clean while she slept. A sharp pain in the stomach sent her flying into one of the two toilets available. Her bowels only stopped when they also had inverted. Carefully she covered her efforts with the available dirt; there were no flush toilets in hide-outs.

She exited the wash room, determined, like many before her, never to drink again. Her determination was astounding. In seconds she had found a bottle of fruit wine, opened it and found a corner to sprawl in. Christian came over to sit by her side.

"That won't do you any good. Let me get you some bread. Hannah did some baking earlier." He disappeared for a short while and returned with a plate of bread and cheese, there was also an apple. Holan supped more wine, but noticing his disapproval, she put the bottle down and tried a piece of the bread. It was good. Her inverted belly called to her, so ravenously she fed it. Crunching the apple now, she turned and looked at Christian.

"How are you?" she asked, softly.

"Not good," he said, tears welling up in his eyes. "Did they really catch her in a net?"

Holan nodded and told him everything she had seen. "They've had her for over twenty four hours now. I dread to think what they're doing to her."

"It will be worse than they've done to anyone else…" Christian choked, and then continued. "Much worse. Will you risk going to the Arena when they put her up?"

"How could I not?" said Holan. "Will you?"

"Nothing would keep me away…" he said, defiantly.

Once again, Christian's fear would be overcome by his love for Madalene. For a while they sat together in silence, sharing the fruit wine.

"Why did you shoot Alan, Holan? You loved him. You always have."

"You loved Madalene, maybe more than I did. What would you have done, Christian?" Holan could not say more than that, even now, she could not fully understand her reaction. Christian simply nodded in response.

A loud noise came from the entrance and suddenly the air was filled with cheering. In burst Elgin, his long white hair flying behind him, like a lion's mane.

"I've left Bertha behind to look after things and come down here to see if I can help," said, Elgin, in his familiar booming tones.

Against her will, Holan had to smile. Some things in life were permanent and safe. Elgin was one of those things. Suddenly, she found herself crying and was unable to stop. Elgin came straight over and she found herself pulled into one of his renowned bear hugs, which only made her cry harder.

"Let it out, girl," he said to her, in what passed for his soft voice. "Let it go."

193

He held her tightly for what seemed like hours, but was in fact only minutes. Hannah had walked over carrying a mug of spiced wine, Elgin's favourite drink, and a huge plate of cheese and bread,

"Your bread, Hannah? I've come to a good place then. No-one handles flour like you do. Put them there, Hannah." Elgin let go of Holan and pointed to an ancient table nearby. "And give an old man a hug. I swear you get prettier every time I see you. If I wasn't so in love with my Bertha, you'd tempt me to be unfaithful."

For the first time since their arrival at this new hide-out, Holan saw Hannah smile and she did indeed look pretty. Why had Madalene always referred to Hannah as an old crone? Manoeuvring his bulk into a small chair near the table, Elgin began to eat with a speed that articulated his hunger. Many army members now came over, greeting Elgin with delight. He spoke to them all as they came, joking with some, commiserating with others. Holan watched him with wonder, the old man knew the right thing to say to everybody and the room seemed brighter and cosier because he was in it. And yet Elgin's eyes showed he had sorrows of his own to contend with and knowing his fondness for Madalene, Holan had no doubt that her loss was one of his sorrows.

As if he had caught her thought, Elgin began to speak, addressing himself to everyone in the room. "You are not the only one's mourning her loss." He didn't need to say her name, they all knew of whom he spoke. "Are we ever likely to meet *such* a woman again? Whoever named her 'The Dark Goddess' named her correctly; yes we have heard that name in the North. Ah, but was she not adorable. Weren't we all secretly in love with her, men and women?

Heads nodded their agreement with his words.

"Damn woman didn't seem to be afraid of anything, but they'll make her know fear before she dies…"

A chill ran through Holan. She hated to think of Madalene's terror, but her sister was not super human. Pain would defeat her just like it did everyone else. Without thinking, Holan spoke.

"We will honour Madalene's memory. We fight on."

A stunned silence greeted these words, but Elgin was smiling fondly at her.

"I don't know what to do, Elgin. I don't have any of Madalene's abilities, or her contacts," she said softly so the others couldn't hear her.

"Then do things your own way, that's how it should be when a new leader takes over," he said, not so softly. Now everyone looked expectantly at Holan, waiting for the words they wanted to hear.

She wasn't good enough. Madalene had understood Torrin and Alan's predicament and sympathised, despite knowing their hatred for her. *She* had been unable to control her passion...Maybe this was the way to make some kind of reparation. Besides which she had nothing left to lose.

"Tomorrow we go back out on the streets and clear them, just as we have been doing. It's not much, but it's a start. When we finish we'll hold a feast to commemorate those we've lost, and that includes Alan, even though he died at my hands. It was a moment of madness and I'll pay for that moment forever... The council must begin planning future strikes, as they did so successfully before. Understand clearly, I cannot be 'The Dark Goddess'..."

Luke and Adrian came up and heartily slapped her on the back. Elgin watched approvingly.

"If she can't be 'The Dark Goddess', we'll have to give her a new name," said, Luke, smiling innocently.

"You know, I think you're right," said Adrian, with a wink. "How about 'Easy Lady', or after last night, 'The Dark Drunk'.

"How about I give you two something?" said Holan, setting about the two of them with her fists, as for the first time in two days, laughter filled the room.

Chapter 24

A Bleak Relationship

Peter sat in an armchair near the bed; silently he watched Madalene sleeping, listening to every soft breath she took. Her face was peaceful and contented, but from time to time spasms crossed it and he knew her dreams were troubled. Occasional mutterings came from her lips, something about babies, but nothing comprehensible.

As if she sensed him watching her, she woke. He smiled at her.

"Good Morning, my love. How are you today?"

"I'm fabulous thank you." She sat up and yawned, "How are you? Not that I care."

Her eyes were hollow black caves of yearning. He knew she was craving the drug, longing for a return to oblivion, but would never admit it. What a fighter she was, anyone else would have submitted to his will long ago. Every day he spent with her, he became more and more besotted.

"I'm totally devoted to you as always," he said, laughing at the frown that appeared between her brows. "Shall we eat?"

He knew her answer before she spoke it, but forced her to get out of bed and helped her into a wool wrap. He then led her to a small dining table nearby that had been set with various dishes.

"You know I'm not hungry. Why make me go through this charade every morning?"

"Why not? You know how much I enjoy your company. As we're soon to be married, you'd better get used to taking breakfast with me."

The hollow black caves that were her eyes grew darker and she almost spat at him, "Marry You! Whatever gave you the idea that I liked you that much? It can't be my sparkling company; the

Naztrolone you keep giving me doesn't exactly make me congenial. Nor do you, come to think of it."

She always found a way to hurt him. Hiding his feelings, he said, "I'm not stupid, Madalene. I know how you feel about me. Nevertheless, you are going to marry me. Surely you don't want to remain a widow for the rest of your life."

This time he hurt her. Her face twisted with grief and it took several minutes for her to regain her composure. Coolly, she looked him up and down, and then said, "If you lost all your gold, would you settle for sawdust? You're mad if you think I would marry my husband's killer. There's only one ceremony I want to attend with you. Your funeral."

"Given time you'll learn to love *me* and forget your pathetic husband, Bren. I'll make it happen, and you'll be unable to prevent it." He was striking out, because again she'd hurt him. It was a sensation he wasn't used to, people vied to please him usually, and had done so for a long time.

"And will you also make me forget my step-daughter, Hayla? Whatever you do to me, be assured that I'll never forget either of them, and you *will* pay for what you did."

"Sit down, Madalene," he said, sharply. "Stop trying to frighten me with melodramatic threats, you're unable to carry out. Now eat some food or I'll withdraw your fix."

He passed her a bread roll and a small pot of butter. Lifting the lid on a silver dish, he placed lamb's kidneys on her plate and smiled as she retched at the sight of them.

"What are these? Bits of your victims brought up from the torture chambers."

"If I could get hold of your Provoke army members, they would be. Alas, they continue to elude my clutches." Seeing Madalene's smile of joy, he realised he should have kept quiet.

"I've trained them well, *Shadowman.*" This last word said with such mockery, he winced. "Maybe they're dining on bits of your Sanctum Guards, I do hope so."

197

"That's not nice, Madalene. If you want that fix, and I can see how badly you do, you're really not going the right way about getting it."

Looking directly into his eyes, she smiled again and said, "I can do without it." But he knew she couldn't. Even as she defied him, she was trembling.

Carefully, he placed a piece of kidney on a fork and lifted it up to her mouth. To his surprise she accepted it and began to chew. It was the first thing she'd eaten in days. Without warning she spat the food into his face. Furiously, he reached for her, but she'd picked up a knife and she stabbed his hand with it.

"You bitch," he cried, throwing his tea in her eyes, temporarily blinding her. "Guards." he yelled.

Four men entered the room. They saw what she'd done, and quickly knocking the knife out of her hands, they contained her and waited for further instructions.

Wiping kidney pieces off his face, he smiled, menacingly, "Madalene appears to have forgotten her manners this morning. Hold her hand out for me, the left one."

She was expecting to be stabbed in retaliation; he could see it in her expression. Wrapping his bleeding hand in a linen napkin, he grinned; Madalene was in for a shock. She was trying hard to keep her fist clenched, but the trembling was getting worse. One of the guards, a huge, powerful man, forced Madalene's hand open with ease, and kept it open. Peter moved up to her then and knelt down by her side. She looked at him rebelliously, but said nothing.

"You guards can be my witnesses. My dear Madalene, I was going to do this in a more civilised fashion. A little breakfast, some pleasant conversation, I even had a rosebud to give you. But you make everything so difficult."

A knock came at the door and Vertex entered. "Ah Fatboy, just in time. You can witness this too. I'm about to formally ask Madalene to be my wife." Vertex was unable to hide his shock.

"Yes, I know you thought I only wanted to use Madalene's genes to make children, but she's quite a catch as they say. And it wouldn't do for any children we had to be illegitimate. Wouldn't do at all."

Madalene was as startled as Vertex, but still said nothing; she simply looked fiercely at him.

"That's no way to look at your future husband. If you're not careful, I might change my mind."

Putting his hand into a pocket, he pulled out a ring made of gold, and stunning pink diamonds in the shape of a rose. It was a rare piece of jewellery and extremely valuable. "Though you endlessly try my patience, I love you, Madalene, and have done so for a long time. Will you do me the honour of becoming my wife?"

Peter's heart was beating fast and for a few moments he felt vulnerable. To his delight, the powerful guard, who held Madalene's hand open using only one of his big hands, anticipated her answer and clamped his other hand over her mouth. Quickly Peter forced the ring onto the third finger of her left hand, and then nodded to the guard.

"Break the hand," he said. "That way the ring gets to stay there. Don't let her hand go until it's completely swollen. If we have to keep breaking the hand to keep the ring on, so be it."

The guard grinned maliciously, as did his fellows. One by one, he snapped Madalene's fingers, and then broke every other bone in her hand.

"Wrist as well. I don't want to take any chances," said Peter, revelling in what he saw as a victory over her.

Aside from a few grunts, Madalene had tried not to make a sound, but when her wrist was broken, the scream from behind the hand was loud and clear.

"We'll take that as a *yes* then, gentlemen. Well congratulate me. I've just got engaged."

The guards grinned and cheered him loudly. They would be well rewarded and they knew it. The powerful one was obviously due for a promotion, putting his hand over Madalene's mouth at such a critical time was inspired. Vertex muttered his congratulations, but seemed stunned at what had just happened.

Peter stood and went to kiss Madalene on the forehead. From out of nowhere, she pulled her other hand free and slapped him hard. His head reeled. The guard who'd been holding the hand looked horrified, as well he might, redeeming himself, only just, by grabbing the hand back quickly.

Through tears of pain, Peter said angrily, "As you can see, Madalene is overjoyed, but also overwrought. She needs somewhere to rest quietly. Isn't there a small locked cupboard on this floor?"

"It's just outside your door, sir," said the powerful guard. "It's tiny though and filled with junk."

"Perfect for Madalene then. Chuck my wife-to-be in there as you leave. I have to talk to Fatboy here. We need to discuss the annihilation of the Provoke army."

As the powerful man removed his hands from Madalene and went to pull her up, she spoke. "Before this gorilla clamped my mouth, I might have said yes just to make your life hell. Now you'll have to drag me to our *wedding*," at that word she spat at him, then trembling and in obvious pain continued, "In chains. And you'll need to make certain I can't speak. I'll never marry you willingly. Never."

"Oh that can be easily arranged," he said, more casually than he felt. "Silver chains to match your silver gown, and maybe a silver gag strapped down hard over your tongue. I'm sure we'll all hear a 'Yes' and a 'Promise to obey', whether you say the words or not. Take her away."

Unceremoniously, the guards bundled her up between them and removed her. Peter heard the door being opened in the corridor, the crash as Madalene was shoved into the cupboard and the sound of a key being turned. He could also hear muffled obscenities, in which Madalene cast doubts on his parentage.

"Feisty thing my fiancée, isn't she?" he said, turning his full attention on Vertex.

Michael Vertex was horrified by what he'd just witnessed. How could Peter have proposed to Madalene? Why? It wasn't something Peter needed to do. He remembered the conversation about Madalene being the best woman Peter could find to bear his children, but at the time hadn't taken it seriously. It seemed to be the sort of conversation you had when you were drunk and a bit maudlin. He'd assumed that in reality, Peter would quickly tire of Madalene and her behaviour. There was even a chance that Peter would throw her his way, before sending her to be tortured. He'd very much wanted that to happen...

"You can't marry, Madalene, Peter," he said, without thinking. "The people won't like it."

Peter looked at him in surprise, but said nothing. The look indicated that he was to continue. Michael hesitated; Peter was at his most dangerous when he went quiet.

"They want to see Madalene in the Arena. The papers are full of stories about her. They're quoting her history *and* exaggerating her recent activities." Sitting nervously down at the table, he placed an egg on a plate, nervously prodded it with a fork, and then reluctantly finished what he'd been saying. "The people think Madalene is being tortured at the moment; getting her come-uppance. How are they going to react when they find out you intend to marry her?"

The surge of anger that raced through Peter was apparent, it made his skin flush and his lips curl. "I don't give a damn what the public wants, or how they react. I'm not obliged to please them. On the contrary, they're obliged to please me, or suffer the consequences. Unlike previous government *my* power had not been gained from the approval of the masses. I *will* marry Madalene and the people will watch and be happy for me. They're even going to help me pay for the event with extra taxation. Who gave the papers the instructions to malign Madalene? Who?"

"It was Stephen Drake, your new press officer. He thought his initiative would please you. The man believed he was doing what you wanted, Peter..." Michael said, knowing exactly what would happen next.

As expected, Peter yelled for the guards. They entered with speed, eager to please him as always. "There's a Stephen Drake in the press office. Go down there and shoot him."

Asking no questions, the guards left immediately to do Peter's bidding. Michael made no comment, he'd stupidly opened his mouth and now poor Stephen would suffer for it. He had few friends in the Sanctum as it was; Stephen was one of them.

"You will put a new person in that post by lunchtime, and they'd better be good enough to deal with the damage caused by this Stephen Drake. If not they'll share his fate."

"Of course," Michael said, resignedly. "What's going on, Peter? I thought you'd spend a few weeks getting Madalene out of your system, and then send her to the torture chambers and the Arena."

"What I do with Madalene is none of your business. I intend to marry her as soon as arrangements can be made, and there will be no objections to this, not even from you. Do I make myself clear?" Peter suddenly chuckled, maliciously, "Could it be that you want her for yourself? I remember how you used to feel about her. It's laughable to even imagine her with you, Fatboy."

Michael was used to his spiteful comments. It was pointless to respond to them. "You know I will do anything you say. I just thought you should be aware of public opinion. I didn't say it was my opinion also. Nevertheless, I admit you've taken me by surprise. Let's discuss the wedding arrangements then." Casually, Michael picked up a chunk of bread and dipped it into the cold, mangled egg on his plate.

Peter sat down next to him and began to visibly relax. "I want to hold the wedding in the Arena. I'm sure the irony of that will please you. Everyone who's invited will attend the ceremony, and then a lavish reception afterwards in the Palace ballroom. Somehow I think a honeymoon will be out of the question." A deep sigh came from Peter's lips, "I'm still hoping there's a way to make Madalene cooperate, but if not, I'll carry out my threat. She'll be dragged in and chained to one of the stakes during the ceremony. We'll decorate the stakes to keep up the wedding theme, cover them with thorny roses perhaps. There'll also be celebrations held on every street. I may even open up a small section of the Arena to the public.

So they'll get to see Madalene in the Arena after all. The only problem with that might be security."

"It sounds good," said Michael, adding, "Do you intend to keep giving her Naztrolone? If you want her to have strong children for you, surely it would be better if she was drug free." It was an incredibly brave thing to say and he shuddered to think what Peter's response might be.

Peter looked thoughtfully at him, but before he could speak they both heard frantic screaming coming from outside the room. "She's reached the point where she desperately needs another fix. I didn't think it would be long in coming. It will be difficult to control her, but you're right, for once. *You're* going to wean her off Naztrolone for me."

"Me! I'm not trying to be difficult, Peter, but how am I supposed to do that? Everyone knows that it's nearly impossible to get someone off Naztrolone." Michael wanted to add that it had been the wrong drug to use on Madalene in the first place, but he didn't dare. "Madalene could die or go insane during the process. Your bride wouldn't look good snivelling and dribbling her way through the ceremony. You'd be a laughing stock."

Peter glared at him, "The wedding will take place in two months time. You have until then. I need not remind you of the consequence of failure."

"I'm well aware of my fate if I fail," said Michael, snappily, looking down at his plate. "But don't go blaming me if I succeed and she's *too* difficult to handle."

Expecting a terse response he looked up, but Peter had left the table and gone to the door to speak to the same guards he'd seen earlier. Stephen Drake was dead then. A moment's sorrow hit him, but he let it pass. This was not the right time for grief. Michael saw Peter hand them a packet of white powder and issue brief instructions. One of the guards asked a question and Peter returned to the table, poured a glass of water and took it back to the guard.

By now the screaming had reached such frantic proportions, Michael covered his ears with his hands. Seconds later, they were removed by Peter. "It works quickly. We'll not be troubled by the noise much longer. Now you can see why I've decided to take Madalene off the drug."

Michael was about to say more on the subject when, mercurial as ever, Peter's thoughts turned to other matters. "I hear the Provoke army is still causing problems. Last night they destroyed my beautiful statue in Hyde Park, and they continue to clear my Sanctum Guards off the street every night; I believe fifty have been killed since we captured Madalene. As for the northern part of the army, they're running amok under the direction of Elgin and Bertha. I thought the army would collapse without Madalene, but it appears not. There's a chance they could ruin my wedding day and that must not be allowed to happen. Call a meeting of the Inner Sanctum for this afternoon; we will discuss strategies for finishing off the army *and* the writing group once and for all."

"Destroying the army will not endear you to Madalene," said Michael, resentfully. Peter was issuing one instruction after another, forgetting that he was still trying to carry out the dozen instructions issued the night before.

"No. But it might win her respect, and with respect comes love. Madalene understands the rules of engagement, she always has. Anyway, I am not asking *you* to deal with the army. You have your task. Get on with it."

Wasn't asking him to deal with the army now, but it was only a matter of time…Michael rose from his chair, preparing to leave, and then he stopped. A sudden idea struck him and for a few seconds he struggled with it: then resolutely he sat back down again and said, "I need assistance. With your permission, I'm going to call Sam File. You remember him, he's the man you made your Head Consultant when you set up the Sanctum's private hospital. If Sam agrees to help me get Madalene off Naztrolone, I'd like to have her taken there immediately."

Peter looked thoughtful. It was obvious he didn't like the idea of losing Madalene, however temporary. Michael willed him to agree. Sam File was probably the only man who could withdraw the drug from Madalene, and keep her sane and healthy at the same time.

"I'll call Sam and insist he takes her. You are to get Madalene to the hospital. I want guards inside the hospital and in the grounds as well. If the Provoke army got word she was there, they might attempt to rescue her. I cannot allow that to happen."

Impulsively, Peter strode out and began to issue fresh instructions to his guards. Reluctantly, Michael followed and watched as they pulled Madalene out of the cupboard and started to carry her down to a transporter. She was unconscious by now; her broken hand in such a mess, Michael wondered how Peter was going to put a wedding ring on her finger. Probably he'd put the ring on the other hand, and then break that one too. It would certainly be an innovative wedding rite. Turning, he found Peter had gone back into the room and closed the door. With a scowl, Michael hurried after the guards.

The call to Sam was brief. Sam File was a no-nonsense sort of man, and he made it clear that taking Madalene off Naztrolone could be fatal.

"Why on earth did you give her Naztrolone? Madalene killed my son you know, and his wife, Arleen. Hedgewick shootings. I ought to *let* her die, but why should she have an easy death? Just you make sure when you execute her, it's as horrible as you can make it. I want to enjoy every moment."

Peter made no mention of the wedding in case Sam changed his mind. Obviously like the rest of the public, Sam believed Madalene's appearance in the Arena wasn't far away. In a way that was now true, but he'd be shocked when he got a wedding invitation. Peter smiled at the thought.

"I'm going to have to substitute lesser drugs into her system to start with. That's never been tried before. It might just work. They'll be expensive though."

"I'll pay the price. Just do whatever it takes Sam," said Peter, coolly. "By the way, she has a valuable ring on a badly broken hand. You can fix the hand, but make sure the ring stays there." Sam began to ask questions, but Peter ignored him and ended the call. If Sam fixed the hand, he could put her wedding ring on that finger, but if Madalene continued to cause trouble, he'd have the hand broken again.

Left alone in the room, he felt strangely bereft. Then her first husband, Bren, came to mind, and Peter heard once again the words he had spoken. 'I marry the most beautiful woman who ever lived and I'm the envy of every man around me. They have their showpiece wives, but I've got the showstopper... the showstopper...

Peter smiled in satisfaction, "I have her now. I have the showstopper. Not you. She's mine."

Chapter 25

Deception

For a long time there'd been endless pain and intense craving, and every time death approached, she'd held her arms out longingly; only to be ignored. Finally, with barely enough strength left to breathe, she sensed change. Her survival no longer depended on Naztrolone. As for Heaven? It could wait.

"Madalene? Can you hear me? Squeeze my hand just a little if you can."

The voice was Sam's. She didn't know the man, but throughout her ordeal she'd been aware that everyone called the owner of that voice, Sam. Squeeze his hand? With what? Her muscles had forgotten how to function, and yet her hand moved.

"Good girl. Yes, good." She heard someone exhale noisily and realised Sam had company. Someone she knew and didn't like much. Well didn't like at all actually. Peter Shadow. It had to be, the hairs on the back of her neck were standing up.

Sam now addressed, Peter, "You were right about her being a fighter. The withdrawal process has been traumatic - for both of us. Nearly lost her several times. Should be okay now though. Worst is over."

Peter's voice was cold, "She doesn't seem to be better, she's not even awake yet. How can you be so sure?"

"Good grief, Peter. Didn't you hear me? She almost died several times. Yesterday morning I was certain she'd gone. Madalene's unlikely to wake for several days yet. Nevertheless I can tell you now she will recover. Maybe not her left hand, your men did a good job on it. I have to say that I'm glad about that. It's her shooting hand isn't it? The hand that killed my son and…Arleen."

What you don't know is I can shoot with either hand, she thought to herself. There might come a time when them not knowing that fact would be an advantage.

"Never mind her hand; it's her sanity that worries me. Will she be normal? Mentally that is."

So Peter was afraid that withdrawal might have left her insane. Interesting, and something else she could use to her advantage.

"I thought you'd be more worried about the babies," said Sam, indignantly.

"What babies?" The tone in his voice indicated that Peter thought Sam had mental problems of his own.

Madalene tensed. Of course, she would have been given a thorough medical examination before the withdrawal programme started. Don't tell him, she urged silently. Please don't tell him. A forlorn hope, because even if she could have shouted her plea, Sam would never have kept it a secret.

"Well I presume they're your babies. How long has Madalene been in your custody? Four months now. Well she's approximately four months pregnant. If you didn't touch her, then one of your guards must have. Have you had sex with Madalene since she was captured?" These words were typical of a medic, but a gasp at the end indicated that Sam felt he might have gone too far.

An angry response quickly followed. "Not that it's your business, but of course I've had sex with her. The first night and every night since. Do you want details involving times and orifices, Sam?"

"That won't be necessary. Forgive me, Peter, I went too far. I thought that you knew about the pregnancy. Thought it was the reason for withdrawing the Naztrolone. You've been using it to control Madalene, haven't you? You should have come and seen me. There are better, less addictive drugs available for that purpose."

Peter's attention was obviously not on Sam's words. "Are you sure about this? Why did you say babies and not baby?" The anger gone, replaced by early elation.

Inwardly she groaned, and then was aware of cool air circulating around her stomach. The skin had been exposed so that Peter could see for himself. A hand caressed her belly. She did not know which man touched her.

"See, the bump is small, but you can feel the hardness of it, and there are two hearts beating in there. Madalene's lost so much weight in such a short time that she's not as big as a normal mother of twins would be at this stage. If we want the twins to survive, we're going to have get Madalene eating and keep her eating."

This time she recognised the hand that touched her; felt the trembling and suppressed excitement that beset its owner. Defiantly, she decided to refuse to eat anything, even though she knew that if he had to, he would force-feed her. *Everything* she did would be controlled by him now. Her only hope was a miscarriage. Maybe the babies had been damaged by the Naztrolone and subsequent withdrawal from it. That hope was quickly quashed.

"Have they been damaged by the drug?" said Peter, unable to hide the concern in his voice.

"No. The heartbeats are strong. Here, listen for yourself.

Cold metal on skin, ice in her veins and no way to react to either of them. Followed by silence and then an exclamation of joy. That joy hurt her more than the withdrawal process had ever done.

"I hear them. One son would have been enough, but two…"

"They might not be sons, Peter, said Sam, warningly. "We won't know until they arrive. I presume we won't now be seeing Madalene in the Arena until after the birth."

"Oh, she'll be going to the Arena and soon, but not for the reason you think." Peter said this with some force.

"Pardon?"

"Don't ask questions. You'll find out soon enough. I'm going to be a father and that pleases me enormously. Nothing must go wrong. Your only role in this is to make Madalene better quickly."

Sam snorted, "She is going to get better, but not quickly. It will be weeks before she's fully recovered and even then there might be relapses."

"If you don't want to appear at the Arena yourself, I suggest that you speed things along. Madalene is to be back with me in a week. See to it Sam."

Peter's footsteps were heard moving away and the tension inside her eased a little. Another fight was brewing and she did like a good fight. If she had her way, he would not become a father. It would be a small triumph, but a triumph nevertheless. Sam's voice whispered in her ear.

"Don't think this is over. Once the babies are born, He'll tire of you. Your reprieve is temporary, believe me."

She wasn't surprised at his words. She'd already got the gist that she wasn't Sam's favourite patient. The needle roughly jammed into her arm affirmed that. Before she could consider the implications further, she fell asleep.

Exactly one week later, she was fetched by Michael Vertex, a man she hated nearly as much as she hated Peter. She'd seen him before of course, but only now her head was clear did she actually remember him. He carried her into the bedroom; she'd previously occupied, and dumped her unceremoniously on the bed. Carefully she considered her position. Her sight was fine, as was her hearing. Mentally she was as good as she'd ever been, if not slightly sharper. Her broken right hand was healing so quickly, she knew Peter would be able to add a wedding ring to the monstrosity currently attached to her finger. She'd not be able to fire her rifle accurately with it again though. On the negative side, she was weaker than any newborn, and her speech was slurred with a tendency to stutter. It was a minor defect; she could live with and given time would probably improve.

Vertex, she couldn't bear to call this animal, Michael, had fetched a white bed gown and he began to undress her. Her hatred could not be concealed.

"You remember me at last. I thought I'd been forgotten." Casually he squeezed her breasts. "Now do you remember me properly, or do you also need to see this?"

A grin crossed his ugly face as he exposed his manhood. She had an immediate urge to castrate him, but not the strength to do it.

Besides it was important that everyone believed she was subdued and no longer a danger. The plans racing through her brain wouldn't work unless she created a false sense of security.

"N-Not much t-to remember from the l-look of it." Well she couldn't let them have it all their own way.

Covering himself up, Vertex laughed and then mimicked her, "If Peter w-would allow me t-to use it. Y-You'd remember it f-fast enough. Fortunately for you, I can't touch you...yet."

Ignoring her shudders of revulsion, he put the gown on her, making sure he touched as much as possible. Then he lay her down and moved away.

"Peter's made me responsible for your welfare, as if I didn't already have enough to do. So you'll have to get used to me touching you. Well I suppose you'll want feeding. Guards," he yelled.

Instantly, four guards came in carrying trays of food. They put them down on the small dining table, and then left the room. Every one of them flashed a look of hatred in her direction.

Vertex noticed and smiled, "Oh, they're not fond of you. Not fond at all. Your army's giving them quite a hard time at the moment. However, you'll be pleased to learn that we've finally managed to infiltrate them. An attack's been planned on the Lyric theatre, where a gala performance is taking place tonight to celebrate your wedding nuptials. We will of course be awaiting their arrival with great pleasure and even greater force. It's a shame you can't be there, but Sam forbade it, said you'd be prone to infection and that might hurt these babies."

Gently, he raised the bed gown and trailed his fingers across her stomach, then sleazily ran them lower. "Shame. How ironic if you'd been killed by your own army. How amusing as well."

"I-If you don't g-get your hands off me..." Talking was so difficult, so tiring.

"You'll what? Tell Peter. The man's still worried about your mental health; he'd never believe I dared touch you. So t-t-tell him."

211

Vertex was probably right, but a little too full of bravado. She knew if Peter caught him touching her, there'd be trouble. A noise at the door made him remove his hand and lower the gown quickly.

"Ah, Fatboy and I see my fiancée's with you. What a joy to have you back with me, Madalene." In his hand was a massive bunch of red roses. "For you, the mother of my babies."

"I-I…"

"You love the flowers. I knew you would. The trouble with you is no-one's ever treated you like a proper woman before. I intend to rectify that. Sam's informed me that you need to stay in bed: he's also told me that sex won't hurt the babies, so no worries on that front. Now I'm not going to make you sit at the table, but you have to eat something. I've been told they found it impossible to get you to eat in the hospital. That won't be the case here."

Going over to the table, Peter carefully selected a bowl of soup and brought it over to her. "We'll start gently, move onto solids later."

The look in his eyes was strange, almost soft and loving. Lifting a spoon up to her mouth, he said, "Only the soup, Madalene. If not for your sake, remember our babies need nourishment."

This Peter was so hypnotic and bewitching, she almost wanted to please him, but the thought of food, after so long not eating, made her feel sick. It wasn't even defiance, she genuinely could not eat. "P-Peter…" The first time she had spoken his name kindly and he knew it. Encouragingly, he smiled at her. "I-I can't. Maybe I-later…"

"No. They neglected you in hospital. That will not happen here. Open your mouth and let me put the food in."

A kind of desperation crossed his face and she could tell that for once he knew she was not defying him, "Y-You don't understand. The d-drug, the illness. T-This…it's n-not my f-fault."

The familiar cruelty returned to his expression. "What I understand is that you refuse to eat and provide nourishment for my babies. I will give you one more chance. Take a spoonful of soup, or I will find a different way to feed you."

212

If she cooperated, he would leave her alone and she needed to be alone to think. Her army were going to walk into a trap tonight. If she could get word to them… But how when her own situation was so hopeless. Her mouth opened wide, but as the spoon came towards it, her brain rebelled and her mouth closed again. The soup spilled down the white cloth of the bed gown.

Peter was furious, "I've never seen anyone force-fed before, and I look forward to it. You know what to do, Fatboy. Get on with it."

A vicious look crossed Vertex's face, "I'm sure the guards would be better at this than me. My podgy hands would make me clumsy. I could cause harm… They have been instructed on use of the equipment…"

"Stop blathering, Fatboy. Fetch the equipment and bring the guards in here."

Vertex left the room and could be heard talking to the men outside.

"It doesn't have to be done, Madalene. Not this way. You've suffered enough. Take the easy way out and eat something. If you don't like soup, I'll fetch you something else."

Again that softness that spoke of genuine concern for her. This man was truly psychotic, changeable as storm winds. "I-I can't…Tomorrow…I'll t-try t-tomorrow." Damn this stutter and the slurred speech, it was making her sound pathetic.

"Then forgive me, Madalene," he removed the roses from her lap, placing them on one of the bedside tables. "This has to be done and will be done three times a day or more, until you eat properly again and make my babies fat and strong."

Vertex returned, carrying a thick pipe made of rubber with a large funnel inserted at one end. "This was found in a museum. I believe it was last used on suffragettes nearly a hundred and fifty years ago. Still it looks good enough to use again."

The guards followed Vertex into the room, one of them carrying a large jug of steaming liquid. "Its weak porridge," explained Vertex, looking intently at her. "We've added a tiny amount of sugar to make it sweeter, not that you'll get to taste it. Well Peter, will she eat what's on the table, or do you want her to have the porridge?"

That Vertex was also a torturer was clearly on display. This was the stuff he did best. She wanted to thwart him, especially after his crudity earlier. All she had to do was eat the soup and watch his face crumble. But then she'd end up pleasing Peter and she didn't want to do that either. Eat the soup, she told herself. It was too late. Peter had given her time, but seen no sign of acquiescence. His only thought now was for his babies.

"Feed Madalene the porridge," Peter said, again that mix of cruelty and reluctance in his voice. "Don't look at me like that, Madalene. You have to be fed."

Peter moved to a nearby armchair and Vertex took another one by his side. For a moment the guards did nothing. Madalene watched them, warily. They wanted to hurt her so badly, it radiated from them, like heat coming from a kettle.

"Begin." Peter waved his hand.

The guards included the powerful man who had broken her hand, his face was gleeful. Violently they forced her down onto the bed. Then while two guards held her still, the powerful one picked up the tube and forced it up her nose. Tears ran from her eyes and her nose bled so much, she thought he'd broken it. Give me the soup was the only thought she was capable of as the pipe was pushed down the back of her throat and into her gullet. She couldn't breathe and began to fight as she panicked, but she was held still with ease. The feel of the pipe was indescribable as it eased down into her stomach. But then suddenly she could breathe again. She could not mentally handle this invasion of her body, so still she struggled.

Worse was to come. The porridge was poured into the funnel and her stomach ached and heaved as it filled with liquid. For a while, she thought it would never stop. With the jug empty, or so she thought, the powerful man roughly removed the tube. Her nose was bleeding profusely and her throat raw with pain. She tried to get up, then realised the guards were now chaining her to the bed.

"You can't get up, Madalene," said Vertex, his face flushed with pleasure. "We have to keep you there until the food's absorbed. An hour should do the trick."

She tried to say something, but was unable to speak at all. It hurt to try. Her eyes searched out Peter and found him. There was no longer any sign of compassion or regret. He had enjoyed watching her being force-fed as much as Vertex had done. No doubt having discovered such a treat, he would use it on others. Instructing the guards not to leave her alone, he stood, preparing to leave. Vertex stood with him.

"I hate to leave you like this, my love, but I have a show to attend tonight and there are preparations I need to make. Your army means to attack this event, so we have to be ready for them. With luck your sister, Holan, will be joining us for dinner tomorrow. Won't that be nice? I do hope she's fond of porridge." He laughed at his pathetic joke, and then noticed her look of scorn. Slowly he walked over to the bedside, and never once did she let her eyes leave his face. To her satisfaction, she saw that she had unnerved him. If he thought that one bout of forced-feeding was enough to weaken her, he was mistaken. His reaction was swift and vindictive. "You do realise that you haven't eaten nearly enough, Madalene. This process will have to be repeated at least two more times today, supper and a light snack." The guards around her grinned at the prospect of humiliating her again, the grins blurring as her strength ran out. The room began to spin and she tried to focus on Peter to stop it. His face was also blurred, but just as her eyelids closed, she spotted a tiny hint of sorrow on his face.

Madalene braced herself as the guards prepared to give her breakfast. The pain in her nose and throat was so excruciating, that she did not think she could endure being force-fed yet again. Fortunately the guards had changed during the night and these men were a lot gentler with her. Even so, the process was just as agonising and humiliating. She had to find a way to persuade Peter to stop this and let her feed herself again. Even being fed by the hideous Vertex would be preferable.

She was lying on the bed, chained and with a full to overflowing stomach, when Peter entered. He smiled with delight when he saw her and dismissed the guards immediately.

215

"Ah, I see you've already eaten. I was hoping to have breakfast with you," he said, sardonically. He meant he'd hoped to watch her being force-fed again.

To Madalene's shame, she heard the words, "N-No m-more, Peter, I'll eat p-properly. At the t-table with y-you." They were whispered words, squeezed from damaged vocal chords, but she saw he'd heard them and was surprised.

"Well, that's good news. Prove it to me though. I'll bring you something to eat, and if you manage it, no more force-feeding."

She wanted to protest that her stomach was bursting at the moment. He knew the guards had only just finished feeding her. Her voice was not prepared to co-operate a second time. Peter headed for the table and returned with a slimy chunk of snail on a fork.

"It's a very fashionable food at the moment," he said, popping it into her mouth. "Eat and swallow it, then no more force-feeding."

She retched violently.

"Now that's no good. Come on; chew the flesh with your teeth."

She tried to swallow it quickly, but it wouldn't pass her mutilated throat. Using her teeth, she attempted to make the mass in her mouth smaller. Sweat stood out on her brow and her heart was beating rapidly.

"Most of your army managed to escape us last night. Somehow they were forewarned. You'll be pleased to hear that we did manage to pick up ten of them, the ones who couldn't run as fast as the others."

This should have been bad news for him, but Peter seemed delighted and pleased with himself. Why? She increased her efforts and again made an attempt at swallowing. It simply wouldn't go down her throat. Looking into Peter's eyes, she saw that he had known from the beginning her throat would be too sore for swallowing.

"Are you sure you can eat that?" he asked in feigned, solicitous tones.

216

She thought of that thick tube being inserted into her nose again and strained hard to swallow. To her horror it went the other way and began to seep past her lips and onto her bed gown.

"Oh well," he said, happily. "I'll see you for dinner. I might even do the pouring. And by the way, we have a guest for dinner – your son, Jinn."

.

Chapter 26

Disbelief and Doubt

Christian was distraught, hardly daring to believe what he'd just heard, what they'd all heard. Yet the radio broadcast couldn't have been clearer, Madalene was finally making her appearance in the Arena. It was going to be a special event for elite spectators, namely the entire Sanctum and their wealthy supporters, though mention had been made of a small selection of the public being let in. It couldn't be true. Couldn't be. The silence and shock around him showed that others felt the same way.

Every day, since her capture, he'd dreaded hearing this news. And as time passed, his only consolation had been the thought that Madalene was proving difficult to break. Never once had he imagined that instead of being tortured, Madalene was writhing around in Shadowman's bed…And she must have been good at it… Madalene was going to the Arena to *marry* Shadowman. Worse, she was said to be carrying his twins.

The broadcast had instructed people to take Madalene to their hearts. She was a reformed person who regretted her past and bitterly rued the day she'd set up the notorious Provoke army. Madalene had betrayed them. Bitter tears came to his eyes; the tears blurred his vision, so he didn't notice that Holan had come over, until she sat down by his side. As usual she'd been drinking, but it looked like the news had sobered her.

"She took us all in, didn't she? All the time we thought she was some kind of female protagonist, she was actually working for Shadowman," he said, adding angrily. "I wish we'd succeeded that day we tried to hang her."

"Don't be stupid, Christian. If Madalene had betrayed us, we'd have all seen the inside of the Arena long ago. No hide-out's been touched, and she's the only one that knows the whereabouts of all of them. The last captured member of the army is *her*."

"Then why is she marrying him? Why is she carrying his babies? Shadowman isn't stupid. He wouldn't invent stuff like that, not even for propaganda purposes." Even saying it made him feel sick.

"I don't know," said Holan, dejectedly. "I hardy believe what we've just heard myself. All those months wondering why she hadn't appeared in the Arena and now this."

"He raped her, hurt her, that's why she's pregnant." Forlorn, but nevertheless it was hope. "To protect the babies, she's agreed to marry him."

"Perhaps..." said, Holan, tentatively. "But there's something between those two, in spite of the fact that he's at least four years older than her. It started when we were at school."

Christian saw Holan's eyes fill with recollection and steeled himself to hear what she had to say. He hadn't known that Holan and Madalene had been at school with Shadowman.

"The hatred between them was over the top, melodramatic you could say. But they both seemed to enjoy it, even when it escalated. They say that love and hate follow each others footsteps...Haven't you ever wondered...?"

"Wondered what?" Christian asked, feeling a tingle of apprehension run down his spine.

"Look over there, where Jinn is sat discussing this same piece of news with Ellyn. What do you see?"

Christian looked, but all he saw was Jinn chatting as intensely to Ellyn, as he was doing to Holan, and as others were doing all over the room. "Jinn and Ellyn talking like us and everyone else in this damn place. What am I supposed to see, Holan?"

"Study Jinn and think," said Holan, quietly.

Again Christian looked at Jinn. Sensing he was being watched, Jinn turned and looked back, questioningly. Only then did Christian see it...It had been there all along and he'd never noticed, until now. Christian mouthed 'Are you okay', Jinn nodded and turned back to Ellyn. "He's..."

"Yes he is, isn't he? The spitting image of Peter Shadow. Same grey eyes. Same facial expressions. Everything's there, except the arrogance and the brutality."

"Shadowman is Jinn's father?" The revelation shocked him. Again he looked over at Jinn, but now he knew the truth, the facts were undeniable.

Holan nodded, smiling at him gently and sadly. "You love Madalene, don't you? And you imagined that one day she would stop grieving for Bren and notice you. I bet you've even imagined her as the mother of *your* children, despite the fact that you're at least ten years younger than she is."

Christian nodded his head, but the lump in his throat prevented speech.

"I've often spoken of my sister as a dangerous woman. What I've never said is that she was a crazy and dangerous child. I know the reasons she murdered my father, she told me them, and she *was* justified in what she did. There's no denying that. But basically my mother and father were kind, decent people. Madalene twisted them up like knots on a piece of string, until they had nowhere to go. How could they love her?"

Despite his sorrow, Christian was attentive. It was interesting to hear a little of Madalene's history. He stayed silent hoping Holan would continue.

"This hate thing with Peter Shadow continued for a long time. She twisted him up the same way she did our parents. Did the same thing to his friends too. Whenever they could get hold of her she was beaten or abused, which as they were older and bigger than her was often. I couldn't stop it, no-one could."

Christian looked up as Holan went silent. She looked deeply ashamed of herself. He went to say something comforting, but she was continuing her tale.

"Madalene's mental state got so bad, Mother and Father began to discuss putting her in an institution. The only reason it never happened was my Mother's fear, that if they found out Madalene had been beaten; they'd take me away as well."

Holan sighed, "I shared a room with Madalene and one day I saw her diary, hidden at the bottom of the wardrobe. I shouldn't have, but I read it anyway. Mostly it was the sort of puerile junk you'd expect from a twelve year old, but then I found something completely different. I can't remember the precise words she used, but I was stunned to read that she was imagining what it would be like to fuck Peter Shadow. I'm sorry if that shocks you, Christian, but it was the word she used."

"I don't believe it. That's not a word she ever uses, though just about everyone else does."

"She wasn't saying it, Christian. Just writing the word in what she thought was her private diary. It confirmed my love-hate theory. Anyway, a few months later, Madalene went missing after school one day. We were so worried, we called the police out to look for her, and those were the days when we had a police force, not Sanctum Guards. After all Madalene was a twelve year old girl, albeit a crazy one. They couldn't find her, but the next afternoon she walked in as if nothing had happened, though her school uniform lay in shreds, her throat was scarred and she was covered with cuts and bruises. When asked where she'd been, she angrily told us to mind our own business. The police questioned her, but nothing could persuade her to talk. Not even Father, who gave her a harsh beating later, when the police had gone."

Christian interrupted her. "That was brutal! Didn't it occur to any of you that something awful had happened to Madalene? That she needed time to recover before she could talk about it? Well, did you *ever* find out what had happened?"

"Yes, Father was brutal, but *her* arrogance drove him to it. When the beating started, I hid in the bedroom we shared. The screaming could still be heard, but at least the sound was muffled. Then I spotted Madalene's schoolbag. Again, I shouldn't have, but I opened it. Inside I found her knickers, covered with blood and torn to shreds. I was fourteen, and girls of fourteen talk a lot about this stuff... Madalene had had sex, and the blood I saw showed it was her first time. Later, when she was lying face down on her bed, her back more bloody than usual, I questioned her, showing her the evidence I'd found. "This is why you won't tell anyone what happened. I know because I read your diary. You said you wanted to fuck Peter Shadow, and now you've done it. You can't deny it. I

221

have the proof right here. Did you mock him when you'd finished? Is that why you got beaten?" I expected her to blush or cry, deny it, something normal."

"And did she? Deny it?" Christian didn't like what he was hearing, but was fascinated nevertheless.

Holan stared at him for a long while, as if reluctant to complete the story, "Madalene glared at me and then said, 'So! I had sex with Michael Vertex too, you know the one they call 'Blubber boy', and with Edgar Heaton, and with Barton Lacey…' She reeled off a list of names, all Peter Shadow's friends. Then seeing my shocked face, she laughed, hysterically. 'I loved it. Couldn't get enough of it. Does that satisfy your incredible nosiness?' So many. How could she have…with so many? It had to be that she wanted to please or impress Peter, or at least that's what I thought at the time."

Christian was horrified. Surely the truth of the matter was that Madalene had been raped. But why hadn't she told anyone? And why tell Holan, her sister, that she'd enjoyed the experience. Then he realised it had been an act of defiance, the only way a twelve year old knew how to deal with what had happened. Holan had been too young and inexperienced to recognise it. As these thoughts raced through his head, he realised, Holan, was still talking.

"She never spoke of it again. When Father wasn't looking, I threw the underwear on a bonfire he'd made, thinking to spare Madalene further trouble. I couldn't save her from pregnancy though. The disgrace attached to a twelve year old being pregnant has always been enormous, so Madalene was sent away and Mother went with her. When they returned Mother pretended Jinn was hers, but no-one was fooled, it was well known that Madalene was his mother. Watching Jinn grow up, I often wondered which of the boys involved was his father. It's only since he's been with us that I realised Peter's the one. Face it Christian, she could be marrying Peter Shadow because she wants to. Damn I'm tired, I need a drink."

As Holan walked away, Christian felt strangely consoled. He was certain now that Madalene wasn't doing anything willingly. She'd been raped again and was being forced into a marriage she didn't want. If he could organise seats for the public section at the wedding, maybe he could find a way to rescue her. It was a slim hope, but hope nevertheless…

222

"They're putting a show on at the Lyric theatre to celebrate Shadowman's engagement. Madalene will be there. It's our chance," said Christian, excitedly.

"Our chance to do what?" said Holan, trying not to shudder. She knew exactly what he was going to say, he'd done nothing *but* talk about rescuing Madalene in recent days.

"Our chance to rescue Madalene of course. Come on, Holan. You said it was suicidal to attack the wedding ceremony, think how much easier attacking the theatre will be. The tickets I'm trying to procure for the wedding won't be necessary." Flinging himself down besides her, he smiled happily.

Holan sighed. Christian envisioned Madalene as a damsel in distress, and himself as her knight errant. Madalene, a damsel in distress? The idea would have been laughable, if the whole thing wasn't so bloody tragic. In her own mind she had no doubt that Madalene was marrying Peter Shadow willingly, but nothing she said mattered. And Torrin wasn't helping; he positively encouraged Christian's maniacal ideas and she didn't quite understand why. Unless it was simply that Torrin wanted to atone for betraying Madalene. An attack on the Lyric was nearly as suicidal as an attack on the Arena, especially if it was done at a time when Peter Shadow would be there, security for the event would be paramount.

"Don't look like that, Holan. You love Madalene more than I do, and you're not afraid of danger. Hannah will plan this out properly for us, I know she will…"

"Hannah will veto the idea. Look Christian, if we want to commit suicide, wouldn't it be better just to take our knives and apply them to our wrists?" He simply smiled at her and shook his head. She didn't seem to be able to dent him; he looked like a little boy waiting for Wintertide. "Let's put it before the whole army and see what they have to say. But understand this, Christian, there's a lot of doubt circulating about Madalene at the moment. You weren't the only one who thought she'd betrayed us. You and your immediate group of friends, Luke and co., Hannah, Jinn and Ellyn, and me, of course, are about her only supporters at present. The men we picked up the other day aren't helping. They say they've seen Madalene being driven to the Sanctum's private hospital for a check-up and she was looking well and happy."

Christian scowled. "What men? Will and Rawl? We don't know them well enough to trust them yet... Yes I was there, they were about to be shot and they had been badly beaten. What I don't understand is why they hadn't been shot already. It's not like the Sanctum Guards hang about when they're in a killing mood."

"Rawl said the triggers on the weapons got stuck..."

"Yeah, and like how many times has that happened before. Very convenient and damned lucky, don't you think?"

"I might if it didn't turn out that they were also members of the original group, Christian." Rawl and Will were nice boys and had settled in quickly. Nothing they had done had given her any cause for doubt.

"Torrin's never seen them before and he was ranked nearly as high as Alan in the original group. I've never seen them before and neither have you." Christian's pleasant mood seemed to have vanished.

"People greeted them like old friends."

"No. *They* greeted people like they were old friends, there's a difference."

"Stop being difficult, Christian. Our army's grown so fast; can you say that you know everyone in it? You're being defensive because it's Madalene they're talking about."

In the end, the vote to attack the Lyric theatre was swung by Jinn. He'd argued that it wasn't fair to judge his Mother's actions when she wasn't able to defend herself. At that point they'd swung into action. The plan was so simple, it could possibly work.

There was no chance of getting into or near the Lyric theatre itself. A quick reconnoitre had revealed that full security was already in operation there. However it was clear that Shadowman intended to show Madalene off to the crowd before entering the theatre, and therein lay their only chance. The couple would be brought to the entrance, probably in one of Shadowman's luxurious transporters. As they stepped out, they would be exposed to the crowd for several minutes, if the length of red carpet was anything to go by. Obviously the couple would be surrounded by guards, but if pandemonium was suddenly generated by several, well-placed smoke bombs, then armed members of the army would get a chance to grab Madalene and throw her into a transporter of their own, one left nearby. Hannah explained all of this and added extra details, warning them that success required concentration on their goal. That goal was to retrieve Madalene; it was *not* to make an attempt on Shadowman's life however tempted they were to try it.

The whole thing was still suicidal in Holan's opinion, and as far as she could see the people in the greatest danger were those who'd volunteered to grab Madalene, namely Luke, Adrian and Torrin. Strangely, Christian hadn't volunteered for this task and she resolved to ask him why at the earliest opportunity. The pandemonium makers were also at great risk; these were Rawl, Will, Adam, Mark and Jinn. She'd tried several times to dissuade Jinn from taking this particular role, but as the action involved the rescue of his Mother, he wasn't having any of it. So much for being leader, she thought, people seemed to do what they wanted, with or without her say so.

Walking through the hide-out, Holan noticed that everyone was busy doing something involved with the Lyric theatre action, except Christian, who was sat in the kitchen, chewing on a piece of bread and drinking potato whiskey.

"And what are you going to be doing on the night, Christian? You know, the night we rescue your great love." All the sarcasm she could manage went into her voice and she expected nothing less than a sarcastic retort.

"We were good in bed together, weren't we, Holan. Why don't we do it anymore?" He'd obviously had more than one glass of the potato whiskey.

"It was traumatic after Madalene was captured. It didn't seem right somehow. Besides you'd only have been thinking of her. That's quite off-putting for a woman you know."

"You always knew I was in love with your sister and you didn't let that put you off before. I don't suppose there's any chance…"

"Not one," said Holan, laughing at his cheek. "We're better off as friends. Sex complicates things."

"It's nice though," said Christian, with a lustful sigh.

As Holan walked away, she realised that Christian had distracted her, so that he didn't have to answer the original question. When she turned back to the kitchen, he'd gone. Almost immediately she bumped into Jinn and Ellyn. They were holding hands and looked rather sweet together. Lately they'd been the butt of several jokes, especially from Luke and Adrian, but even the usually quiet, Adam and Mark, had been joining in, and Malcolm had also had his say. The hand holding had started the jokes, then Jinn and Ellyn had been seen kissing, and finally the couple had taken to sleeping in the same bed together. Luke and Adrian had gone wild, joyfully complaining about how noisy they were, and aping Jinn's groans of lust and Ellyn's squeals of joy. And of course the invites to Ellyn to try a real man, had increased enormously. Holan smiled; under Ellyn's influence, Jinn had reddened, but taken it all in the good spirit it was intended in.

"Holan," he said, stopping her in her tracks. "We will get Madalene back won't we?"

"Of course we will, Jinn. With you as one of our pandemonium makers, we're bound to."

His face twisted in anguish, "Don't do that, Holan. That's the sort of platitude you used to give me in my schooldays."

Giving him a hard stare, she said, "What we're doing is akin to suicide. There's too much luck involved for my liking. I would gladly pull this action and begin planning something with better odds of success." His face fell, as did Ellyn's, who still stood holding his hand.

"You want your Mother back badly, don't you, Jinn?" said Holan, with some sympathy now.

"She's never liked me much, but that doesn't matter. It's good when she's proud of me. I'd like us to rescue her, and for her to be proud that I was involved in it. And if she's pregnant with twins like they say she is, she'll need me to look after her."

Tears came to Holan's eyes. Madalene might not love or care for Jinn, but undoubtedly he loved her.

226

As leader, Holan had to stay behind and coordinate the action. Twenty men and women were involved this time. It was meant to be twenty-one including Christian, whose idea it had all been in the first place, but there was no sign of *him*. Holan was furious, when she got her hands on him; he'd better explain himself fast, otherwise she'd turn him into a eunuch. Near her sat Ellyn, acting as theoretical co-coordinator. Ellyn had wanted to be part of the action, but Holan had been worried that she'd distract Jinn and put him in danger. Ellyn was reading a picture book. Seeing this, Holan was just thinking that she ought to teach the girl to read, when Christian burst in, his face burning with urgency.

"Quickly. Fetch your weapons," he said with a shout. "We've been betrayed. They know what we intend to do. They're waiting for us. If we hurry we may be able to pull everyone out."

Holan moved quickly, as did Ellyn and the others. "What are you playing at Christian? Why do you think it's a trap, now at the last minute?"

"You wouldn't listen to me, so I undertook my own investigation. Rawl and Will are traitors, just like I said they were."

"Don't be stupid, Christian. They've gone out with the others." Even as Holan spoke, they were exiting the hide-out.

"Only to make sure that army members are recognised when they appear at the Lyric. They'll probably use hand signals. I know what hand signal I'm going to give them." Christian ran a finger up and down the trigger of his weapon, making his meaning clear.

"And why should I take your word for it?" said Holan, exasperatedly. "You have no proof."

Reaching a hand into his pocket, Christian pulled out two cards and almost threw them at her. "This is what I've been doing, Holan. I knew you'd never believe me, so I found you proof."

Holan glanced at the cards, and then stopped in shock. The cards were Sanctum Guard identification; the photographs on them were Will and Rawl. "Run," she yelled. "We've got to get to the Lyric before anything starts."

Nearing the theatre, they separated and began to walk casually. A few suspicious looks passed their way, but by and large they went unnoticed in an excitable crowd. With ease they sent Luke, Adrian, Torrin and their back up team, off to the hide-out. Ellyn managed to find Mark and the men guarding his back, but as a loud roar went up from the crowd, everyone realised they were too late to reach Jinn, Adam and *their* back ups.

A large transporter drove up to the front of the theatre. Holan watched with trepidation as guards exited it and then stood aside. Peter Shadow came into view. He smiled for the crowd and then extended his arm to the transporter. Holan could hardly breathe as she anticipated seeing her sister again, but it wasn't Madalene who followed Peter, it was Michael Vertex instead. The disappointment of the crowd was audible. Hearing it, Peter spoke up,

"I understand that many of you have turned up tonight hoping for a glimpse of my beautiful and quite notorious fiancée. Alas, I am as upset as the rest of you, but Madalene is indisposed and cannot be here tonight. I'm sure however that a wonderful show awaits us and Madalene would want us all to enjoy ourselves." With that, he began to walk down the red carpet, stopping from time to time to talk to members of the crowd.

Indisposed? Holan had seen the look Michael had given Peter, when he'd heard those words. An evil chuckle had been the response. Madalene *wasn't* participating readily in Peter's schemes. Christian had been right to want to rescue her. Looking up in horror, she saw Rawl raise his arm twice and Will raise his once. It was the signal. A whistle blew, and before anyone could use the smoke bombs, Jinn, Adam and the men watching their backs were surrounded and held at gunpoint. Members of the crowd screamed with fright, but curiosity kept each one of them rooted to the spot. Holan moved quietly away, and signalled, unobtrusively, to the remaining army members to do the same. Getting away was a slow agonising process as none of them dared draw attention to themselves. Everything had to look natural, and they prayed that neither Rawl nor Will spotted them. Christian returned to her side when they were safely out of sight, as did Ellyn.

"They've got Jinn," said Ellyn, beginning to sob.

"Not here Ellyn," said Holan, harshly. "Don't draw attention to yourself, we're still in danger."

"Madalene didn't turn up. This is my fault. I instigated this action. We've lost Jinn, Mark and the others for nothing," said Christian, bitterly.

"We'd have lost all of them if it hadn't been for you, Christian. I was so stupid trusting those bastards. Madalene wouldn't have made a mistake like that...And you *were* right to want to help Madalene escape. From the look I saw on Michael Vertex's face tonight, I have a feeling that Madalene's having a really bad time at the moment."

Chapter 27

A Much Loved Son

"Well this is cosy. Here I am about to have lunch with my future wife and stepson," said Peter Shadow.

The words might have been pleasant, but the tone was not. Jinn sat trembling at the table; facing the man they called Shadowman. The man who had killed Bren and Hayla. The man who from his look, intended to kill him. Feeling he was being watched, Jinn turned and looked over at the bed. When he'd been brought into this room, she'd been sleeping, and seeing how content she looked, Jinn had been convinced that those who called his Mother a traitor, were correct. Now she was awake, he saw something different. Madalene was pale, so devoid of colour she was almost transparent. Her eyes were dull and black. Her nose was badly swollen and a thin trickle of blood ran from the right side of her lips.

"M-Mother…?" he said, tentatively. A faint smile of reassurance, that increased the trickle of blood, appeared on her face.

"Y-You'll b-be okay Jinn…"

Her voice was hoarse, her words whispered, and never had he thought to hear his mother stutter like that. "What have you done to her?" he said, angrily. His terror temporarily forgotten. "What have you done?"

"Now, now, Jinn. Mummy's not well at the moment. It's upsetting, I know, but believe me I'm doing everything in my power to make her better."

"You're torturing her. That's why she's like this." Again he looked over at the bed. The agonised expression on Madalene's face was unmistakeable. If the army could see her like this, not one of them would dare call her traitor.

"Oh, the overactive imagination of the young. Your Mother hasn't been near my torture chambers. What you're seeing is due to

230

a little drug habit of your Mother's that had to be dealt with. She's a withdrawing addict," Shadowman said this to him, with a look of sympathy that indicated he was sure Jinn had come across this before.

Bren had got so angry at Madalene for taking drugs. Jinn had always been afraid that Bren would throw his mother out of the house if she didn't stop taking them. He remembered his own disgust when she was being sick everywhere; how she couldn't control her bowels, so she smelled bad all the time. Worse, he remembered the violence of her temper. Never had she looked as bad as this, but Shadowman's empathy seemed sincere.

"Come Jinn, help yourself to food." Delicious smells rose into the air as lids were taken off dishes.

"I thought we were waiting for Mother to join us..." Again Jinn looked to Madalene for guidance. He was hungry and longing to eat, but would not do so without her permission. Madalene used her hand to indicate that it was fine for him to go ahead.

"Your Mother will get her lunch in a minute. You'll see. Now eat. I know only too well how ravenous young boys can be."

Something about the way Shadowman said this was disturbing, but as he piled food onto his plate, Jinn followed his example. There was so much food to choose from. Breads of different varieties, plates of beef, pork and lamb, some in sauces, others not. Kidneys, liver, sausages, pies, potatoes. Dishes of fish and dishes of eggs. Shadowman even poured him a glass of beer. After a swig of beer, Jinn got stuck in. Food was so plain in the hide-outs, he couldn't help himself. He was just getting second helpings of everything, watched by a highly amused Shadowman, when four guards entered, carrying a steaming jug and a strange contraption.

A gasp came from the bed. Looking over, Jinn saw pain and dread clearly outlined on his Mother's face.

"G-Get him out of h-here P-Peter. G-Get him out...H-He mustn't s-see this..." Madalene's desperation was clear, but Jinn didn't understand its cause. It was something to do with the guards and that contraption, but what?

231

"Leave him alone, Madalene. The boy's enjoying his food. He'll be happy when you're fed too."

"G-Get him o-out…"

Jinn's fork hit his plate and involuntarily he ran to his Mother's side. There had been no mistaking her distress. A guard grabbed him and hauled him roughly back to the dining table, forcing him to sit back down on his chair. Jinn went to get up, but was pushed down a second time.

Shadowman chuckled in a chilling fashion, and then said, "If you get up again, you will annoy this man. If he is annoyed your Mother will get hurt, because in his annoyance, this man will be rough with her. Now stay where you are and watch."

The guard nodded his head in agreement with Shadowman's words and moved back to the bedside. They began the force feeding process and Jinn saw the guard who had grabbed him, shove a tube viciously up Madalene's nose, blood poured out of it and she was clearly in agony.

"It would have been worse if you had angered him further," said Shadowman, sagely.

Worse? How could this be worse? He couldn't help himself, Jinn sobbed like a baby.

"There, there," said Shadowman. "Don't take on so. It looks cruel, and I will have that guard reprimanded for being so rough, but it's actually a kindness. Your Mother finds it physically impossible to eat. She'll die without nourishment and so will her babies. This is the only way to feed her. Once she gets strong she'll be able to eat normally again. You can see for yourself how thin she's become; surely you wouldn't let her starve to death."

"How many times a day do you do this to her?" asked Jinn, watching as they began to chain Madalene to the bed, and still unable to stop crying. "W-Why are they doing that to her?"

"The food has to stay in her stomach, so she needs to be kept still until the food's digested. I see that Madalene gets fed at least four times a day and occasionally throw in a snack. It looks painful, but I

232

believe she's beginning to enjoy being fed this way. Your Mother always was a little strange."

The guards chuckled at these words, as they continued to secure Madalene. Wiping his tears away, Jinn looked at Madalene and saw that she had reached the limits of her endurance. Whatever Shadowman said, this *was* torture. Then he noticed her mangled hand, still bandaged, but the ring could be clearly seen. It was held tight by a finger swollen to twice its normal size. It wasn't hard to guess what the proposal had been like. 'Will you marry me?', 'No'. Ring shoved onto finger, crack of a hammer. 'I've changed my mind, the answer's yes!'

Suddenly Jinn felt calm, from out of nowhere surfaced a part of him that was purely and uniquely formed by his Mother. What he was going to do was futile, nothing more than a gesture, but it wasn't as if there'd been any hope for him in the first place. He'd seen that after Shadowman's announcement that they were to play 'Happy Families'. Shadowman's only family lay inside Madalene's belly.

Thoughts of Ellyn came into his head and with them more tears. Who would look after her when he was gone? He'd never understood why she had chosen to be with him when there were so many good-looking men in the army, most of whom had tried it on with her. But she had, and recently they'd taken their relationship further, despite enduring incredible torment for it, particularly from Luke and Adrian. Just the thought of those two made him smile. They were clowns who lightened the mood whenever things got serious. And despite their constant tormenting, they were the friends who had helped him cope with the capture of his Mother. They would look after Ellyn for him. A thought entered his head. What if he had made Ellyn pregnant, but didn't know it? They'd never used protection. It was a nice thought and provided him with the final bit of encouragement needed.

Taking a deep breath, Jinn grabbed one of the meat cleavers, leapt up, and in seconds had it pressed against Shadowman's throat. "Let's see how you like it," he growled, frightening himself with his own menace. "Eat, and don't stop eating until I say you can." The guards left the bedside and moved slowly towards him. "Make any move and he dies instantly. Believe me I'll do it. I have nothing to lose."

233

"You've got nowhere to go, son. Put the cleaver down," said the guard who'd grabbed him earlier and hurt his Mother.

"Then come and get me, but his throat will be sliced first. You! Don't stop eating." He forced a sausage into Shadowman's open mouth. "Chew it. Get it down your throat. Now for some kidneys. All of them, I think." Strangulated noises had been coming from the bed since he'd started this. He knew Madalene was trying to stop him, but couldn't speak after the abomination that had been done to her.

"H-He wants this, J-Jinn…" Desperation had forced her voice to the surface, though it made a strangely eerie sound.

Jinn dared not look at her; he couldn't afford to lose his concentration. The guards had moved closer and they were alert, he could almost smell the adrenaline pouring off them.

"Y-You've given h-him the excuse h-he needed to kill y-you…"

Shadowman's look was malicious and triumphant. Jinn knew he had been tricked. To avoid antagonising Madalene, Shadowman needed to keep Jinn alive, unless a reasonable excuse for killing him could be found. Jinn had just provided that excuse. He realised that even the cleaver in his hand had been cunningly left on the table. Madalene had been deliberately force-fed in front of him. He had walked into a pre-arranged trap laid by a manipulative, evil man, and was now beginning to panic. Shadowman finished his mouthful and gave him a pitying smile.

"And what shall I eat next, Jinn?" he asked, as if it was a game.

"M-Mother. What shall I do? I don't know what to do." The cleaver in his hand trembled violently and Shadowman's smile grew broader. The guards tried to rush him, but Peter signalled with one hand and stopped them. Why had he stopped them? Because this was just a joke to him. Mid-afternoon amusement. It was frightening.

"M-Mother," he almost shouted it this time. Her voice came to soothe him and though it was still hoarse, she'd found the strength to make it more audible. He could tell it hurt her to do so.

"S-Stay calm, J-Jinn. I-I'm proud of y-you and...I l-love you. T-The knife's at his t-throat. U-Use it...Quickly. N-No hesitation..."

The power had run out, her voice faded, but a glance at the bed showed him that one of the guards had gone over and stuffed a cloth into her mouth, the cloth they'd used to wipe her clean after feeding her. It was the lapse in concentration the guards had needed. As they rushed him, he desperately pulled the cleaver across Shadowman's throat, but he was unused to blades and flustered, he left behind a scratch, nothing more.

Peter grabbed the cleaver off him and cut a deep slash across his right arm, disabling him instantly. Then the guards had him.

"That's how you cut someone's flesh, boy. You have to put pressure on the blade. Your Mother should have taught you this. Do I have to do everything myself? Take him to the chambers. It's time he learned some manners. It's rude to attack your host during a meal."

There was time for one last look at his Mother. The cloth was still in her mouth and there were signs of blood seeping through it. But her previously dulled eyes sparkled with pride. He had waited seventeen years to be acknowledged by her, and it was worth waiting for. Holding his head up bravely, he smiled at her and said, "Don't let him destroy you, Mother. Be strong..." It was enough.

'Don't let him destroy you, Mother...' the words went round and round in her head. Peter Shadow had destroyed her a long time ago, not this time however, please not this time. Though he was doing a pretty good job of it, she had to admit. The use of the drug followed by its withdrawal had severely weakened her. Force-feeding was humiliating and unbearable. It leeched her spirit like nothing else could have done. "And y-yet, though it's i-intolerable, he's actually s-strengthening me," she said to herself.

Unchained and temporarily left alone, she paced the room. Her legs shook with weakness, but she forced them on. 'Don't let him destroy you...'

"He w-won't destroy m-me, J-Jinn, but if I'm t-to have a chance o-of saving you, h-he must b-believe I am d-destroyed." Again she paced. It would take time to regain her physical strength. Her only weapon was mind games and Peter Shadow was better at them, always had been.

Hearing the guards outside stand to attention, she returned quickly to the bed and lying down, closed her eyes. His footsteps could be heard approaching the bed. She waited till he was near and then opened her eyes.

"You look hot, Madalene. Are you unwell?

Careful not to overdo it, she put a weak smile onto her face. "Y-You are m-making me i-ill, Peter. I'm w-worried about m-my son and I-I get hurt every time y-you have me f-force-fed." It actually wasn't that difficult to make her eyes well with tears and the effect was surprising. Peter sat down on the bed beside her and took her hand. A genuine look of concern was on his face.

"He tried to kill me, Madalene, and you encouraged him. That hurt me more than his feeble efforts at torturing me."

"M-My mind is n-not right at the m-moment. Y-You know that. H-He's my s-son, I reacted a-according t-to my instincts. Sadly, I k-knew he couldn't u-use a knife. I-I trained h-him remember." Now she let the tears run, controlling them so only a few fell. "T-Tell me how they're h-hurting him. I-I know you'll e-enjoy doing that and I-I need to know."

The concern on Peter's face increased. His psychotic nature was favouring his nicer side at present. "I'm not the monster you think I am, Madalene. I do what I have to, to get what I want. You are just like me in that respect. If your knife had been at my throat today, you would have killed me without blinking. I'll be sad when I finally break you, but it will be a lot safer for me, don't you think?"

Her laughter was actually genuine, and he laughed too. "If I h-had got t-to the cleaver, i-it would have flown directly f-from my hand t-to your heart."

Strangely there was no guile in what happened next. Suddenly Peter bent down and kissed her tenderly. This was her chance to play, but it had to look and feel real. Peter was an attractive man and like her in many ways, how hard could it be? Reaching up with her arms, she pulled him down and gently caressed him. Her attempts to remove his clothing were a failure, as her hand was healing, but not healed. Taking over, he removed his own clothing. He then helped her out of the bed gown and lay naked by her side. The look he gave her was tender and loving. With difficulty she gave him a tender look of her own; the loving bit was too hard.

"Are we really going to do this without any force on my part? I'm not sure I can manage without that bit."

"Y-You have to b-be g-gentle now I'm p-pregnant. Get used t-to it."

"I'll hurt you again, Madalene, you know I will. The game isn't over yet."

"I'd expect nothing l-less from y-you, but I'll h-hurt you if I g-get a chance t-to. Let's just enjoy a t-temporary truce. One h-hour of 'n-no-mans land'."

"You don't make life easy for me, do you? I never know what to expect when I see you."

She'd done too much talking to reply, so she simply kissed him. She'd heard the phrase 'Sleeping with the Enemy' and now understood what it meant, an easy way to gain an advantage. Men could be so stupid.

They spent an hour exploring each other's bodies and using them as they willed. Nothing was taboo, but everything was done gently. For a while they napped, and then Peter fetched wine for himself and juice for her. One hour became two and then three. Contentedly they curled up together, each reluctant to let the other go. Finally, Peter said the words she'd hoped to hear.

"They're torturing Jinn at this moment. For your sake, and for the pleasure you have given me this afternoon I will stop it, Madalene. He still goes to the Arena though. After your non-appearance, it needs to be so. Again, for your sake, I will get my best marksman to shoot him. His death will be fast and painless."

Though he was naked, she watched him walk to the door and issue the instructions that would save Jinn from torture. She breathed a sigh of relief. A few more sessions like this and maybe she could get Jinn a reprieve. Hell, when she'd finished fighting the government there was a good career waiting for her – whoring. She must have already begun to lose her mind, but the afternoon had been like a dream, she had to admit that she'd enjoyed every moment of it. Maybe she could make it last all evening. Peter was still talking to the guards, but would be back soon.

The moment Peter turned around however, she saw that 'no-mans land' time was over. Three of the guards followed him back into the room, carrying the tubing and funnel. The other one had obviously gone to fetch the food jug. The guards leered at her nakedness, but in that she felt safe. Peter would never allow them to touch her.

"Get dressed Madalene. If my guards molest you, it will be your fault," said Peter, as if her nakedness surprised him. "It's dinner time."

Chapter 28

A Broken Woman

Sitting next to a roaring log fire, Peter sipped mulled wine and smiled contentedly. Outside the windows a blizzard wreaked havoc, which meant it was going to be a white Wintertide. Two more days to go, and he was actually excited. Usually Wintertide bored him, and generally he worked through the day, but this year he had Madalene. This year, Wintertide would be different...

Vertex sat opposite him, nibbling at spice pies and gulping down glass after glass of mulled wine. For the moment, Peter ignored his friend, fixing his gaze firmly on the woman who lay dozing on the sofa. Most of her body was covered with a blanket; even so, there was still her beautiful face to admire. She was skinny though. Her belly had begun to swell and it looked ridiculous on such a skeletal frame. Looking at her, it occurred to him that for the first time ever, he was happy and content. It was an unusual feeling.

"See how peaceful she looks, Vertex. We'll have no more problems with her. Finally, she is broken." As he watched, Madalene stirred and sighed, but she did not wake up.

"You can't be sure of that," said Vertex, spluttering crumbs everywhere in his haste to speak.

"And why is that, Fat boy?" Peter said, reverting to the use of the hated nick-name. He didn't like this jarring of his good mood.

"What if she's playing a game with you? Want's you to think she's broken, so she can fight back when she's stronger. Remember our schooldays. Madalene was always at her most dangerous when she went quiet." Vertex seemed desperate. Now why was that? Did Vertex begrudge his happiness?

"You have a point, but I think I know her better than you do. She *is* broken, and she will stay that way. You should be happy for me; Madalene has come to love me as she should have done all along. She knows we're meant to be together."

239

Vertex's face had a sour look about it, "Are you going to continue feeding her with the tube, now that you are *so* in love with one another?"

"Madalene had to be force-fed, because I could see that she intended to use starvation to kill my babies. That it turned into an enjoyable form of torture was a benefit. And when I saw how that torture was gradually breaking her, I continued it. But now it's no longer necessary. I'm teaching her to eat properly again." With a sly smile, he added, "She's struggling to eat enough though, so the guards are feeding her with the tube in the evenings to help maintain her strength."

Last night, he had sat by her side and inserted the tube himself, slowly and gently. She had lain still, not quite able to hide her horror, but looking at him with trust. That had moved him. When it was done, he'd stayed by her side and talked. Later when the soreness had left her throat, she'd talked back, and the stutter had, surprisingly, almost gone. Later still, they'd made love and once again he'd felt the affection that had grown between them. Madalene was everything Bren had said she was and more. In another age she would have been a superb courtesan. She never failed to give him pleasure and always left him wanting more. It surpassed the violent sex he still enjoyed with the breakfast girl and other women.

When they'd finished, he'd carried her down to see her son, Jinn, as she'd requested and left her there for several hours. When he returned, her gratitude had been astounding. She'd smothered him with kisses and hugs and had continued doing so, even though he'd clearly stated that Jinn *would* die in the Arena, two days after the Wintertide celebrations. Quietly, she'd said that Jinn had brought it on himself, that she'd never loved the boy and would be glad to be rid of him. This would have been suspicious, if he hadn't already known of Madalene's dislike for her son. When Madalene professed to have little more than affection and an interest in the boy, he'd allowed her free access to Jinn, telling the guards to carry her down to see him whenever she wanted.

They'd made love again. Afterwards, she'd begged him not to make her go to the Arena and watch Jinn die. The boy was her son and if she was seen coldly watching his death, the public would hate her. Adamantly, he'd refused. The public needed to see the woman who was to be his wife. What better occasion than this? Her

240

devotion to him would be clearly shown by the fact that she'd chosen him above her son. Madalene had complied instantly. No sharp retorts or snappy one-liners. It was at that moment he'd known that she was finally broken.

His recollection was broken by Vertex, who seemed determined to make him doubt and put him in a black mood.

"I've been torturing people for a long time, Peter. I know when someone is broken. Speaking as a friend, I tell you clearly, Madalene isn't broken; she's playing some kind of game. When I talked to her this morning, she was hostile and contemptuous…"

Peter glared at him and shook with anger, "Maybe because you can't keep your fat, grubby hands off her. I know what you do to her, my guards tell me everything. I permitted your groping sessions, because they humiliated Madalene and I knew she would hate them. But no more. Touch her again and I will put you in Partlin's hands, he would love to torture *you*. You're implying that I am stupid, that's reason enough to send you to the chambers. Don't think I can't live without your friendship, Fat boy."

Seemingly taken aback, Vertex hastily poured the remains of his mulled wine down his throat, and then heaving his bulk out of his chair, he went and fetched more. "Forgive me Peter. I can't deny I have feelings for her, and memories of her body plague my mind. She's your prize and for a while I wanted to forget that. My envy has overcome my better nature. I won't lay my hands on your property again. As you say, Madalene is broken and will give us no further trouble. I wish we could say the same about her army, they are still causing problems and apparently most of the original Provoke group have now joined them. I beg your tolerance while I ask one more question, then I will leave the two of you alone. "When you look at Madalene's son, do you ever wonder at his resemblance to you?"

"Have you gone completely mad, Fat boy? What are you implying now?"

"That maybe you already have a son. Madalene had Jinn when she was thirteen years old, which means anyone of us could be his father. He most resembles you." Vertex looked at him bravely and questioningly.

241

"What is *this* nonsense? The boy looks nothing like me, and no son of mine would be as pathetic as Jinn. If you're saying what I think you're saying, then I'd guess his father was Robin Jones. We all knew that paedophile was fucking Madalene on a regular basis, that's why the bastard turned on us."

"Robin didn't have grey eyes," said Vertex, stubbornly.

"How should I know what colour eyes Robin had? Unlike you, I wasn't interested in the colour of other boys' eyes. Get out Fat boy. You've spoiled my good mood; I hope you're satisfied." Vertex looked like he would have run if he'd been capable of doing so.

Shaking with fury, Peter swallowed the rest of his wine and then petulantly threw open the large windows in the room, letting the snow rush in. Suddenly an arm went gently around his stomach. Angrily he turned, his anger fading as he came face to face with a dishevelled Madalene, more beautiful in a sleepy state than he ever could have imagined.

"Why so angry, Peter?" she asked, with a yawn.

"Vertex has made me angry, not you my love. I've told him that if he touches you again, he'll go to the chambers."

"I'm glad," she said, smiling at him. "He makes my skin crawl when he runs his hands over my body, tweaking and nipping as if he owns me. Thank you, Peter."

Her other arm reached for him and then her eyes went wide with shock. "What is it, Madalene? What's wrong with you?" As he wasn't deliberately hurting her at that moment, he was concerned.

Again her eyes widened, but this time a slow smile spread across her face. Removing her arms from him, she pushed her light woollen trousers down slightly and raised her jumper.

"Not now, Madalene," he said, with a light-hearted grin. "A man can have too much of a good thing."

"No. That's not my intent, unless you wish it." For a moment she stood still and concentrated. "Yes. There it is again. Give me your hand."

242

She grabbed his hand with her newly healed left hand, the pink diamond ring sparkling brightly on it, and placed it against her stomach. He was puzzled. What kind of insanity was this? Then he felt a clear thump hit his hand, the thump repeated itself. Quickly, she grabbed his other hand and placed it on a different part of her stomach, now both his hands were feeling tiny thumps. For a moment they disappeared and he looked at Madalene with wonder, reluctant to remove his hands from her. She didn't speak, but her eyes had filled up with tears. His own joy was immense.

"They're kicking. They're kicking me. My sons! They have to be boys, they kick so hard." Now he knelt in front of her, like a worshipper at an altar and reverently moved his hands over the tight skin of her stomach, until he felt them kick again. At that moment he would have given Madalene anything she wanted, except her freedom. He even would have set Jinn free for her, but she did not ask it, proving that he was right to say she was broken. His desire to possess Madalene had also been right; she was the only thing that made him truly happy.

Still on his knees, he gently reached for Madalene's finger and removed the ring. "I'm going to ask again, Madalene. I won't pretend that I'll stop hurting you. And I won't be happy until every member of your army's dead, including your sister. Knowing this. Knowing that I killed Bren and Hayla. Knowing what happened in our youth. Will you set aside all animosity and marry me?"

He waited anxiously, it hadn't exactly been a romantic proposal, but it had been an honest one. She looked down at him and was silent. His heart beat faster. If she refused, the ring would be replaced on her finger and he would use the heavy candlestick nearby to break her hand again. The force-feeding would be resumed in all its fullness, and he might even send her to the chambers for a while. If she refused…it would break his heart.

"Of course I'll marry you," she said, smiling again. "Well stop gawking at me and put the ring back on my finger. I've got used to it being there. There is a condition however…"

Ah! Now came the conditions. Free Jinn. Leave my army alone. No more force-feeding. Set me free to fight you again. He braced himself, anger already creeping out of his crevices.

"And that is?" he said, striving to remain calm.

"I choose my own wedding gown and you don't see it until our wedding day. It's unlucky for a groom to see what his bride will be wearing."

The breath Peter had been holding exploded from him in a burst and he found himself laughing. Madalene was indeed compliant and broken. It was that idiot, Michael Vertex that had made him doubt it.

"I'll need the best dressmaker you can find and if possible some white silk. I'm not exactly pure, but white silk will compliment my dark hair, don't you think?"

Peter replaced the ring on her finger and then returned his hands to her belly. Again he felt the kicks of his children and delighted in them.

"You do me honour and bring me great joy, Madalene. There is a ream of antique silk in one of the attics. I will send my men to find it. Then we will find the greatest dressmaker in the land. The dress will be started tomorrow. Hate can become love, Madalene, you'll see."

"I already know that, Peter. Are you tired of my belly yet? It's getting cold with all these windows open."

Reluctantly, he released her and pulling up her trousers and lowering her jumper, he carried her to her room.

"It's suppertime," he said, laying her down on the bed. "I have an important meeting to attend, so the guards will have to feed you tonight." A look of dread crossed her face. Peter called the guards in and beckoned to one of them, a handsome man in his early twenties. "This is Damian. He's a new man, but I trust him to be as gentle with you as I've been, if not more so. Damian was training to be a doctor, before he decided to earn money and become a Sanctum Guard." Damian smiled politely at Madalene, but she could not hide her distress. However gently it was done, she hated being force-fed.

Peter sighed; the meeting was important and would go on throughout the night. He was about to revoke the right of the masses to an education. In future only the wealthy would be educated; the rest of society would be unwitting slaves, capable only of manual labour. It would save a fortune and reduce the numbers of those who questioned his choices, but it was a contentious issue. One he intended to force through. After all, the majority of the Provoke army were the educated poor. He would not suffer such opposition any longer. Still it was his meeting and he could do as he pleased.

"I'll hold your hand, Madalene. You'll see how gentle Damian can be."

Damian was so gentle, Madalene hardly flinched and before he'd even extracted the tube, she'd fallen asleep. In front of his guards, Peter felt her belly and was rewarded with more kicking. As much as he loved Madalene, these babies were more important. Madalene hated the feeding and he wanted to stop it to please her, but he couldn't, the babies needed food and he had to admit he enjoyed watching her being force-fed. For the foreseeable future it had to continue, but he would allow only Damian to feed her, the young man had been incredibly gentle.

Madalene shuddered as Peter left her side with the guards in tow. She hated having to do things this way. She was what they called a hands-on sort of person. Hands on a gun, bang you're dead. Hands on a bomb, boom you're dead. This pretence was killing her. She'd thought her true profession was whoring; after all she could sigh, moan and fake orgasm after orgasm. Damn, she could give a man pleasure with a look, she was that damned good. But in the last couple of days, she'd discovered a hell of a talent for acting. The stage wasn't just beckoning, it was yelling at her to get over there.

She'd not only got to see Jinn, she'd also managed to formulate a plan which might save him. Best of all she'd found a way to get messages to her army, and she planned to escalate this war to a greater scale than ever before. One day Peter Shadow would be her prisoner, and the first thing she planned to do was shove a tube of rubber down his damned throat and pour a can of laxatives into it. She was troubled however. Whether she liked it or not, there was something indefinable between them, something that had made the pretence easier. Smiling, she thought who would have guessed that might be a complication, and then she recalled her meeting with Jinn.

"Madalene! I mean Mother. What are you doing here?"

Jinn's face was badly swollen and he moved stiffly. Turning him around, she winced. His back was bloody and lined. The boy had been flogged. Carefully, she lifted the tatters of his shirt and sighed with relief, only four lashes, painful, but not enough to cripple him. It looked like she'd got the torture stopped in time.

"I don't know how long Peter's going to let me stay here, or if he'll let me return. We need to talk quickly, Jinn."

"What's there to talk about?" he said, dejectedly. "You can't save me."

"He's sending you to the Arena, two days after Wintertide. I've sent a message to the army to be in the Arena on that day…"

"How?" Jinn had turned and was now hugging her. She was a little uncomfortable with this, but said nothing to hurt him. "He's torturing you. That tube…the funnel…the chains. I couldn't bear to see you treated like that." Tears ran freely down Jinn's cheeks.

"S-Stop that," she'd said harshly, ignoring the slight return of her stutter. "N-Neither of us has time to feel sorry for ourselves. I can endure the things he does to me. You must endure too."

Wiping his eyes, Jinn nodded and waited to hear what she had to say.

"There's a young girl who brings Peter his breakfast, and is violently raped by him every single day. She also endures, but she hates him with a passion. This same girl bathes me and does my hair. Mostly we're watched, but the guards usually stand at a distance so we're able to talk. It was risky, but I decided to trust her. She took a message from me to Holan and brought me one back, verbal messages you understand. She's a brave girl; she knows if she's caught she'll be put to death, and I offer her nothing for doing this, but she tells me that she would prefer death to the mistreatment she suffers. Yesterday she brought me news that the army will all be in the Arena waiting for you. They're trying to find a way to smuggle their weapons in, but may have to go unarmed."

"Will Ellyn be with them?" Jinn said, with a wistful look on his face.

"How the hell am I supposed to know that? The messages that pass are brief and abrupt. Listen, I know it feels like you're badly hurt, but you're in a better state than most people who go to the Arena. You're problem will be the hand chains, you'll have to run with them on."

"Run?"

"Yes run. And as soon as I have left this cell you are to begin running up and down it until you drop. You need to be fit and fast."

"Fast?"

Madalene was exasperated, was she not explaining this properly? "Jinn, are you being deliberately stupid? Let yourself be taken to the stakes. Cry and wail a little. Stumble. Make yourself look weak and afraid, it shouldn't be hard to do. I'll create a distraction, and when I do you are to run. Holan and the army should help you at that point, if they can."

Jinn's face showed his relief and joy. She had to make it clear that it wasn't going to be as easy as it sounded. "The likelihood is that you will be shot as you are moving. All I give you is a tiny hope of freedom and a chance to make life difficult for the Sanctum. Do you understand that?"

He looked at her and she saw full comprehension in his expression. "I understand, Mother," he said, fearlessly.

Her pride in him was enormous. He saw it and smiled.

"What have I missed?" she said, with a loud sigh. "What have I missed?" Suddenly they were hugging again, and this time she was not uncomfortable with it. "He thinks I'm a broken woman, Jinn and he's partly right. It's important that he believes this to be true. It is the only way I can move against him from the inside. Whatever I say or do will not be the truth. I have told the army the same. They are not to even think of rescuing me, they are to concentrate on you. I will look cold and like I do not care, but my heart will break if you get shot."

Shortly after that, their time together ended. She'd told Jinn much, but not everything. She hadn't told him that Peter Shadow was his father. Nothing would induce her to tell him that. She had thought of telling Peter in a bid to save Jinn's life, but pride had stopped her. She hoped she would not regret her pride, two days after Wintertide.

Chapter 29

An Unexpected Turn of Events

It was the week before Wintertime, and the members of the Provoke army were lounging in their new hide-out. There'd been such a huge increase in their numbers, with many new members coming from the original group, that Holan had decided to make the change for everyone's comfort.

Festive spirit was thin on the ground, despite attempts to decorate the main living area with holly branches and assorted paper decorations. The trouble was that it was too cold to take action against the Sanctum, and there was nothing else to do. Being members of an outlawed army meant they couldn't even visit their families. The street patrols continued of course, but only a few people were needed for them. Holan sighed as she played a game of Jostle with Luke, Adrian and Torrin. It involved moving packs of carved wooden figures around a board in an attempt to knock other player's figures off and lessen their packs. Winner was the last person with figures left standing. It was a mindless game, but one they had been reduced to for entertainment.

"There must be something we can bomb," said Luke with a yawn. "Or someone we can shoot." At this point, Adrian knocked four of Luke's pieces off the board. "Bastard. You can't take my pieces when I'm talking."

"I just did, and look, you've only got two figures left," said Adrian, smugly.

Holan looked up at the ceiling, if these two were starting then she was going elsewhere. It always escalated, usually finishing with Luke and Adrian wrestling on the floor like small boys.

"It's too cold to run amok, Luke," said Torrin, still running his figures round the board.

Holan knew Torrin was only trying to create a distraction, but in the process he knocked one of Luke's two remaining figures off the board.

"That doesn't count," said Luke, trying to put the figure back, only to have it snatched out of his hand by Adrian. Holan knocked Luke's final figure off, and the infuriated Luke started to shout at all of them.

Holan was about to leave him to it, when Ellyn came over to speak to her. Holan was convinced that Ellyn was in the early stages of pregnancy, and had come seeking her advice. As unquestionably this was Jinn's child, Holan would do whatever it took to keep Ellyn safe and well. Seeing Ellyn, Luke and Adrian, who both adored her, settled down.

"Come on, Ellyn," said Adrian, kindly. "Sit down and join us. Luke's out of the game. Would you like to take his place?"

"You don't want to play with Adrian," said Luke. "He cheats. Come and have a stroll with me instead. We'll find Annie and then go outside for a while."

"Isn't Annie avoiding you?" said Adrian, with a wicked smile. "It was really stupid of you to get caught with Shola. I mean, Shola's beautiful, but Annie's got a fantastic pair of..."

"Legs?" said Holan, before they started again. Torrin looked over at Holan and smiled. Lately, Holan had become surprisingly close to Torrin, she smiled back at him. If she stayed cool, she believed she would have a new lover before too long.

"I'd love to go outside, Luke..." said Ellyn.

Adrian's derisive laughter interrupted her. "The last thing you want is to go outside with Luke. You'll bend over to make a snowball and he'll jump you. The poor boy's so deluded he thinks females of every age desire him. I'll take you out for air if that's what you want."

Luke's response was agitated and immediate. "Don't go with *him*, Ellyn. Adrian thinks rape's an honourable profession. Look at poor Clara; she's still traumatised from taking *air* with him."

"She's tired from the good time I gave her," protested Adrian.

"Will you two give it a rest," said Holan, trying not to laugh. The sound of people entering the hide-out distracted her. Looking over, she saw that Christian and Malcolm had returned from their patrol. They had a young girl with them, around fifteen years old. Malcolm was holding her warily. Everyone went silent.

"Who the hell is *she*?" said Holan.

"She says Madalene sent her and she needs to talk to you," said Christian. "If she's a spy, we'll deal with her."

"We don't shoot little girls," said Holan, standing up and walking towards him. Ellyn followed her.

"I need to talk to you, Holan," said Ellyn.

"Not now, Ellyn. Let's hear what this girl has to say first."

The girl seemed terrified; she kept her head down and didn't look up until Holan was right in front of her. "Y-You look like her," she said, quietly.

"Like who? What do you want? Speak up; we have little patience with outsiders." Holan didn't mean to be harsh, but memories of Will and Rawl still haunted her.

"You look like Madalene, only not as kind…"

"Madalene, kind!" For a minute Holan was taken aback, then she realised the girl was being serious.

"I can't stay; I'm on an errand and have to return to work quickly. Are you Holan?" said the girl, anxiously.

"I might be," said Holan. "What can I do for you?"

"Madalene asked me to give you a message. Jinn is to go to the Arena, two days after Wintertide. She wants the army to be there and ready to help him."

Holan was taken by surprise, so was everyone else in the room. People began to crowd the girl, unnerving her. "Give her some space. Come, sit down here and tell us about Madalene. What's happening to her?" Holan led the girl to a comfortable chair nearby. Then they waited, some more cynically than others. Luke and Adrian smiled encouragingly at the girl, but others muttered that Madalene was a traitor; who cared what was happening to her.

Hearing this, the girl said angrily, "If you saw what was happening to Madalene, you would *never* say those things."

In hushed tones, the girl spoke of how Shadowman had kept Madalene controlled with drugs. How he'd made her pregnant and suddenly withdrawn the drugs, an act that had nearly killed her. She told them about a proposal of marriage that had led to Madalene's hand being shattered in order to keep the engagement ring on her finger. And finally, she told them about the daily force-feeding.

Holan almost collapsed with grief. Madalene must have lost whatever sanity she had left. Her sister could have withstood any amount of pain; she'd experienced enough of it in her lifetime. But not humiliation...not humiliation. Looking around she saw that those who were not in tears were looking ashamed, the one's who had called Madalene a traitor. Luke and Adrian seemed sombre for once, and Christian looked... It was hard to describe how Christian looked. It was a mixture of terrible sorrow and fearful anger, emotions too powerful to control. Finally she realised the girl was still speaking.

"Madalene says you are to concentrate on getting Jinn free. Forget about her. Whatever you see her say or do, don't believe it. I'll come again in two days time to find out what you've got planned. I've taken a terrible risk coming here. I must go."

Holan regained her senses, "Luke and Adrian will take you back. I know you don't want them to, but they'll make sure you're safe." For a moment, she glanced over and saw Ellyn, white-faced and full of hope. It was a miniscule hope, but how could Holan take it away from her. "You have our thanks, and you are welcome here anytime. If you need refuge come to us."

"One more thing," said the girl. "Madalene says that many of you will think this is a trap, despite the fact that I found the hide-out, because she told me where it was. She told me to tell Hannah to loosen up a little and not be such a sour-faced crone."

Hannah was standing nearby and began laughing. "She's come from Madalene alright, and despite every word we've heard, they haven't broken her yet. Tell Madalene that Hannah still thinks she's a dangerous maniac."

Laughter broke out and the mood in the hide-out changed. As Luke and Adrian led the girl away, bantering as usual in a bid to win her favour, Holan sank into a chair and looked at Christian and Torrin. None of them spoke. Their horror at Madalene's predicament did not allow it.

Now Wintertide was over, everyone's attention was given to the rescue of Jinn. Holan had no intention of risking the whole army, but she did need enough army members spread around the Arena, so that whatever direction Jinn decided to run in, someone would be there to help him. Ellyn would not be coming with them; she was too emotionally involved and could prove to be a liability. This mission was far too dangerous for a pregnant young girl. Weapons would have to be smuggled in under overcoats. Of course random searches were always carried out, but they were likely to be few and far between in this atrociously cold weather. It would be incredibly unlucky if everyone smuggling in weapons got caught.

The girl had returned twice more, each time carrying further instructions from Madalene. Holan noticed the girl look shyly in Adrian's direction and wondered what had happened between them. For goodness sake, couldn't Adrian leave any female alone? That young man had way too much testosterone. A glance revealed Luke caressing Annie. Luke was no better. She had a new name for the pair of them - The Testosterone Brothers!

"It's not going to work," said Hannah. "Jinn will be shot the moment he starts running."

"Madalene knows that's a likelihood, but she's hoping the distraction she creates will draw attention away from Jinn long enough for us to help him."

"The trouble is that it's unlikely to draw everyone's attention. The guards will stay alert."

Hannah was right of course, but for Ellyn's sake, Holan pushed the scenario. "Not if we shoot them."

Hannah sighed and ran her fingers nervously through her hair. "They'll be too many. With Shadowman present, security will be at its maximum. Bear in mind that to help Jinn we need to be at the front of the Arena. The exits are located at the back. We'll have the crowd to get through."

"The crowd will be panicking and we're the ones with the guns," said Holan, desperately trying to find responses for Hannah's arguments. "I can't disagree with anything you say, but look at Ellyn's face, Hannah. We have to try."

The Arena was crowded. Singly and in pairs, members of the Provoke army came in and made their way to the front seats. Holan and Torrin entered, entwined like a loving couple. Nearby stood Christian. From time to time, he glanced over and scowled at them. The guards on the gates had been searching every third person; once the army spotted the pattern, they'd been able to bring in their weapons. It helped that no-one in charge seemed to believe that anyone coming to see the shows would want to bring in weapons. The searches were made to confiscate alcohol and recreational drugs; in that way crowd trouble could be prevented.

Holan's eyes were drawn to the decorated box in the VIP area; it was raised above the stands and had a low safety barrier, allowing the privileged people sitting there to be seen by the common crowd. Beyond the box she saw Luke and Adrian in position, and slightly further away were Malcolm and Mark. She'd wanted to leave Mark behind; Adam would be part of this show, as would other members of the army. They couldn't save them all, but Mark might not see it that way. The girl's voice echoed in Holan's ears.

"*Madalene thinks that other members of her army will be involved in this show. She says don't even think of rescuing them. They'll be too badly hurt to run. You won't succeed. Jinn is capable of running.*"

It was a leader's decision based on cold facts; Holan knew many would view it as self-interest, Madalene wanting to save her son. It wasn't a decision, Holan would have made. She'd have tried to save them all. "And probably lost everyone," she said, with a loud groan.

"What's that?" said Torrin.

254

"Nothing." Madalene was right. Help the person who could be helped, and if Madalene was guilty of self-interest, then so was she. Jinn was her nephew, she loved him and didn't want to watch him die. "Oh look. Here comes the band."

Not one band, but several marched into the Arena, each of them playing different, but confluent tunes. As they finished there was a fanfare. A deep hush fell over the expectant audience. Into the box filed ministers and other well-known people. When they were seated, Shadowman entered with Michael Vertex at his side. The crowd cheered wildly. Holan and the others did the same, they had to. The Arena was a natural auditorium, as Shadowman spoke everyone heard him.

"Welcome all of you," he said, in clear, accent less tones. "I hope you had a good Wintertide."

Holan scanned the area. Sanctum Guards were everywhere, not only surrounding the box, but also mingling with the crowd. This was going to be a lot harder than they had thought.

"Now to introduce you to the woman who has captured my heart and is to become my wife."

A buzz of excitement started, and people began shifting to get a better view of the box, eager to see the notorious woman they had heard so much about. Holan was no different. She noticed that the army members were also eagerly awaiting the appearance of Madalene. None more so than Christian, whose face was ablaze with excitement.

Then, suddenly there she was, dressed in a Roman-style gown that fitted snugly and exposed her pregnancy. Her dark hair had been curled and piled high on her head; holding it together was a diamond tiara that sparkled erratically in the weak, winter sunshine. Her face was expressionless, but Holan noticed that she smiled at Shadowman, as he came forward and took her hand.

"Meet Madalene," he said. "My Dark Goddess."

Holan heard the gasps. That was the army's nickname for Madalene. Christian had invented it, and he looked shocked to hear it spoken so publicly. It must have been revealed by tortured army members. The gasps were concealed under a storm of foot stamping. Madalene smiled for the crowd and they went wild.

"She looks beautiful," said Torrin. "But so cold and uncaring…"

"Don't believe what you see. Think only of what she's asked you to do."

A look around revealed that some of the army members had seen the smile, Madalene had given Shadowman, and were beginning to think this was a trap. Holan hoped they kept their nerve.

As Madalene took her seat and Shadowman joined her, the show recommenced. Acrobats and jugglers replaced the bands, and were themselves replaced by troupes of dancers. Finally there came a choir of nearly two hundred people. It was brilliant entertainment, but Holan was unable to concentrate; her attention remained on her sister. Madalene sat laughing and joking with Shadowman, occasionally pointing out something that had amused her. She kissed him lightly from time to time, and he responded by rubbing her bump.

"Don't believe what you see. Madalene has her own game to play."

It was difficult *not* to believe that she was watching two people who genuinely loved each other. Nearby, Christian was obviously undergoing the same emotions. His pain was clearly on display.

"Torrin," she whispered. "I want you to wander off for a while and settle our army members down. Tell them they have to believe Madalene hasn't betrayed us."

"He has nearly broken her completely. It's only a matter of time…"

Was she already broken? Could they trust messages from someone who had endured so much pain and humiliation? Who doubted now?

On a single note from a cornet, the prisoners were brought out. Adam came first, and there didn't seem to be an inch of skin left on his body. He had to be supported by two Guards. Tears came to Holan's eyes immediately. Then one by one, those who had been part of the back-up team appeared, most of them also having to be dragged in. Of Jinn there was no sign. He was evidently being dealt with separately.

The prisoners were placed against the stakes in the centre of the Arena, and chained down. Guards holding rifles in their hands entered and took up their positions. Now, there was complete silence, broken only by the sudden sound of laughter, Madalene's laughter. Holan was shocked, how could Madalene show men about to die, such disrespect? A drum roll began. The Guards raised their rifles.

Adam's head lifted and he looked towards the box, the anguish on his face plain to see. "We loved you, Madalene..." he said, loudly. "We loved you..."

The guards fired. Adam screamed wildly, and then fell silent. The others died at the same time. Holan looked to see Mark's reaction. Malcolm had hold of him and was dragging him towards the exit,

Mark was screaming, "I'm going to fucking kill Madalene." It was drawing attention.

"Don't believe what you see..."

"I'm going to cut that fucking bitch's head off." Guards moved in to intercept Mark, but to Holan's relief, Malcolm had reached one of the exits

Once again a single note sounded and Jinn was brought into the Arena. Holan saw that he had been hurt, but not as badly as the others. As Jinn approached the stakes and saw the dead bodies of his comrades, he began to stumble and wail loudly. Holan hadn't expected him to react so badly. How could Jinn run, when the time came, if he was immobilised with terror? Looking intently at the box, Holan saw Madalene stood by the low barrier, coldly watching Jinn's entrance. There were mutterings from people nearby; it was well known that Madalene was Jinn's mother.

"Save me Mother, please. I'm too young to die," shouted Jinn, in desperation.

Holan kept her eyes on her sister. Madalene was running her thumbs over her fingertips, again and again. Holan immediately

257

recognised the gesture; whatever Madalene had planned was about to happen.

"Jinn…" The word was spoken so croakily, it was barely audible. Nevertheless it floated around the Arena like a butterfly. Madalene leaned forward and then fell over the barrier into the crowd below. There was a crack of broken bones, and harsh piercing screams came from the area where she had landed. Shadowman leapt off his seat and began shouting instructions. Guards from all over the Arena began rushing towards the spot.

A different yell was heard; Holan looked back at the Arena and saw Jinn running in the direction of Luke and Adrian. The Guards were chasing him, but Jinn was fast. Luke and Adrian leapt over the barrier with their weapons to hand, and began shooting as they ran. Holan raced to join them, as did Christian, and Torrin, who was just making his way back to her. It was ludicrously easy; the pursuing Guards were slain in an instant. With the other Guards fully occupied, they surrounded Jinn and led him back to the barrier. All they had to do was get themselves over the barrier and out through the exits. Other army members rushed to join them.

Everyone's attention was still on the area where Madalene had fallen, they were going to make it. Holan looked up at the box to see what was happening. Shadowman had gone, but Michael Vertex was still there, and he was aiming a telescopic rifle in their direction. Who was he aiming at? She realised *who* too late. A shot was fired and it struck Jinn in the back. She grabbed the boy before he fell, Luke and Adrian helped, and between them they got Jinn over the barrier. Christian and Torrin were already on the other side to receive him. Others arrived to shield them and they headed for the exits.

"Ladies first," said Adrian, gallantly holding his hand out to help Holan over the barrier.

"That would be you then, Adrian," said Luke with a smile, that faded as a bullet slammed into his chest.

"No," said Adrian, in panic. "Get over the barrier, Holan! We have to get him out of here. Hold on Luke! Think of all those women who'll be sad if you're not around to laugh at."

Luke chuckled, and then coughed up a lot of blood. "They'll still have you," he said.

Holan leapt over the barrier and reached out for Luke. A man called Frank had run back to help her. The Guards had finally realised what was going on and were heading their way. Already clouds of bullets were flying towards them. Adrian leapt over the barrier and grabbing Luke out of Frank's arms, he ran with him to the exit. Holan followed, with Frank behind her. The crowd had now thinned and as they made their way to the exits, they were chattering excitedly. Through the mist that seemed to have seeped into her brain, Holan finally realised that it was not Jinn's escape they were talking about. It was Madalene's.

Chapter 30

Retribution

"How could she do this? My reputation is in ruins! The public laugh at how easily I was duped. I thought Madalene loved me." Peter was distraught.

They stood in the room where he'd kept Madalene. Now every part of it lay in ruins. In his hands, Peter held the bed gown she'd worn and periodically he stroked it, as if the act would bring her back. Michael had never seen his friend like this before; he was beginning to wonder if slipping a sedative into Peter's drink might be a good idea. In the state Peter was in, he would send the entire Sanctum to the Arena as punishment for Madalene's loss. Michael chose his words carefully. 'I told you so', were not among them.

"I don't think that her original intention *was* to escape. The fall was simply a distraction to give her son, Jinn, the chance of freedom. The decision to run came when she landed. What worries me is that she knew her army members would be there."

"A guess?" said Peter, his interest sparked by Michael's words.

Michael breathed a sigh of relief. He'd chosen the right thing to say. Which didn't mean he could afford to become careless.

"I would have thought so too, if her army hadn't been so well organised. Their weapons were cleverly smuggled in, and they spread themselves uniformly around the Arena."

"That could have been organised without Madalene's knowledge," said Peter, beginning to calm down a little.

"Then why didn't the army members go into action when their friends appeared? You heard the words of the young man who was dragged out of the Arena. We all heard them. He'd obviously been ordered to stay put and wait for the appearance of Jinn. Madalene knew Jinn would be the only prisoner capable of running. It would have been useless to waste her efforts on a failed bid to save the

260

others. Only she would have been capable of making such a heartless decision." Michael had known all along that Madalene wasn't broken, and that she would attempt to save her son by any means possible. It was why he'd taken along his telescopic rifle and endured Peter's scorn for doing so. He'd had no intention of letting that boy escape. Madalene had been hostile and unkind to him, and she'd almost ruined his friendship with Peter. She deserved to lose her son.

"And she prepared for this by persuading me not to torture her son..." Peter faltered and madness returned to his eyes. "She's good, isn't she? I truly believed that she loved me, or at least was beginning to. It was there in her eyes - I saw it." Angrily, Peter tore the bed gown in half. "It wasn't faked, Fat boy. She *does* have feelings for me."

Tread carefully, thought Michael. "There's always been something special between the two of you. Even in the beginning I knew it, but you and Madalene are too alike to be together. The games between you would continue into old age, you hurting her, her hurting you. Surely there must be someone else you could fall in love with. Madalene isn't the only beautiful woman around."

"Madalene is special; there's no other woman like her. You know it. You desire her as well. Not only that, she's carrying my sons and I want *them* back. I've felt them kicking, Michael, it would hurt too much to lose them." This wasn't conversation, this was an order that it would be perilous to disobey.

Michael took a risk, it was important that Peter considered a possibility. "Don't think about them, Peter. The first thing Madalene will do is have them destroyed. She's mentioned it often enough in my presence. She would have starved them out of her body if you hadn't force fed her, you know that. And she didn't think about them when she leapt out of the box, she didn't care that a fall like that could kill them." The 'mentioning it often' was a lie, Madalene had barely spoken to him at all, except for some choice name-calling. It had the desired effect however. Peter was incandescent with rage, and this time it was directed, correctly, at Madalene.

"If Madalene has harmed my sons, she'll pay dearly when she's in my possession again. I'll have her tortured unremittingly and it will be done by you Michael, because you'll make sure that she stays alive through it. Your work has always been more exquisite than Partlin's." Michael was taken aback; Partlin's brutal ways had always pleased Peter more, than his own subtler methods. "I'll have Madalene sent to the Arena, thinking the release of death lies ahead of her, and then have her returned to you for further torture. We'll mess her mind up, using the occasional bout of kindness. And if you can work as well as I think you can, I'll use her as a brood cow. She'll produce children until she has no more eggs left. I will..." It seemed that, like a child making threats, Peter had run out of ideas. Michael was bracing himself for the 'calling her names' bit.

Peter walked through the debris of the room, kicking broken bits of chair out of his way and wading through feathers from torn cushions and bits of broken porcelain. "Get the Inner Sanctum together and give them the following instructions. I don't feel like facing those idiots today. I have a feeling I'd send them all to the chambers, and I can't do that, I need their help. There is to be no leave for any of my Sanctum Guards. They are all to be involved in the search for Madalene. Routine duties are to be overlooked. I want Army troops detached to look for her too. A people's police force is to be set up; those who join are to be paid well. They are to offer a two million engle reward for her capture alive. That should gain someone's attention."

"Two million engles!" Michael almost choked.

"I don't intend to pay it. The recipient will be quietly disposed of. Use the papers to advertise the reward, and make it imaginative. Let the public know how this much money could change their lives. There's to be nowhere left for Madalene to hide."

"What if she's left the country and gone to Ireland? A boat sailed there last night." The thought had only just occurred to Michael.

Peter's look was ominous. "Then we'll invade Ireland and tear the country apart until we find her. I never liked the Irish anyway. It was only a matter of time before I took their country off them."

Madalene's escape was about to wreak havoc, possibly between countries. "What about the Provoke army?" said Michael.

"Forget them. We can deal with the army anytime. Finding Madalene is more important."

"What if they're hiding her? Surely she'll turn to them for help," said Michael, reminded that there was still the matter of how Madalene had got instructions to the army, when she was locked up in this room, to be dealt with. Someone must have helped her, but who? He was determined to find out.

Peter laughed, "What? And 'get her fucking head cut off'? That young man won't be the only one feeling like that. I don't think Madalene will go near her army. My only worry is them getting hold of her before we do. They'll kill her and I don't want that."

Michael had to agree. He didn't want that to happen either. Madalene was infamous, she couldn't hide for long, and Peter had promised that he would be allowed to do whatever he wanted to her, provided he kept her alive. Already thoughts of what he'd like to do to her, were racing through his head. He could hardly wait.

Madalene lay hidden in one of her underground haunts, a place she'd originally set up to hide old people while she arranged for their transfer to Ireland. She was badly bruised and had broken her left hand again. She was also exhausted and grieving deeply for a son she hadn't known properly until the end.

She'd never planned to escape, and the fact that she'd got away still bemused her. Two people had cushioned her fall, and at least one of them had broken bones, she'd heard them snap as she landed. At that point, the urge to escape had become overwhelming; she'd pushed her way through crowds of bewildered people, terrified by her reputation. Of course she'd been as conspicuous as hell, but a young woman had been persuaded to hand over her hooded overcoat. Not exactly persuaded, more coerced. The woman had probably got hypothermia, but it was a small price to pay for such a nice tiara - she could sell the thing, or wear it next time she went out.

Despite the huge numbers of Guards, the coat had got Madalene safely out onto the streets. However, before leaving, she'd seen Michael Vertex shoot Jinn in the back, as the boy reached the barriers. To her relief, army members had got Jinn safely away, but Madalene knew Jinn wouldn't survive a wound like that. His death was only a matter of time.

All along, Michael had known that she wasn't broken and was planning to rescue Jinn. He was also the bastard who'd convinced

Peter to carry on force feeding her, when she'd almost persuaded Peter to stop it. Well she certainly intended to repay Michael for his kindness. Abuse of her body, torture, death of her son…The damned list was endless. Repaying Michael was a priority. Peter had just been edged off her wish list.

At first she'd found a drain refuge and hidden there. Unused to exercise, she'd been horribly weak and breathless. There she remembered her laughter and Adam's response, and she wept unashamedly. The laughter had been the subterfuge which had allowed her to stand by the barrier. Peter would have never permitted it otherwise. But Adam wouldn't have known that, all he'd seen was betrayal by a leader he'd loved and admired. Mark had seen the same thing and so had the others. She had a feeling that any reception she got from her army would involve rope and a lynching again. She'd heard Mark's words, *"I'm going to fucking kill Madalene."* They'd shocked her, because usually Mark didn't speak. *"I'm going to cut that fucking bitch's head off."* Almost certainly Mark would act on his words. Quiet people always did.

When darkness fell, Madalene had cautiously made her way through streets that were being patrolled by, either Provoke army members, or Sanctum Guards. The Provoke army had no knowledge of the hide-outs in ruined underground stations, or how to get to them. As far as she knew neither did the Sanctum. For the time being she was safe.

The babies kicked, reminding her she was pregnant. "Okay you two. There must be something here I can feed you with." Getting to her feet, she hunted and found a barrel of dried biscuits and some dried milk, it was a start. Where tracks had once run, she made a small wood fire, found a drum of water, and then made a large pan of hot biscuit porridge. It wasn't easy with one hand, but she managed. She resolved to sort out her left hand once she'd eaten. Another quick hunt revealed a jar of sugar and a jar of herb tea, there was also flour for bread making. The porridge looked nasty and reminded her of the stuff she'd had poured down the rubber tube. Retching violently, Madalene began to eat. It wasn't easy, but she didn't stop. She needed strength, and not just for the babies sake.

It was probably habit, but afterwards she lay down to make sure the food stayed in her belly and began to think. She couldn't remember how far into her pregnancy she was, and her body gave her few clues. She'd remained thin, and for a twin pregnancy her bump was small. They'd captured her at the end of July hadn't they? If that drug induced hallucination had been anything to go by, Peter had made her pregnant instantly. Five months gone then. Perhaps she should get herself to Ireland and return when the babies were born. Superwoman couldn't do a lot while she was pregnant. And what better vengeance could she have, than to bear the babies and leave them where Peter would never find them.

The idea was appealing and she was definitely ready for a period of rest and recuperation. Then images of Bren, Hayla and now Jinn came into her head. Her response was to get angry. Who needed a holiday, when you could have more fun at home? There was another choice: find a back street abortionist - if any remained when Peter had in effect wiped them out - and get rid of the babies. Quickly she dismissed the idea: if it came to it; the babies were serious bargaining power. And when she thought about, what did pregnancy stop her doing? Running, climbing, quick getaways. It was possible to work around all those things.

Wasn't she a 'one woman war machine' now she couldn't contact her army? "Well you've been here before," she said to herself. "And look how well you did."

Peter had new policies coming thick and fast and no longer cared for public opinion. No education for the majority of citizens was just the beginning. Peter Shadow was about to be more perfidious than anyone could have imagined. He had to be stopped, or at least delayed.

She'd overheard Peter and Michael talking about a conference that was taking place at the Greyfriars Hotel, in Colchester. It had been arranged to finalise plans for education changes, and would be attended by ministers from the Outer Sanctum as well as four of the eight Inner Sanctum members. The event was three weeks away and it was a good place to start. Bombing the place at the right moment would leave the Sanctum needing a recruitment drive. And if Michael Vertex was one of the four Inner Sanctum members, all the better.

If the Sanctum had given up watching her old home, she could return and pick up everything she needed, including a replacement for her lost rifle. She had a similar one hidden under the back shed.

It was erratic and needed reloading after four shots, but it would do. When she was ready, she'd sign in early at the hotel, as a partner of one of the ministers, waiting for her husband to join her. There were so many ministers attending, she shouldn't be asked too many questions, especially if she donned a long blonde wig and stylish clothes, all of which she could buy or steal. She'd also need a stylish bag to carry her explosive devices in. Immediately after this attack, she'd commence further actions. She'd bomb minister's homes on an almost daily basis. She'd bomb parts of the Sanctum building itself, if she could find a way in.

Peter had publicly named her Dark Goddess. How apt, when she intended to bring death and destruction down on him. And yet, there was no denying the bond between her and him. A bond it would hurt to break...

Chapter 31

The Hunted

A day had passed and there was still no sign of Madalene. The army had been expecting her return, ever since the events at the Arena. Many of them planning a less than friendly reception for her. Holan was worried: it had been a long drop from the box to the ground, and Madalene was pregnant. What if she was lying somewhere, badly hurt and in need of help?

Holan tried to get people to go out and search for her, but many simply refused. In the end, only Torrin, Christian, Malcolm, Hannah and a few others had gone. Ellyn and Adrian would have done the same, but they had troubles of their own. Holan also went searching, but with no luck. Perhaps it was better this way. Until the strong feelings against Madalene faded and the army members saw reason again, it wasn't safe for her to return to the army. While many agreed that Madalene had not betrayed them, few could forgive the laughter that had caused Adam so much anguish before his death. Anguish that had been seen on the faces of all those who had died.

Malcolm came in as dawn broke. "I've found signs of her," he said, his weariness from being out all night obvious. "She used one of the drain refuges, Holan. The one nearest the Arena. We were stupid; it should have been the first place we looked. There were patches of dried blood on the ground, half a bottle of wine's been drunk and several other bottles are missing. It doesn't appear that she stayed long; I guess she waited until darkness fell and then moved elsewhere. Possibly to a different drain refuge. Hannah's checking them out now in her usual meticulous fashion, which means she probably won't report back for a week or more."

Christian and Torrin walked over and joined them. "Were you able to track her beyond the refuge, Malcolm?" said a worried Christian. "I know you're a talented tracker, you wouldn't have stopped just at the refuge."

Malcolm smiled, making his rugged face look positively handsome. "I couldn't track her far. There were signs of blood, near what was at one time a train station, in Piccadilly. And there were signs of blood moving away from there. After that, nothing."

"Has she gone to our old hide-out then?" said Christian. "That's not far from there and she wouldn't have known we'd moved."

"That was the first place I went to. She hasn't been there. I don't understand why she's hiding from us."

Torrin's face was grim, "I do. Mark's quiet, but I know he intends to kill Madalene the moment she shows her face, and there are many prepared to help him. Madalene knows this too, that's why she won't come to us."

"Well this is like old times," said Holan, with a hollow laugh. "Everyone wanting to kill Madalene." She thought of Alan and flinched. It always hurt to remember him, and what she had done.

"That doesn't make sense. You told her the Provoke group were going to lynch her and she came to *that* meeting, totally unafraid. Why would she hide this time?" said Christian.

"She wasn't pregnant last time, nor was she broken. I saw the change in her, Christian. She's been damaged and this time I don't think she can be cured," said Holan, sorrowfully. The signs had been there for all to see, the effects of it yet to be discovered. If the mental damage was too great, it would be dangerous to let Madalene live…No, she wouldn't consider that possibility.

"We're *her* army. She should be with us. If she thinks it's too dangerous for her here, I'll take her up to Elgin and Bertha, they'll care for her, they love her," said Christian. As do you, thought Holan. "I want permission to go out now and hunt for her, Holan."

"Permission?" said Holan. "When have any of you asked my permission for anything? "It's too dangerous in the daytime, Christian. Wait till night falls."

"I'll go with him, Holan. He needs someone to protect him from his crush on Madalene. Sweet though," Torrin smiled familiarly at her.

Christian noticed. "So you two are together now?" There was no animosity in his voice, only a hint of wistfulness.

"Danger and sorrow again," said Holan, wryly. "It happened between the two of us before, remember. The difference this time is Torrin had genuine feelings for me, and is not secretly in love with my sister. Don't look like that, and don't ask because you're not getting an answer." It was there on Christian's face. Was he as good in bed as I am?

At that moment Adrian came in, virtually carrying Ellyn, who was so distressed she hardly seemed aware of her surroundings. The girl was holding unread newspapers, which she dropped onto the floor. Holan pushed through the crowd, who had instantly surrounded them, and were already asking questions. Christian and Torrin followed her. Like a small child, Ellyn saw Holan, and beseechingly, held her arms out for comfort. Holan pulled Ellyn into her arms and held her tightly while she sobbed uncontrollably. Holan's own tears fell into the girl's hair. The news was bad.

"He tried to hang on...I told him about the baby...His face never looked so happy..." Ellyn couldn't continue. Everyone in the room stood silently, tears wetting their faces. Ellyn's sunny nature had made her loved by all of them, her pain was their pain. Jinn had not been loved in this fashion, but he had been respected by all of them.

Holan felt like a hole had been punched through her chest, she could hardly breathe with the pain of Jinn's loss. Images of him growing up flooded her brain. The fun they'd had together when he was older and visited her flat. His pain on finding out his mother was in fact his grandmother, and his desperate longing to be acknowledged by Madalene as her son. Her resentment at him following Madalene around like a lapdog, and ignoring her...

Finally, Ellyn ceased crying. Softly she said, "He told me about Madalene. Said I had to know the truth. Jinn was made to watch her getting force-fed. He cried while he was telling me about it, he'd never seen anything so horrible. Adrian was with me at the time, weren't you Adrian?"

Adrian looked grim as he began to talk, his eyes dark with pain. "Peter Shadow really loves Madalene. He couldn't risk antagonising her by killing her son without an excuse. Jinn was so angered by the force-feeding, he took a meat cleaver to Peter's throat and sealed his fate. Madalene's laughter in the Arena was part of the plan to help him escape. There was no other way to prove herself trustworthy enough to be allowed to stand by the barrier and create a distraction. On the word 'Jinn', he was to stop playacting and run."

Adrian threw a dark glare around the room. "Mark. Get here now." Mark was nearby and had heard every word. "If you still intend to kill Madalene, then you go through me first. Follow the movement of my lips. It was planned that Madalene laugh at Adam and the others, and Jinn said this part of the plan hurt her the most."

Mark scowled, but Holan could see that he was struggling with his emotions It was the same with those who had become Mark's allies. To alleviate the tension, Holan passed Ellyn over to Torrin's care and gently embraced Adrian. The man felt like a rock. "Luke?" She dreaded his answer. Luke was the comedian of the army, a man who could put a touch of brightness into any situation.

"Luke's holding on: probably due to the huge number of female army members that have taken up residence by his bed. They're willing him not to die. The bullet missed his heart, so he has a chance. The next two days are critical, if he makes it through them, he'll probably live. Anyway, look after Ellyn. I'm going back to Luke's side, if I can make my way through his harem. What do women see in him?"

"We'll bury Jinn tomorrow night, Adrian," said Holan, softly.

"Where?" said Adrian.

"Madalene would hate this, but I'm going to dig up my mother's grave and put him in with her. She was more Jinn's mother, than Madalene ever was. The Death Gardens, Marlton Village. Eight o clock. You know where to go."

Adrian had only just left, when a gasp came from Mark. He was sat on the floor, looking at one of the papers, Ellyn had brought in. "They're offering two million engles for information that leads to the capture of Madalene."

Holan was stunned, two million engles was a fortune. Peter Shadow wanted her sister back, urgently.

"It's not just for Madalene," said Christian. "He wants his babies as well."

"And we can't protect her, because she won't come to us, while she thinks we'll try to kill her," said Torrin, in frustration.

"I wouldn't have gone through with it," said Mark, tearfully. "It was her laughter that angered me, and Adam's reaction to it. I felt like she'd betrayed all those who worshipped her, including me. I was so wrapped up in grief and rage; I forgot we'd been told not to believe everything we saw. We have to find her, Holan and protect her like she protected us. I'm the reason she hasn't come back. This is my fault."

Holan closed her eyes with relief. Finally Mark had seen sense. She almost heard a click, as the army reunited. "We have to be careful. There'll be Sanctum Guards, Secret Force members, and just about every citizen in the land who could do with two million engles looking for her. If we're lucky, she'll come to us of her own accord, but I doubt it."

No-one paid any attention to the plump woman staggering down the street on ill-fitting heels. And that, thought Madalene, is the way I like it. The hour was late, but she'd achieved what she wanted, at a cost. She was utterly exhausted, the staggering was no act. Underneath her coat, clinging to her body like an over-adventurous stranger was her new rifle, and the shopping bags in her right hand held enough explosive to blow up half of London. Two men passed nearby and looked at her with contempt.

"Care to help me gentlemen?" she asked in a gruff voice, laughing as they quickly moved away. Shortly after that, she was back underground.

Cold biscuit porridge awaited her on the platform. She wanted tea, but was too tired to make a fire; instead she poured some nettle wine into a mug and drank that. Then, after carefully hiding the explosives, she wrapped herself up in about five blankets for warmth, and settled down to eat some of the cold porridge. Her throat was not healed and it still hurt to eat, but she forced down enough for revival. Her plan was progressing, and having seen that there was a two million engles reward on her head, she was determined to see it through. Peter had no intention of paying out

271

that sum of money, but he was certainly eager for *her* return. Hadn't she always said that a woman had to play hard to get.

Already she was booked into the hotel, as mistress of an insignificant minister called Clary Johnson. She'd heard him mentioned, in derogatory terms, during a conversation between Michael Vertex and Peter. What mattered was that the hotel recognised the name, and they had. Clary would be surprised to find one of his mistresses waiting when he arrived at the hotel- a quick piece of research had revealed he had many of them. By then, her bombs would be in place, and she would be long gone. After that, Clary would find himself victim of an even bigger surprise.

Slowly, Madalene removed her disguise, trying to remain under the blankets as much as possible. The padded coat was left on for its warmth, as were the thick wool stockings, but the buck teeth, the thick glasses, dreadful woollen hat and blonde wig came off. She forced two more spoonfuls of porridge down her throat, and then lay down to sleep.

A noise stirred her. Thinking she'd imagined it, she rolled over to get comfortable and went back to sleep. No. Someone *was* in the tunnel, or was it more than one person? It was hard to tell, given the disorientation of sleep. Carefully, Madalene reached for her rifle and then slid off the platform, and went as far back under the ledge, as she could go. It wasn't the best hiding place, but most people wouldn't think of looking there, not when they had the whole ruins of a train station to search instead. Now the noise came nearer and this time she heard weapons being cocked. Sanctum Guards then. What the hell had induced them to come down here? Had someone been so alert, they'd seen her enter the tunnel? Torch light appeared, she shrank back as it was shone under the ledge.

"Nothing there," said a voice, she knew well. Torrin Spice. What the hell was he doing here? Looked like the Provoke army wanted her badly enough to hunt her down. Well they weren't going to find her, however well she'd trained them.

"Here, Torrin," said Christian.

She might have known he'd come as well. So where was the last of the glorious trio, Alan Moore, her favourite of the three?

"She's not here now," said Christian. "But she's been here and recently. Look at this."

Madalene heard Torrin climb onto the platform. "She's been out and about in disguise then," he said.

"And sleeping here by the look of the blankets. They're warm, she hasn't been gone long. We could still catch her if we hurry. This disgusting muck must be all she has to eat, perhaps she's gone looking for food," said Christian, a hint of excitement appearing in his voice.

"Then if we wait for her here, she'll return shortly."

"It's too cold to wait here, unless we make a fire, and if we do that, Madalene will see it and run off. Let's go back to the hide-out and tell Holan, we've found where Madalene's hiding. Tomorrow night we can come back better equipped, and then we'll wait. Holan will probably want to come with us," said Christian, shivering noisily.

"We can't come back tomorrow. Jinn's funeral's taking place in Marlton Village at eight tomorrow night. Though we could come back here when we return. If we catch Madalene asleep, it'll be a lot easier than trying to catch her awake. You know what she's like," said Torrin, a hint of apprehension in his voice.

"She has the right to attend the funeral," said Christian, sombrely. "She was his mother. Let's try to catch her tomorrow morning. If we're early enough we may find her asleep."

Madalene heard them leaving, but stayed where she was until she was certain they'd gone. By then she was so cold, she'd begun to go numb. Heaving herself out from under the ledge, she bundled herself back into the blanket pile. She'd seen Jinn get shot and knew the wound was fatal, but wasn't it human nature to hope, that in cases like these, you were wrong?

"If anything goes wrong, Jinn, I want you to know that you were the outcome of a prolonged and violent rape. I didn't allow myself to love you; you always reminded me of that night. Big mistake, none of it was your fault. It was mine, and now I'm paying for it, because I can finally see what I missed. I should have loved you and I'm sorry

that I didn't." Tenderly she'd taken him in her arms and cradled him like a baby, stroking his hair and kissing his cheeks. "Listen Jinn, if there's an afterdeath, I'll come and find you. I swear I will make up for every single slight I have given you."

"Don't worry about me, Mother. I'll run faster than you've ever seen me run before. And when I'm free, I'll fight to make you free too. Then I'm going to take care of you and our new babies. I'll be the man of our family." Jinn had smiled at her and then cheekily added, "And we will love the babies, in spite of who their father was."

The memory of his care and love made her tremble and then shake violently. Something broke inside and her grief poured out in torrents. Scared that such grief would tear her apart; she wrapped her arms tightly around her chest and held on. *"If there is an afterdeath, I'll come and find you."* Mindless of the cold, she stood up and fetched one of her knives; there was something she had to do. Holding out her right wrist, she examined the scar that made the word 'Bren', and then carefully she carved Jinn's name into the flesh below it. She cut too deeply and her head began to spin. Satisfied at last, she was about to return to the blankets, when she fainted.

When she came to her senses she was freezing, and for a moment she couldn't understand why she wasn't under the blankets. The pool of sticky blood around her right hand reminded her why; instantly she was violently sick. It was disgusting, but she dragged herself over to the cold biscuit porridge and shoved spoonfuls of it down her resistant throat. Vengeance required strength. But first she had a funeral to go to.

Chapter 32

New Life

Why the hell were *they* still here? It was half past nine; the funeral should have been over long ago. Madalene shook her head; the pain in it was terrible, as was the pain in her stomach. Something was wrong, but when had that ever stopped her. Ahead lay the majority of her army, and she noted how their numbers had swelled since her capture. Only they weren't her army anymore, they were the enemy. Listening to the conversation, she realised the difficulty of digging a hole in frozen ground had caused the delay. Jinn's body had been lowered into the hole. Now it was just taking an age to fill the damn thing in.

A painful spasm tore so hard and fast through Madalene's body; only sheer willpower stopped her screaming out loud. Almost doubled up, she watched Ellyn tearfully lay a wreath of evergreen leaves on the finished grave. Holan said a few words and finally, to Madalene's relief, the army began to disperse. Another spasm struck and she had to shove the sleeve of her coat into her mouth and bite down hard, even so she almost passed out.

It rankled that Holan had chosen to put Jinn's body with her abysmal mothers'. Why hadn't they burned his body instead and scattered the ashes somewhere nice?

Madalene waited, and then waited some more. No further spasms occurred, though her stomach ached, and her headache was getting worse. Finally, believing it was clear; she walked over to the grave and knelt beside it.

"I knew you would come," said a voice behind her.

She reached for her rifle, but it was snatched out of her hand. Snarling, she turned.

"No Madalene. This isn't the time for violence or threats. You've come here to mourn your son."

"Well if it isn't, the handsome Christian Peek," she said, mockingly. "Are you here on your own, or are others waiting nearby to assist you?"

"I'm alone," said Christian, studying her warily. "Torrin and Holan have gone to wait for you in your hiding place. I was going to go with them, but then I had a thought. What if Madalene had been there last night, hiding from us? She'd have heard our conversation, which means she'll be at the Death Gardens when she thinks we've gone, probably an hour later. And here you are."

"Very clever, Mr Peek. I'm impressed." She began to laugh at his unexpected ingenuity. It made the pain in her head worse.

"You have to come back with me, Madalene and face your army." He looked like he meant business. Well so did she.

"Oh, I can't do that. Haven't you heard, I'm to be married soon? Peter Shadow and I will be playing 'Happy Families'." She rubbed her stomach to emphasise her point. Christian knelt down by her side and lifted her left hand. She flinched violently. The hand was in a bad way and not healing properly.

"It's true then. Shadowman smashed your hand to stop you taking the ring off your finger. Quite a proposal. I can't imagine how he'll top that at your wedding." He lifted her other hand, and she saw him cringe at the word 'Jinn', freshly carved into her skin. It was seeping, but she would not cover it with bandages.

"I'm sure whatever he thinks up will be delightful. It will be interesting to see how his guests react, when he force-feeds me at the wedding breakfast." Suddenly she became angry. "Why the hell should you care, Christian? You hate me too. Once before you tried to lynch me. I won't let that happen again."

"You've got things wrong, Madalene. I don't hate you, and the Provoke army's not going to hurt you," said Christian, quietly, as if he spoke to a child.

"Yeah, Alan Moore's planning a surprise party, and Mark's making me a 'Welcome Home' cake." Did Christian really think she was that stupid?

"You don't know?" said Christian, with a strange look.

276

"Know what?" she said, puzzled by his expression.

"Alan's dead. Holan flew into a rage when she learned he'd betrayed you. She didn't stop to think. Her gun was in her hand and she shot him."

"You're lying. Holan loved Alan too much to do something like that." Madalene was stunned by this news. Homicide was obviously in the family's blood and considering how violent their Father had been, that was no surprise.

"I'm not lying. She almost killed Torrin too, but now he's one of us and he's proved his worth many times over. Holan drinks heavily to ease her pain, too heavily. If you were around you could help her, I know you could. We made her our leader, when we decided to carry on without you, but she's not like you and she knows it. She'll gladly relinquish her control. Come back to the army, Madalene. We need you." Christian grabbed her shoulder, desperately. She shrugged him off.

It was hard to believe what she was hearing; she'd been so convinced that *she* was the army's latest enemy. Her body began to tremble badly; it wasn't possible to hide it from Christian. She didn't like the look of concern on his face, and she didn't want his pity. "Everybody wants me, but nobody trusts me. I saw the reaction in the Arena, the widespread doubt, *and* I heard Mark's furious words. Even though I told you all not to believe what you saw, that you had to let me do what I needed to do. And don't deny there was a plot to deal with me on my return to the hide-out." She watched Christian's face and saw that she had been right not to go back. "I thought so."

Christian began to plead with her. "Everyone's seen sense, even Mark. Jinn told us the truth before he died. Most of us never doubted you..." Christian stopped and tried a different approach. "Luke's dying, Madalene. He was shot shortly after Jinn got hit. It would give Luke so much pleasure to see you again." Christian smiled, "Do you remember our pot of engles? It still exists and there's a lot of cash in it. Luke was always convinced he'd be the one to collect it..."

Christian's face started to fade from view; she didn't hear his last words. Fierce bursts of pain rampaged through her skull. Her stomach had settled, her head had not. Like a banshee she began to wail, making Christian stand up and take a step back.

"No-o-o. I'm tired of constant condemnation. If I return there'll only be something else to berate me about. I'm in Hell, Christian. Hell! The army can't save me from it, no-one can. You don't understand." Her right hand was holding onto her head tightly, but she heard his response and the anguish in his voice.

"Madalene? What is it? Do you hear me? The army can save you from this pain and we will. Let us help you. Remember we're all prepared to die for you, even me, the biggest coward in the army."

The pain eased slightly and through it she groaned, "This isn't about preserving the people of this country anymore, it's personal. Maybe it always was. You don't know the history between me and Peter Shadow. If I'm mad, he helped make me that way. Though he didn't do it alone, his friends helped him, many of them now an integral part of this government. Then there was my Father and others, but I've dealt with them…"

"I know you were gang-raped at the age of twelve," said Christian, interrupting her. "And I know Jinn's father was probably Peter Shadow."

"Holan been telling tales again? Did she also tell you that she read my diary, and saw an entry that said I wanted to fuck Peter? She assumed I'd willingly had sex with all those boys. She made a mistake. I wanted to fuck him *up*, Christian, fuck him *up*. You know what I'm like. I stupidly offended Peter the first time I met him. How was I to know he was Head Boy and a big-shot in the school? After that him and his friends started to bully me. Because I refused to be frightened of them, like everyone else, they increased the lengths they were prepared to go to." She didn't know why, but through her pain, she told Christian the whole story. Afterwards, he was physically sick.

"I spent years trying to forget the whole thing, and other traumas came along to take its place. Then we get a new government. And low and behold, look who's leading it, Peter Shadow, and with him his boys. You can't imagine the joy I felt. Realising what he was up to, I fought to curb his excesses, always hoping others would rise. People muttered and grumbled. Little pockets of resistance were

278

everywhere. But every time they rose, he destroyed them. Somehow the pathetic Provoke group survived, and that, I think, was because you were led by a man like Elgin. So I turned to you for help. You were all I had. Now I don't need help." Surely she'd made her point this time.

"You're pregnant, Madalene. You need our help more than ever. Direct us, and we'll do your fighting for you. When you've given birth and are strong again, then you can change your mind." It seemed that nothing would persuade Christian to leave her alone.

"No. Tell the Provoke army that you've seen me, and they're to leave me alone. Keep harassing this government, don't stop. Emulate Elgin and Bertha and their people. Tell Holan that before too long, I will be the new leader of this country, and then everything will be alright again. Now, give me back my rifle, Christian. I've found a new hiding place and I need to go there and rest."

Christian handed her the rifle and then looked thoughtfully at her. "I'm younger than you by at least ten years, but I want to take care of you. I want to make you happy." To her surprise, Christian's voice nearly broke with emotion. "There are things you don't understand about me. I've never forgotten the night you picked me up from my shame and made me feel better about myself. The night I first met you I was angry and hostile; I wanted to see you destroyed, but my heart thudded with excitement every time I looked at you."

Looking into his unusual, but earnest eyes, Madalene forced a smile through her pain. "I'm not stupid, Christian. I know how you feel about me. I thought in time you'd outgrow it. There are so many pretty women who sigh at your looks, and long for your beautiful eyes to turn on them."

"My 'beautiful' eyes see only you. Don't mock me, Madalene, or treat me like a child."

To Madalene's surprise, Christian raised her up, and put his hands on her face. Then suddenly, he kissed her deeply and passionately. The pain in her head still plagued her, but she found herself responding. Perhaps it was because this kind of love had eluded her ever since Bren's death, though there'd been mystifying moments with Peter that had felt like love. She needed to remember what it was like, before she got embroiled in the hatred which burned so fiercely inside her, it consumed every other emotion. In seconds she removed enough clothing for him to touch her, and he did likewise.

"It's too cold to be naked," she said, laughing at the reverent way he handled her breasts. "Five minutes only, or we'll die of hypothermia."

"I only need two," said Christian, with a cheeky grin.

It was the lovemaking of people in an extreme situation, fast, intense and pleasurable. Madalene smiled contently as she prised Christian's hands away from her breasts, and refastened her clothing. Sex seemed to have eased her pain, better than any drug could have done.

"Now will you come back with me?" said Christian, his delight clear on his face.

"Well I've never been asked anything quite as nicely as that before, but I still say no. It's time to end this and only I can do it." Picking up her rifle, she began to walk away. When Christian tried to follow, she sent a warning shot to his feet. "Stay where you are. I'll meet you here in three weeks time and give you another chance to change my mind."

"You won't turn up. You're trying to get rid of me, but you're not well, physically or mentally. Can't you see you need looking after?" Christian's joy had become anxiety.

"Eight o clock in three weeks time. I will be here. Behave yourself and you get another two minutes. And don't forget to bring me a present from your winnings."

Christian looked puzzled, "What winnings?"

"The engle pot. Tell the boys what you've done and you'll win the engle pot. I don't mind what you tell them we did, as long as you don't get too inventive." Blowing Christian a kiss, Madalene left, and this time he let her go.

Madalene had use of a stolen transporter. Jumping into it, she drove to a deserted farm on the outskirts of Marlton Village. It was a place she'd known about for a while. The meeting point of one of those pockets of resistance that had been wiped out quietly in the night. Looking around the grounds earlier, she'd come across a shallow mass grave that marked the event.

Everything she required had been transferred to this place, so she had no need to return to the tunnel. Holan and Torrin were in for a long wait. The explosives and detonators were safely hidden in a nearby barn, where she'd also discovered a storeroom that held ample supplies; potatoes, flour, wrinkled apples, turnips, swedes, aging cheeses and wine. Life had certainly improved over the last twenty four hours. The Provoke army didn't want to kill her after all, and she'd just had sex with a gorgeous man, ten years younger than her. Making a small, contained fire, Madalene reheated some soup she'd made earlier. Unexpected sex had given her an appetite, so it was easier to get food into her stomach. To accompany the food, she opened a bottle of apple wine and drank most of it.

Nearby, on a broken table, lay a small box. She'd found it under a pile of compost in her greenhouse. It contained a syringe, needles and a variety of drugs. It would be good to get high, she thought, to escape for a while, after all the pain she'd suffered recently. She chose a white powder called Sonambulam. It had been bought cheaply from a sailor, a long time ago. Sonambulam's effects were similar to opium; it brought peace, contentment, and would give her a feeling of well-being. Quickly she mixed the drug with water and drank it down. The effect was immediate. Now nothing mattered, not the deaths of Jinn and her family, not the Provoke army, not Peter Shadow, not Michael Vertex. She didn't care anymore. At some point the world faded from sight and she slept.

There was a persistent tapping noise, she tried to ignore it. It was probably trees dancing in the wind and hitting the broken windows. Suddenly Madalene woke with a start; it was trickling she heard, not tapping. Her waters had broken; the babies were coming early, *too early*. Her contractions started with no let-up, less than two minutes between them. For a while all she could do was writhe about in agony, and then the first baby came, it slid out of her body with ease and was so tiny it looked like a child's doll. She tried to snatch it up and protect it, but the second baby followed with speed. It seemed surreal; neither child made a sound, the only noise in the room came from her. It was hard to move, but she managed to crawl across the

281

room and fetch a blanket for them, and then she crawled back again. Just as she wrapped the babies in the blanket, she gasped in pain and pushed out the afterbirth. It was over, but the babies were still silent. They weren't breathing. One at a time, she picked them up and slapped them hard, and then she cleared their mouths with her fingers and tried to blow life into them. Nothing worked. "Breathe damn you. Breathe." She didn't stop. "Breathe babies. Please breathe." Morning came and went, still she carried on, but the bodies had gone grey, and slowly the realisation hit her that they were dead. The threads of her sanity were stretched to breaking point and she knew it. What little reason she had left, she needed. She put the babies' bodies down and covered them with the blanket. She couldn't cry, but she did sleep and when she woke up it was dark again.

As weak as she was, she finally acted. Wrapping the bodies up in some dusty sheets she'd found, she placed them outside, in fresh snow she hadn't seen fall. Then she bathed in cold water and dressed in fresh clothing. The afterbirth was burned on the fire and it made the room stink. Madalene didn't care; mindlessly she tried to scrub blood off the floor. The bloodstained blanket was tossed to one side; she'd deal with it another time. Without tasting a thing, she forced food down her throat and drank another bottle of wine. Again she used Sonambulam, but this time it wasn't strong enough to douse the extremity of her emotion, and to add to her pain, her breasts had begun to leak.

By the time morning came, she'd decided what to do. A small measure of strength had returned and she needed to act quickly before it faded. An injection of Xybille helped. Carefully she placed the bodies, wrapped like two tiny parcels, into the transporter. Beside them she put an even tinier package. Then she drove to London. She wore no disguise and wasn't bothered about being caught.

Near the Sanctum building, she stopped and waited. Though a few people passed by, she went unnoticed. As a Postal transporter came into view, she loaded her rifle and stepped out directly in front of it. The driver stopped at the last minute. Pointing the rifle at him, she walked up to his window.

"I have urgent packages for Shadowman. They're labelled and he must get them this morning. Trouble is my transporter's failed me.

Can you put them in with your delivery?" His expression showed that he saw the madwoman she had become.

"No I can't. You can't stop me like this, without authorisation," said the apprehensive driver.

Pushing her rifle closer to his face, Madalene said, "This is my authorisation. Tell Shadowman that Madalene returns his gifts. They are unwanted."

Recognition appeared in the driver's eyes, but already Madalene had pushed the three packages onto his lap and returned to her transporter. Before he could summon help, she'd gone.

Chapter 33

Conclusions

"You saw Madalene! Why didn't you say there was a possibility of her attending the funeral? I could have waited with you and persuaded her to come back with us." Holan was frustrated and disappointed. She'd spent a freezing night, in a disused train station, desperate to see her sister again, and now Christian was telling her that he'd known all along Madalene might appear in the Death Gardens.

"I wasn't *certain* she'd come, it was just an idea I had. If I'd been wrong and she'd gone to the train station instead, you wouldn't have been happy, Holan."

"I'm not happy now, and I would have sent Torrin to guard the train station just in case. Next time discuss your ideas, Christian." Holan was trying to calm down, but she'd had a lot to drink and was missing Madalene more than ever. "So how was my beloved sister? Crazy as ever?"

"Crazier. Madalene's in a bad way, Holan. She needs help." Quickly Christian recalled his encounter with Madalene, and he left nothing out.

The hush that had fallen over the army was broken by Adrian, who began patting Christian on the back. "This'll set Luke's recovery back by months," said Adrian, chuckling. "Still it looks like you're the rightful winner of the engle pot."

"He doesn't get the engles," said Malcolm, "until we get the details *and* Madalene's word on it. And if she says he was rubbish, he doesn't get it at all."

"Yeah," said Mark, shyly joining in. "We need proof, Christian."

"Stop it," said Holan, most definitely not amused. "This isn't a joking matter. From what Christian's told us, Madalene's seriously unhinged. Her time with Peter Shadow has obviously affected her

284

more than she realises, not to mention the effect of Jinn's death. She may well be out of control."

"It's the talk about becoming leader of the country that worries me," said Torrin. "She'd be scarier than Shadowman. Many of you haven't seen how manic Madalene can get. I have, and it's terrifying."

"You have *never* seen her lead this army," said Adrian, protectively. His words echoed by others. "She fed us, trained us, looked after us and gave us pride. Even if she was totally deranged, she would still be the best leader this country's ever had, and I for one would support her. I know Luke would too."

"I would also support her," said Christian, joining in the argument. "But she isn't manic or out of control, she's not well. Look, I'm meeting Madalene in the Death Gardens in three weeks time…"Holan could have predicted the hooting and laughter that accompanied this statement. To his credit, Christian flushed, but continued. "She's probably aware that I intend to bring all of you with me. When you see her, you'll be as worried about her as I am."

"We can't wait that long, Christian," said Holan, firmly. "I don't know what she means by 'It's time to end this and only I can do it', but it could have a big impact on what happens to us and to the country. The hunt for Madalene goes on, and we have to be more thorough in our searches. I'm going to ask Elgin and Bertha to come down and help us; hopefully they'll bring some of their people along as well."

Picking up a bottle of spirits Holan walked away, hearing Christian getting plaudits behind her. No-one wanted to hear about the problems Madalene might cause them. Not when there were important things like her sexual behaviour to discuss instead. Ellyn gave Holan a sympathetic grin as she passed, and she smiled back. Ellyn was getting bigger every day, and though it was a delight to have her with the army, Holan thought it was time to find her a place of safety. Yet another problem to deal with. Madalene would have probably sorted Ellyn out, the minute she heard of the pregnancy. Big deal, *she* wasn't Madalene.

Sinking into a chair, Holan became emotional. The army always forgot that she'd grown up with Madalene. They didn't understand the danger Madalene presented to herself and others around her; you ducked when she exploded, and checked you were intact when she finished. No, the army viewed Madalene as a heroic figure, brave, kind, willing to listen to any problem, keen to laugh and joke with them. And she was all those things and more, but her head wasn't right and never had been. Damn it. All Holan really wanted was to do, was to hold Madalene in her arms again and look after her. "Don't lose it, Madalene. Not now," she whispered to the bottle, before opening it and downing the contents.

Peter studied the parcels in front of him. He was aware that they had come from Madalene and was intrigued. Security had wanted to check them out first, to be certain they were safe. He had refused. If these packages were explosive devices, he'd know nothing the minute he opened them. However, he was convinced that Madalene would never attack him in such a cowardly fashion; she'd be far more direct. Vertex wanted to be present when he opened them, but again he'd refused. Whatever was in these parcels was between him and Madalene.

Carefully, he unwrapped one of the larger packages. *"Tell Shadowman that Madalene returns his gifts. They are unwanted."* No! No! No! A tiny, stiff body fell into his lap. This couldn't be happening. In shock, he reached for the other parcel, knowing already what he would find. Another stiff body appeared. Perfectly formed, both the bodies were boys - his sons. Retching violently and shaking like a man with palsy, he made himself open the small parcel. Out rolled a stiff finger, and on it was a pink diamond ring.

She had maliciously killed his sons, and rejected his love in the most horrific manner possible. His heart didn't break; it shattered into a million pieces. What had he done to deserve this? Hours passed by, but he couldn't move. Voices came and went through the door. He told them to go away, he wasn't to be disturbed.

"Peter? I don't care what you think, I'm coming in. I know you'll be angry, but I'm worried about you." Vertex, entered defiantly, then stopped and stared at him in horror.

"What has that bitch done to you? Are those your...Are they what I think they are?" Vertex moved carefully past him and headed for the drinks cabinet."

Bitch? Did he mean Madalene? Cerulean eyes, dark hair? A sparkle of light, from the ring, caught his eye, as Vertex opened the curtains, letting in daylight. *"Of course I'll marry you. Well stop gawking at me and put the ring back on my finger. I've got used to it being there..."* She hadn't meant one single word.

"Here drink this. It's strong, pear wine. Let me remove the er...packages from your lap. Fuck! She cut her finger off to remove the ring?"

No-o-o. Peter held his dead children with one hand; his other gripped the finger.

"Put her finger down Peter, and then you can hold this glass. The alcohol will ease your shock." Without volition, Peter did as he was told, and accepting the glass he drank deeply.

In moments Vertex had the glass refilled. "Unbelievable. After all the kindness you showed her. She'll pay for this, I promise."

Warmth surged through Peter's body and it was accompanied by hatred of such force, he shook from it. "We have to catch her first Fat boy. Something no-one seems able to do, not even when she appears in daylight, totally undisguised, right outside the Sanctum building. Have all my people gone blind?"

"That's better. Be angry, Peter. You deserve to be angry." Vertex refilled the glass again.

"Get these abominations away from me." He threw the bodies to the ground, but looked regretfully at them. Vertex went to take the finger. "Wait. I want that ring. She'll wear it again before she dies. No-one rejects my gifts. No-one."

"A good idea, Peter. She has other fingers you can put it on, at least I hope she has. It will infuriate her to have to wear your ring again."

"Are you implying she wouldn't want to wear my ring, Fat boy? What is so wrong with me, that she wouldn't want to wear my ring?" The pain of rejection entered his emotional arena.

"You misunderstand me. I meant that chopping a finger off to remove a ring is an extreme..."

287

"Don't get in any deeper, you've said enough. We will try a different way to find Madalene. I want you to send out squads of Sanctum Guards. They are to blow up schools, hospitals, universities, homes. Get snipers out as well; they are to kill ordinary people going about their daily business. I've got plenty of Madalene's possessions, we can scatter them about after these events: proof that it's Madalene's work. Reports are to indicate that she's insane and wild; that she's extremely dangerous and no-one must attempt to tackle her on their own. Raise the reward to four million engles, on condition that she's captured alive. I want the public to hate Madalene as much as I do." Peter beckoned Vertex to fetch him more wine. The public would never hate Madalene as much as he did at this moment, but by the time he'd finished, she'd have no-one to turn to. Even Elgin, who continued to elude him, would turn against her.

"Brilliant, Peter. Mere sightings of her will bring reports flooding in; we'll have her locked up again in days. Even better, the people will turn against her army, and we may even pick up the remains of the original group. Anyone suspected of any association with Madalene will be turned in. It will be quite a witch hunt." Vertex's face quivered with excitement.

"There's a danger that seeing this, her army will hunt her down and destroy her, but I want Madalene to be captured alive. She must be alive, Vertex, otherwise how do I repay her for this?"

"Your little breakfast whore doesn't think the army will harm her. Their attitude towards Madalene seems to have changed for some reason."

"My breakfast girl? What has she got to do with anything?" Peter was puzzled.

"She betrayed you; Partlin's currently showing her the error of her ways. Normally I despise the man, but that girl deserves his brutality. Messages did pass between Madalene and her army; your breakfast trollop was the messenger."

Another betraying bitch, not that he cared about this one. Partlin was welcome to her. Madalene was a different matter entirely. He thought of the long afternoon he had spent making love to her. She

288

hadn't been feigning her emotions, he was certain of it. He ached to have more of those times and felt a sudden need to be alone again.

"Leave me, Vertex. Come back later with news, I want my squads and snipers on the streets as soon as possible."

After Vertex had gone, Peter suddenly noticed the labels on the floor. Picking them up, he read them. 'This child is named Bren'. 'This child is named Jinn'. 'Do I want to marry you? No!'

"Good Madalene. Very good. Soon however, you will have no choice in the matter. Vertex salivates at the thought of torturing you, but I have different plans. Partlin will take care of you for a while, and when he's finished, you will beg to marry me. Then I'll make sure you spend all our married life, regretting the day you did this"

"I told you she'd gone crazy. She can't distinguish between the Sanctum and the public anymore. People hate her and they hate us because of her. She has to be stopped. She's a menace." Holan was desperate, what the hell was wrong with Madalene? Why had she started to attack ordinary people?"

"No! She's ill. I don't believe Madalene's doing this. It's Peter Shadow's work. He's trying to damage her reputation, and he's succeeding if even you believe it." Christian looked at her in defiance, his jaw jutting out so much; she thought it would fall off. Well he would defend her, wouldn't he? His feelings for Madalene had never been fully hidden.

"Christian's right," said Hannah. "I've never liked Madalene, but she wouldn't attack the public like this."

A booming voice came through the entry way. "Holan, my dear girl. What's going on down here? It's like a war zone outside. Have your army gone mad?" Elgin emerged into view, with him came Bertha and many others. In seconds Holan found herself enfolded in his arms and could have wept with relief that he was there. No longer did she have to feel so responsible for everything.

"The army's not involved in whatever's going on. This is Madalene's work. I think she's lost it, Elgin. We have to stop her." Holan felt tears run down her face, she'd dreaded this happening ever since Madalene had re-entered her life.

Elgin spoke softly to her, "Don't be so quick to judge, Holan. That girl wouldn't attack the public."

"Tell Elgin what she was like the last time you saw her, Christian." She hoped he would back her up, but should have known better.

"She was ill and mentally unstable, but how could she be otherwise after everything she's gone through? Being pregnant can't have helped." Christian looked at Holan, apologetically.

Elgin looked at both of them and then turned his attention to Bertha, who simply nodded her agreement with him. "Well there's only one way to find out, Holan. Get your army onto the streets and stop whoever's doing this, Madalene or the Sanctum Guards."

"I've been doing that, Elgin, but the most unlikely places are being attacked. Eight children, all of them under five years of age, were shot yesterday at a Sanctum nursery. Peter Shadow wouldn't do something like that, not to his own supporters. It has to be Madalene." The nursery business had hurt her more than anything. That Madalene could be pregnant and harm small children was the biggest sign her sanity had gone."

Torrin spoke up, "Madalene's possessions have been found at every incident. It has to be her."

Elgin smiled, and it was a smile of relief. "So she's not only gone mad, she's also become careless with her possessions. Come on, Torrin, don't be so stupid. Madalene's done something so unforgivable, Peter Shadow wants her destroyed, starting with her reputation."

Holan realised that he was right and for the first time in ages she smiled with relief. "If it's not her, then where is she? What's happening to her? Christian said she drove away from Marlton, which means she could be anywhere in the country."

"Or," said Elgin, "She could be hiding in Marlton itself. What do you think, Bertha?"

"Insane or not, this isn't Madalene's work. I know that for sure. Now the explosion at the Greyfriars Hotel, that kindly removed half

290

the Sanctum and led to the loss of Barton Lacey, Shadowman's deputy, *that* was Madalene. It has her hallmarks all over it."

"There, my dear wife knows everything, and I believe she's right. Madalene has struck a huge blow, but against the Sanctum only. Now didn't you tell me, Holan, Christian had a meeting with her tomorrow."

Christian gave Elgin a worried look, and then said, "She won't be there. I thought she'd expect me to bring the army along, but now I'm not sure. If she sees a hint of anyone else, she might run off."

"Ah, but she won't see anyone with you," said Elgin, cunningly. "If she is in Marlton, then I believe she's hiding in a disused farm that used to be home to some friends of mine. They established a resistance group of their own and were slaughtered for it. I put out a rumour that the place was haunted, to keep bloodthirsty sightseers away. Madalene's not afraid of ghosts and almost certainly she knows the place, there's little Madalene doesn't know of. While you meet her in the Death Gardens, Christian, the rest of us will go to this farm. When she returns from your meeting we'll have her, and then we'll know the truth and react accordingly."

Holan reached out and held Elgin tightly, her relief was enormous. "Forgive me for taking advantage of your husband, Bertha, but I've needed comfort like this for a long time."

"Don't worry, Holan. Help yourself. There's more than enough of him to go round. In fact there's rather too much of him, I think it's time he lost some weight."

"Bertha!" said Elgin, in dismay.

"Northern food," said Bertha to Holan, laughing. "Don't worry, Elgin. I'm sure our beloved Madalene will still adore you, despite your increased girth."

Holan smiled, happily. Somehow everything was going to be okay, and tomorrow she would see her sister again.

"Vertex! Put the whore down and get your massive backside out of bed. We've found Madalene."

291

Michael groaned and pushed the young girl on top of him away. How much longer would this go on? Reported sightings had come in from all over the country, all of them false. Nevertheless, Peter had made him investigate every single one. The only true sighting had come from the Greyfriars Hotel in Colchester, and Michael believed Madalene herself had made that call. Fortunately, he'd been delayed on his way over there, arriving just as the hotel was torn apart by a massive explosion. It didn't bear thinking about. As it was, over half the Outer Sanctum had been caught in the blast and, much to his delight, so had Barton Lacey, which made *him* second in command, whether Peter liked it or not.

"Open the door, Fat boy, or we'll kick it in. Don't worry about your modesty. Your blubbery body disgusts me with or without clothing."

Peter was becoming increasingly erratic; Madalene had almost destroyed him with the contents of those packages. He'd stopped sleeping and refused to eat. One minute he was spewing out a list of vile reprisals against her, the next minute he was excusing her actions.

"She didn't mean to destroy our children. Sam File says she miscarried them and no-one could have prevented that. Madalene's probably so distraught at this moment; she doesn't know what she's doing."

How on earth did you blow up a hotel, without knowing what you were doing? Peter had even set the breakfast girl free. In a way Michael was grateful to Madalene, she'd damaged Peter so much, it gave him a chance to grab control of the government. He'd endured Peter's insults and ill-treatment long enough. Peter would get what he deserved, and despite her help, so would Madalene. He'd already discussed the matter with John Fletcher, Chief Commander of the Sanctum Guard, and the Inner and Outer Sanctum's were virtually under his control. His chance for power was almost there, but he had to move fast, before Peter regained his senses.

The door to his room crashed open and Peter entered, angrily. "We've found Madalene at last. I thought you might like to be there when I capture her, but if it's too much trouble."

"So where's she supposed to be this time?" said Michael, realising at once that it wasn't wise to talk to Peter this way. His coup had not yet taken place.

"Am I boring you, Fat boy?" Peter gave him a searing look, as if his thoughts were on display. "Several sightings of Madalene came in from Marlton. Sanctum Guards have checked out the area and they believe she's hiding in a disused farmhouse. There were signs of her living there, such as drugs, weapons and clothing, and there were also signs of heavy bleeding, which can only be the miscarriage. At the moment they're waiting for her return and I've sent them reinforcements. I've also sent the Army units based in Aldershot to help them, to make sure no more mistakes are made. If you and I hurry, we can get there in time to see her recaptured."

Michael knew the farm. He'd been there when a hard-core resistance group had been destroyed. The capture of Madalene would destroy his one chance of leadership, unless John Fletcher, Chief Commander of the Sanctum Guard was prepared to act immediately.

Chapter 34

The Madness of Hatred

Madalene sat on the floor in a corner of the room, rubbing her face against a bloodstained blanket in an attempt to catch the scent of her babies. She'd killed and killed again lately, but it hadn't eased her pain. There were a few more to kill, namely Peter Shadow and Michael Vertex: after that it was over. After that she didn't care what happened.

Her head hurt, and flashes of the past presented themselves against her will.

"Hello Madalene. You weren't trying to get away from us were you? That's not very sociable. We're going to do things to you no-one else has dreamed of. Bad things, Madalene. Bad things for a bad girl. Arrogant bitch. You won't be so arrogant when we've finished with you." Peter Shadow tearing the clothes from her body, while surrounding boys with hostile faces, mouthed words that promised pain. Their faces merged, becoming her Father.

"You little bitch. You've hurt your Mother, again. I'm going to beat this wickedness out of you." Her Father's idea of good parental practice.

"Everyone has the right to die when it's their time, not before…" Images of those she'd killed entered her wounded mind. Had she really used such an idiotic and pompous phrase?

The images began to change with terrifying speed. *A rope being placed around her neck, because she was dangerous. A tube shoved up her nose. The stiff bodies of the babies she tried to bring to life. Failing because she was a killer; killers didn't give life, they took it. Burning bodies pouring out of the Greyfriars Hotel.* The papers blamed her for so much death and destruction; she couldn't remember what she'd done and what she hadn't done. She wouldn't have gone into a nursery school and killed small children, just because their parents were Sanctum members, would she?

Her eyes went to the place on her hand where once she'd had a finger. It hurt badly. Had insanity led to her cutting off her finger? Did she still know what she was doing? She needed to get a grip. Peter's government was damaged, but given time he would resurrect it. Her work wasn't over yet.

Michael Vertex killing her son with a shot from his rifle. Michael Vertex running his fingers all over her, inside and out, his bad breath reaching her nostrils as he rolled his tongue around her ears.

"Shall I help you with dinner, mummy?" Hayla's smile. "I'm not your mummy, I'm the Princess Madalene, whose been rescued from wild beasts by your daddy."

"How was your evening, darling, you look exhausted?" Bren's smile. "Elaine was fine, but let's not talk about her at the moment."

"It doesn't matter that you never loved me." Jinn's smile. "...my heart will break if you get shot."

Thoughts of her family gave her strength. Thoughts of Michael Vertex added hatred to that strength. Putting the blanket down, she stood up, it was time to meet Christian at the graveyard and almost certainly the rest of her army would come with him. She smiled at the thought of seeing Holan again, and getting to speak to the others. Only lately had she realised how much she missed them.

"Hello Mr Peek, handsome as ever I see. So tell me, where's my army hiding, I was certain they'd accompany you."

Christian's unusual eyes fixed on hers and there was a strange look in them. "I lied, told them I was meeting you next week at this time."

"And we know the reason for that Mr Peek, don't we?"

"I haven't come here to have sex with you, Madalene," said Christian, irritably. "I was worried about you. You seem to have been a busy woman lately."

"I have been busy. Attacking the public's quite exhausting. There's so many of them to choose from." She smiled and moved closer to him.

"Don't lie to me Madalene. I'm not a fool. I know what's been happening isn't your fault."

Moving closer, she began to stroke his hair, then ran her fingers down his body. He trembled, but stayed still. "Two minutes isn't a long time, Christian and there's no need to worry, I'm not pregnant anymore, my babies are dead. Be a good boy and get your trousers off."

She was pushing him and she knew it. His face was alarmed, but to his credit he was trying to hide it. She began to undo the buttons on his trousers. "I'll be gentle with you, Christian. Don't look so apprehensive. Have you stopped loving me?"

"Where's your finger gone, Madalene?" said Christian, nervously, as she fumbled with the buttons.

"Oh, that thing. Do you know what; I never liked the ring on it, too big, too flashy, and too pink. Because I'd broken my hand again, I couldn't remove the damn thing, so I cut the finger off instead and sent it to Peter."

"You did what?" Christian pulled away from her.

"Yeah, not one of my best ideas, my hand's hurt terribly since. Still Peter Shadow was probably relieved to get the ring back; it was a *very* expensive piece of jewellery." Again she moved on Christian, like a predator stalking its prey.

"Madalene! You're insane. Stop that. Don't touch me." She smiled at his panic.

"I'm insane, so what? It doesn't bother me and it shouldn't bother you. It's not my mind you're after."

"Tell me about the babies, Madalene. What happened to the babies you were carrying?" Honestly, he really needed to calm down. Why did this stuff matter so much to him? It was her business and she'd dealt with it.

"I sent them back to Peter too. Well I never wanted them and he did, so I thought it would make him happy." Christian began to cry and her feigned nonchalance broke. "I didn't deliberately hurt them,

Christian. I miscarried. The fall from the box in the Arena, the drugs I'd taken, having sex with you, who knows what made it happen?"

Reaching out with her hand she felt that he was hard and ready for her, but in spite of this he backed away in horror. "Well you're no fun. You used me, won the engle pot, and now you've lost interest. Men!"

"All this killing's your work! I thought the Sanctum was responsible." He pulled a pistol out of his pocket and aimed it at her.

Now she backed away. Angrily she said, "I blew up the Greyfriars Hotel and killed over half the Sanctum's members. I've blown up homes belonging to members of the Sanctum I've recognised. At no time have I touched the public. How can you doubt me?"

"I don't know what to think anymore..." Looking helpless, he dropped the pistol, then came over and pulled her into his arms. Suddenly and roughly, his desire took hold of him. He began to pull off her clothing and she helped him.

"I'm sorry, Madalene. I don't know what comes over me when I'm near you. I shouldn't have touched you, you're still bleeding below." His face was hot and flushed, but his look was that of an adoring puppy.

"Don't apologise, Christian. That must have been at least fifteen minutes. My how you've improved. Next time I'm hoping for half an hour." Suspiciously, she added, "Have you been practicing in the last few weeks?" His indignant expression made her laugh. "I'd carry on, but I'm freezing. I notice you managed to keep most of your clothes on."

"It was only in my hurry to get to you. Will you come with me back to the hide-out, Madalene? I can see you're not well, mentally or physically. We can help you." His eyes said the words his mouth could not, 'You're crazy and I can't handle you by myself'.

There was nothing she could do to mollify him, because he was right on both counts. "All of this is nearly over, Christian. I've broken the back of the Sanctum. Now I need to put it out of its misery."

"We'll help you finish off the Sanctum. Come back with me."

"Okay, Christian, I'll come to the hide-out and speak to my army, but first I need to sort a few things out. I'll return tomorrow, or the day after and then you can all cluck over me, fretting about my state of mind and how ill I look. I have news to give you anyway."

Christian did up the last button on his trousers, he was smiling happily. "What news, Madalene?"

"I needed the experience of the Army, the nation's army that is, and finally I've got it. Have you ever noticed how reluctant they've been to help dear Shadowman? He was lucky there were enough thugs around to form his Sanctum Guard or he would have been in trouble." Madalene was having difficulty getting her shirt re-buttoned; Christian took over from her, his hands unable to resist her breasts as he did so.

"After blowing up a barracks full of men, I thought the Army had no love for me. I was wrong. Several members of the Special Forces were sent to find me after I blew up the Greyfriars Hotel. I thought that they'd come to kill me and attacked them. Luckily they overwhelmed me quickly, because they'd actually come with a very interesting proposal."

"Why did they come to *you*, Madalene? Shall I help you get your jumper on?" She smiled, how on earth was he going to put her jumper on, with his hands still wandering over her body.

"It turns out, that unwittingly, I've rescued elderly relatives of some top Army personnel, in particular a lady called Ivy, who happens to be the grandmother of General Walters, or Kenny, as I like to call him. They've also been watching our army's antics and have been impressed by what we've achieved. They propose a coup led by me and the Provoke army, with their help."

Christian had finally got her dressed and now he stood back looking at her in amazement. "Will they run the country when Shadowman is deposed?"

"No. They want me to be in charge, until everything is stabilised, then they want me to step down and allow a return to democracy. Don't look so worried, I've no intention of running this country, I believe Elgin would be a much better option, especially with Bertha at his side to guide him. I've told General Walters that, but at the moment he's insisting I take leadership. I'll give you more details when I come to the hide-out. Now I have to get moving, Christian, before I get the urge to ravish you again."

"Are you going back to the farmhouse…?" Christian gasped, as she looked at him in horror.

"How do you know about the farmhouse? Tell me, Christian, how?"

"Elgin came down to help us look for you. He realised you'd probably stayed in Marlton and guessed where."

"Where's Elgin now? I need to speak to him and Bertha, urgently."

Christian pulled a face, reluctant to speak, "Okay Madalene. They've gone to the farmhouse to wait for your return. Everyone's there except for Luke. He's still in hospital, but he's chasing female medics, so he's on the mend. Yes it's a trap, but only because I told them how ill you were and they all want to help you, especially Holan."

"They've seen the stuff in the papers and want to find out if I'm responsible. Don't lie to me." However, she couldn't help feeling glad that her army were at the farmhouse.

Christian obviously thought she was about to run off because he said, "Ellyn's there and she has good news for you. She carries Jinn's child. We're trying to look after her, but she's nearly as wilful as you are."

Ellyn pregnant with Jinn's child! How had that happened? Why the hell didn't Holan have the girl locked up somewhere safe? For Madalene's part, she intended to tie Ellyn to a bed for the rest of her pregnancy. No harm must come to *that* child."

"Quickly, Christian. My transporter's over there. We're going to the farmhouse."

He stood staring at her, not understanding that he'd said the right thing. "Okay," she said, laughing. "If you want another fifteen minutes, we can spare the time, but this time it's your clothes that come off, not mine."

Christian gaped at her, and then began to move. Honestly, the young had no stamina.

Madalene studied the scene from above and at a distance. Her army were sat on the ground with their hands on their heads, surrounded by a huge number of Sanctum Guards. Nearby and spread around were the Army members, her new allies. The dead and dying had been left where they'd fallen. As she watched, a transporter rolled up and out of it stepped Peter Shadow and his fat henchman, Michael Vertex. Peter immediately began shouting that they had to get everyone out of sight, or Madalene would see what was happening and run. She had no intention of running. She'd always thought matters would be settled in the Sanctum building, looked like she'd been wrong. Matters would be settled here and now.

"Looks like everyone's been having fun," she said to Christian. "I want to play. Take my transporter and go to Liverpool. I'll give you a contact number, the people you talk to will get you to Ireland."

"I'm not a coward anymore, but it would be madness to go down there. I have to get you to safety, Madalene."

"You don't understand, Christian. I am mad and I have every intention of going down there…"

A branch snapped nearby, her rifle fell instantly into her hands. Elgin and Bertha appeared, followed by a weeping Torrin. All of them were injured, but not badly.

"Madalene?" said Elgin, quietly for once. The bear hug he gave her was pure 'Elgin' though. "We've been waiting for you."

Bertha came forwards and also hugged her warmly. "We didn't know the Sanctum had found your location as well. They were waiting here when we arrived, we didn't stand a chance. We need to get you out of here at once. You can come up north with Elgin and I.

Strangely, Torrin came over and embraced her, "I'm sorry, Madalene," he said.

She knew what he was apologising for and shook her head, there wasn't time for grudges. "You have nothing to apologise to me for. Christian here's told me what a good soldier you've become. I'm

300

glad you joined my army." He was still wary of her, but she made no comment.

"Holan's down there," he said, pointing to bloodied body near the barn. "She's so badly hurt, I don't think she's got long to live. We can't help her, Madalene. Come let's get you to safety."

Not Holan too! Enough was enough. Madalene's head began to feel like it would burst. She needed to take action. "I will not run and hide. I've finished with that. A good leader doesn't leave their army behind."

"Be sensible, Madalene," said Elgin, the familiar booming returning to his voice. "It's *you* they want. Can't you see you're too important for us to let you commit suicide? What can you do with only a rifle? The entire Sanctum Guard is down there, including their Commander, John Fletcher, and there's an Army unit with them."

Boldly, Christian put his arm around her. "Listen to them, Madalene. They're right. If Shadowman doesn't capture you, then you've won."

"How the hell have I won if all my army's in the chambers being tortured? I persuaded them to fight for me, so I'm responsible for them. Holan needs medical help, Ellyn's down there, I can see Adrian with his hands on top of his head and there's Malcolm and Mark. I will *not* leave them to their fate. Use my transporter and get out of here, I'm going in to help them."

Bertha looked at her sympathetically. "You've been through a lot, Madalene, you're not thinking straight. Grab her boys; we're taking her out of here."

"No-ooo!" In moments she was held tightly. "Wait. You've given me an idea. But first, I need to talk to someone."

Elgin had tied Madalene's hands behind her back. Accompanied by Bertha, Torrin and Christian, he pushed her towards Peter Shadow. Bertha, Torrin and Christian kept their weapons trained on her at all times. Sanctum Guards surrounded them as they came forward. The Army kept its distance. A cloud of doom settled over the Provoke army members as she walked through them, so for their benefit, she gave them her most radiant smile. Ellyn mouthed her name and started to weep, Adrian urgently whispered words of comfort to the girl. Near the barn, Madalene saw Holan and not far from Holan lay the dead body of Hannah. Raising her head, Holan looked at her and began to cry, bitterly.

It wasn't part of the plan; nevertheless, ignoring Peter, Madalene forced her way over to her sister. Elgin and the others feigned anger; they kept their weapons trained on her and followed. Peter watched with amused interest, but did nothing. Michael Vertex looked angry, but also did nothing. As Madalene knelt, her hands still tied behind her back, Holan laid her head back down and smiled through her tears.

"I thought you were leader of this outfit," said Madalene. "What are you doing lying down on the job?"

"I knew you'd turn up and take over, so I thought I'd have a rest. I missed you, Madalene." Holan's face had gone a terrible grey colour and her breathing was harsh.

"I missed you too, Holan, though why I missed you is hard to say. Stay awake and keep talking to me. I'll get you help as soon as possible." Madalene's voice cracked with emotion, but she continued, "So many bad things have happened; I need your nagging to keep me going."

"You're coming apart aren't you? I can see it in your eyes. Hold it together, Madalene, you haven't finished yet." Holan's face twisted in agony and she cried out.

"I can't hold it together, Holan. Not anymore, not without you..." An inner part of Madalene began to wail.

"I-I can't stay with you. I think I'm dying Madalene..." Holan reached out with a bloodied hand and stroked Madalene's cheek gently.

"Take my strength from me. You can't die...I'll go mad if you die."

"No change there then." Holan's grin was weak. "Did you know Mother was going to call you Alene, then she realised your nature and added the Mad bit?"

302

"Very funny, Holan. Very funny…" Holan's eyes closed. With difficulty, Madalene bent her head to Holan's chest and found no movement. A roaring filled her ears, her heart pounded and her eyes filled with blood, not tears; a price would be paid for this. She trembled as the final threads of her sanity loosened. Not yet! Not yet.

"Get me over to Peter," she hissed at Elgin and the others, ignoring their sobbing. "And dry your damned eyes. We mourn later. For now we have some negotiating to do."

"Madalene," said Peter, looking at her with delight. "My condolences on the loss of your sister. Shame, she would have been a star attraction in the Arena. You look terrible, and you're skinnier than ever. I'll have to make sure you're fed, before I send you to the chambers, though my favourite torturer, Partlin will be disappointed at having to wait; he's so looking forward to getting his hands on you."

She smiled brightly at him, "How nice to see you, Peter. Remind me again why I jumped out of that box. I hate to say it, but the engagement's off. I trust you got your ring back and the other gifts I sent you."

His pain was clear, but he hid it quickly. "How rude of me not to thank you. I intend to do something equally as nice for you."

"I don't doubt it," she said, still smiling as if they were old friends who hadn't met in a long while.

Peter turned his attention to Elgin and the others. "Hand her over then. I've waited a long time for the pleasure of *your* company, Elgin, but I can wait a little longer. We shall extend the game between us. You, and those with you, can go free."

"I don't think so," said Elgin. "You put a four million engles reward on Madalene's head if she was captured alive. We don't want your money. Instead we want the lives of every man and woman sat around you." A collective gasp of dismay came from her army members as they realised the exchange was her for them.

"That's a lot to ask for when you're surrounded by my people, and the delightful Madalene is right here in front of me," said Peter, with a chuckle.

"Do you see the guns we have pointed at Madalene's head?" said Bertha, without any trace of emotion. "If you refuse us, we will kill her before your eyes. Why should we care about the death of this crazy bitch? We simply want to use her life to free our army." Each weapon clicked in readiness and she saw the alarm that appeared on Peter's face.

Torrin shoved his pistol into her face, making it bleed. The hate in his eyes looked real. "Once I was part of a group of people who tried to hang her. She's too dangerous to be allowed to live. Elgin might be bluffing, but I'm more than happy to kill her."

"I was also part of the lynching mob. Madalene dies if you won't release our army," said Christian, his attempt at hatred not so good. In fact not good at all.

Madalene held her breath, she'd told them to shoot her if Peter refused. Would they do it?

"Then go ahead and shoot her," said Michael Vertex, irritably.

Peter turned to him in horror. "Arrest this man," he shouted to his Guards. They didn't move. "I said arrest him. He knows I want Madalene taken alive."

The Guards remained still. Something big and unexpected was happening. She had to react quickly.

"What is wrong with everyone?" said Peter, in confusion. "Explain this to me Fat boy."

"My name isn't Fat boy. It's Michael. Michael Vertex. They're deceiving you and you can't see it, because you're so obsessed with this bitch. Everything I admired about you has gone and it's her fault. Before we left today, I spoke to John Fletcher; he's agreed to help me. I hold power now, not you. Guards, take Peter into the farmhouse, while I deal with this situation."

Madalene looked at Elgin, who nodded and pulled the loose ropes away from her arms. His rifle now pointed at Peter Shadow. The others turned their weapons on Michael Vertex. Madalene was fast, in seconds she'd pulled a knife and stuck it into Michael's groin.

"Let me handle this for you, Peter. Call it an unengagement gift. This animal needs neutering." Pulling her knife out, she struck again in the area of Michael's manhood. She struck true. He fell to the ground in agony. Bending over him, she licked his face and tweaked his nipples. Above her Elgin kept Peter at bay, and Peter was now able to keep his Sanctum Guards in check, though a quick glance showed the Army were moving forward to assist Elgin. She had time for some fun.

"I'm all yours big man," she whispered into Michael's ear. His eyes looked at her in horror. "Do you remember shooting my son, Jinn? This is for him." She thrust the knife near his heart, but not into it. Blood poured from his mouth, but she kissed him anyway. "You were the only boy who didn't manage to rape me and you know it. You were flaccid and had to pretend. I thought it was hilarious, you gave me my only moment of joy that day." Tears poured from Michael's eyes, as she mocked him. "You're still inadequate. Your coup has lasted seconds. Mine will last longer with the Army on my side." Satisfied at last, she slit his throat; it was time to turn her attention elsewhere.

Standing up, she saw the looks of horror around her. Her face must be covered in blood. Wiping it with the back of her hand, she threw back her head and howled her triumph like a wolf. The Army had done their work efficiently; the Sanctum Guards were mostly disarmed. Peter seemed to assume it had been done on his behalf, and then he saw her army members being helped to their feet and looked confused. Howling again, she moved towards Peter.

"Let us deal with him, Madalene," said Elgin, moving to intercept her.

"No!" she screamed. "He's mine. My business alone."

"Let it be, Madalene," said Bertha. "We will see justice is served on him."

"We will. My justice!" Her head filled with images of her loved ones, Robin, Bren, Hayla, Jinn and Holan. One by one the threads snapped. Reaching Peter, she began to push him around, whirling furiously on those who tried to stop her. "Raping me when I was twelve years old - Guilty. Murdering my friend, Robin Jones - Guilty. Murdering Bren, the man I loved - Guilty. Murdering and raping, Hayla, my daughter - Guilty. Murdering Holan, my sister - Guilty. Murdering Jinn, my son and yours, if only you'd known it - Guilty."

Peter finally reacted. "Jinn was *my* son...*my* son. You should have told me." His look of anguish failed to move her, Peter should have seen the resemblance on their first and only meeting. She continued her attack with greater ferocity.

Adrian, Mark and Malcolm had come over, and with their help, Christian and Torrin were finally able to grab hold of her. They weren't going to stop her shouting. "I haven't even mentioned your crimes against the public – Guilty. Guilty. Guilty." They began shushing her, trying to get her to calm down, but she couldn't, the violence inside her was building not subsiding.

"We will deal with him, Madalene," said Elgin, sorrowfully. "He will pay for all these crimes. But it must be done properly; he was leader of this country after all."

Looking angry now, Peter glared at her, and then addressed the people standing around them. "You fools. You think *I'm* evil, look at her. You say things were better before I came to power, think back to what this country was really like, before you judge me. Do you seriously think your lives will be better with this psychotic, 'The Dark Goddess' as you call her, in control? A woman who can destroy her own babies, then wrap them up in paper and return them to me as unwanted gifts."

She heard the gasps of shock; she hadn't thought that story would go down too well. Her knife rested in the palm of her hand, they hadn't thought to disarm her. She stood still, knowing that sooner or later her captors would relax and lose their hold on her. "I was glad to get that muck out of my body," she said, overjoyed to see the hurt on Peter's face. More gasps of shock. Hell, people were so damned sensitive where babies were concerned.

Peter seemed to have got into his stride, "This is a woman who chopped her own finger off to spite me. Look at her hand. She sent the finger to me in the post, not the act of a sane person." Taking a deep breath, he smiled at her and continued. "Your lives were put at risk to save a boy, who had I known he was my son, would never have gone to the Arena. Madalene killed him. If she'd told me the truth, Jinn would be alive now. Don't you feel horror hearing this woman howl like an animal? And that, after killing a man, so brutally most of you couldn't even watch? Look at her, what little sanity she had has gone."

His words had the desired effect; conversations rose around her, the noise getting louder and louder. Peter smiled at her triumphantly, and then said softly, so only she could hear, "Hayla squealed like a little piglet while my men raped her. Squeak. Squeak. And Bren wept and cried as he listened to it. You'd have stabbed him in the spine yourself if...

Nothing could have held her at that point. With a ferocious scream, she leapt at him. Again and again she stabbed her knife into his body, his limbs, his face, licking the blade between slashes to taste his blood. Images of the past once again came into her mind, but this time they were muddled and confusing. *Her Father was gently trying to teach her how to use a rifle. Peter's friends were flirting with her, not hurting her. The babies hadn't died, they were still inside her, she could feel them kicking. Peter had his arms around her and she felt safe with him. Her wedding dress was being fitted, it was made from antique silk and she felt beautiful in it..........* Strong hands grabbed her and pulled at her. Why were they pulling her? Was she in danger? Looking on the ground she saw the body of the man she'd felt safe with, the man she was going to marry. His body and face were a tangled mass of ribbons of flesh, but his eyes were intact and they stared at her victoriously.

Without warning he began laughing. "We're the same you and I. The same..." His laughter got louder and louder, hacking her senses in the same way her knife had hacked his body. Her knife...She was responsible for that tangled, bloody mess...

Pulling herself free, Madalene ran past frightened faces into the farmhouse and slammed the door behind her.

Elgin entered the farmhouse, cautiously. Madalene was curled up in a corner, looking like a lost child. It was heartbreaking, there was no reaction to his presence, not even when his foot sent an empty bottle flying. He'd thought of bringing Ellyn in to see her, hoping it might help. Now he was glad he hadn't done, Madalene looked beyond help, and Ellyn would have been devastated to see her like this. Bertha came into the room, followed by Christian, Torrin,

Adrian, Malcolm and Mark. The General of the Army accompanied them. They all stopped and stood still, silently staring at Madalene in disbelief. The grief on Christian's face was terrible.

Elgin sank his big frame down next to Madalene and pulled her into his arms. "We will look after her until she has recovered. She has done us and this country a great service. With drugs and the right treatment, she will be herself again. Yes, she will be herself..." Tears ran down his cheeks, falling onto Madalene's face, to his surprise she stirred, and focussed her gaze on him.

"Elgin?" she said, in a wooden voice. "I don't want to live. Kill me."

"There's been enough killing today, Madalene," he answered, sobbing openly.

She turned her plea to the others, but they too refused her.

"Then I'll do it," she said, weakly raising the knife in her hands.

"Wait," said Elgin, looking around the room in desperation and suddenly spotting a solution. "Christian, bring me over that box of drugs."

Christian complied, looking at him doubtfully. "What are you going to do?"

Elgin ignored the question; there wasn't time to answer it. "You deserve to die gently, Madalene," Elgin said, prising the knife out of her hands and laying it on the floor beside him. Ignoring the protests that started, he studied the box and extracted a packet of green powder. The amount seemed about right. "Mix this with some water for me, Bertha."

"How much of it shall I use, Elgin?"

He loved the way she trusted him. Smiling he said, "Use all of it. This is meant to be an overdose after all."

Bertha mixed the powder as instructed and returned it to him. Carefully he filled a syringe with the solution, and then looking into Madalene's unfocused eyes; he stuck the syringe in her arm and released its contents.

"That's…" her eyes closed and she went limp in his arms. The others gasped, but he began to laugh.

"A very strong sedative. It should keep you unconscious long enough for us to get you to a hospital. Mad and dangerous you may be, but I have a feeling we may still have need of you."

The End

Printed in the United Kingdom
by Lightning Source UK Ltd.
136398UK00001B/95/P